THE QUEEN OF FROST

L.B. DIVINE

First paperback edition January 2025

Paperback IBSN: 979-8-9873957-8-3

E-Book IBSN: 979-8-9873957-7-6

Cover by Kelly Carter

Map by Natalia Junqueria

Editing by @kmortonedits

❀ Created with Vellum

BOOKS BY L.B. DIVINE

THE PRINCE OF SNOW SERIES

The Prince of Snow

The King of Flames

The Queen of Frost

The Queen of Fury (Novella to be released)

French Translation by Edition Celeste

LE PRINCE DE GLACE

LE ROI DES FLAMMES

THE HEIR TO THE EMERALD CROWN DUOLOGY

The Heir to the Emerald Crown

The Heir to the Ashen Throne

To anyone who has had to let go to come into their power, and to anyone who has ever had to become empowered to let go.

Author's Note

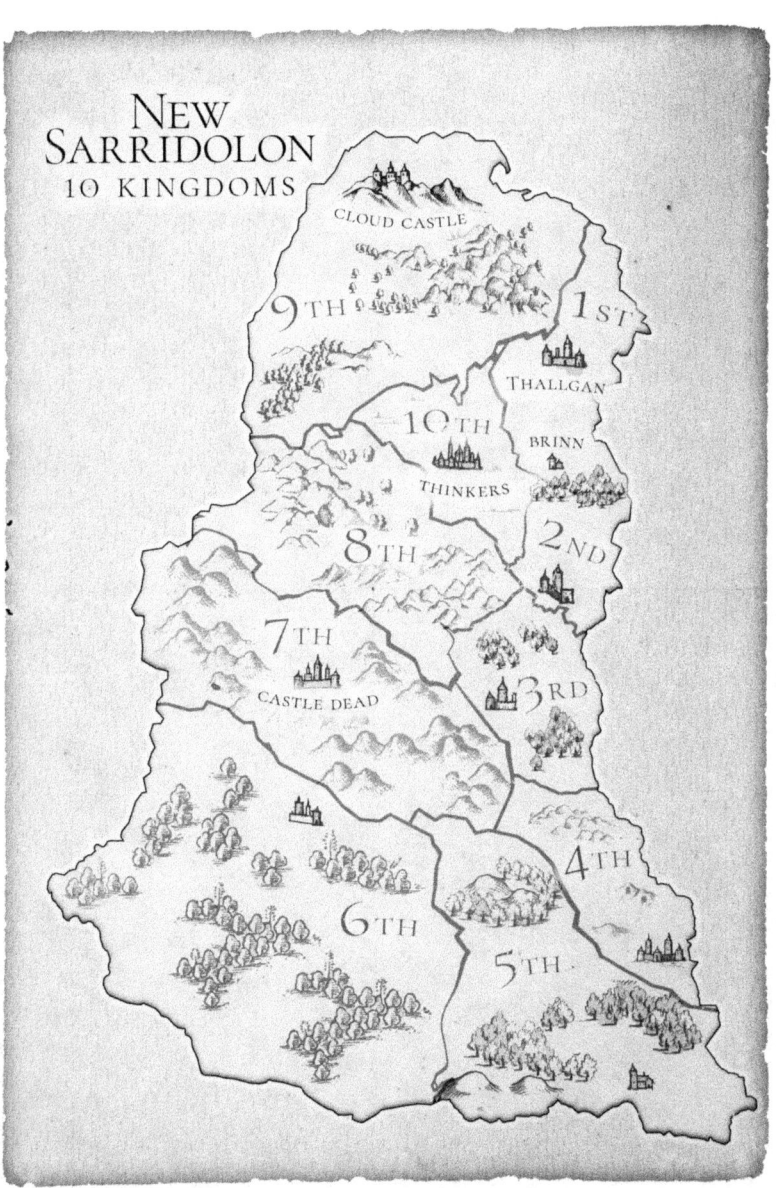

The King of Snow is coming.
He will Rise from the death of his Father.
The Ten Kingdoms will fall.
Fire will scorch the lands.
A Violet Queen will Reign, and the light that holds the Kings of Old will go out.

The Dragon and his Queen
Many years before

Ciara Regavine breathed shadows.

They curled around her, whispering. She played with them, her hands lifted into the air and her fingers spread for them to dance around. She did not call upon them, and she had not for many years, instead she just let them purely exist.

Shadows were as natural as the light, a commonality she saw and felt beyond her own power so deeply that it only brought her confusion when she saw others look upon it and fear. They were curious, as the sun was when it awoke in the morning to touch all around it.

She knew as well as anyone that they could be dangerous if they were not controlled, but that was not what she was doing here. She was commanding.

And she would not relinquish control.

Not to anyone.

Terrify, but not attack.

Intimidate, but not touch.

It was a risky game, to toy with such immense and dangerous power but never have the strength to wield it.

But that is precisely why she did it.

And why the dragon was so afraid of her.

Winding down the marble staircase, just beyond the dungeon of the castle, Ciara began to slip on her mask. It was as easy as changing her clothes and as brushing her hair. She knew it too well all of these days, for she never had any other choice than to simply wear it.

And wearing it was a strength within itself.

Another reason that the dragon was *so* afraid of her.

She had too much on the line as of late not to indulge his curiosity. She needed to hear what was in store for her, to get guidance on all of the other darknesses which were coming her way.

Everything had a price. All power had a push and pull.

She heard his chains rattling before she stepped down, and she knew that it was to be completely and utter fun to see him yet again.

The Queen had left Cian asleep in his chambers and managed to avoid his pest of a friend Cyril as she made her way to see him. It would be worth it, these lies and deceptions. She would tell him eventually. Cian that was.

He just had to earn her trust first. He almost had the other day when he nearly ruined himself at the ball to prove his loyalty, but then he had not completed the task to completion and had failed as a result.

It was a pity, because she was so rooting for him to win. And she never rooted for anyone but herself. She was not sure who wanted this more, *him or her*?

There was one way to find out.

As she made her way down the final stair, he was already waiting for her. He was predictable. She liked it that way.

"Hello old friend," she said, not breaking eye contact as she curtseyed.

The disrespect was out in full force this evening. She did

not even try to hide it. He was her inferior, and she was his superior. He better get used to the hierarchy.

Rumbling responded first, before his beautifully sinister voice wrapped around the chamber like fire. "My, my, the Queen of Fury paying me a visit, to what do I owe the pleasure?"

She stood upright, her black lace nightgown so informal for the black obsidian and diamond encrusted creation that sat atop her flaming hair. She had been preparing her questions all evening, knowing that she had to ask him something that was maddening but would be preventive.

"Well?" he hissed, his mouth leaking smoke similar to her oozing of shadows.

"Prophecy. I wish to know how to see the truth from the lies."

"How interesting," he growled, his talons flexing and scraping against the marble. "To see the truth from the lies is a skill which many want to possess."

"It is a good thing I have so many friends in high places then," she deadpanned.

"Only Ciara Regavine would dare to dream to ask a dragon a question and then compliment him as if he were her servant."

She bit her tongue. "What will this knowledge cost me?"

"There are many things I want," he hissed. "I will give you an option this evening."

She had danced this dance with him numerous times. Always getting and giving in return. But she would *never* give him certain things which he never asked for. That she knew he wanted above all else. To unleash such a danger-ously clever and powerful adversary would be a death sentence to all, and she had worked too hard to terrify but bring about peace. He would shatter everything if he—

"My two options are as follows. I will tell you how to see the truth from the lies if you either, release me—"

She paled. He had never asked before... The ramifications of such a thing would—

"Or I will have you listen to your own fate."

Ciara was never afraid. Of anything. Yet right now, she could consider this the closest she had ever felt to such a thing. It was foreign and she hated it, being terrified. Heart pounding, she laced her hands in front of her black lace nightgown so that he could not see them shake. With an inhale, she replied, "My fate."

She would not ask questions. She would not let it affect her—

"I understand that you have a friend, Ciara."

Her shadows stilled. Frozen in time. Her doing. Always her doing... Everything was always her fault.

"Your friend will be very important, beyond this life and into the next."

She could have sworn a tear escaped from her eye. She had sensed this, she had known he was special—

"But, your friend will face many challenges, and you will know the chess pieces which you have to move to ensure that he survives them."

There it was again, that suffocating feeling that—

"When the blade drops, Ciara—Queen of Fury and of the Ten Kingdoms—you will be the one to take it to the heart."

She was on her knees. She was not breathing, she could not think—-

The dragon stepped closer, his white scales somehow shimmering in the darkness like a rainbow. "To see the truth from the lies deary, you must ask yourself the question that many do not know or wish to understand."

She breathed through a sob, suddenly not caring that

she stood before one of the most ancient creatures to ever walk the continent.

"You must ask yourself—when unleashing the deepest and darkest parts of yourself—what is the cost?"

"What is the cost?" she repeated, dumbfounded.

With a puff of smoke, he began to rumble in laughter. "What is the cost, my dearest Queen? The age old question to which I have always wanted to know the answer to."

"What is the cost?" she demanded, her fiery hair matching the flames which sprouted out of his nose.

"You tell me, Ciara." He began to shift backward, his white scales looking gray in the haze of smoke which began to shroud him. "You tell me."

A Letter from the King to
The King of Snow

ear Dalton Saphirrus,

  I hear you have the same powers as your ancestors, Cian Saphirrus. Not only do you share his namesake, but I find poetry in the fact that you too have the power of snow and ice and all things winter. Such a pretty thing, to be able to create snowflakes with your hands, and ice storms with your heart. I always admired that about Cian, the fact that he had a gorgeous party trick to bring with him whenever he saw fit, but that it could be so devastating as well.

  Which brings to me something as peculiar as the universe itself: love. This might seem as a strange transition, as how does speaking of one's elemental gifts possibly relate to love itself?

  Well, Dalton Saphirrus, King of Snow, I believe that you know the answer to this.

  I write this letter, not to praise you of the gift's that remind me so much of Cian Saphirrus, but to tell you of what I have done.

  Of who I have, rather.

  Charmaine Grimes resides at my current residence. You

may ask Randolph Eniar all about it, another king with another gift. She will be staying here until I see fit, until she shows me what she truly has capabilities of. In truth, she has evaded me many nights, and many days.

Her gifts, you might understand, are clever.

I look forward to seeing you on the battlefield one day, Dalton Saphirrus, King of Snow.

Until we meet again,
King Finn of Sarridolon

PART ONE
THE ICE PRINCE

CHAPTER ONE

Heartbreak was a searing pain that took only prisoners and left the rest for dead.

There was an enigma to the term—heartbreak—for it was an emotion that did not scar the entire world, only those lucky enough to fall headfirst into anything that mattered more than a little bit. It was a catastrophic sense of free falling into the distance, plummeting from the sky to the ground with nothing to latch onto, and breathing for the first time after nearly drowning in the sea. It was ballistically complex, irritatingly unfathomable, and completely and utterly the most beautiful emotion to ever grace humanity.

Charmaine Grimes thought of all of this as she stood at the precipice of Castle Dead and prayed to the Gods that she would die.

The Seventh Kingdom was not unlike the others she had passed through on her way away from the First. The hills and streams still rolled downward, the mountains still rose steady, and the flowers in the fields still blew in the wind. She had imagined the continent to look a million different ways throughout the span of her eighteen years of life but never could she have imagined the sheer vastness that was before her.

For she would know, she had traveled it. Days on end in that carriage had left her broken; that time with her thoughts and fears a true manifest of the pain that settled deep within her chest. *Where were my friends? Were they even looking for me?* She tried to push the thought aside but it continued to creep in, the battlement between her and her anxiety a constant struggle.

She had nothing left, but she thought she had her friends in the First Kingdom. Never did she dream of having Dalton—but for one moment in the rose garden—she had felt as though everything between them had been real. There had been no root of the lily, the titles and politics once forgotten.

Instead, it had been nothing but the rush of energy between them.

And the cost of relishing in it had been the ultimate price.

Bone weary, Charmaine put one foot in front of the other as she entered the castle gates. The black metal gleamed pure gloom despite the sun shining. What struck her the most was the sheer amount of flowers that stood in the gardens at the forefront—ones which had her heart aching for the familiar scent of Randolph Eniar.

But what was so peculiar about this place? Not only was it anything other than home—the opulence dark, the people terrified like they had been during Ronan's reign, but more-so the fact that an eternal winter seemed to have sprung on them. The snow fell daintily, just as it did daily.

And Charmaine tried to push aside the familiar brush of wind and the feeling that she got when she thought of snow.

And she continued to do so every time he began to cross her mind.

The screaming, the horror, the promises, the draw—she knew she was a survivor, but she would not withstand this place if he crossed her mind for too long.

Instead, she diverted. Just as she knew he would do.

Someone would come for her. She knew it in her heart.

And until then, all she could do was grin and bear her situation.

And get stronger.

That would be critical to her survival.

And Charmaine Grimes was a survivor. The toughest of them all. She knew it.

She just needed everyone else to know it too, but in good time.

Yes, good things take time.

She dreamt of Randolph throughout the journey, trying to channel his fearless energy. She had never seen Randolph be afraid of anything, lest it was something of his own creation. It took everything in her not to look down at her healed hands now, knowing there would be no burn marks but still a powerful memory. He had burned her and the pain that he had flaming in his amber gaze had been strong enough to overtake the physical pain of the injury.

The emotional pain? It was much worse.

Shaking her head, she tried to push off the memories of the First Kingdom. Everything from the screams that had erupted from the King of Snow to this very moment was almost too much for Charmaine to bear, along with everything else she had endured in the last few months.

Flanked by two mercenaries, she tried to stand tall as she prepared to greet whatever destiny had in store for her.

The castle stood tall, the pillars and staircases far grander than that of the First Kingdom. Despite her shaking hands,

Charmaine could not ignore the power that besieged her. There was also a sense of warmth here, a heat that continually burned within her as she approached the inner halls. The stone was a deep red, grand and dazzling in rubies and diamonds.

She tried to picture Randolph here, for she knew he hailed from the Seventh, yet she had a hard time doing so. He was not one for dalliances in the Gods.

With a squeal, the mercenaries beside her grabbed each of her shoulders as they walked her to her chambers. They climbed the grand stairs quickly, as if they were afraid of being sighted by someone.

If Charmaine were brave, she would ask them who they were so afraid of.

The mahogany chamber doors opened slowly and she was shoved inside. The mercenaries in unison hissed, "We will come to collect you when he is ready to see you."

Without a second glance in her direction, the door slammed.

Charmaine sucked in a deep breath, nearly falling over at the shock of being thrown so abruptly into chambers in this foreign castle. She turned around toward the rest of the chambers, ready to inspect and begin to cultivate an escape plan when she froze. The dagger that Dalton had given her at her side remained, the power of her invisibility strong enough to keep it cloaked. However, she realized suddenly that it might have to break her cover, if she would have to use it to defend herself.

Before her stood a girl—probably her own height—with amber eyes flecked with gold, brown hair that flowed to her waist, and a ruby crown. The girl's lip had been busted on the side and her dress clearly had been worn for multiple days. Her dark brows were furrowed, though she did not appear angry.

But what had Charmaine's soul ripping to shreds was the familiar wrapping of florals that curved from her fingers up her forearms, disappearing beneath the black wrinkled gown she wore.

The name escaped her before she even had a chance to think, and the recognition that spread across the face of the girl that could be the female version of her best friend was so heart wrenching that Charmaine nearly collapsed.

"Randolph?" she asked, so quietly she was not sure the girl heard her.

But the girl did. Her voice sounded strong despite the golden hue that wavered in her gaze. "How do you know my brother?"

CHAPTER TWO
MANY YEARS BEFORE...

The Queen rested her hand gently over her undignified stomach, dreaming of feeling the child that was taking root within her. She had been two weeks late in her courses, and today was the day that she was going to tell her husband. It had been much too soon for her chambermaids to really notice, and she had been quite clever the past few weeks in her routine to keep it a secret, but she was certain now. She had never been a day late in her courses in her entire life and she was certain.

She was with child.

She had never dreamt of this day, but rather, she thought often of what it would mean to the world to bring forth a new life. All thoughts that could consume joy however, only existed in the shadows of her mind. The Queen knew the reality of the situation, the gravity of what was going to befall the Ten Kingdoms soon. She knew that there was going to be a darkness that took over, for there had been shadows building in the corners of the continent for many years.

Well, since Queen Ciara had died.

And was born.

They had never left, she was sure of it.

The Queen of Fury's efforts were valiant, losing her own life in the process, but they had been for nothing. The crackling of darkness that had been reported was not shared with the citizens of the kingdom, no, the council of Thinkers had warned the rulers of New Sarridolon weeks prior that the situation was escalating, but to remain silent.

The Queen knew that if one wanted things to go away, it was best not to just simply ignore it.

With a sigh, she clasped her hands behind her back. She knew that she was simply just biding her time with her husband, the King, who she knew would be thrilled at the news. However, part of her mind wondered if that is truly what he would think.

He knew just as well as she did the state of the world, and she was certain that like most things that they would be in agreement.

The child was not safe here, at the castle.

There were a few young king's and queen's recently born in the Ten Kingdoms, and even hearing that news had frightened her.

The babe in the First Kingdom frightened her most of all. It was King Ronan who was most adamant that magic needed to be outlawed, that they were not safe from any infiltration at any level.

She did not agree, nor did many, but the Seventh had acted so strangely as well. Though it was not in line with Ronan's outburst about the fears of the average citizen's potential wielding of elemental magic. No, it was something deeper, as if both of them were haunted by different demons.

Shaking her head, she took a deep breath after a moment's pause.

She knew what she was to do, for the world was not safe for a royal child. And she deemed those who had royal children recently: the Seventh, the First, the Sixth, the Fourth... Well, they were all bring children into this world with a crown on their head and be left to clean up the messes of their ancestors.

No, if she was going to be a mother, she was going to be a damn good one. She was going to give her child a chance.

Lifting her gaze, she stared out at her kingdom from the balcony of her study and made a vow.

A silent one.

A powerful one.

One that could not be seen.

And then she turned around to tell her husband the news, praying that he would forgive her for what she had just done.

CHAPTER THREE

Vengeance is not born, it is forged. And for Dalton Saphirrus, he forged dreams of nothing but violet eyes and a sword through the chest of all men who stood in his way.

Everything reminded him of her.

The laughter that still somehow existed in his court. The silent moments of kindness when nobody is watching. The humility.

It was everything. He should count himself lucky to live in a place like this where there were so many things to cherish and enjoy. Except when he thought about it...like really thought about it, it only brought him sharp shooting pains. Like being stabbed.

Or what he imagined that it would be like to be stabbed. He had never had the pleasure.

Standing at the head of the council table, he threatened to freeze another apple and chuck it at the next man who denied his request to send troops after *her*. The King had sole power in the First Kingdom, yet he needed the unrelenting support of the nobles in order to gain the traction he needed to send the men who took *her* to their graves.

He was losing his Gods-damned mind, and there was nothing that could be done but play tyrant to all of those who continually pissed him off.

"King Dalton, we must be reasonable—" Lord Peach started, only to be silenced by Dalton's rising hand. He had gotten rather good at this the last few weeks, instilling fear in idiot men who thought they could control divinity and destiny.

"What is unreasonable?" A voice cut through the air like an arrow, and landed directly in his head, bringing him back to reality.

Dalton quirked his head behind him, allowing for the breakthrough of an encroaching smile upon his face. "Ah, my wife, so nice of you to join us."

Elena strode through the council chambers, a lace blood-red gown clinging to her body and accentuating her perfection. A sapphire crown was displayed atop her head, an ornament and reminder to the men of this kingdom that she was the Queen consort.

Despite the fact that Dalton knew at every moment she was rereading that Gods-damned contract between their kingdoms, looking for a way for them to be free of one another and Ronan's everlasting stink.

"Lord Peach, may you reconcile us again with whatever it was you were demanding of my husband?"

Lord Peach, per usual, was white as a ghost.

Loser.

"Do you not know how to speak to a woman my lord?" Dalton asked, the disgust at the six members of the privy council unjustly wavering in his voice. "It is quite easy you know, you simply just open your mouth, and hope that some words fall out of it."

Lord Smith spoke, suddenly feeling brave. "I think what Lord Peach is trying to say, my dearest King and Queen, is that we must be reasonable that a commoner of the First Kingdom is not our greatest priority at the moment. Rather, it is the mercenaries."

Within a nanosecond of speaking his final word, Dalton was upon the man. Ice coated his fingers, spreading quickly on his shirt as he fisted the collar of it in the palm of his hand. "She. Is. Not. Just. A. Commoner."

"My lord—" Lord Smith chattered out, his breath hitching ever so slightly as he clearly acquired frostbite.

"Apologize." A command.

"I am sorry my lord, I did not mean to disrespect."

Dalton dropped him, though the ice did not disappear. It remained, a reminder that this was unfinished.

Striding away, yet keeping his gaze on the entirety of the room, Dalton spoke slowly. "You listen to me you fucking bastards, today and tomorrow and the next day, I am King. My ancestor, King Cian, brought this kingdom to the light and saved the world. But I think you are forgetting that his wife was the one who tilted the neck of the crown, and made this dynasty, this court, her own."

Nobody spoke.

He continued.

"I can be two men. *Fuck*—I have been two men. I have been pummeled, destroyed, attacked, brutalized, and treated like vermin. And all of you half-wits stood by and turned a blind eye to my misfortune because it suited you." He breathed in deeply, snowflakes spewing out of his mouth on the exhale. He knew it was brutally cold, but Elena herself did not flinch. She was used to this. Used to the new him. Maybe she even liked it. He was not sure he cared. "But I can be this man. The man born of snow and vengeance. I can be the man forged out of these defeats."

He took two steps forward, speaking so closely to Lord Peach that he himself was almost convinced that he was about to commit a murder on his own privy council. "My ancestor was married to the Queen of Fury, yet it is the King of Vengeance I can become."

With a hand lifted, snow began to fall from the ceiling. Ice was cracking along the walls, building and building and building and building...

And as soon as it had been created, it fell away. Dalton could feel the ice melting away, just as it had when he had lost *her*. The impetuous of all of his issues, for he had lost everything but it was as if they could have been saved together. They could save one another.

Just like everything else, he had failed.

He had lost control.

He was everything his father had said that he could be and everything that he ever had been to him.

A failure.

Unworthy.

Better off than a bastard but undeserving of everything that he had ever had. And then Dalton left, striding from the room filled with councilmen so unlikable that it was becoming contagious.

He heard a few insensible men open their mouths, maybe to stop him, maybe to tell him once more that the threat was still at large, maybe to tell him that he was a bloody idiot and knew nothing of the world...

Well, he would hear none of it.

So he strode from the room.

Elena standing there in his wake, speechless.

And went to find a glass of champagne.

CHAPTER FOUR

Into his chambers he went. The eternal power struggle within him needed to be addressed in complete silence, and alone.

Although, deep down, he knew that the last thing that he wanted was actually to be alone. He so very deeply craved to be accompanied. But his criteria for a companion was very specific at the moment. They were to have violet eyes, raven black hair, and always a look of hesitation upon their face—

Hands shaking uncontrollably, ice poured from his fingertips in raw chaos. Running nervous hands through his dark hair, he felt his power turn to dust and dew as his hands came free. Bent over, he held himself in closest regards and let his mind wander.

That is what his room had become for him once again, a sanctuary from chaos. And frankly, a prison not unlike the one which he had recently escaped.

Crowded. That is how his mind felt. Far too crowded for being alone in an empty room.

Flashes appeared from his life, all twenty years of it. As

he approached the apex of winter, his twenty-first birthday on the horizon, he suddenly felt the weight of his years as if they were measured in decades rather than months.

"Stop," he whispered to himself. "Silence!"

Unanswered, the buzzing continued. This had never happened to him, never fully committed to the madness that lived within him. Voices from the Kings of Old, that is who he deduced he was speaking to. Flashes of swords, red hair, and a face very much like his own existed in his eyes. Swarmed with feelings of loss and a pain unlike any other, Dalton lifted his gaze to stand. The weight of months of destruction: the continent falling apart, hateful violence existing around every corner, powers reigniting like it had one hundred years past... All of that followed him as he opened his stride and made his way over to his dresser.

Grabbing the sides of the piece of furniture, Dalton hoisted his chest upward and gazed upon the face of someone that he barely recognized.

Hallowed cheekbones, dark circles under his dark blue eyes, tousled hair that he once recognized that now seemed like it belonged to someone else... The reality was clear for Dalton Saphirrus.

He was *nothing* without Charmaine Grimes.

The tightness in his throat was bound to her, he knew that for certain amidst everything else. He was at her mercy, his body physically begging him to go to her. Wherever she was.

But he knew one thing for certain, he would find her.

Because that is what Cian would have done, and he knew now more than ever that it was the role of destiny which he was to play.

He was to be the King of Snow.

So the King of Snow he would be.

CHAPTER FIVE

Charmaine woke up as she did everyday for the last two weeks: full of terror and sadness. There was a tinge of regret too, for she never got to say the things she needed to say before she was ripped from everything she had grown to love.

Before she was ripped from *him*.

This castle was another reminder, something which was terrifying within itself, for everywhere she looked she only saw Randolph. Oddly enough, she could picture him here as a royal. Growing up here in this dark castle, it was no wonder that Randolph often found himself more haunted than most.

Most haunted from *him*.

Before her thoughts were able to wander too far into the abyss, she found herself interrupted by the slamming of her large oak doors as the silver snake walked in. Or at least, that was what she was going to call him.

Silver hair was the only thing that was even comparable to him. For when she had originally seen him two weeks ago when the carriage doors open, she thought she was seeing things, but upon further inspection he was far too wicked to be hers.

Or what had almost belonged to her.

Bairre, he had called himself. A servant to King Finn and a wielder of shadows within his own right. But there was something about him that led Charmaine to believe that he was not what he seemed to be.

He was, by all accounts, a mystery.

And one that she was determined to crack.

"Charmaine Grimes, we have to move," Bairre said. "I have already approached the Princess, and we should find you some dressing gowns per the King's request."

The Princess. Charmaine's stomach dropped at the mention of what she knew. There had been no time in the last few weeks to even process much of anything.

Reine Eniar was exactly like Randolph, in every sense of what made him, well *him*, at his core. And if she could not be the one to stop King Finn with her fire, who could? She had been trapped here for many months, her own home becoming a prison. Charmaine had not had much time to really talk to her, to get to know her, but what she had seen had made her convinced that if Charmaine found a way out of here...

Well, Reine would be coming with her.

"He is not the King of anything," Charmaine found herself saying before she had even a moment to think it through, her mind still wrapped up in Randolph's sister. "He is the King of nothing, for he was murdered by his daughter Ciara..."

But she did not get the chance to finish, for Bairre had her pinned against the wall with shadows clawing at her hands and feet before she could even inhale her next breath.

"There are not many rules here, Charmaine Grimes," Bairre hissed, walking closer to her in a manner which was eerily calm. "But the only rule which I could possibly concoct is one that will keep you alive for all of eternity in this place. I would know, for it is the reason I have survived here as long as I have, and the reason that I have kept my youth."

With another step forward, he leaned so close that he was nearly touching her ear with his lips. It was romantic when it had happened to her last, with Dalton Saphirrus of course intimate in the way that caused her to lose her breath.

This was a warning, all romance devoid in the nature which he hissed. This was darkness in a person, no light here. Her mind wandered to how Dalton would react to such a scenario, if he were here to witness it. If they had been taken together, is this something that would have happened? She had to think that Dalton would protect her from everything, but Bairre... the King? They were forces with power so great that she was not sure if snowflakes were the cure.

Who could stop them from whatever they were planning?

She was not sure if she knew anything anymore, lest the answer.

"Her name is the only thing that will keep you alive, I suggest you keep it to yourself."

"What are you—"

"If I explain everything now, Charmaine Grimes, just know that you become collateral. It is better that I know what I mean, and that you simply just spend time in your solitude wracking your brain as to what I am even speaking of."

"How does that make any sense?" she asked, irritation flooding her. Sure, there was probably some safety in not understanding what was truly at work here, but there was also no immunity in feeling completely and utterly lost. And that is what she was... Lost. Alone. Fearful.

Even though she refused to show it.

And then with a flick of his fingers, his shadows brought in a gown that looked like a nightmare itself. The dark tendrils of fabric hit the ground softly, elegantly. But it was the corset, covered in gems so dark that Charmaine could only assume that she was to be wearing obsidian itself.

Very different from sapphires.

And mostly definitely not Saphirrus blue.

CHAPTER SIX

Carinthya Saphirrus knew nothing but the fact that she had absolutely ruined everything. She knew this was an unspecific judgment that she had passed onto herself, but she knew that it was the truth at its core.

She knew as much too that the Ten Kingdoms were out of control. Finn had done something two weeks prior, something that had shaken the continent to its core. It was a violation. It was something that she could not put her fingers on, but knew nonetheless that it was happening.

Straightening the front of the white silk gown she wore, she continued onward. It was unusual that Finn demanded that she dress for any occasion, so she was already feeling the pain and suffering which usually came with their one on one interactions.

Something was not right about this decrepit castle. The energy—the air—it was as if it were deliberately horrifying. Carinthya could not stand the sound of her own heels clicking on the darkened stones of the castle halls. It was maddening, to listen to nothing but the sound of ones breath on the promise of a false freedom. Callum, the boy who had worked at the castle, had promised her nothing, but Bairre seemed to have promised her everything. Not that Callum would do her any good, for he had disappeared and had not been seen since. She had meant to ask Bairre about him, but a part of her did not want to expose any weakness. Callum had been the closest thing that she had to a friend, and it would completely wreck her if she were to find out that horrors had befallen him.

She nearly tripped over her own two feet at the idea of Bairre. He had not come to her chambers since he nearly choked her to death those weeks before. So she could throw her idea of asking him a bloody question out the window. Useless.

She was not sure if he entirely meant it, but something within her knew that he did. Maybe, deep down, some part of her knew that she deserved to be killed for her actions. What she thinks she had done, it was despicable. To give up any information was one thing, but to endanger...

Shaking her head to rid herself of all things terrible, for the moment at least, she took another step forward and realized that she now stood outside the great hall. The obsidian doors gleamed in the moonlight, and if it was any other day, any other life, she would have known that this place was beautiful.

But it represented nothing but a prison of impending death. Something which she could never escape.

She was completely and utterly alone. Nothing was here for her. And she had to do everything she could to get back to her home. Too long had she sat in the shadows.

And with that she threw open the black doors of the Seventh Kingdoms chambers and stepped toward the threshold, only to pause once more.

For it was the girl with violet eyes that stood before her, shock ridden all over her face.

"How?" The words came out of Carinthya's mouth before she even had a chance to stop and really look at her. To really look at her.

She was definitely the girl from the Saphirrus Orb, and everything about her was even more gorgeously divine in person. Her black raven curls fell effortlessly down her shoulders, her violet eyes more poignant and curious in person, her lips soft and poised as if to ask a question herself...

"How are you here?" she asked, her voice unsteady still.

The Violet Queen paused, her face ghostly pale. Carinthya noticed in that moment how she had dark circles under her eyes, as if she had not been sleeping. She knew that feeling all too well, and her mind started to wander to if she would be able to sneak her any of the sleeping draft she took—

"What is this?" the Violet Queen asked, her voice much unlike Carinthya's. It was soft, but there was power behind it. Clearly, it was masked by confusion, but Carinthya would never mistake softness for power ever again.

Especially being that she was a Saphirrus.

Nobody was ever to be underestimated. Her parents might have been terrible ones, but they taught her how to survive. To endure.

Hopefully the Violet Queen had learned the same things in her life leading up to this moment.

Out of the shadows, King Finn stepped forward. Alone. Shock rippled through Carinthya, for it was rare indeed that he would ever meet with others alone. He always brought reinforcements.

Where was Bairre?

"I have awaited many years for this moment," he said

with a whisper, his eyes never leaving the queen. "So long I have dreamt of two royals, together, like this."

"Like what?" Carinthya asked.

"At my mercy," King Finn hissed. "Tell me, girl, what is your name?"

"Charmaine Grimes," she said, lifting her head high.

"And tell me, Charmaine Grimes, why are you here? Do you know?"

Charmaine—the Violet Queen—glanced around. "I do not know why I am here," she said after a moment's hesitation. "Who are you?"

"Ah, a question for a question, what a fun game. I am going to play too, but only if you promise to answer."

She nodded. Not a clear vow, but a vow nonetheless.

"You may have heard of me, being that I know your background." He paused, considering. "Have you ever been to the First Kingdom's hall of portraits?"

Charmaine's cheeks reddened. Interesting.

And Carinthya's heart fluttered. She had not thought of that place in so long.

"Why?"

"Now child, you told me you would play along," he said with a *tsk tsk*.

"Yes, I have been to the Hall of Portraits."

"Do you recognize me?" he asked, stepping backward so that she could gaze at his stature. He wore dark pants and a navy blue tunic. A mockery of Saphirrus blue, Carinthya imagined.

Charmaine's violet eyes widened in shock and disbelief, though Carinthya caught a sense of deception rushing through her gaze. This girl was a good liar, a natural survivor, but Carinthya recognized the likeness that also lived within her. She was not sure she entirely believed this ruse of whether or not Charmaine was truly shocked to see the king here. Maybe, somehow, she already knew. "I thought you were dead," she whispered, her face turning a horrifying shade of gray. "Queen Ciara...she..."

"It is your turn to ask me a question darling," he drawled.

"Did the Queen of Fury not kill you?"

He smiled in a feral way, his teeth nearly fangs in his own mouth as he said, "It would appear not."

Carinthya, despite her best efforts to remain silent and invisible, snorted. This was the game he played, torturing with the truth but never telling the specifics. He had told Carinthya the same thing about his daughter when she had come here years prior, and she never got anything different out of him.

As he spun around, he seemed to remember that she was there. "Oh, I almost forgot why I called this meeting, I was having such fun with you, Charmaine Grimes."

Grabbing Carinthya's arm, she gasped, and he dragged her forward so that she was only standing a centimeter away from the Violet Queen.

King Finn nearly purred, as if he was at the center of something that nobody else was, and was having fun watching it unravel. "I am going to propose that you ask one more question, Charmaine Grimes, before we retire for the evening. I know you have already met our dearest host, Reine Eniar."

Carinthya paused. *Why in the name of the Gods would he have them meet already? What was he getting at—*

"So it better be a good one," he growled before he stepped back, letting the Violet Queen really look at her.

Carinthya did not break eye contact, and instead began to search the girls face. What was her purpose here? Why had she been dancing with her brother? What was the significance of her coming to the castle?

Charmaine opened her mouth, taking a deep breath, before asking, "Why am I here?"

King Finn cackled, throwing his head back. His red hair bloomed in the candlelight as shadows began to encroach closer and closer to him. Taking a few steps toward Charmaine, he rested his hand on her shoulder and whispered in her ear loudly enough that Carinthya could hear.

"You are here, Charmaine Grimes, because Carinthya Saphirrus told me exactly where you were," he said as he lifted a finger in-front of her face, and pointed to Carinthya herself.

Charmaine's face paled, and a look of betrayal was so apparent on her face that Carinthya could feel the pain.

"I am sorry—" she started, trying to find the words. It had been so many years since she had apologized for anything, but she knew she had been wrong.

"You see, Charmaine Grimes, I needed Carinthya to tell me where you were because you are very special to someone who I need to see."

"No—" Charmaine said in one breath, so quiet and filled with terror that Carinthya gasped. She did not know exactly why she had been looking at the orb that day—

"Carinthya knows him too, but never would have told me without you being a part of my grander plans." King Finn paused, tilting his head to the side. "I know you have a very special ability, Charmaine Grimes, one that it is my understanding that you do not know how to use very well. Or so my intelligence has told me."

"I do not know what you are talking about—" she said, taking a step backward, her dark gown ruffling behind her.

"I think you do, Charmaine Grimes," King Finn said, stepping forward so that she was no longer one step away. "How you disappeared during the fire of Brinn, where I was looking for you. How you disappeared from the ballroom, when I was searching for you amongst the castle. King Ronan told me that you were there—"

Carinthya felt like she was going to vomit at the mention of her father. At the mention of her brother. At the look of fear on this girls' face. It was clear Carinthya had made a grander mistake than she had ever realized.

Charmaine Grimes was not a queen, she was a girl.

A girl with power.

One that King Finn wanted for his own gain—

"How you disappeared from me multiple times, only to be caught in plain sight it would appear." He chuckled, darkness swarming around them.

"What do you want with me?" she said softly, her voice unwavering but quiet.

"Two simple things my dearest child. I want you to use that special little gift of mine on my armies."

"Is that all?" Charmaine said, now laughing. What was so funny?

"And I want you to bring me the King of Snow."

CHAPTER SEVEN

It had been many hours since Cyril had laid eyes on Dalton, which was problematic for many reasons.

The last few weeks had been tumultuous between them for obvious reasons. Dalton was keeping it together, as best as he could. He knew that the draw that existed between Dalton and Charmaine was—at this point—doing more harm than good.

Not that it had ever done good really, for they had never quite figured out why the Gods were driving them together so aggressively. There was something between them for sure, that was clear.

The snow that still fell from the sky in the tiniest of waves was a constant reminder of the power that had exploded across the continent. And any that had any sense at all would know that this was not just a cause of the impending winter that would unleash upon them all.

No, rather, this was something deeper than that. A power that had never been awoken before, and now set loose upon the continent.

Dalton Saphirrus, it would seem, had unleashed upon them all at last.

There had been a weight sitting upon Cyril's old shoulders for many weeks now, something stirring in the shadows of his mind that he could not put a finger on. That was how he knew that some prophecy was brewing, something grander than what he could even imagine.

Great.

Splendid.

But as he was overcome with the sudden urge to find Dalton—to tell him something—he knew it was time.

Time for what, he was not sure.

But he would tell him what he could.

He always did. And always would.

Standing up slowly, Cyril began to make his way down the corridor toward the King's chambers. He had heard among the servants that it was where Dalton had retired after a minor outburst in the council meeting.

Lord Peach was a real pain in the ass, and quite the wet blanket, so Cyril silently prayed that he was the one who had the pleasure of awakening the king within Dalton.

Walking with purpose now, his arms swinging wildly, Cyril reached Dalton's chambers. Without a knock, and praying that Dalton was fully clothed—because you truly never knew with him—he did what he did best.

He barged in.

And then it hit Cyril as if he were being crushed by a stone, falling from the sky so fast that he did not even have time to look up before he was gone.

That was the memory.

The moment.

Before he knew what he was doing, before he realized the turmoil and the actions that these consequences would have, he was moving toward him with his hands extended.

Dalton's name was at the tip of his tongue, but he forbid himself from even speaking a word. He did not know how much time his body would give him before the Thinker rules would come out, and he did not know if Dalton would even know what he was getting at. It was imperative that the boy understood him.

If not, it would all be for nothing. This was far graver than Cyril had ever imagined. Suddenly, the urgency that he had felt was clear. The Gods were giving him a window, one that he must take on a leap of faith that his heart would only slow, not completely stop.

His time was not done yet, Cyril knew this for sure.

After weeks of agonizing over the prophecy, rethinking each and every moment over the last months, Cyril had finally been in a place where he was to give up. However, as he had turned the last few pages of Ciara's journal, rereading and reading and rereading... Well, he saw it. The line and the word of what she had been planning to do all along.

What she never had the chance to do because her life was snatched from her at the hands of her father.

Cyril would not even think it, not even let it burden him. He could not risk not saying what he had to say.

"Cyril?" Dalton asked, all humor devoid from his voice. Cyril knew now that Dalton could see the look on his face.

He knew he would be there, or he would not have made his way. Dalton remained very few places this day, plotting and broken. He also looked very different these days, his dark hair curling against the sides of his head like the shadow king that he was capable of becoming. He was eerily familiar in this state, looking more and more like Cian than Cyril could bear.

His friend, it would seem, had transcended lifetimes to cure the world of King Finn once and for all.

When that letter had arrived, detailing who had

returned and why, Cyril's bones had shook, his breath rattled without even thinking. The darkness that was encroaching on their world was beyond anything that Dalton had ever experienced, and Cyril feared for him.

He feared for Charmaine too, but feared more for what would become of Dalton if Finn never let her come home.

Pushing away the thought with a groan, Cyril looked directly into the eyes of his king who looked very much like his best friend of a century ago.

The voice that spoke to him was immediate and sharp. "Cyril, has something happened?"

Without partaking in the usual banter that Dalton was without expecting, Cyril marched over to him. He could feel the sweat building on his brow, his breath more ragged by the second. It was almost like when he had heard the contents of that letter, but now it was real.

And Cyril had a solution. A way to stop him.

Gods forgive him for what he was about to do.

With a shaking hand, he placed one on Dalton's left shoulder. With another shaking hand, he put another on his right.

"Are you alright, Cyril?" Dalton asked, his dark hair and voice so much like Cian that Cyril wanted to cry out at the memory of his lost friend. But this was no time for grief, and only hoped that Dalton would not take it too hard.

"You need to give it to her," he whispered, his eyes pleading that Dalton would understand. That he would carry these words with him. He knew he was leaving, he knew that he was plotting an escape.

A rescue mission.

And he hoped that this would be the impetuous, the defining moment that would lead to him finally taking the leap after weeks of considering it. Cyril knew Dalton like he knew every line on his own two hands. Dalton would do it.

He would just need a push.

A very large one indeed.

"Cyril?" Dalton asked, his voice becoming more concerned, raising an octave as Cyril began to sink to the floor.

Clutching his hands to his chest, he felt as though someone were standing on it. A great weight relieved off his shoulders, but now forced to weigh on him in other ways.

The Gods, he knew, were displeased. He had broken the cardinal rule, but so swiftly that he knew that he would not be dead.

Not yet, anyway. They had given him this window, and he was to take it.

"Go to her," Cyril groaned out, his voice strained and his face hot. Tears streaked down his cheeks as Dalton coaxed him to lay down.

Screaming erupted from the King, his own fear over-taking him.

But Cyril did not want him to fear.

He wanted him to understand.

He wanted him to go.

To carry those words with him.

And get her back.

Chapter Eight

For the first time in Reine's life, she felt truly and utterly hopeless. Losing her brother had been one thing, but something that she had resigned herself to recovering from over time. She dreamt of finding him again one day, that hope staying alive within her like a flame of a candle that flickered.

The fire had never gone out for her there, but this? Being captured and at the mercy of a king which everyone had thought was dead? This was something that was completely and utterly inescapable for her, that feeling of being stuck.

One that she was never quite sure that she would make it out of.

So these past few nights, she did what her brother had once told her to do when there was darkness that shrouded her. She focused on what she could control, focused on dreams.

And last night she dreamt of ferocity.

The heat of the world was not hot enough in Castle

Dead. The walls were not dark enough. The flowers did not bloom enough.

This place was never just that for her: enough.

Reine thought of herself as such a thing, a concept of royalty. But never had she ever thought that her entire life would be subjected to awaiting the return of her brother. Plain and simple: he should have never left to begin with. She understood wildly how difficult it had been for him, growing up and being forced against his will to be as he was.

They had both been subjected and forced to do unspeakable acts. They had burned, they had hurt, and they had killed in the castles in order to stay alive. Father had been damningly difficult, something which she was understanding now was not an enigma among the Kings of New Sarridolon.

Difficult men—she realized more and more each day—were not the apex of society. They were merely the surge of power.

And when that surge was over, well, those who had it wasted away to nothing.

Though it was women who were destined to rule this continent. She had known it from the moment she was a little girl.

Ciara had done it.

And she would do it too.

So she dreamt of ferocity, and smiled as she thought of burning down the whole world.

And when she closed her eyes, she dreamt of the girl with violet eyes, for she knew she had that power within her too.

It was just going to be a matter of when it erupted.

CHAPTER NINE

Randolph Eniar paced back and forth in Dalton's chambers, not sure how he really ended up here at all.

It had been a whirlwind the last two days. Cyril had collapsed, Dalton had explained, on the precipice of explaining something to him that the Gods obviously had forbid. And the cost, in most cases for a Thinker to disobey like that, was their life. However, someone (or some God, Randolph was not sure what the intervention was), let him get out a few words before he fell.

However, he was still alive.

Dalton had been feverish in despair, rightfully so. There were so few relationships where Dalton really let the other completely in. And Cyril saw all.

He was a good man. Randolph prayed when he could for his return to health.

But this form of Dalton was a rare one indeed.

Not even Randolph knew if he could control him, especially since Elena had employed him for such a task that he was sure he was to fail.

Opening his mouth to speak out and try to make sense of what Dalton had just said, he found himself once again interrupted.

"Have you ever fucked up so badly that you're not even sure that you really fucked up at all?" Dalton twirled a lock of his black hair incessantly. This was what it had been for the last hour, nonsense, nonsense, and more nonsense... Speaking in riddles and walking in circles around one another. Literally.

Randolph's fists were clenched at his side—a rather natural disposition for him at this point—so it was of no cause of concern for the King of Snow.

"You know, I do not appreciate that the blessed Gods did not even give me a choice in the matter of my new hair color. What if I liked having white hair?"

"The longer we sit here, the longer we lose sight of her." Randolph was tired—per usual—but he knew what Dalton was doing. He was stalling. Going to escape on his own.

Find her. That was Cyril's message.

All the confirmation that Dalton needed that he needed to leave.

Randolph had seen the power explode out of Dalton, causing this nearly eternal flurry and the darkness of winter to linger over them like an ever looming storm. Randolph would never forget the sight of his friend—yes, friend—sitting up after Charmaine had been taken to a pile of frost and snowflakes, only to recognize that Dalton had transformed. That scream that had escaped him, it had been one of the deepest and rawest power that Randolph had ever encountered. Something primal that he could never take back.

Dalton had mentioned before that the white hair had been some sort of manifestation of his power and energy. His aura had been exploding with it when Randolph had met him when he was inducted into the knights. But now? Now it was like an ever-lit candle. It was always there and on, but it did not shine like it once did. The light had gone out, at least partially.

That was what happened when someone you loved leaves you. It scars. It burns. It ignites and it dulls all the same.

Randolph knew the feeling deep in his bones.

"You think I do not know that, Eniar?" Dalton snarled, finally breaking character. "If you have not noticed, I cope by ignoring. I ignore your ass. I ignored Cyril's ass, and look how that turned out for me. Very regrettable, might I add. I ignored Charmaine's own feelings for the sake of keeping myself together these last few months. There is nothing but ice in my heart, despite my teddy bear disposition. Did you know that, Eniar?"

Randolph stood. "I never once thought you had a teddy bear disposition, Dalton."

"Are we on a first name basis now?" Dalton egged on. *Say it. Say it. Say it. Say it.*

Lips pursed, Randolph paused. "I need to go home, I am wasting time sitting here. We need to get home. To get to her. You know what the letter said—"

"And what exactly are you going to do when you arrive home? Take me to the tattoo parlor so we can get matching sunflowers on our asses?"

Randolph snorted.

At least Dalton was getting somewhere.

"We leave at the end of the week. It is decided."

"The week?"

"You need to brush up on your drawing skills," Dalton said casually, throwing a paintbrush that had been sitting in his back-pocket this whole time toward Randolph.

"Drawing?" he asked, confused.

"Make yourself useful and draw me a map."

"Of what?" he said, perplexed by Dalton's order.

"Of everything I am going to need to know to get her back."

"You cannot be serious, we cannot enter the Seventh Kingdom without a plan—"

Dalton took two steps toward him abruptly, so close that Randolph could see every freckle across his cheeks and nose. He looked very much like stardust when he had white hair, but now he looked something of a nightmare reincarnate with his dark features. Something that had haunted him as a child after he read a scary story, he was sure of it. "I am not sure why you are making things difficult for me Randolph, either you do this for me right now or I am leaving of my own accord without any information. And I can only guess that would go badly—"

"You cannot leave on impulse! We need to think, how are we going to get her back? What awaits us—"

Ice crackled on the floor beneath them, and Randolph refused to look down to acknowledge it. To acknowledge Dalton was to give him even more power than humanly possible, and he needed to remain in some semblance of control. The fate of the Ten Kingdoms was resting upon the actions of this young King, and Randolph could call him nothing but utterly unhinged.

Well, there may be a few more words that he could call him—

"I am leaving," Dalton said, snowflakes puffing out of his mouth nonsensically. "Now. And there is nothing you can do to stop me."

And then he spun and turned, leaving nothing but frost in his wake.

—

Randolph had thought, by all accounts, that Dalton was not serious.

Normally, he operated on complete chaos and all-talk, most would say. But when both Lawton and Elena thundered into his room nonsensically, hours after their exchange in the council chambers, Randolph knew that he had royally fucked up.

"You are kidding me," Randolph said as they both stood before him, flustered beyond all means. "He did not—"

"He is gone," Elena said, tears welling in her eyes. She took a step closer to him, and Randolph felt that familiar sensation of butterflies in his stomach rise once more. "Did he tell you he was leaving? We were supposed to have time to prepare, to convince the council of our operations so that we could have support—"

Randolph stood, mouth agape, and all that Cyril whispered was. "You knew."

"I did not know—"

Smack.

A hand collided with the side of his face, strong and filled with complete and utter rage.

Elena had hit him.

She had hit him hard.

"Elena—" Lawton gasped, rather horrified.

"He lives with his heart, Randolph! Not with his head! How could you be so stupid—"

"ELENA!" Lawton roared, and Randolph's head popped up at the sound. Lawton never yelled, lest at a Queen. "He could not have possibly known that Dalton was serious..."

"Dalton is always serious, that is the problem, Lawton! It is the fact that you never know when he is kidding...that is the issue!"

Randolph had to agree.

As they continued to bicker between themselves, and bicker at him, Randolph pushed it all away. The uncertainty, the shock of realizing that the truly had left, and the fear that lived within him at what he would find when he returned home. What lived within the Seventh Kingdom now was yet to be determined, yet as he thought about things, he realized once and for all that he had already decided what he was going to do.

Turning around so quickly, leaving them to their business, he threw together a few things in a pack which he could strap to his horse, Gregoria. It had been some time since he had ridden her, for he did not want to burden her with too much weight.

And if he knew one thing, Dalton was fast.

And he was going to have to catch him.

"And where do you think you are—"

"I am going after him."

"Then I am coming too," Lawton protested, putting his hand on Randolph's shoulder.

"So you are both just going to leave me then?" Elena's eyes welled up, but it was more with understanding than it was anything else. This was the part of duty that Randolph knew that she hated, and technically, she was still the Queen consort of the First Kingdom, despite her protests to the title and their mutual desire to dissolve the marriage.

Randolph stepped forward, suddenly feeling bold despite having royally messed up nearly everything. He legitimately lost his king. Nothing could be more shameful than that.

And he had called himself a knight...

"Elena LeClair, you are the strongest person I know," he started, looking her directly in the eye. "You have survived so much, and kept your head high the whole time. That is what royals do, but more than that, that is what you do. I trust nobody but you to keep the First Kingdom safe while we go after Dalton."

She smiled softly, breathing in deeply and closing her eyes. Resetting herself after feeling so much emotion so quickly.

"Then bring him home quickly, for messing with Lord Peach is not nearly any fun if you cannot freeze him to the floor."

CHAPTER TEN

L awton did not know how it was possible that Dalton Saphirrus and Randolph Eniar could have any type of discussion without creating some sort of incident on the continent.

It was so fascinating to him, to observe how different they were and how they clashed as so. At first, the difference between the two was physically relevant, being that Dalton looked like snow itself and Randolph always embodied more of a harshness. However, now the lines were blurred.

Maybe they were closer together in ways that even Lawton did not understand. And maybe now they were finally starting to see eye to eye, despite the consistency of the bickering and the frustration. Lawton did not have any siblings, but he figured that what they had was not too much different than that.

Randolph and Lawton had departed as soon as the moon was high, carrying nothing but what could fit on their horses.

The Kings new dark hair helped make him more conspicuous, but Lawton knew that the King of the First

Kingdom had this aura to him that could not be hidden. That's how Randolph had discovered that Lawton had power in the first place, his aura shining merely too bright... or something like that.

The King's aura was bright white, almost as if he had casted a spell of winter wonderland around him. Randolph on the other hand was dark, smoky.

Lawton would expect nothing else from either of them.

Dalton had not gotten very far, despite leaving before them. Lawton would not waste precious seconds recounting all of the ways that he thought that the King of Snow could have gotten distracted along the way. It could have been anything. A snowflake. A stray cat. A gust of the wind. Simply just getting lost in thought.

There were many reasons for Dalton Saphirrus to stop along the way, however, there were many reasons for him to keep on going, and never give in.

Randolph and Lawton followed silently for a few paces, and then nodded to one another in confirmation that they would jump in order to get closer. They were not speaking, but it did not take a genius to figure out where in the name of the Ten Kingdoms they were even going. Obviously, she had violet eyes, black hair, a recently deceased brother—

A hand smashed into Lawton's throat, pinning him to the wall that had been behind him mere seconds ago.

Dazzled in flowers, Lawton was surprised it hurt this badly to be choked out by something so physically beautiful.

"Dear Gods! THORNWOOD!" Dalton yelped, peeling his hand off Lawton's throat as if it had burned him to the touch. "Do not ever sneak up on me like that again..."

"I...was...not...sneaking!" Lawton choked out, his throat raw. "If there are...marks on my neck...my king... I will have you hanged..."

"I am so sorry," Dalton said, coming over to him

cautiously. Clearly, Dalton had no idea how to comfort another at the fault of his own hand. "I did not mean... Hold on! You will have me hanged—"

"Think," Lawton said hoarsely. "Think next time you try to kill a random person you hear behind you..."

"Thinking?" A voice like snow and ice said with a dark chuckle. "Eniar has never thought about anything in his life, but I appreciate the sentiment."

Randolph rolled his eyes, two fingers burrowing into them in a manner which Lawton thought looked rather painful. He would have commented, ordinarily, but he thought it unwise given how he was still catching his breath.

"Dalton, I did not mean—"

Dalton held up a long icy finger, frost dancing on his skin like icing on a cake. "Rule number one on our journey Eniar, you must stop lying to yourself. I scared you, you did not mind it, the end."

Lawton made a strangled sound that he hoped they interpreted to sound like a laugh, because it was.

"I am working on it," Randolph hissed.

"If this is working on it, I am worried for you my dear friend." Dalton took a step toward Lawton, concern etched in his eyes despite the fear of the moment. "So, I assume you are coming with us? It took surprisingly little time for you both to catch up to me, though I must say I could have had a bit less fun sneaking out of the citadel—"

Randolph moaned, and all Lawton could do is smile.

"Excellent then. Here are the rules. One, do not lie to yourself. Two, do not lie to me. Three, when we get there and all hell breaks loose, we get Charmaine Grimes out of Castle Dead."

Randolph moved to interrupt, but Dalton sealed his lips with a mere wiggle of his dark eyebrows.

"He is not rather fond of rule four, but let me inform you, Lawton Thornwood, it is the most important."

Grumbling ensured as Randolph lips began to grow red, clearly an attempt to melt off the ice-seal which had impaired his speaking abilities.

"Rule four is quite simple—and the most important as I just mentioned"—He paused, breathing out a puff of snowflakes dramatically—" If you, or Rand here, get to Charmaine first. You leave. Without me."

Lawton gaped, unsure what to say. To leave the King in any capacity had to be against some sort of knights code...

"So, are you coming?"

CHAPTER ELEVEN

And so they walked on.

Or rather, the horses did.

When they had snuck up on him—badly, he might add—he had heard them put their horses behind the three. Luckily for them, they brought one for him as well.

That was part of why they had been able to catch up to him, he had simply walked out of the castle. He was tired of waiting for life to take him by storm, he was the lightning bolt, the catastrophe to get everything into motion.

It was time he started to use that to his advantage.

Dalton could not help but enjoy the company, though he made sure to remind each of them that he was merely a pain and completely and utterly unhinged. It was his silent way of communicating, for he felt as though he was on the cusp of some villainous spur that he could not and would not contain. The power within him was surging in bursts, somehow worse than it had ever been when he was embodied snow itself.

The dark hair was not a relief, but rather the burden of darkness.

Power bloomed within him, coming in waves. Sometimes it reminded him of its presence with some additional snowflakes falling in an already winter scenario, other times it was more like a feeling. Anxiousness is the only thing that he could describe it as, though he was not willing to admit that to anyone just yet. It was as if a weight was sitting on his shoulders, demanding to be felt and heard.

Per usual, he decided if this was what true power was, he did not want it.

Randolph and Lawton rode together side by side, and Dalton found himself grateful that he was in front of them. It was easier to eavesdrop this way.

And it was easier to think without interrogation.

Dalton knew that if he slipped too much, if he appeared too pensive, Randolph would know all.

Dalton, for all it was worth, was scheming. And he did not think in earnest that he would be one to make it out of Castle Dead.

He was willing to embrace that, willing to do that, as long as it meant that Charmaine was without harm.

As he let the thoughts surge and run rampant, he caught himself lost in thought. It may have been hours, or minutes. Who knows, he was never truly that good at mathematics.

"Are we just going to walk there then?" Lawton asked, his voice filled with cheer despite almost dying earlier at the hands of Dalton. A surge of power had come over him suddenly, despite hearing them. If he would have simply appeared, the effect would not have been the same.

It was a power move, not against Lawton, though Lawton had been the one to feel its wrath. Literally. It was so that Randolph would understand that Dalton would overturn every stone, look through every forest, let nothing stand in his way.

Charmaine Grimes was to return home. No matter the cost.

"Well, technically, we are riding," Dalton snickered, not bothering to look backward at him. "Why do you not just jump us there, that would be easiest."

Lawton huffed a sigh. "I have been practicing, in complete seriousness, but it is nothing to write home about."

"Well, good then, for I am not about to turn around," Dalton sneered. He knew what Lawton was actually saying, but could not miss an opportunity to once again remind them that there would be nothing on this continent to turn him around.

He was getting to her.

And she was coming home.

And that was that.

"How far can you make it?" Randolph asked in sincerity, after a moment's pause.

"I think I could do a mile, at most, but I am not sure what I could do after that."

"Do emotions bring it out of you more?" Dalton found himself asking.

"Pardon?" Lawton asked, curiosity creeping into his voice.

"Do you find that, if per se, you are upset... well, do you have more power then?"

Dalton heard Randolph's breath hitch. Did he know what he was talking about then? Or was he truly alone in all of this?

"To be honest, Dalton, I do not know." Though, Lawton did not sound very convinced of his own "honesty".

"Are you sure about that?" Dalton asked, swiveling his head around to face him.

Lawton was biting his lip, cheeks flushed, and blue eyes

haunted by some sort of memory. "Well, the first time that I ever jumped... It was complicated. It was not rage or anger per se, but a surge of high emotions. I suppose it is exactly like you are referencing, though I have not thought of this moment in quite some time."

"Were you able to control it?" Dalton asked, curious and nervous for his reply all at the same time.

"Not at all, actually quite the opposite. But I am wondering now if that had to do with inexperience, rather than the power taking over me."

"Interesting," Dalton said, putting some stock into that thought. When his power erupted, it had been explosive. Both when it first came out, and next when Charmaine was taken. Was he just incapable of channeling it? Or was that something that he had not even really attempted? Could the well of power be challenged, and better yet, controlled?

Randolph cleared his throat, obviously eager to remove himself from the potential of this conversation. Though, Dalton already knew the answer to any questions that he had for Randolph regarding power. Dalton was certain that if he was bad at controlling his power, well, Randolph was so much worse.

"Where are we staying this evening?" Randolph's voice cut through the air like the sound of reason that he somehow was. "Are we to pause at a tavern? Resume in the morning? It is going to get dark soon, and Dalton, well, it's rather cold."

"Then make it warm, Randy boy," Dalton said lazily, urging his black stallion forward. "Show us some control."

CHAPTER TWELVE

Shadows curled around the make-shift throne room in complete and utter agony, as if they were straining against the power of King Finn himself. Maybe it was rejecting him, the shadows that were stolen were in fact stolen after all.

Maybe they too wanted to break free and go home to people who loved them.

Charmaine Grimes kneeled with her hands tied behind her back, her face tilted upward by the long shadow covered finger of King Finn, and wished that she could find the courage to go where the shadows might. Silently, she made the vow to herself, if an opportunity arose that she would follow them.

"Speak to me, girl. What can you tell me of Dalton Saphirrus?" Finn's voice cut through the air like a shadow itself, bone-chilling and frightening. He loomed over her like a giant, though he was probably not much taller than herself if she were to stand next to him.

What could he possibly want with Dalton? His power? Was the eternal winter around them not enough evidence of what brewed underneath the prince's skin? Her mind wandered to dark, darker, and the darkest places. Fear clutched at her chest, threatening to burst forth with tears at the thought of causing anyone else that she loved harm. James, her father, her mother, her friends... They had all suffered at this point because of her mere existence. Finn had been after her all this time. And there was nothing that she could do but to endure. But what she would not do? That was most important.

Charmaine pursed her lips, contemplating what she could give away that would not lead him and her friends back in the First Kingdom to their deaths. There was so much that she could say about Dalton that she was truly not sure where to start. How much time did Finn have to listen to all of the things that she could say about Dalton Saphirrus? A smile began to curl at her lips.

Nothing she would say about Dalton would be information that he cared about.

"Well?" he pressed, nearly snarling in her face. His red hair appeared a shade darker today, almost duller. Was it possible for him to age? Or was this a part of him now, that he was just less bright than the average person.

Definitely less bright than Dalton Saphirrus. Nobody quite shined like the King of Snow.

"He is a great kisser," she said matter-of-factly, followed by a short laugh.

Bairre behind her snorted, his shadows skirting across the floor as if they too were laughing. She had forgotten that he was there to begin with, always lurking in the darkness.

Yet, he had a brightness to himself as well.

Unfortunately, King Finn did not share their sentiment.

The shadows curled around her neck like a fist, oxygen depleting from her instantly. Trying to move her hands to go for her throat, to provide herself any relief, Charmaine began to sob inadvertently. He leaned close to her face for a second, snarling, and she blinked as if he were going to hit her.

No.

She was over this.

Being weak.

Being stuck as the girl from Brinn.

She was so much more.

She had to be.

Nobody else would be hurt at her expense.

According to Finn, she was worth something. Something more than just being in love with the King of Snow. She was a piece of this grander prophecy, just did not know how yet she was to fit in.

But she was determined to figure it out.

And she would not break.

As her breath slowly came back to her, she realized that this was all true and not some mantra that she was telling herself to get her emotions under control. If Finn wanted her dead, she *would* be dead.

But why was she alive?

And what power did she hold here?

She decided, then and there, that she had some semblance of power. And she was not talking of invisibility. She was talking of politics, something that she had been well-versed in when it came to Dalton Saphirrus.

"Stop," she choked out. "Stop."

"And why should I stop?" King Finn screamed, his voice deep and rumbling. Hands clutched at her throat, suddenly, a physical reminder that he was not some mirage of power. He was really here. Somehow, and against all odds.

"Because..." she gasped out, her body shaking uncontrollably. Out of the corner of her eye, she saw Bairre step forward. If he was worried, clearly something was massively askew. "Because you . . . You need me."

He paused, as if a victim of his had never spoken such a thing aloud before.

Glancing to where Bairre stood in the shadows, he growled, "Bairre, come here."

Walking with a level of casual that Charmaine had only ever seen on Dalton after he had gotten up to complete and utter mischief, Bairre strode over but with a hint of caution. "Yes, my liege?"

"Where are Phillis and Meriki?" Finn spat.

Bairre only replied with, "Out."

Finn swore, and she could have sworn that he also had the word useless thrown in with a plethora of other colorful language choices.

With a thud, Charmaine dropped to the floor. Her knees hit the ground with a *crunch*, her pain there however nothing compared to the shadowed marks that she knew now lived on her throat. Hands grasping, she made a move to look up at King Finn.

She would not falter.

She would not fear.

She was strong.

She was power.

She was loved.

With all the hatred that she could muster, she met King Finn's gaze. She tried to imagine, in that moment, what she would look like to the king who had come back to life. She was sure that it was pathetic, but there was no way of telling such a thing. So she did the only thing that she could do, look at Finn as if she was the most powerful being on the continent.

She looked at him as she imagined Dalton to look at him. Like he was nothing,

Like he had just made a huge mistake.

"He will come for you, you must know that."

It was an empty threat, but a threat nonetheless, and the only thing that she could dangle. Ambiguity and haunting promise wrapped in one.

"And who might he be?" Finn asked, nearly snarling.

"The King of Snow."

Faster than he had dropped her, he looked away.

"Get her out of my sight, Bairre."

Throwing his hands up in the air, his shadows raced toward the door, eager to leave the situation. The heels of his boots thundered in an echo as he made his way out of the room, as if he had never been there at all.

In this moment, Charmaine Grimes knew one thing.

She had won.

For now.

CHAPTER THIRTEEN

In the depths of the castle, the dragon awoke. It had been many weeks since he had been last visited by the King of Snow, and even longer since he had been summoned to speak by the Queen of Fury and her husband. The first King of Snow, he had been.

However, these *new* rulers, they intrigued him. Randolph Eniar was stoic, especially, given the rumblings among the Gods about his power. But he could sense the power that lurked within him. It did not ooze, no, it was the definition of control. Even more impressive and important than he could have ever imagined, another twist in the long tale which he could write about his life. Though he had spent most of it in the dungeon.

Dragon to dragon, this was something that he knew that he would need to wait to see erupt over time.

Kai, the only dragon left in this world, paced back and forth and dreamt of none other than Dalton Saphirrus.

The complete opposite of control.

And frankly, far more intriguing.

There was something about the boy, white hair gone and his heart shattered into a million pieces, that intrigued him. It was the same level of heartbreak that Cian had when Ciara had disappeared from the world after destroying her father.

They were far too similar for coincidence. And it drove Kai mad.

Or at least, what the world had understood at the time for the destruction of her father. A part of Kai was twisted over the fact that she had died for nothing, and he did not have soft spots for many humans. But there was some centripetal force that seemed to connect Dalton, Ciara, and Cian. It was beyond Kai how it could be, other than their relationship as royalty of the First Kingdom.

A problem that he could ponder another day.

For that was the least of his worries. And he did not have many.

The Saphirrus men were many things in life, but they were not disloyal. And if Dalton was anything like Cian, he would do what he needed to do to get the woman of his dreams back. But Kai could not help but feel the flames begin to trickle up his spine every time he thought that today would be the day that the young king would call on him.

Of that, Kai had much experience. That desperation to be free. Oh, it had been so many years. He had been visited by the young and old king, many times throughout his life. At first it had been desperation, the driving force behind trying to get her back and bring her home. Over time, however, the forces that drove Cian seemed to lay more with pure admittance and a lack of fullness.

Ciara herself had been electric in more ways than one, her shadows nearly spurting lightning they were so charged with ferocity. Kai admired her because they were more the same than they were different, him and her.

But this was the first time—with Dalton Saphirrus—that a promise of release had been given. And Saphirrus' were many things: chaotic, broken, maybe a little bit crazy, but they were *not* liars. They were true to their word.

Scraping his claws on the ground impatiently, sparks flew up and the cobblestones began to burn where he had made contact. This was what he had been subjected to, making sparks out of stones. He was a great dragon, one who had ruled the continent for so many years prior to any one of importance coming along. And now he amounted to nothing.

But Dalton Saphirrus was going to change all of that. Change fate. Change the heavens itself.

Kai was sure of it.

Looking up at the grand staircase that sat before him, he pondered once again his long-lost friends Cian and Ciara.

"Were you thinking about me?" A voice chided from the darkness that surrounded him, laced with the night sky and shadows darker than the ones from which the voice sounded.

Chains rattling, Kai stood without warning. It had been a hundred years since he had last heard that voice, a century worth of waiting and rumbling. He looked forward to the Saphirrus boy unleashing the signal, one which he would come forth and be able to seek his vengeance.

Freedom.

However, this was an alternative that he could live with. One that he may even...prefer. He could wait a while longer, as long as the voice that lived in-front of him was not a part of his memory and was actually very much alive.

Shadows blistered around his shackles with a death-like stillness, and Kai found himself rumbling a laugh from the pit of his stomach as he gazed upon the familiar face which he dreamt of so many nights and moments for the last one hundred years.

"I knew you would come, but I figured it still be sometime," Kai hissed, but not without fondness. "Now, where are we off too, my love?"

CHAPTER FOURTEEN

An adventure with Lawton Thornwood would have been one thing.

An adventure with Randolph Eniar would have been questionable at best, but he could have managed it. Another thing entirely but not out of the question in terms of ridiculousness.

But *this*? Ten Kingdoms.

An adventure with the two of them?

Gods.

Dalton was not sure he strong enough for such a feat. Especially with his patience running thin and his power running thicker and thicker in his veins by the minute. Them joining him had been a part of his grandest scheme yet, a ploy to get them both to follow him willingly to get Charmaine back.

He thought that he bickered and was a nuisance. But no, Lawton Thornwood had taken the title within the first few hours of their journey together. There was not one stone left unturned when it came to Lawton.

And it brought Dalton an insurmountable amount of

joy to see just how much Randolph could not deal with Lawton's chaos.

Dalton was taking notes.

Maybe this could be great fun after all. However, his patience was running thinner and thinner as they approached the unknown roads that laid before them. The draw had been waning, but as they approached the edge of the First Kingdom last night and entered the Tenth Kingdom, he could feel the tug beginning to yank once more.

Dalton could only describe it—to himself, as surely he would admit this to nobody else—as an invisible string that jerked ever so slightly every few hours. It was almost like a heartbeat, though very far away and faint.

But the inconsistent beating reminded him that she was still there, and hopefully she could still feel what he could feel.

With all of this in mind, they charged on for hours. The sun beat down on them relentlessly a cooler day as they made their way across the Tenth Kingdom. With every step getting further and further way from all he had ever known, a weight was added. It was the ongoing realization that all that he could see before himself, the mountains rolling and the grassy plains ahead, all did in fact belong to him.

They were his responsibility. All of which *actually* belonged to him was now well behind him. However, all of which that he was going to save still stood before him. It was vast, vaster than he ever could have imagined as a child.

And all of it was in jeopardy.

With a startle, he looked behind him as he heard a large crashing sound. Before he could stop himself, he found his lip curled upward and his eyebrows furrowed in the utmost level of irritation.

"What. Are. You. Doing," he spat out, each word filled with more and more agitation by the second.

Lawton swung off his horse in one motion, the dapple mare not moving even an inch. Clearly, she was used to whatever nonsense went along with journeying with Lawton Thornwood.

"It appears in my mad dash to follow your Majesties," he said, his voice sounding further away as he leaned down to pick up the sacks that had fallen from the sides of the mare. With a grunt he rose and repeated, "It appears that in my mad dash to follow your Majesties this morning that I did not tie my knots quite tight enough."

Randolph, emotionless, merely just blinked in irritation.

Dalton, however, possessed no such subtleties.

"Maybe you should not have dashed," Dalton said, resetting his white mare. "Maybe you should have just not come at all."

"And miss all the adventure?"

Dalton clutched the reins tighter, his knuckles turning white. "This is not a game," he said. "She is not a game."

"Dalton," Randolph said, finally speaking for the first time this day. "He knows this is not a game. *She* is not a game."

"Charmaine Grimes is my friend," Lawton said, sounding genuinely hurt. Dalton almost felt bad. "I want her to get home safely, that is why I am here."

"Then why can you not just jump us to her?"

"I have already told you, your Majesty. I wish it worked that way," Lawton whispered, yet Dalton and Randolph looked at him as if he had yelled. The power in his voice was there, commanding and stern, despite it acknowledging those he spoke to. "But I do not think I could manage a jump from our Kingdom to the Seventh your Majesty."

"You do not have to call me that," Dalton said, refusing to look back. His temper was already volatile enough, he did not need to yell at anyone else. At least for the moment. He needed to stay focused on the mission.

Focused on getting her back.

That was what truly mattered.

"But I do," Lawton said. Dalton could tell that he was smiling, just by the sound in his voice. "Because whether or not you like it, Dalton Saphirrus, you are going to be the one to save us all."

Dalton snorted at that, though he hated how right part of the statement was. "And I am lucky, I suppose, to have two valiant companions. Just think of the songs that they will write about us boys."

"Oh once was a boy with two kings, who hated one another yet loved one another's friendship. Oh once was a boy with two kings, who traveled across New Sarridolon in search of the king's girl..."

"I hate this song," Randolph muttered as Lawton took it from the top.

"You should sing that for the Old Dead King who is no longer dead," Dalton muttered irritably.

Though he had to admit, it had a nice ring to it.

CHAPTER FIFTEEN

It had been a few days since Dalton, Randolph, and Lawton had gone after Charmaine. Elena had been waiting patiently for some type of letter or sign, but nothing had appeared.

Quickly, she realized that she was probably waiting for nothing.

Even though she had been upset when they had initially left, she quickly realized that they were right. She was the only one who could hold the First Kingdom down, control things and steer the Lords in the right direction. She might not have a frozen fist, but she did have power.

She was, by all accounts, the Queen of the First Kingdom.

Dalton and company would want to be discrete and move quickly. Her mind immediately went to tales that she had heard of royals in the olden days running from kingdom to kingdom in secret, staying at taverns and hiding out in the woods.

She imagined that this was very much what they were to be doing, arriving in secret. And writing a letter as a result of that would be plenty stupid. They could not be caught. They could not fail.

The fate of the world depended on it. That much she was sure.

So it was to her utmost surprise that she found a letter on her nightstand after a long day of Queen-ing, addressed to her.

"Dalton?" she questioned, for it did look like his handwriting.

Sure enough, it was.

The letter fell out of the addressed enveloped draped in winter wonder. The paper was stark white, and she could have sworn that snowflakes dripped out of the packaging without causing any water damage. It brought a smile to her face, as everything Dalton always did.

DEAREST ELENA, *my darling wife, and my moon to the ocean.*

Did you practically vomit as you read that? It took everything in me not to projectile myself as I wrote it. I am not sure when my return will be, nor do I have a clear plan as to what I am even going to do. However, my plan is relatively straightforward.

I am to collect Charmaine Grimes and return with my head attached to my body.

Simple enough, I am to hope.

I expect that I will have two accompaniments to this journey. I know that Randolph will not be able to help himself, especially given the location as to where my journey is going to take me. Additionally, where Randolph goes, Lawton Thornwood must follow.

So, in order to ease your suffering, oh darling best friend and wife-counter part, I am going to do one thing that you very much will like and one thing that you will very much not.

The first piece of this is that under my pillow there is a document shrouded in magic. Please take care of it and read it closely. I annotated it myself, so that you will not miss the piece of information that you oh so very need to read. I will let you take care of that in my absence. You are far better with delicate things than I.

The second piece of this is what you are not going to like, but it had to be done. Please forgive me, but with the world about to tip on its axis I was left with few choices. I have heard rumors that the other kingdoms surrounding the Seventh are in danger, and the whispers amongst the councilmen have only clouded my fears. My first choice for aid would have been Titan, but with his proximity to the problem I am not sure this is wise. Therefore, it is with my deepest regret, that I have invited your mother.

And with that, I leave you to your devices, for I can only imagine the look on your face, and I am suddenly very glad that I am hundreds of miles away.

With love,
Dalton Saphirrus

"My mother is coming," she said softly, barely audible.

Greyson froze, and she had forgotten that he was even waiting at the door. "Queen Maria...is coming...here?"

"I am going to *kill* Dalton Saphirrus," she growled, running a hand desperately through the top of her fiery curls. "How could he possibly—"

"Elena, calm down, we will get through this—"

"Because I have no choice in the matter!" she shrieked,

nearly falling backward on her bed in exasperation. "Can I run away and leave the duties to you, Greyson?"

Greyson laughed, genuinely sounding more like a friend than she had even though he was capable of. "No, Elena, that is not plausible. Also, I think Dalton is already very far away."

"When the hell did he even write to her?" Anxiety flooded within her. She loved her mother, she did, but there was so much pressure to be perfect. What would her mother think when she arrived only to realize that everything was askew? The king was gone, she was desperately searching for a way for the two of them to be in harmony with one another without being married, her best friend was her guard, she had been in love (in some regards) with a commoner, and she somehow found herself dreaming of the murderer son the Seventh Kingdom?

Her mother would not survive this news.

She was not quite sure how she was surviving it herself.

"Elena?" he said, looking at her lost in thought.

In the next breath, she was running over to Dalton's side of the bed. Lifting his pillow, she held her hand and let her magic blare out. There was no water in-front of her, yet she felt the moisture in the air and let it flow out of her in a singular breath.

Standing and watching in awe, Greyson moved closer as if to see what she was doing. Shock reverberated through him as he saw her hand glowing a light blue, and the piece of parchment appeared just as Dalton had said it would.

"Dalton does not make anything easy," she choked out in a laugh. Opening the document, she immediately saw his scribbled handwriting and gasped.

This was exactly what she had been looking for.

Glancing up to the sky, as if talking to Dalton some-where else, she whispered as she moved the parchment closer to her chest, "Damn you Dalton Saphirrus, for all that you are."

"What is that?" Greyson asked. "What does it say?"

Elena smirked at him, her hair surely looking like fire blazing in the sun. "It is my way out of everything, my key to freedom."

Holding up the letter to Greyson's face, she smiled. "My husband may be king, but we were also best friends as children."

"And?" He asked, his eyes squinted as he tried to look for whatever it was that Elena had just seen.

But she was so excited—and so utterly pissed that he had kept this from her from Gods knows how long—that she could not bare to utter the words to Greyson of what exactly he was looking at.

No, this was something she was to bring to the Lord's tonight.

And then she was to check-in on Cyril. Tell him all about it. Despite him not being able to hear her.

"And it is the key to my happiness, my freedom." In one fell swoop, the document rolled up, and she smiled for the first time in months. "Long live the King."

CHAPTER SIXTEEN

After a long day of riding through aimless fields and forests, all under an ever graying sky, Lawton Thornwood found himself with a pen as they took a rest. He had been writing for weeks now, ever since King Titan from the Sixth Kingdom had left. They had exchanged a few letters back and forth, their conversation before he left after Dalton's coronation had left much unsaid. Titan was to be a great friend, play some role in his life that had no destination that he could predict.

What was it that Titan had said to him that night before he left? He had made some reference to the Thinkers, and them having some sort of entanglement.

Shaking his head from side to side, Lawton brought himself back to center and began to write.

Dear Titan,

Your Holiness. I hope this letter both finds you well, and finds you. I have been thinking about your last correspondence for a few weeks and have been debating sharing it with my legion head. Frankly, I do not want him to see the rest of our letters, for I fear his eyes might fall out of his head at their promiscuity and provocative nature.

And that is not saying much, nor am I insinuating that there is anything inappropriate amongst us. Rather, he is quite conservative.

There is a reason that rats flea before him when he scurries down to the dungeons.

Although, I have found that I extremely enjoy our correspondence, he may not feel the same, especially if I am telling him it contains information which is privy to our kingdom affairs. Even though it is, I just do not feel as though I am up to being verbally assaulted and then praised. He does not handle secrets well, it would seem.

I digress.

The kingdoms have been in a bit of strife for the last few weeks. My dear friend, and King Dalton's close...whatever you want to call her...was captured from the castle in a very public display of violence. It was an invasion, and the prophecy and rumor mill within Sarridolon must be as crazy here in the First Kingdom as it is in the Sixth.

Have you caught wind about anything regarding our dearest friend Charmaine yet? My heart is in pieces thinking about her, and I only want her back with us. I will not get into the details, Titan, but she is more important to me, and the world, than I think anyone realizes.

I look forward to hearing from you and seeing your script on the page.

YOUR HUMBLE FRIEND,
Lawton Thornwood, Knight of the First Kingdom

LAWTON WOKE up from his nap later that afternoon, the snow dancing on his face in gentle kisses, and was completely and utterly horrified by seeing what his King was holding.

And Dalton Saphirrus, by all accounts, was completely and utterly speechless. The letter that he was holding was certainly some sort of mirage. He held it as if he could not quite believe that it was real.

"You wrote this?" he asked again, his voice rising in octave. "And he wrote you back?"

"Well, that is the thing, your Majesty," Lawton said, rather unsure of himself, still groggy from sleep. Dammit. There was no hiding from this now. So much for secrets. "He has not written me in over a week. I am getting worried."

"Maybe because you left the castle, where you should have remained," Randolph barked.

Lawton flashed him a frown.

Dalton loved it, though he would never admit it. Jesting was fun, something that Lawton knew all too well.

"The owls find me wherever I am; if he wrote, he would have used one, and I would have received it."

"When did this even begin?" Dalton asked, curious. Love—well in this case, companionship—was something that fascinated him, clearly. Lawton guessed that it always had. How does it happen? How does it choose who it infects?

And why did it hurt so much?

"At the ball, he knew something, clearly."

"Titan loves his thinkers," Dalton snorted. "Cyril says it is an abuse, to know too much."

"Cyril is wise," Randolph said.

"Cyril is a pain in my ass," Dalton retorted, but Lawton could see with everything in him that he did not mean it.

"But we learn much from those who are the biggest pain in our asses."

Snorting, Dalton mused, "That is the truth if I have ever heard one."

"Has he taught you anything...about power?" Lawton ventured, finding that there were never any opportunities to talk to Dalton Saphirrus one-on-one. This might be his chance to learn something. Anything.

"What are you really asking me, Lawton?" Dalton asked, a dark eyebrow raised inquisitively. "Are you referencing yourself?"

"I was told all of my life that those with power are royal born," Lawton said, moving his two hands outward as if to gesture to an invisible Randolph and Dalton. "And of course everyone's power is varying, for Randolph's fire does not give us eternal summer or warmth."

"Now where would be all of the fun in that?" Dalton said, sticking out his tongue and catching a snowflake.

"I am not sure whether any of this is truly any fun at all," Lawton said solemnly.

"My Gods you are a depressing creature," Dalton said, huffing strands of hair out of his gaze so that he could look at Lawton unobstructed. Turning his attention to the letter again, he sighed. "What in the name of the Ten Kingdoms do you two even talk about? How did this even happen? My Gods, Titan had asked at one point to sleep in my bed. You could not have—"

"DALTON!" Lawton shouted before covering his mouth instinctively.

"My, my," Dalton said, rather impressed that he had been yelled at it would seem. "I did not know you had it in you. Little obedient knight you are not, Lawton Thornwood."

Despite his best efforts, Lawton felt his face go beet red.

He was not embarrassed often, but there was something just so plainly ridiculous about Dalton that had him stumbling into verbal traps left and right.

Lawton had spoken to Dalton many times in the course of his life, but there was something about him just being a king that had him off-kilter. Watching Randolph and Dalton jest had Lawton feeling rather confident that he could manage the king's behavior by proxy, however, clearly he had underestimated both him and his tongue.

"I am intrigued, sire, by the royals of this continent. I always have been, and I fear that I always will be."

"Titan was not born with powers, though that does not make him any less worthy of his crown than you may think. He, and his forefathers and daughters, receive a blessing from the land itself."

"As if the land is alive?" Lawton realized how stupid he sounded as soon as he spoke.

Dalton, though, did not seem to find the question as such. He lifted a hand, snow pieces dancing and the winds picking up peacefully. "All of us have some sort of elemental based blessing. Titan's is merely that the land bestows some of its beauty upon its rulers, though the Gods have never given his kingdom more than that."

"And the other kingdoms?"

"We do not have all day to be telling stories of the Kings and Queens of Old, Lawton."

"I would not say my power is elemental based," Lawton ventured, thinking back to what Dalton had just said. "I mean, jumping?"

"Is it not?" Dalton asked, raising a dark eyebrow playfully. "You move through time and space it would seem, faster than the winds itself could carry you and appear everyday and every night like the sun and moon."

Lawton moved to protest as Dalton said, "I would say you are just as elemental as the rest of us."

"And what about Charmaine?"

"Charmaine..." Dalton stiffened at the mention of her voice. Lawton continued, "And I, have powers. She is clearly not royal, not a drop of royal blood lives within us."

"Cyril had pondered this a few weeks prior to my coronation, and I asked him to stop searching for an answer... where Charmaine was concerned."

"You asked him to stop?" Lawton said, floored that there was no explanation, for Cyril surely would have discovered an answer.

"She was in a lot of pain," Dalton said softly, not looking at him. "I did not wish to find something, maybe some evidence that she does not come from where she thought she did, and cause her more devastation. Take it from me, there is only so much in your heart that can be smashed repeatedly before it can never be made whole again."

Turning his head to look at Lawton, he said, "I do, however, believe that the Gods bless those who are worthy. And for whatever reason, Lawton Thornwood, you and Charmaine are amongst those who deserve the gifts that they have. Not all royals have gifts, and maybe that is for the best."

"It seems that destiny has funny ways of connecting people," Lawton chided, appreciating seeing the King of Snow in another light, as much as he was grateful for the opportunity to have a moment like this. Maybe the Gods did choose him for this. However, then it begged the question: Why?

The tree-line behind them suddenly rustled, and a plethora of inked flowers burst through, followed by Randolph.

"Where did you get off to?" Dalton asked, not turning around. He always knew who was behind him it seemed. Another gift of his, perhaps?

"There is a tavern, just a few miles past this bout of forest," Randolph said, waking into the thicket. "If we leave in the next hour or so, we can get there before it gets dark."

"In such a rush to share a bed, Randy boy?" Dalton stood as the snow began to trickle down.

"More like get out of the cold," he muttered, breathing smoke into his hands, rubbing them vigorously together. "Come, let us keep moving."

As they made a move to follow him, Dalton turned around and Lawton realized that he was still holding the letter. Waiving it incessantly in-front of his face, he smacked him on the head with it and whispered just low enough that Randolph could still hear, "I still want all of those details later. Mind-boggling!"

CHAPTER SEVENTEEN

The first leg of their trip had been rather leisurely, as had been their exit, however, Dalton was beginning to crumble. As the hours drug on, he found himself slipping away from the calm and control that had started with him when he had decided to leave the castle. Rather, when Cyril had urged him to leave and find her.

And now Dalton was irritated.

Clearly, nothing else was new.

Not only had his entire mission been thwarted by Randolph and his goon sidekick, but they were not moving fast enough. He was beginning to pace, was already not sleeping, and could not feel fucking anything in his chest. He had felt something earlier, a steady tug, but the last few hours since they had entered the Tenth Kingdom had her silent.

When she had been at the castle, he could feel her. Constantly. He could not put his finger on it, the feeling that coursed between them, but when he saw her last, they had all but confirmed between one another that the stars were driving them together for some Gods-forsaken reason.

It was challenging enough to be a royal, but to be a royal in love with someone who was not a part of the Gods royal was utterly impossible.

Why did the Gods hate him, truly—

"Your Majesty, are you alright?" Lawton Thornwood stood at the edge of the clearing, coming into frame and eating an apple. They were leaving in a few minutes, yet he seemed to be the only one who was feeling any sort of urge to rush.

"Where did you get that?" Dalton said, gesturing to the fruit.

"A tree," Lawton said with a smile, taking a big crunch. "Would you like one yourself?"

"Fetch me one," Dalton ordered, not caring if he was being rude. Lawton would do as he was told. He was the King after all. "But be quick about it, we have wasted far too much time this day anyways."

"Of course, your Majesty," he said before he scampered back into the wood, taking another rather large bite from his apple before he disappeared.

"You do not have to order him around you know," Randolph scoffed, his irritation blatant. "He would have gotten it for you if you would have just asked nicely."

"I am not sure why you think I care what comes out of your mouth," Dalton shot back, though a familiar twinge of regret pulsed through him.

Is this what it was to have black hair? To feel things? To experience regret and not be able to push it away?

He wanted his icy heart back.

The *real* icy heart.

Not whatever game he was currently playing.

And he thought he looked better as a blonde anyway.

"I know what you are doing," Randolph said, preparing

to lead the horses toward the clearing to be mounted shortly.

"And what is that, my dearest kingly friend?"

"Avoiding. Causing issues. Wearing thin. Testing me on purpose."

"That is a lot of things to do at once, Randolph." Dalton turned around, his face facing the forest. "I am not sure if I am capable of such a feat. I am not so talented."

"Oh, but you are." Randolph stepped forward, the horses leaning forward to eat the grass before them as he made his way over to him. Rubbing his flowered hands together, he whispered just loud enough that Dalton could hear. "I think you are capable of more than you lead on, I learned that you know, that day we went below the dungeons."

Fear flashed in Dalton's eyes, as it mirrored in Randolph's. "You are a fool to speak of that in-front of me. You do not know the weight—"

"I know the gravity of what you did, I just have not been able to figure out what you sold to get it. I understand you got the name from the diary, but to have to confidence to actually go through with it..."

Dalton snorted, but did not look away.

"What gave you the confidence?" Randolph asked, an amber eyebrow raising inquisitively.

"Delusion," Dalton retorted. "You would be surprised what you can accomplish when you live your life in a fantasy land."

"And is delusion going to rescue Charmaine as well? We do not necessarily have a plan."

"I do not see a reason to plan, Randolph, because I know the second we get into that castle all hell is going to break loose. That is why I only have us a few directives."

"The dragon should have just given us a ride there—"

Dalton's eyes nearly popped out of his head, and all he could do was wildly wave his hands back and forth while spitting "SHHHHHHH" out of his mouth. "What in the name of the Ten Kingdoms is wrong with you?! I swear he can hear us!"

"From below the castle? Which is over a day's ride away?" Randolph was smiling. Actually smiling.

Was he winning? Dalton had not been keeping score between the two of them... But fuck.

"I will call our friend when we need him. I will only get one shot at this I am afraid, and I am not wasting it on hitching a ride."

"Do you think she is alive?" Randolph asked, suddenly timid. He had known that Dalton had been searching for the diary in secret, but to actually pull this off.. Gods. A dragon was not a power that could be wielded so easily and so casually. Dalton was out of his mind. "Can you, I mean, can you feel anything?"

Dalton inhaled sharply, the frost-bitten air stinging his throat as it traveled through him. "I feel her, on and off though. I would know if she was gone. There has to be a reason that King Finn is back, something larger that we are not seeing."

"Well, is it not obvious that he wants some sort of revenge?"

"But Ciara is gone," Dalton protested, confusion written all over his face.

"Maybe it was never anything to do with Ciara. You know the stories, Dalton, just as well as I do. He was a mad king himself, something similar to the likes of both of our fathers. I find that we actually have a lot in common with Ciara." Stepping backward, Randolph made his way back over toward the horses as Lawton reappeared with a green apple for Dalton.

"Here you go, Dalton," Lawton said, no anger or irritation present in his voice. "Are we ready to go now?"

Handing over the reins to both of them, Randolph smirked. "It has been a long few days, and it is getting late, how about we get a pint?"

CHAPTER EIGHTEEN

Titan, King of the Sixth Kingdom, had just received a letter.

Casually, he strode toward the white owl which now sat at the railing of his chambers balcony, and extended his hand as the creature plopped it into the palm of his hand.

"Thank you, darling," Titan said to the owl, before it squawked and began to fly away from which it once came.

Before he had the chance to open the letter however, his gaze followed the stunning beast. As he was about to tear his eyes away from the gorgeous site, his eyes caught something.

The sky was—Purple? Orange? Something that he had never seen before in his sea of pink within the kingdom. The Sixth Kingdom was notorious for its gorgeous botanicals, for his entire castle was surrounded not with armies and guards but with cherry blossom trees and tiger lilies. The aroma of flowers was sickeningly gorgeous, so suffocating that his kingdom thrived in the areas of healing and medicinal herbs, to which were then supplied to the whole continent.

However, the more he squinted, the more he realized that this was no sunset.

No, the sky was burning.

Overcome with sickness of the mind and heart, Titan clutched his chest in dismay. They—whomever they were—were here. They had arrived in his kingdom, breathed the air of the pink flowered trees, and touched the green grass which billowed so freely.

They were rotting his kingdom from the inside out, and they had only just arrived. He had time to get his people out—

But would remain when they finished tearing through this kingdom? And they moved onto the next? Titan could only assume that this was the plan, for there was no other reasonable explanation as to why they had come here first.

Clearly, they were to make their way around the continent. Titan just had the pleasure of being their first stop.

Falling to the ground, the letter hit the marbled pink and cream-colored stone with a silent thud, as the King of the Sixth Kingdom made his way toward the door.

"Guards!" he yelled. "Guards! Help me!"

Dashing around the castle, Titan found himself utterly paralyzed with fear. His guards had dispersed, nowhere to be found.

But somehow, he knew that they were alive. He could feel it.

Instead of panicking, he slid on the mask that all royals had and took a deep breath before saying with all the might that he could muster, "Who goes there?"

One second.

Two seconds.

Three seconds.

A body materialized in-front of him. Red hair. Dark robes. Shadow like black mist evaporating off him.

No, it could not be. He had heard rumors, but nothing like this.

"King Finn?" he asked, his voice cracking halfway through the title. "How are you—""

"King Titan of the Sixth Kingdom," King Finn said, his voice more horrifying than Titan could ever have imagined from the childhood stories of the evil king. "Join me, or die."

CHAPTER NINETEEN

The tavern was everything that Randolph wanted, but not necessarily needed. He knew from everything that had ever happened in his life that drinking was not a viable coping mechanism, there were much better ways to deal with whatever he was feeling.

Like fighting, perhaps.

Yelling. At Dalton. That always seemed to help things along.

But this situation, the traveling, the company. Gods, he needed a drink. All in good fun. Just to take the edge off.

He had no room to leave his wits behind him. This was certainly not an indulgent sort of trip.

The tavern that they had stumbled upon had a dinky sign out front crafted entirely of maple wood, something that the Tenth Kingdom was known for. Although the Tenth had no governing king or queen, it was governed by the Thinker Castle that sat within it. There was something oddly home-y about the entirety of the kingdom. The terrain, the woods, the idea that not just one family ruled it

—Randolph could not put his finger on it, but he felt at ease here. Almost like he was out of his own body.

That was the only way that he could be relaxed, he realized with a silent chuckle, to actually not be himself at all.

They had shoved open the door after finding a stable boy to man the horses, and immediately made their way to the tavern to find something to eat.

And most importantly drink.

Randolph strode through the tavern as he made his way to the bar where they were serving pints of ale. It was rather metaphorical, that the most sound member of this absurd trio that had banned together to rescue Charmaine, and quite possibly, save the world, was tilted on its side.

It was unlike him, to lose to control.

Rather it was like Dalton, who had somehow become the axis of this grouping, that was keeping everyone together. They lived to please him, Randolph realized, for everyone on this continent lived to please him. He had kept his mask on tight these last few weeks, but earlier it had begun to crack. Whatever Randolph had walked in on between Lawton and Dalton had felt like the old Dalton. Cheerful, chaotic, and menacing. But just a few moments after that had come and passed, well all sense of everything had shifted once more. He had become irrational, difficult, and challenging beyond reason.

Dalton Saphirrus was far more of a King than anyone else even realized.

He was more than that.

This place, this world, hung on every word he said.

Randolph realized with a start that this was the truest thing he knew in his life.

"What can I do for you?" the tavern holder asked.

"Three ales," Randolph said, gesturing toward his traveling companions behind him. He nearly chuckled at the sight of Dalton looking rather askew behind him, very much out of place. The King of Snow stood with an ethereal aura to him, whether he realized it or not.

Hoisting two into his left hand and one in his right, Randolph made his way over to the standing table that Dalton and Lawton had settled at. Discreetly, it was located in the far right corner of the tavern, away from prying eyes.

"What are you looking at?" Dalton sneered, his cloak up over his dark hair.

"You," Randolph shot back, not missing a beat. "You look absolutely ridiculous with that hood on."

Lawton slurped his ale, clearly trying to keep a chuckle within.

"I think I look fantastic, very pretty even." Dalton smoothed out the sides of his hood in a dramatic fashion. "Black is my color, you know?"

"Is it? I rather thought your color was Saphirrus blue," Lawton chided, clearly giving him the side eye.

"Nobody's color is Saphirrus blue, you nitwit," Dalton said, smacking Lawton upside the head.

"No reason to get violent now," Randolph hushed, though he found that he was somehow very much at ease, despite the ramifications if they were to be discovered. If King Finn found out...

No, he would not let his mind wander to such dark places. It had taken so long for him to crawl out of them these last few months, there was no reason as to why he needed to jump back in head first.

They were going to get her. They were going to get her back.

Maybe if he kept repeating it then it would become reality. What the hell was that called again—manifestation? Cyril had tried to tell him about it once, he had tuned him out.

Anything he had ever tried to manifest had turned to ash before him.

Clearly, he was not doing it right.

Though there was a creeping sensation that existed within him that terrified him more than the rest, something that he had been pushing down over and over again.

Reine.

She had to be there.

And he was going to get her out too. No matter the cost.

Charmaine and Reine. Charmaine and Reine.

He repeated their names in his head over and over like a prayer as he took a few more sips of his ale.

Maybe he was getting the hold of this manifestation thing after all.

"Eh, trying to forget something?" Lawton asked, pensive himself.

Randolph only replied by gazing across the table at his king, who also looked positively stumped on whatever it was he was working through in his mind.

"D—" he started, only pausing because he was afraid of saying the name out loud. It was true that many across the Ten Kingdoms had actually no clue as to what Dalton really looked like, but it was nerve-wracking all the same.

"Yes?" Dalton said, glancing up faster than Randolph had anticipated. Whatever daze he was in, it was over physically, but still lingered in his dark blue gaze. "You can speak my name, or should I have a code name?" He paused, squinting his eyes as if he were trying to see something. "You could call me Mordred, I think it encompasses how hideous I am!"

Dalton's dark references were not lost on Randolph, though clearly Lawton had not been schooled to the same accord. The history of Mordred was a long and dark path that none should venture in history. Even as a joke,

Randolph was left concerned that Dalton would even bring up such an evil. Clearing his throat, Randolph took another sip before he whispered, "Are you alright?"

"*Hmmmm*," Dalton hummed, much to his own amusement. "You know, not many people dare to ask me that question my lord. The contents of my head are a funny thing, I am not even sure what madness you could even dare conjure that is even close in comparison."

And then he wiggled his eyebrows.

Always a game.

"You are a rare jewel," Lawton said softly, gazing upon the king like he was just that. A diamond in the rough.

"Ha!" Dalton said cheerfully before becoming somber. His voice began to drift as if he were in a dream. "I said that once to Charmaine, you know?"

"My king..." Randolph whispered so low that none other could hear them. "Perhaps it is getting late, and our minds wander too far with drink in hand. These are not times to be easy and merry."

Setting down his ale, Dalton replied, "Yes, perhaps we should be wise this evening, and a warm bed could bring us good."

Randolph suddenly became flooded with sadness, knowing just as well as they were all plagued with nightmares.

"The sooner we wake up, the sooner we can be on our way," Dalton said in finality, and with a wink he added: "To bed we go, gentlemen."

And as he moved to walk toward the staircase, he collapsed.

He knew that Randolph loomed at his side.

It normally would have brought him some random shroud of concealment, but instead it only reminded him of his failure. Earlier, he had felt it brewing within him. All of that darkness and sadness that had controlled him when he let his mind wander for even a second. It had come out in his naming. Maybe he was turning evil. Maybe that was the reason for the slight eternal winter outside of these walls. Maybe it was the reason for his dark hair.

He was becoming darkness somehow, it was taking over him every step he took closer to whatever destiny lay ahead.

Tossing and turning, sweat built up on Dalton's brow. The bed was made of pure straw, so different from the goose feathers that typically laid underneath his mattress. And his mind, well, his mind was the problem.

His mind was always the problem. It wandered this night, to dark places, as it had every night that she had gone.

And the dreams turned to nightmares.

CHARMAINE SAT ON THE STAIRCASE, though Dalton did not recognize the castle which they were at. It was black on the exterior, no rose bushes in sight, and the moon that hung in the sky was a dark pink, shining ominously where the sun once was.

"Char?" He found himself asking, filled with hope.

"Dalton?" she replied in question, flipping around her head to gaze upon him. "What are you doing here? Have you come to rescue me?" Tears welled up in her eyes.

He paused, though his legs jerked as if they wanted to run toward her. "I am not sure," Dalton said, extending his hands to take a good look at them. "I do not think this is real, darling."

"It has to be, you cannot tell me that you do not feel it."

"Feel what?" he asked.

"The draw, it is pulsating."

Dalton could feel it, but it did not thunder. It was as if it were dormant. Dying.

Taking a step closer, and then two more, he hoped he could reignite it.

"Charmaine," he half-growled, that power between them still silent.

Violet eyes glanced up to meet his own gaze, his sapphire blues reflected in the pools of her eyes. Though he could not help but notice that he could not touch her. It was like a repellent magnet, this thing between them.

A dream. He realized with a curse. It was a dream.

As if she could tell, Charmaine began to evaporate. His mind losing his grip on manifesting him before her as he took a deep breath in and out, in and out. "Charmaine," he whispered, sadly extending a hand to live momentarily beside her face as she began to leave in front of him. "Do not leave me."

"Come and get me," she cried out. "Dalton, come and save me."

"I am trying—"

"You are not trying hard enough," she said, before completely vanishing before him.

Half-collapsing to his knees, he sagged downward, only to be met with another materialization before him. One that was so vivid he was not sure how his mind could have conjured it.

Red hair was knotted behind his dead, a Saphirrus crown atop his head, and eyes filled with pure envy. It was none other than King Finn that had materialized in-front of him.

Breathless, Dalton tried to rise to face him, to demand that he give Charmaine back from wherever he had just taken her. Cursing, he found shadows wrapped around his ankles and knees like shackles. "What have you done with her?!" he screamed, his throat suddenly raw. Was he suffocating?

"Dalton Saphirrus," King Finn said with a bow in mockery. "I look forward to your arrival."

❄

"DALTON!" Flowered hands and a worrisome blonde stood overtop of him, their brows riddled with concern. "Dalton Saphirrus, wake up!"

"Keep your voice down," Lawton's voice said in reason. "If anyone finds out here that we have the King—"

Sitting up suddenly, Dalton shut them up as he heaved.

"Too much to drink?" Randolph asked, though there was no humor and sarcasm living within his voice.

"My dream—" Dalton said, leaning over into the pail that had been sitting at the bottom of his bed frame. "He had her..."

"He?" Randolph asked, alarmed.

"Finn..." Dalton stood, hands shaking and legs wobbly. Making his way toward the door, he nearly tripped over his own two legs. He was totally going to vomit. "He has... he has taken everything from me... Charmaine... my sister... the mercenaries took both of them. Gone. They are both gone because of him. Because he wants something with *me*. With this power." The words came tumbling out of him in a strained manner, like something was standing on his chest.

He was not sure what time it was, but nobody now lingered in the tavern for drink. Voices sounded from behind him, echoing memories of being chased as a boy by Cyril. Though, he was not running toward anything right now.

He was running toward something.

Thrusting all of his weight into the door, once and then twice, it exploded open.

"Dalton—" A voice sounded behind him. Randolph's voice. Lawton trailing close behind. "Dalton..." Dismay filled the air, and Dalton breathed in an icy breath.

A snow storm. No—a blizzard had erupted in the Tenth Kingdom.

One of his doing he was sure, though he barred the question anyways. "Did I do this?" Dalton asked, the sweat from his nightmare causing his dark hair to begin to stick coldly to his skin. He looked down at his hands in disgust. "I... I did not mean too—"

Randolph took a few strides toward him, hesitantly as if not to spook him. Lawton stood at the doorway, still behind him, as if to leave this moment to just the two of them. Two king's stuck and entrapped by the gifts that the Gods had given them.

"Dalton, please take my hand and come back inside..."

"I have to make it stop snowing... I have to get to her. *He* has her." His voice was broken, pleading with Randolph despite knowing the truth of the moment. This was not the time to leave, especially with the storm of his own creation raging on. If he did not get his power in check, he could kill them all, make the whole journey unsafe for passage.

"Dalton, take my hand. Let me help you." Randolph's voice was pleading, his hand extended in friendship.

Dalton raised his hands and blasted Randolph with all of the snow that he could muster around him. Exhausting poured and seeped into every crevice of his body. Flames ignited in-front of him as quickly as he had thrown his power in that direction. Smoke began to rise, his flames incinerating any of the snow which Dalton had so carelessly conjured.

Beginning to shiver, Dalton took a defeated step toward

him and threatened to collapse. "Randolph, I do not want to be like this anymore."

"I know, my friend," Randolph said, his hands expelling a warmth that went straight through to Dalton's icy heart. "We will get her back." A promise. A vow.

Or rather Dalton wanted to be. Needed it to be.

"Make it with me," Dalton growled, the blistering cold still swarming around him. "We get her out. No matter the price that I may have to pay."

Extending a free hand, Randolph grasped it in his hand. "I vow this, Dalton Saphirrus, that I will aide you in your retrieval of Charmaine Grimes, no matter the cost to you."

Thunder erupted from the sky in response, as if the Gods did not approve of such a union and understanding.

Or maybe that was the way which they chose to express their acceptance. Their support.

And Gods, they were going to need it if they were to accomplish this goal.

Holding the door to the tavern open, Lawton ushered them inside, and they made their way back upstairs. "Oh boys," he said, rather sad yet filled with his usual chipper sarcasm. "What am I going to do with you?"

CHAPTER TWENTY

Dalton's whole body seized.

Randolph stood in-front of him, just paces away. He could see his mouth moving, his inner fire pulsating beneath his skin that screamed "fight", "change", "shift". But no matter what he said, no matter how many tears fell from Charmaine's gaze, there was nothing that could be done.

She was losing the battle within herself, fear gripping and taking away from her as it did everyone. The only thing that could take a power given by the Gods is the thing that inhibited everyone from becoming what they were always meant to be. The one thing that was always in the way of greatness, that you had to conquer in order to get stronger.

Fear.

And it had taken her too.

Dalton blinked, his body frozen with the same thing that now gripped her. The one thing that he hated more than anything, because it took so much and never asked for permission nor did it give anything back.

And then Dalton succumbed to the fear. And then every-thing went dark.

THEY AWOKE the next morning cold.

Dalton paused as he freshened himself up, looking very much like a young child now instead of a king. A cracked mirror lived in the corner of the room, no larger than his left hand and hanging above a pail which he assumed to be some sort of sink. A glass gallon bottle, which he assumed had contained some sort of liquid at some point, also lived in the corner.

Without turning around, he spoke directly to Randolph and Lawton, who had been hovering at the window all morning, very concerned about the snowstorm that his little dream had created last night. "You do not know the limits of our power, I cannot imagine it being some bottomless well where we can untap the magic of the world at our disposal—"

Heat flared from Randolph's fingertips in the form of a flame. Dalton could see the reflection in the dinky mirror. "Why not?" Dalton touched his black hair, his eyes eerily dark and full of wisdom this particular morning. Unusual. "I believe it gives and takes."

"It?"

"Power."

Randolph huffed a laugh.

"I do not think the blast would have taken me like it did if there was not a wall between me and unlimited power." Silence rang between them, deafening. It was unlike any of them to speak of Charmaine being abducted so freely, but his dreams continued to change things. They lived more vividly every night, more real and haunting than the last.

Had changed everything. "I like black hair, it suits your aura better."

Dalton looked at Randolph like he was just slapped, but then his features softened, and he began to laugh. "Randolph Eniar, did you just insult me with a compliment?"

"I could never compliment you," Randolph replied dryly. "But the white suited you more, even now when I look at you I see the power of snow coursing through your veins."

"I know it did not leave me," Dalton said, puffing out air with snowflakes so that Randolph could see for himself. "But it left me all the same. Maybe it is outside now, and that is just where it can live. Away from me."

"Maybe it was time it went away, moved on to plague someone else." Dalton smirked at Randolph's candor, though without his usual covering he looked not so much ethereal but utterly damning. "Then who did it go to? The squirrels outside?"

"Where did Ciara's power go to? When she died?"

"What do you mean?" Randolph said with his whole heart nearly pounding out of his chest.

"Well, you do not think she got to keep it, do you? When she died?"

"Why are you asking this?" What did Dalton have up his sleeve?

"Just something I read once, in a diary, when I was looking for a name."

Randolph knew what he was referencing, but this was a dangerous conversation anywhere. He knew the secret deal which Dalton had made before they left the castle, and to even utter the name, let alone speak it, was enough to make Randolph's skin crawl. Dragons, it would seem, were not to be messed with.

History had told them as much.

And the dragon himself had confirmed as much.

"Tell me you did not bring the diary with you—"

Dalton smirked, evil basically coursing through him. "What's the phrase: secrets—secrets are no fun unless you share with everyone?"

"I have most definitely heard that before..."

"So have I," Dalton said, leaning forward. "And I think it is stupid."

"What the—"

"You two are very cryptic you know, but you also lack complete discretion. It is quite fascinating, are all royals like this?" Lawton interrupted, a smirk plastered ever so discreetly on the side of his mouth.

"You might be royal for all I know," Dalton said, turning around and putting his hands on his hips. "You have that little suave thing going on. Maybe you are a secret child of a crown, a kingdom, within Sarridolon."

Randolph scowled.

"You know they exist, they have to," Dalton pondered, sitting down on the awful bed once more. "Nobody is perfect. Or maybe you are, and that is why you were blessed."

In a blink, Lawton was right next on him, not even a sound arising in the air. "Tell me again how nobody is perfect," he said with a raised eyebrow.

Swearing uncontrollably, Dalton stood and shook off his clothes as if they were covered in dust. "My Gods, Lawton! I take it all back—every compliment I have ever given you—this power of you is not blessed, it is quite creepy. Please never port yourself next to me again, my Gods."

Randolph sat across the room, trying to hold in a chuckle.

"What the fuck are you laughing about, Randy boy?"

Dalton spat, though he could not hide the fact that his snarl was transitioning to a smile.

"Dalton Saphirrus, are you smiling?" Randolph questioned, looking rather smug.

"I do not smile," Dalton retorted, forcing himself to pretend like he was back at court. "I simply had a slip up of the face. It happens to the best of us, I am human after all."

"*Hmph,*" Lawton said, still sitting on his bed. "So, when do we get to leave this place?"

Dalton moved to look out the window. "It does not look like it is going to be stopping anytime soon—"

"It is ok," Randolph said softly. "Though we do not want to wait too long, to rouse suspicion."

"We have to get to her," Dalton said. "We cannot delay, especially of my own doing."

"I say this respectfully, but Dalton, if we leave now we will both freeze."

"Do we part ways?" Dalton asked, though he knew the answer.

"We made a vow," Randolph said. "And I do not know what you know about me Dalton, but a part of that should be the fact that when I promise something, I do not break it."

Extending a hand, Dalton clapped his palm on Randolph's shoulder. "You may be a dingus, Randolph Eniar, but you are my dingus."

"I am not sure that is a compliment, your Majesty," Lawton said, unable to keep the smile out of his voice.

"And you," Dalton said, striding back toward him. "You scared the absolute shit out of me earlier, and I did not like it, but I know for a fact that the Gods sent you to meet me in this life because we need one another. In whatever capacity that is, I am unsure. But I have walked these roads alone before, and I refuse to do it again."

Walking back over toward the window, Dalton said with command, "The Thinker's Castle is about a half day's ride from where we are."

"The Thinker's Castle?" Randolph asked, alarm rising slightly in his voice. "Why ever would we subject ourselves to more philosophical torment?"

"Because maybe they can help me turn this off, and I can send word back to Elena about how to help Cyril." Dalton's voice broke slightly at the sound of his friend's name, and he found no argument from either Randolph or Lawton. "And maybe, just maybe, they can tell us something about what evil we are about to face."

CHAPTER TWENTY-ONE

Bairre stood before Carinthya with the Saphirrus orb. He had been in her chambers for about half an hour, presiding over her—or something like that.

"What are you doing here?" she asked for the third time.

The first two times he had given her nothing, simply walked around the room and looking at the effects as if he were searching for something, though he kept coming up dry. After a moment's pause, he sighed, looking extremely bored.

Though she knew that this was a farce. He was anything but bored. And straightforward.

"I need you to look into this." Extending the orb toward her, he raised a silver eyebrow in his direction. "But be careful not to touch it, I would hate to explain to Finn why we are playing with it."

"Why?"

"Well, because it is yours, precious. Or your families I should say." He paused, taking a step toward her as his shadows wrapped themselves around the room. "It is silencing, Carinthya. Finn is not here, but I cannot be too careful."

"Where is he?" she asked, her voice wavering as she commanded herself to stand taller.

"Conquering," he whispered sinisterly. "But the other two are still here, and I refuse to have them thwart me. I have put in too much work over these years, waited too long, and will not have those nimwhits getting in the way of what I want."

"And what is that? What exactly do you keep referencing, but refuse to tell me the specifics of?" she asked, her voice gaining strength as he came closer. She had to get confident, adapt, it was the only way in which she was going to survive this.

Survive another day here.

Survive him.

"Well, if I reveal my plans to you, who is to say that you will not spoil all the fun?"

Before she could reply, he continued, "I saw the way you ratted out the Violet Queen, though I do know that you were unaware of what you were truly doing. Still, it is unnerving to subject someone who is utterly powerless into something that is so sinister. Reminded me to never make an enemy of you, gorgeous."

Carinthya nearly vomited at the wave of guilt that smashed over her, coating her so much that she felt as though she might just drown. "I never meant to hurt her," she said. "I have not—"

"Been able to rectify things with her? Carinthya, honestly, you have been stolen here but have you lost all sense?" Bairre made a *tsk* noise with his mouth, his tongue clicking in reprimand. "There is much pain that lives in her heart, even before she got here, but you? Oh dearest

Carinthya, you think you are the stars, but you are the night sky."

"The night sky?" she asked, puzzled by his analogy.

"You conceal, and you hide, and you bring about darkness with no fault of your own." He took another step forward, and this time she did not step back. "Do not engage with Charmaine Grimes in the next few days, it is very important for my plans that you both have distance. Your time will come to talk to her, I promise you that. I cannot promise, however, that the two of you will find peace. I think about all you have in common is your brother, and I am not sure what even he would say when he finds out what you did to the love of his life."

Opening her mouth to rebuttal, to say that she felt as though it was important that she did talk to Charmaine, that she apologize—she was silenced.

The love of his life.

How had she been so daft? If she ever got out of here, ever got a chance to speak to her brother again, he would never forgive her for what she did.

And she could never forgive herself.

Holding out the Saphirrus orb, Bairee smirked, his gray hair looking like moonlight. If she was the night sky, maybe he was more a part of her story than she even realized.

"I need you to look into this and find the King of Snow."

"And then what?" she asked, her voice trembling. She was terrified to look into this evil object again, and to see her brother. It would only lead to more guilt. "Why should I do this for you?"

"Carinthya, my night sky, you are not as selfish as I know you are being right now." He extended the orb once more. "Now look into it and tell me where he is. Let us get this over with, so that I can move to the next phase of my plan."

CHAPTER TWENTY-TWO

Elena was having a lot of nightmares.

Well, that is what she was calling them.

It always started the same. *By drowning.* She had never had a fear of water before, but it crept through her mind like some sort of evil and would not relent. She would wake up there, alone in the freezing deep blue seas off the coast of the continent. The waves crashed around her, bringing her down every single time she reached the surface to take another breath.

She was alone.

And then she would see something in the distance—no —someone coming to save her. There was a beam of light among the black ocean current, so bright and ferocious that she would open her eyes and fight back a choking sob.

With a start, she would realize that it was fire. Fire was here to save her. She was no longer alone, no longer wondering if she would survive this. Heat and warmth waited for her, wanted to rescue her.

As it got closer and closer, she reached out her hand and heard a voice that sounded so much like one that she knew

whisper through the ocean waves, "Use your power, Elena."
It was commanding, that of a king.

And dressed his hands in tattooed florals.

Fear struck once again, the drowning starting up again, violent instead of peaceful. The flames grew closer and closer, demanding to save her.

And then she woke up.

HOURS LATER, Elena stood overtop a glass of water and twiddled her thumbs.

She *could* do this.

She *should* do this.

She had not practiced her power in many months and she was beginning to grow restless without the usual ebb and flow of the water beneath her hands.

But doing this—trying this—well, she felt as though she was losing a part of herself. Day by day it slipped away like water did when it was spilled over, running away from her and never materializing the same way it had originally.

She could feel that it was different now though, her water power. So much so that she barely remembered anything about it. It used to be a thrill for her, how much she could accomplish and who she could impress. Even a few months ago, running amuck around the castle with Dalton, well that had been great fun after all.

But when she met James—

She closed her eyes, willing herself to go there. She had to feel it, she was certain. That was one of the things that Cyril had talked about to her at length before he had collapsed. She needed to embrace the pain. To feel it. Let it in. Let it erupt.

And then rise from the ashes of her grief.

The first step, she guessed with a silent laugh to herself at her own ridiculousness, was to stand in-front of this here cup.

As she made a move to lift a hand, after who knows how many minutes, she heard a knock followed by the swift opening of a door.

"Elena?" Greyson's voice sounded, confusion filling the air at precisely what she was doing hovering over a glass of water.

"Yes?" she asked, straightening her shoulders and trying to play it off. This was normal.

Sure.

"Your mother has arrived at the gates, would you like to greet her or wait until the morning?"

Elena closed her eyes, taking a deep breath in and out. Running her hands through the front pieces of her hair, she recentered.

Later.

She would work on the whole magic thing later.

First, she had to conquer this.

"Coming," Elena said, trying to put on a face. "She was invited by the King, so as I am the Queen I must greet her."

"Elena—" Greyson pleaded, his voice and gait giving away all that the was thinking. Of course, she always had a choice with Greyson. He would do it, make something up or entertain her mother himself to keep her out of harms way.

No, this was something that she needed to do.

For herself.

And without another word, she strode from her chambers, careful to leave the glass of water where it sat.

Queen Maria was nothing like Elena remembered.

She was much worse.

Well, intimidating that is.

Her mother had entered the castle with a cool and level-headed gaze, her eyes looking forward and not around at anything except what was directly in-front of her. Her heels clicked mercilessly on the marble floors, as if every part of her was fighting to be noticed involuntarily. Her dark hair was swept up in utter perfection, no trace of that gorgeous auburn fire that Elena held.

No, where Elena was all fire, her mother was all that a queen should be.

Graceful.

Calculating.

Stone-faced.

Where mothering was concerned, Elena was not sure that she deserved some type of recognition for her parenting skills, but there was no question that she had prepared Elena for the harsh reality of the world.

"Elena," her mother said, her voice devoid of all emotion and left with straight regal aura.

Elena bowed before speaking, she must be on her best behavior. "Queen Maria."

"Your husband sent a rather peculiar letter, something about a contract and your marriage, and that my presence was required at court," Maria said smiling. She was actually smiling. Only Dalton Saphirrus could bring this sort of emotion out of her mother, as he could any person. "He also mentioned a war brewing on our horizon, something which I have feared for much time."

"He really did not spare any details then," Elena said softly.

"It would appear not," Maria said, surveying Elena's body language before speaking again. "It is an interesting time to be a royal, especially with power, Elena. How has your training been going?"

Elena nearly flinched. She had not as much practiced with her water power, it was almost as if she did not have it at this point. "I will be honest, mother, I have not been practicing much of late."

"You do not take to the training sessions that Dalton endures with the Thinkers of his court?"

"Well," she said, nearly closing her eyes in the fear of being reprimanded, "I have been... struggling since I got here. You know of the attacks, the madness of King Ronan, the death of..."

"A common boy, I understand." Maria's voice was stern but not unkind. How the devil did she know—

"Dalton told you that too, I suppose?" Elena said, barely looking at her.

"No, it was actually Cyril who wrote me a few months back. An update on the Queen, he called it." Maria gestured that Elena begin to walk with her. With one glance back in Greyson's direction—a final plead for help—she followed. "Love is a challenging thing, Elena, especially for a queen. I am sure you have figured that out in my absence, surely?"

"Challenging is one way to put it," Elena said, rather shocked that it was this easy between them after so much time apart. Maybe, just maybe, the distance had been good for them after all.

"It is easy to be young and fall into love quickly, as if you are tripping and falling." Maria walked with her hands laced in-front of her gown, her shoulders set strong and her gaze still facing forward. "I have found in your absence Elena that I have been very harsh on you, and I do not ask for your forgiveness, but often I think I forget what it means to be young and to have power. Though, I do not nearly have the power that you do."

Elena was not sure what to say.

"You do not need to say anything, rather, I came here today because I know you are prepared for all that might cross your path." Maria paused, turning toward Elena and meeting her gaze. With a free hand, she lifted her daughter's chin, and Elena could swear that there were layers of regret behind the Queen of the Fourth Kingdom's eyes.

"There are too many rulers, and too many moments of my life, where I swim and drown in regret. However, Cyril's letter, as well as Dalton's, reminded me that life does not have to be a path walked alone."

"Dalton convinced you of that? Just with his writing?" Elena could not avoid the shock in her voice.

"He is a very special person, Elena, and I regret my next move on the chess game which is the shuffleboard of the Ten Kingdoms."

"And what is your next move, mother?"

"Well, we are going to end your marriage of course."

Elena opened her mouth, star-struck, but her mother continued.

"And I would like you to take me to the dungeon, Dalton mentioned a traitor amongst your staff, and I would like to have a chat with him."

CHAPTER TWENTY-THREE

The forest was thick as they made their way toward the center of the Tenth Kingdom. There was no magic in the air, as there was in other areas of the continent, leaving an eerie and stark quiet which contrasted the usual buzzing in Dalton's ears. He could feel its pulsation though, almost a similar feeling as the draw which had dimmed between him and Charmaine. He knew from experience that it meant that magic was close, as though it was concentrated or drawn to something.

Looking at Randolph's concentration and knowing that Randolph was able to read auras as a part of his professional skill set, Dalton confirmed that his suspicions were correct.

Dalton's gaze lingered in-front of them, almost muscle memory from the last time that he was here.

It ran through his mind in flashes, the memories of being brought here for answers when his hair had began to turn white. *Power flooded through him as he watched her be taken. Her violet eyes shone with straight horror as she realized that she had no power, not while fear choked her and surrounded her on all sides. There was nothing she could do but withstand it and prepare to endure. Dalton let out a scream, one filled with everything that was left both said and unsaid between them, and felt the power of the Gods flood out of him in unadulterated chaos.*

His power had been pulsating through him like a wired current, so vibrant and terrifying, but bound to him in his blood. Aine and Ronan—he felt as though referring them to be his parents was an insult to parents everywhere—had been concerned about his little manifestation.

Or at least, at the time, he chocked it up to parental feeling. However, the reality that he learned upon reflection was that neither Aine nor Ronan had an ounce of parental virtue in their hearts. They were merely concerned for what this meant for the world, especially a world that they had endorsed that existed without magic.

This championship had been faulty, as had been made clear by their assassination by the mercenaries in Brinn.

It was certain, in Dalton's mind, that nobody should try to bottle up magic.

Rounding a turn on the path that had been carved before them, the castle unveiled itself, and Dalton heard as Lawton inhaled a stark breath.

The Thinkers Castle was the creation of dreams greatest inventions. As Dalton Saphirrus gazed upon it, he decided that the universe was truly magical after all. Sitting atop a grassy hillside, that moreso looked like a small mountain, the home of the Thinkers glistened in all of its glory.

Periwinkle stones that shone light blue in the sunlight glistened, reminding him of the depths of what his magic could feel like at its lightest. Suddenly, he was rather jealous that his own castle did not look like this.

Maybe it was time, after all of this that they were about to endure, that he think of remodeling the place.

"Have you ever been here before, Dalton?" Lawton

Thornwood asked behind him, the knights blue gaze filled with wonder.

"Unsurprisingly, yes," Dalton said, though he was not sure why it would be unsurprising. He had not gone many places, save the First Kingdom. "I came here when my power first...well, you know." He paused, thinking of a way to word it without hashing up new memories. "The whole white hair thing was rather concerning to my family."

"I have too," Randolph whispered, causing both of them to turn their heads. "My mother took me here as a little boy. I cannot remember what for though..."

"A place of mysteries and answers alike," Dalton said, trying to sound chipper. Though he knew the reality of this place, an origin of his torture as well as a dark memory. "How about we make a pit stop for some tea?"

"Are we not in a rush?" Randolph asked, referencing Dalton's numerous outbursts no doubt.

"Scared, Randy boy? Of a few old men?" Dalton raised an eyebrow as he trudged forward.

"Yes," Randolph muttered. "And I think you should be too."

THE COUNCILMEN MADE of the four strongest Thinkers in the castle sat in a half-moon at the top of a five-stair staircase that reminded Dalton oh so much of home. He wondered if this was reminiscent of all the castles in New Sarridolon, to sit atop a small staircase and to stand overtop of those who were considered beneath them.

He made a mental note that if he would return home, that the staircases would be blown up. Never would he ever stand a-top and look down at men and women ever again.

"Dalton Saphirrus," the Thinker in the center stood, his

gaze rendered dark as his starlit covered robe shone in the candlelit ballroom. "What brings you to the Tenth Kingdom?"

"Simply passing through," Dalton said, looking at his fingernails.

Bored.

Cyril had taught him numerous times, as he remembered when he was a boy, that one had to play a part here. The Thinkers believed that they knew all, so it was important to remain indifferent, and not give them anything else to latch onto.

"On your journey to where, might the council inquire?"

These were Cyril's bosses. Assholes indeed.

"Randolph Eniar. Lawton Thornwood," the Thinker spoke again, clearly over the allure of the King of Snow being present. "What brings you to the Tenth Kingdom?"

Resist resist resist resist resist resist...

"We are on our way to my home," Randolph said, quipped.

Fuck.

The Thinker on the far left stood. He looked about seventy-five years older than Cyril, if such a thing was even possible. Hunched over with the most wrinkled skin that Dalton had ever seen. When he spoke though, his voice was clear as day.

"You do know, your Kingship, that your home is rather occupied at the moment?"

"I would like to see it for myself, and check on my sister," he said.

Dalton shot him a gaze that screamed: *Stop telling them our business.*

Randolph shot him a gaze right back that spoke: *If we do not give them anything, we will not learn anything.*

Dalton looked ahead, crossing his arms over his chest in irritation and defeat.

Fine.

"Your sister... Reine. What a beautiful mind and a fierce heart."

Dalton could see Randolph nearly twitching. They knew something. They always did. It was just a matter as to what they were going to say—

"Can you offer me any advice, my Lords?" Randolph asked, bowing his head.

But Dalton was the only one truly looking at him to see his shaking hands. He knew what it was like to lose a sister, and wished that level of pain on nobody else.

Fear was controlling enough but put the love of someone you shared blood with, and it became desperation. More dangerous than fear, because when one was desperate, they will resort to anything to survive.

"You will see her," the Thinker on the far right spoke, though he did not stand. His blue eyes shone brightly, so much so that they were nearly white. The color of a sea-glass that was nearly opaque, and very much frightening. "And I suggest when you do, that you listen to her."

Randolph nodded, clearly not trying to drive himself to madness thinking about the implications.

Lawton had been so silent and still, terrified clearly of the power that stood before him, that Dalton almost forgot that he was there entirely. He guessed he understood, though Lawton had been around his own royal-ness, as well as Randolph's plenty. He guessed it had something to do with the lack of familiarity with this place in particular, and these men's eccentric line of work.

"Lawton Thornwood," the center Thinker said. "You are quite the outlier, for you are not royal in birth, but the Gods have blessed you anyways."

Lawton flushed red. "It would appear so, your Majesties."

The Thinker bowed his head, an acknowledgment of respect for the boy. "Trust in that the power that you were given is clearly for a purpose. Use it well, and use it when you know in your heart that it is necessary. You have the ability to turn the tide of this world and to put it on its axis. That type of power is not seen very often. Use it well."

Lawton nodded his head, digesting the information and slight-warning.

"And you," he said, turning to Dalton slowly. "You have much destiny before you, it is crippling to even myself to think and feel what the road has laid before you, and the road that you have traveled thus far. Yet, I am sure our good friend Cyril has told you all about it."

Dalton's heart cleaved in two at the thought of Cyril, currently laying in the castle for telling him to come and rescue Charmaine. "You would be surprised to hear that Cyril picks and chooses what and when he gives his advice."

All four of the Thinkers laughed at once.

"Cyril is one of the better of us," the Thinker said that had not spoken yet. His gaze was of the forest, dark green and warm. "Let me offer you something to take with you, Dalton Saphirrus. You have a destiny in-front of you that I do not even think that Cyril has the capabilities to see, Gods bless him during his time of strife currently."

Dalton winced. The Thinker continued.

"You will be faced with many trials, both emotional and spiritual. It is critical that you face these head on, and do not linger in your own head, like I know that you tend to do." Smiling softly, he took a step forward, and then another. Before Dalton knew it, he was standing in-front of him, his head bowed. "You, Dalton Saphirrus, are going to save the world. The Gods will not punish me to say this, because you need to hear it."

Stuttering, Dalton was not sure what to even say.

"Trust in violets," he said softly, taking Dalton's hands in his own. "And watch them bloom."

AFTER HAVING THEIR BELLIES FED, they found themselves in their quarters for the evening. Despite the Thinker Castle being quite large and speculative, their housing quarters were less than ideal. The three of them were crammed into one room, as they were a traveling party.

Leave it to the Thinkers to be focused on practicality over all else.

As they prepared for bed, and began to settle in for the evening, Randolph found his mind wandering to places that it should not. However, he felt as though it were safe for questions to linger among them.

Journeys brought people closer together. Or so he hoped as he closed his eyes and brought up the question that had been on his mind for some time.

"Did you and Elena—"

"Oh Gods, what the fuck is the matter with you, Rand —" Dalton looked horrified.

"I was just asking, Dalton," Randolph spat. "You two are married."

"We will see for how long," Dalton muttered under his breath. "I did leave Elena a gift under her pillow, she should have found it by now—"

Randolph chose to ignore this commentary, letting his mind wander for a second once again. He had no energy left to dissect Dalton's words, always tumbling out so freely without context and or meaning. At this point, he would figure out what he was saying when everyone else did. So, him and Elena had never done anything, other than be the political alliances they said that they were. A truth in this world, yes, Randolph could handle a truth in this world.

"Are you...jealous?" Dalton sneered, his gaze wandering to Lawton who was ferociously scribbling on a piece of parchment. "And are you still writing to your long lost love?"

"You two are very question-y this evening, do you know that? We have barely made it to the Seventh Kingdom and you are already—"

The wind howled outside the window, a reminder of the winter storm and the impending doom that they were to face.

"You know, your Majesty," Lawton drawled, leaning closer to Dalton across the table that sat in the corner of the room. "You cannot just freeze anything you do not like. That is not how the world works."

"I am blessed," Dalton whispered, sarcasm and serious-ness dripping through every word. "And if the Gods blessed me, then there has to be a fucking reason."

"It does not give you an excuse to abuse—"

"You do not know the first thing about abuse, Lawton Thornwood of Thallgan," Dalton hissed, the tavern suddenly shaking. "Or at least, I hope not."

The glint in Lawton's eye was of complete fear.

This was not what royals were for. Royals were not supposed to be fearful. If they were, they were no worse than their own fathers. But Randolph knew if he said that, if he told Dalton that, he would completely and utterly lose his shit.

So he diverted the only way that he knew how, with chaos.

Chaos, it would seem, is the only thing that ever steered Dalton Saphirrus back on track.

"Did you and Charmaine—" Before he could finish his thought, ice cold hands gripped his throat. This was not a warning, this was an unleashing.

Heating himself with what breath he could manage, he pushed his power toward his throat, melting the ice which was forming on Dalton's fingertips. Lawton stood suddenly and walked in-front of him, and Dalton released him.

"I am sorry—" Dalton said, breathing heavy and going to sit on the bed's edge. "I do not know what came over me—"

Randolph gasped, rather shocked that Dalton was capable of such things but also when he touched him... He could feel the dark powers radiating off him. Suddenly, Dalton's aura had changed from bright blues and snow to shadows and violet hues. Whatever he was driven by, it was not within himself. Not a part of who he was.

So Randolph lifted his head and said, "I baited you. It is my fault. I am sorry I pushed you, I thought we were there and—"

"No," Dalton said, softly. Clearly, the King was disturbed by his own behavior. "No, do not apologize."

And then he said the most surprising thing of all. "We are there, Randolph."

Lawton laughed out loud, his shock audibly reverberating throughout the room. "Who is going to do the honors of sleeping together?"

"And who is going to get the honors of sleeping on the floor?" Randolph said, wavering from side to side, desperate to move on from that moment of darkness.

❄

Shrugging that dim and dreary thought away, he acted on what felt most natural for him. Impulse.

Flinging himself across the room wildly, he landed on the small and uncomfortable bed and whipped his head around to look at a gawking Lawton and Randolph. Their eyes were filled with surprise, and even a touch of humor, but mostly shock.

Now, *that*, is what felt most natural to him.

Within another blink of his eye, Lawton was thrown to the floor as the two began to scuffle. Laughing out loud, Dalton could not help but cackle at the intensity in which Randolph sped toward the bed. Tattooed hands flailing such that his usual terrifyingly stoic mask was completely and utterly shattered.

With a thud and a creak of the old bed frame, Dalton instantly found himself in a different kind of battle. Honestly, one which he would always come to prefer. These demons he could handle.

An entanglement of the sheets, rather than an entanglement of the swords, it would seem.

"Um," Lawton mumbled from the corner of the room which he had been thrown. "I suppose I am going to sleep on the floor then, since... Yeah."

"Randolph George Eniar!" Dalton shouted as he tried to maneuver Randolph with a kick for more space on the bed.

"That is not even my name!" Randolph spat as they dueled for control.

"I do not care! Stop taking up all of the space on the bed!" Feeling extra cruel, Dalton shot ice cold air out of his mouth in one breath toward Randolph's face.

Reacting quicker than Dalton had attacked, flames erupted from Randolph's fingers. They danced eloquently at the tips—a hell of a lot more threatening than Dalton's ice breath had been.

"Um, you guys, we kind of need a place to stay tonight..." Lawton chided from the floor. Dalton did not sit up to see if he was actually looking at them, or could just merely feel the power which they were wielding from the bed.

Touching the tips of Randolph's finger one by one, they sizzled as fire collided with ice. With a hiss, Dalton said, "Then Randy boy here better not take all the covers."

Chapter Twenty-Four

The gates to the castle opened and Charmaine felt the ground quake with dark power.

He was here. Back again.

Great.

Shouting began to become the song in the halls, gripping and horrifying as followers of King Finn began to yelp with excitement and power.

Tears continued to drip down her face, the memory of hours ago still fresher than she would have liked. Finn had been trying to convince her—coerce her—into using her power. It was simple really, she was to make a knife disappear.

Though it was not really simple after all. For Charmaine had learned quickly here in the Seventh Kingdom that there was a price, and a motive, for everything. Nothing was free and everything was costly.

She had not been able to do it, of course. Her mind weighed too heavy, her motivation low, and her fear very much at the forefront of her mind.

Of course, she told Finn none of this. Of the blocks that prevented her from doing what he wanted her to do most.

Despite the terror that ripped through her when he was near, she found some solace in the fact that her mind—or body, she was not sure which was more prominent when it came to her power—did not physically allow her to comply. It had to count for something.

Maybe, just maybe, she would survive this without becoming an implication in the whole thing. Whatever this thing was.

A war against Dalton, *clearly*, in some capacity.

But no, there was clearly some other evil at work here. The way that King Finn had nearly foamed at the mouth when she strained, over and over and over again—

She tried to push it out of her mind, but she had been wracking her brain for the last few days, trying to find his drive.

Where was Bairre?

Sticking her head into the hallway, she thought deeply about what it meant if she were to truly defy Finn. To run from this place.

Did Ciara ever run? Did she ever defy her father in this way when she was a child? Charmaine shivered at the thought. Her family had not been perfect, for all that it was, but she knew that they had her best interest at heart.

King Finn must have been truly awful if it meant that his own daughter had turned against him with a knife in her hand.

It made Charmaine not want to run, to be complacent.

But Ciara did not have the powers that she did, and Charmaine's greatest asset was her ability to fall into all of the things that should make her weak. If nobody could see her, then they could not see her weaknesses.

The only problem however, was that she had a block. It was emotional she knew it, and it came totally out of fear.

Out of fear for herself. For her friends, of whom were now her only family.

Boom.

The doors opened with haste, shadows pouring into the room before her as Finn strode in without as much as a second glance in her direction.

"Charmaine Grimes, I have a new visitor I would like you to meet!" Hands extended, he beckoned his shadows to come forth.

Shackled in chains of death and shadow, the man who came forth was a shadow himself of what he was the last time that she saw him. An array of short pink hair no longer had its twinkle, his eyes lackluster and filled with fear, and his voice nearly cleaved in two without the spark that once burnt so fiercely in him.

"Titan—" Charmaine sobbed, her body wracked with the emotion of seeing the King of the Sixth Kingdom so easily obtained by this monster. If Titan could be taken, what could become of Dalton? Was he alright?

"Charmaine Grimes..." Titan said softly, his lips cracking from dehydration. "What brings you here?"

"How pleasant," King Finn said, interrupting their eye-contact. "You two are already acquainted then."

Before Titan could say another word, Finn's shadows took over. Spinning him around, he began to exit the room silently. It looked painful, to witness moving without complete control of one's own limbs. To be controlled by another was completely horrifying to her, as it was to be anything that she did not want to be.

She would never be powerless again.

She would try.

She would try.

She would try.

She would try—

Finn's voice cut through the air, so much so that she had nearly forgotten that he was there at all. "Charmaine Grimes, we will try again at dawn. You will make the dagger disappear."

"Or what?" she asked, her voice tearful rather than combative. Though she meant it to come out in the latter.

"Or your friend Titan will suffer. Maybe I will take a finger. Or an eye."

Charmaine inhaled sharply.

"You could not—" She shook her head side to side, tears rolling down her face. "Another monarch?! You could not! To commit regicide—"

She would try.

She would try.

She would try.

King Finn stepped closer to her, his eyes dancing with a level of evil that she had never seen before. No, this was different than when Ronan had murdered Gwendolyn. This was different than anything she had seen before. There was a level of control, and fear, behind Ronan's eyes.

But in Finn's? Only murder existed.

"But dearest Charmaine Grimes, I think you are forgetting the stories." He leaned down, facing her eye-to-eye. "I killed my own daughter, for she was the heir apparent to my throne, and a hell of a lot more worthy than myself. There are no boundaries that I will not cross, no rules that I will not shatter. I failed before, numerous times, to regain what is rightfully mine."

"And what is rightfully yours?" she asked, trying to be brave.

She would try.
She would try.
She would try.

"Sarridolon, of course, my child." He extended his arms wide once more, as if gesturing to the entire world. "It has been, always will be, and will once again be mine."

CHAPTER TWENTY-FIVE

Carinthya paced back and forth in her chambers, haunted by all that had befallen her in these last few weeks. She could not even begin to rehash the last few years. She was a pawn in this, something of a symbol and useless as she waited for the moments that were starting now.

Except, one thing had been maddening to figure out ever since she had been taken in the forest those years ago. Snatched against her will, as she had been living in a child-like moment of defiance of her family. Never did she think in a hundred years that the repercussions would be *this*.

To be used like a chess piece on the continent's stage was one thing—although she was not sure that it warranted the punishment from a moment of experiencing teenage rebellion like she had done that night many years before—but it was entirely another to be used as a chess piece against her own brother. Her only remaining blood in this world. And the bloody king who had been prophesied to fix the world, to remake it in his own name, and vision... Well, he was on the other side of the continent.

And the love of his life? Well, she was here. All thanks to Carinthya.

Cursing herself, she lifted her heads to the Gods, and audibly asked them the question that had been hanging on her lips for many years.

"Why?"

"Why what?" A starlight laced voice whispered behind her. She had no need to turn around to see who sat behind her.

"What do you want?" she said, her voice cracking. "Can you not see that I am in the middle of something?"

"And what, exactly, are you in the middle of?" he whispered, curiosity paramount in his voice. "Praying, perhaps?"

"You mock me," she said, exasperated. "I have sinned, just as everyone has sinned."

"Ah, but the difference is Carinthya Saphirrus, is that when normal siblings fight, they may take a toy from one another. Cause one another grief even, maybe pull their hair." Bairre stepped forward, his hair shining like silver stars and his eyes intense. "But you are not normal, Carinthya. You are a Princess, and one to the most prodigious king in the history of the world. A descendent of the esteemed King Cian and Queen Ciara."

"Keep your voice down," she whispered, taking a step toward him with shaking hands. "You know how Finn gets when he hears her name—"

"Then let him hear it, for he is going to be hearing it more and more often as war looms over us like a dark cloud."

Bairre took a step toward her.

Two steps toward her.

"I told you that I would get you out of here. Hell or high water."

"And why is that you suddenly care about me? You are a

Thinker, as you tend to forget, and nothing more than an advisor to the devil."

"But you are forgetting, lovely," Bairre said, a smile across his face. "That the devil gave me a power that I have wielded for many decades. That my age is not a number, none at all, and that I have his utmost trust and support."

She inhaled sharply, rather shocked at his honesty when he normally did not say much at all.

"And I think you underestimate how much I care for you." He intertwined his scarred hands at his front, leaning so close to her that she could smell the shadows shafting off of him. "And how much Finn appreciates my counsel."

Bairre intertwined his scarred hands in the hair of the Princess who had vanished from the world and crushed his mouth against hers as if it was their last moments in New Sarridolon together.

Groaning in both shock and pleasure, Carinthya found herself swept up in an array of emotions that she could not understand.

And she was met with flashes—visions—that could only be the result of the kiss between a Thinker and a Princess. Although she knew it was happening to her, she could not place anything.

Flash. Her brother's eyes.

Flash. Tattooed hands.

Flash. Shadows and red hair.

Flash. Dragon fire.

Flash. Clouds.

Flash. Blood. So much blood.

Flash. A dagger with chains and diamonds.

Gasping, she fell to her knees, choking on the images that had just suffocated her. Looking up, struggling for air, she met Bairre experiencing the same thing.

"What. Just. Happened?" she asked, her voice ragged

and raw. Emotions flooded through her, but the one that lingered among all else was pain. There was to be a war, was there not?

"I always wondered what would happen, should I do that." His eyes shone with pride at his own discovery, the most hard-lined emotion that she had ever pin-pointed on him. "And now I know."

"What do you know?" she asked, her chest heaving. "You kissed me!" Shock reverberated through the air at the words as if they were a sin themselves.

"And we found out so much, thank the Gods that you saw what I did, then."

"And what exactly did I see?"

"War, Carinthya," he said, standing and making his way toward the door. "And soon."

"Wait," she said. "You cannot just leave. You kissed me!"

"You say it as if you liked it."

Blinking, and stunned at his forwardness, she paused. Looking around the room, she realized that it was just the two of them.

Just the two of them.

"Bairre..." She paused again, speechless at more than one thing this evening. "Bairre, where are your shadows?"

With a jolt, he looked around feverishly. Though, when he met her gaze again, there was nothing but joy that spread across his face.

Another thing that she had never seen before: Bairre joyous.

"Carinthya Faye Saphirrus, pack your bags."

"And where are we going?" she asked, her voice so low. Out of fear. Fear of him. Fear of what she saw. Fear of the shadows. Did Finn take them? Would they somehow be punished for this?

"Anywhere but here, Carinthya," he said. "I have heard

many tales in my many years, but the one that has prevailed above all else is your families pension for chaos. I look forward to seeing it reign down this evening."

And then he slid out the door, leaving her to the same silence that had nearly broken her before he came in.

CHARMAINE AWOKE to her hands being tied.

It was the least frightening thing that had happened to her thus far today, if she were to count her dream.

"Stay still," Bairre whispered, merely an inch from her face. His eyes were haunted by the memory of something so deeply troubling that Charmaine actually wished to reach out and touch him. Before all of this: being captured, being stolen, this was something that she figured would be acceptable. That was who she had been, the one to reach out with a hand when nobody else would.

No more. She knew now that this was done, and that she should reach with caution.

But there was something within Bairre that called out to her. Like he knew her.

No, that was *impossible*.

Nobody truly knew her. Not anyone that was here with her, anyways.

But was it?

With a grunt, he yanked her upright. "You are coming to the dungeon with me, Charmaine Grimes, and when we walk down the hallway you best put on the performance of your life."

Shadows quipped around him feverishly. It was as if they were trying to tell her something, despite not being able to speak. Like communicating with a rope over your mouth, it was getting nowhere.

But she could not shake the feeling...

Yank.

Without another word, her wrists began to burn, and she let it take over her. The fear, the anguish, all of the things which she had been bottling in the last few weeks... it came tumbling out in a devastating fire.

Heaving, her breath became unsteady, sweat building at her brow.

She could have sworn she was dying, if she did not know what this was. The panic was taking over, attacking her from the inside out.

It was all things at once, the death of her entire family, the traumatic separation from Dalton, the fact that she could not speak his name...

It poured out of her like water came out of a hot spring, violent and traumatizingly difficult to navigate with nothing to anchor her. With nobody to anchor her.

As they made their way down the halls of the Seventh Kingdoms castle, she was numb to all. Hands extended in front of her, she could do nothing but trip over her own two feet and sob as Bairre pulled her along.

Maybe he was the monster everyone believed him to be after all.

But for giving into his demands, what did that make her?

Blinking, tears beginning to soak her neck and hair, she decided she was not ready to face that question. Though she knew the answer, unspoken for months between her and Dalton.

She was power, she just was not ready to be it yet.

Without warning, they rounded the final corner of the long hallway and Bairre came to a haunting stop so quickly that she nearly fell into him. But her wits were coming back to her, as though her body and mind knew that their travels were over for the time being.

"Go inside," he growled, that mystery from before completely evaporated from his vocals.

Shadows swirled up the door that stood before them like hands, twisting and turning the knob until it swung open with a creak. With all the force that the shadows could muster, she felt them touch her lower back, and fling her through the doorway.

Stinging, her hands and knees throbbed with the impact of her landing. Slowly, she lifted her head, her tears still being blinked away from the walk.

But it was not her who gasped, but the girl who stood before her with the sapphire eyes and the black hair. The girl who she had not had the chance to talk to yet.

Carinthya Saphirrus.

"You must be Charmaine Grimes," Carinthya said, her eyes hauntingly the same as her brother's.

"And you—" Charmaine said, stumbling over her words. However, the girl only smile.

"You look like you have seen a ghost," she said, raising an eyebrow.

Oh, she was most definitely a Saphirrus.

"Well," Charmaine said after a heartbeat. "I suppose I am looking at one."

Carinthya cocked her head to the side, her dark ebony hair shifting with the turn. "Have we met?"

The question was genuine. "No, but I have met your portrait in the gallery of the First Kingdom."

Whatever mask Carinthya was wearing disappeared, slipped even, for just a second before she regained it. "And who might you have had the pleasure of touring that spectacle with?"

"Your brother, actually," Charmaine said, her heart racing just mentioning him. "I was with him—well—before I..."

"Ended up here?" She paled. The light freckles that were sprinkled across her cheekbones suddenly looking dark with the sudden change of her complexion.

"Yes, that is one way to put it," Charmaine said.

Bairre stood in the corner, silent, as if he was waiting for something to come out of this. For something to happen.

"Did you just want us to meet?" Carinthya asked. "You risked a lot by her coming here right now."

Bairre spoke, stepping forward. "I had a few minutes carved out in my day so that when you two see one another it will not be a complete and utter shock to both of your systems."

"How kind of you," Carinthya said, standing slowly.

Charmaine noticed the garb that she wore. It was the finest of silks and the most beautiful royal red gown. Was she even a prisoner here at all? Her mind could not fathom such a thing. If that were not the case, Dalton would be crushed to know that his sister had been living here for years without ever writing to him. Her blood boiled at the thought actually.

She would kill to talk to her brother.

Just one more time.

"Are we to meet again, then?" Charmaine asked, her voice cracking with uncertainty.

Bairre smiled, taking Carinthya's hand in one hand and then reaching for Charmaine's with another. "Of course, I cannot leave the castle without the Violet Queen and the Princess of Snow."

"I am not the Princess of Snow," Carinthya snarled, all venom.

Charmaine was rather taken aback by that, her tone in particular. Did Carinthya not have the power of her brother? Dalton had mentioned as such, but she never actually put two and two together.

"Oh, but Carinthya Faye Saphirrus," Bairre said, still holding both of their hands. "But you could be."

CHAPTER TWENTY-SIX

After whisking away Charmaine Grimes, Bairre returned only moments later. Carinthya wondered suddenly where Finn was, because Bairre would never risk doing something like this without knowing exactly where he was at and what he was doing.

Extending a hand filled with mystery and wonder, Bairre nearly growled, "Come with me, we have a job to do."

"Where are you taking me?" Carinthya's gaze lingered far too long on his silver hair.

"We are going for a walk, stretching our legs merely, but we have to stop by a friend's room first. Everyone must be prepared, and know one another so that when all hell breaks loose, we know who we can trust."

"You think that we just did—Charmaine Grimes and I —are now trusting of one another?" Carinthya could not hide the laugh that blasted out of her. "She looked at me as if I was other worldly."

"I think you are underestimating the hold that your brother has on her. If need be, Charmaine Grimes will trust you simply because of your blood."

"And if we are to get out of here, which surely will be the chaos that you promise, how can you be sure that everything will work out?" Carinthya could not envision a scenario, especially if she were to eventually go home and see her brother, where she would be welcome with open arms. She imagined that he would feel betrayed and abandoned.

And she could not blame him in earnest.

Wandering down the hall silently, Bairre trotted in-front of her with haste. Her heels clacked on the dark floors as he made no noise, as if his shadows propelled him forward. It was almost like he was walking on air.

Carinthya noted how his silver hair was pulled behind his head, not even one shard of hair out of line. He demonstrated and exuded the utmost levels of perfection, though it was a wonder to her where his cracks were.

Everyone had cracks.

But where were his?

As they rounded the corner, Bairre came to an immediate stop. Whose room were they at—

Bairre knocked twice and without warning flew the door open. "Reine, you are coming with us."

Reine Eniar said at the foot of her bed, her back pressed up against the base, and eerily stared forward. Tattoos glistened as the sun shone through the stained-glass window depicting a village burning down, and a shiver went down Carinthya's spine.

"And why is that?"

"Because we need to go somewhere, and dearest Finn was insistent that you were to come with us." He gestured to Carinthya.

Reine only indicated that she noticed her presence by asking, "Then what is to become of Charmaine in our absence?" Carinthya was rather taken aback by the comment. Had she been able to spend time with Charmaine Grimes? Or was she just nearly expressing her concern?

"Scrying," Bairre said, though Carinthya was certain that she caught a hint of distaste in his voice. "Or trying to."

"For what?"

"Things."

"You are so vague, Bairre. I hate it." Reine's voice exuded irritation.

Obviously, she was not a fan.

Carinthya on the other hand was no longer sure where she stood.

As Bairre opened his mouth to answer, the castle shook abruptly. Stones fell from the ceiling, the air thick with war and soot. "Carinthya! Reine! Get down!" he yelled as the walls thundered and shattered with the cry of battle.

Throwing themselves under Reine's bed, the three of them huddled as the castle creaked and groaned, as if it were stretching its legs.

If such a thing was possible.

"What was that?" Carinthya asked, noticing the rumbling slow after a few moment's pause.

"Well," Bairre said, sliding himself out from under the bed first. "It appears we have a visitor. Maybe two, if we are lucky."

CHAPTER TWENTY-SEVEN

Athelred had committed the greatest of sins. He had conspired with the enemy, with King Finn, for the abduction and finding of Charmaine Grimes. He had taken something precious from all of them, but most of all Dalton.

Now, Maria stood in-front of Athelred as he cowered in the back of his cell, and all that Elena found that she was doing was marveling at her mother's display of raw power. Maria did not wield anything but her crown, but oh was it so magical nonetheless.

"Now, tell me, Athelred, how did you come to work for King Finn?" She did not crouch down, to stoop to his level.

For any other monarch, she knew that this strategy would not work. To not display an outright showing of magic... Well, any other ruler would have looked weak.

Yet, this was Maria's gift from the Gods. The look in her eye. The ability to command a room with just one simple look.

And to get men to confess.

Athelred opened his mouth, though his eyes burned

with pure hatred. "He selected me for the job, for my close-ness with the King."

It took everything in Elena not to laugh at that.

"And what was your closeness, to the King of Snow?" Maria's tone was sharp.

"I was his servant," Athelred said proudly, as if he himself was King.

Elena snorted, making her presence very much known. "For a moment."

Maria's hands twitched behind her back, and she saw Greyson out of the corner of her eye put a hand on his sword. Two gestures of silent approval if she ever saw one before.

"And what was your goal, Athelred?" she asked softly, her voice remaining level despite the escalating tension in the room.

"Well, it was quite simple really," Athelred said, trying to sound suave. "I was to get him the Queen of Frost."

There it was. That term again.

"The Queen of what?" Maria asked. "And who might that be?"

Athelred sat up, his sandy blonde hair looking rather gray as he moved into the solemn light in the dungeon. "Charmaine Grimes, your grace. Have you had the pleasure of meeting her yet? Oh wait—"

He paused. Sagging down once more. The shackles on his hands and legs rattled with the motion. "You have not had the pleasure, because he took her."

MARIA HAD USHERED Greyson to take Elena to her chambers immediately, rather shocked at the admission. Elena was shocked too, though she had admitted as she closed the door it was moreso at the idea that someone was capable of such evil through another.

As she turned in her chambers, the door closing with a thud behind her, he could feel the fear festering behind his eyes.

He stood before Elena with all of the nerves inside of him buzzing, alive with fear and excitement alike. He knew he looked like he was about to vomit, as if that this—whatever he was about to say—was a shot in the dark, frankly a shot in hell, but he had to take a chance. To strike while the iron was hot is the only way which he could think of getting a chance, a moment, with Elena Leclair.

He had cared for her for months, since James Grimes had been murdered at the scene of a heinous crime. He was completely and utterly at her mercy, and all he needed was for her to see it. To know it. He wanted to make it clear he wanted nothing from her. He did not wish to act on these feelings and thoughts that he had. It was purely to be her protector. To be for her what she needed.

The world was a dark place, and he wished to be her light.

He would lay down anything on the line for her, friendship or more. That was what it was, to love, he decided. To choose someone and be whatever you needed for them outside of our own interests.

Clearing his throat, he approached Elena slowly. He did not drag his feet, for he was the utmost level of professionalism, per usual.

"Elena," he whispered softly, afraid of startling her.

She turned, her fiery hair somehow softer in the light as she turned from the window which she was staring out. She wore a black gown, and Greyson rather found it to be ironic.

She had figured out the divorce, the split amicably from

Dalton, and now she wore the color of a funeral. But what was she mourning?

"Yes, Greyson?" she asked, suddenly looking much younger. Her voice carried none of its usual weight and flame, rather it was like a sweet song of springtime. A breath of fresh air.

"I felt it—pertinent—your Majesty, to tell you some things that have been on my mind."

"And what would those be?" she asked, her voice remaining in the same tone.

"I do not believe we are fated together," Greyson said honestly, his voice not stumbling when he thought so surely that he was nervous enough to do so. "But I do believe that fate brought us together for a reason."

She quirked up an auburn eyebrow, as if she was unsure what to make of this statement.

Taking a knee, Greyson drew his sword and placed it in-front of him. "I took an oath before Dalton, but because you and him are no longer, I want to make sure that you remain protected."

Her gaze softened, and he could have sworn she was crying, but he refused to look up too long. He could not take rejection for something that he felt so utterly and completely sworn to. "If you were ever in danger Elena, it is now when you are most vulnerable. Your mother has sworn her allegiance to your line, and to your happiness. And because of that, I want you to be—No, I need you to be—safe."

"I appreciate this Greyson," Elena whispered. "But I have powerful friends, Randolph and—"

"Randolph, his Majesty," he corrected. "Cares for you deeply Elena, I know he does. But let me do this. Let me have purpose in this world, because without you Elena, I am not sure where I fit into these ten kingdoms..."

Before he could finish, she kneed down with him and threw her arms around him.

"Thank you," she breathed into his crevice of his shoulder and neck. "Thank you Greyson, for being there for me."

"Always," he whispered, letting the emotion overtake him. "Always."

Chapter Twenty-Eight

S moke filled Charmaine's nose, and she woke up gasping for air. Dangerously reminiscent of her home in Brinn, seconds before her whole world had gone up in flames, she found herself shouting a name that she had not uttered in weeks. Although, it had remained at the forefront of her mind.

It always remained at the forefront of her mind.

He always remained at the forefront of her mind.

"James," she breathed out, sitting upward as quickly as her exhausted and tortured body allowed. Raising an arm to shield her mouth, she rolled from the bed to the floor.

Just as she had in Brinn.

No.

Focus.

Survival.

Her mind wandered to Dalton. *You are a survivor*.

Yes, she was.

And she had escaped fire before.

And this would be no different.

Making her way around the floor, eyes focused on what

was in front of her, she paused despite the danger. The ground was softer than she could have ever imagined when she had hit it, but she quickly found that it was not wood that she was touching.

It was violet roses. Petals.

And they were burning.

Violet roses singed around her, their petals disintegrating as the fires came alive. Smoke whiffed into the air, cursing every breath that Charmaine took as she looked around wildly. This was not the first time that she had woken up in a fire.

James.

Her heart thundered in her chest, eyes growing wide as she made her way to her window.

She had lived this before, in some life and in some way. Had she not?

And who in the name of the Gods had put these flowers here?

As she made her way over to the window, her eyes fully opened to the shadows of smoke around her, she gasped and choked instantly. The smoke caught in her throat, sitting in her lungs as she beheld something so monstrous that she was not sure she was even alive to see such a thing.

Before she had time to fully register its girth, she ducked under the bed in her chambers, as a fireball came smashing into the wall of the Seventh Kingdom's castle.

And for some reason, she no longer thought of James, but instead could see nothing but Randolph. The flames ignited from his fingertips, lightning against the darkness and shadows of this place.

Shaking her head, and crouching low to the ground, she shook her head from side to side. There was no way that Randolph was here. There was no way that Randolph was here.

There was no way that Randolph was here.

As the smoke began to waft more and more, lacing her skin until her body felt heavier and heavier. The violet petals drooped around her, and she wondered once again who put them here, and what they were trying to say, when sleep overtook her.

CHAPTER TWENTY-NINE

As they approached the castle, Randolph had never felt so out of his body. His limbs were heavy, the tattoos on each of his hands weighing thousands of pounds suddenly. The ink was heavy, and for the first time he suddenly wished that it could just melt off him with his flames. The darkest of skies loomed over them, an omen within itself. Should they have just never come at all?

It had been so many years since he had laid eyes on this castle. Last he saw it, it was pouring rain and he had barely been able to get another look before he had taken off on Gregoria.

Now it just looked so ordinary, despite the evil that harbored itself within it.

Black sandstone stood at the bottom of Castle Dead, as ominous as the name his ancestors had given the land to begin with. The whole thing was a ruse, for Randolph would know better than anything, that the interior of the castle was rich and luxurious.

Not a very homely place to raise a family, yet alone to wear a crown.

Dalton took a step forward, the snow crunching under his boots. Randolph immediately put a hand out, preventing him to leave the tree line.

"You cannot just walk in the front door," Randolph hissed. "You would be asking for a fight."

"What if I want one?" Dalton said, squaring himself up to Randolph. His eyes blazed with that Saphirrus fury that Randolph regrettably admitted had not been around much of late. Yes, Dalton was always impulsive and sporadic. But on the journey here, there was some type of resigned-ness to him.

He did in fact create—what would seem to be—an eternal snowstorm, but that was besides Randolph's point.

"You do not want a fight," Randolph hissed, careful not to let the smoke pour out of his nose. "We do not know their numbers yet, and frankly we do not know anything about where they are keeping her."

Dalton's only reply was an audible huff and a groan.

With that, Randolph knew that he had won.

"What if we started something?"

"Lawton Thornwood, if you are suggesting a fight as the King just did I swear to the Gods—"

"No," Lawton said carefully, treading over to them silently in the fluffy snow that continued to fall. "But hear me out."

"What would you have us do?"

"Me? Dalton? Nothing. But you? Well, you can easily create some chaos."

Randolph did not like the sound of this. "You have to be mad. What would you have me do?"

"Pick a window, any window, and launch a fireball at it."

Dalton was smiling now. The most genuine he had in weeks.

Good Gods, someone save him.

"And why would I do that, we would get caught!" Randolph exclaimed, exasperated beyond all measure. They did not come all this way to get captured within six seconds of their arrival.

"Because it will draw them out," Dalton said, as if he was somehow on some other wavelength than Randolph entirely. "And then we can get inside."

"Beyond inside, I can jump us away. You know I can, Randolph, I have been practicing, and this is close enough. I can do this."

Randolph bit his tongue, and then decided to un-bite it. "Just because the Thinker's told you yesterday that your power would be useful and needed, does not mean to attack my childhood home and then jump inside of it. What if this is not the right time? What if they know we are coming?"

Dalton got up in Randolph's face, his freckles looking less and less like constellations and more like fuzzy dots as his own nose touched Randolph's. "You are technically my subject, Randolph Eniar, and I am telling you that as your King I want you to throw a blasted fireball at that castle so that we can all get back what we want."

Randolph gulped, but instead of protesting he simply said, "Please stop touching me."

"Will you do it, then?" Dalton asked, not moving.

Randolph replied with a raised hand, the center of his power beginning to build and flow. He thought of the most painful moments of his life: his father's murder, losing his sister forever, running away, seeing so much pain on Dalton's face every day since Charmaine was taken, the death of James Grimes, the grief that everyone faced after the attack at the castle of Brinn...

The fire grew, and he could feel the heat building on his face.

As it paused, his closed his eyes once more, and thought

of the beauty that he had within his own life. For there was much to celebrate. He thought of meeting Charmaine, hugging her after her brother's funeral, being promoted to the king's services and finally finding even a misplaced version of purpose. His mind even wandered to Elena, and receiving that dignified look of respect that she certainly did not give to everyone.

There was so much good in his life, despite all of the darkness that clouded him. Though, he surmised rather quickly that was the trick to life: to let the darkness come right at you, to threaten to overtake you, and then to let the light in and never let it go out.

Opening his eyes, he could not hide the shock at the size of the fireball that now danced above his hand. Dalton and Lawton now stood ten paces away, and Randolph laughed at himself that he did not even realize that they had migrated away from the splash zone of his power.

Dalton was jumping up and down, quite childish yet so innocent in the gesture. Lawton merely stared, his mouth agape, as if he had never seen anything so magnificent.

With the wink of an eye and then a spin in the other direction, Randolph wound up and threw his concentrated power directly at his old bedroom window.

And prayed that nobody was sleeping in that room.

And prayed even harder that this would work.

CHAPTER THIRTY

Charmaine awoke to the smell of smoke, the absence of rose petals, and a note from of whom she could only assume was written by Bairre.

Get ready to run.

-B

A feeling that unfortunately was becoming habit for her swam within her once more. Fear. But another strange one —a more unfamiliar—awoke as well.

Excitement.

As she tried to pull apart her hands, she was met with only resistance. Gods, she had been tied up. Her hands bound. A groan of frustration left her, for she could not believe that anyone would have the impression from her that she had plans to murder everyone in this castle.

She had admittedly gotten stronger in her defeat since being brought here against her will, but there was nothing murderous about her. Not yet anyway.

Darkness crashed around her, smothering her as she tried to sit up. This was surely some part of a nightmare that she had never woken up from, though she had never had a dream before where she went to sleep and everything felt so alive.

And surely, she saw Randolph out of the cornerstone of her window. There was no way that she would mess that up, even in the wildest parts of her dreams.

But when a shadow lifted her chin, as soft and wistful as the wind itself, she could not do anything but realize that this was reality.

King Finn chuckled in the corner, darker than he had been the last few weeks in tone. He was leaning up against the wall, dressed in full battle garb, though he lacked armor. His fighting leathers were ordained with daggers on each side, and his tunic had a vest of plated chainmail.

Before she had a chance to act—or think, really—he spoke softly. Calmly.

Too calmly for the smoke and ash that infiltrate her lungs.

No, this was most definitely *not* a dream.

"Tell me, Charmaine Grimes, what is your greatest fear?"

Charmaine thrashed from side to side, the shadowed chains on her hands locking into place so she could not move. She would be making no attempts at running this day.

"I do not know why this is relevant—" she started, interrupted by a fit of coughs.

"Fear," King Finn growled, "is just as powerful as fury."

Why was he not coughing?

A motion of the shadows opened the door, and two familiar faces walked in. Carinthya followed Bairre in tail, though their faces gave nothing away. One would think, if they did not know any better, that Bairre was merely dragging the princess of the First Kingdom here.

Now, Charmaine knew better.

Carinthya stood next to Bairre in the room, together they remained stoic as they watched her fall apart before them. She knew though, she knew that this was the impetuous between them. She guessed then that she was to be their sacrificial lamb, as well as she could handle it.

Then so be it.

Bairre did say that it was important that they got to know one another after all.

"I am not afraid of anything," Charmaine said.

"Nothing?" The shadows grew tighter. King Finn's voice louder. "Oh, child, everyone is afraid of something."

"You did not let me finish," Charmaine spat. "I am not afraid of anything, not one man, not one person, not one woman. But what I am afraid of is letting myself be. To be authentically myself in a world that has always told me to be the watered down version of myself."

"And what version would that be?" King Finn asked, his interest surely peeked.

"The ability to be me."

Charmaine did something then that she had not thought she was ever going to do.

She listened to Bairre, and let the change overtake her. There was more to her than what met the eye, she knew it. She just had to believe it. No, not believe it. Embrace it. She had nothing to lose. Nothing to gain. Only potentials existed in this scenario, in this life, where she had learnt over and over again that if she did not strike there would never be lighting.

With the sweetest smile that she could muster, she took a deep breath and steadied her mind.

And then she vanished into thin air.

CHAPTER THIRTY-ONE

Randolph's fire crumbled the walls of his castle faster than he had admitted. As he looked longingly at the place which he had once called home, and before he could start making moves to see what type of damage he had exactly caused, Lawton took his hand and they were flying through the air. They did not jump far, rather they only moved along the tree-line, but out of any viewers from within the castle's plain eyesight. They would be looking directly where the fire had come from, and now they were no longer there.

Randolph was out of his body, his mind and soul no longer bound to the continent but other-worldly. Seconds passed that felt like years, his mind able to wander yet completely rooted in the same moments and flashes that he relived in what overcame him while he slept. It was magnificent, like falling through a chalice of water, yet drowning at the bottom.

Maybe Lawton was blessed by the Gods after all, because that was the only reasonable explanation to *possibly* explain how any of this was possible from a non-royal.

As soon as they had taken flight, he blinked and they were once again rooted. As he turned to count the three of them—himself included—he was overcome with relief.

"Did you doubt me, Randolph?" Lawton said with a smile curling on his lips, as though he was really proud of himself for being able to bring him with him.

"Was this a gamble?" Randolph said, shock and irritation flooding into him as he came back fully into his body. Lightheadedness overcame him in flashes, though he only put his hands on his hips to cope. There was no time for error and no room for any potential disasters to overtake any of this.

He had to remain perfection. Something that he had mastered when he was last here, so he figured that it would not be difficult to slip back into his other shoes.

Turning his head to look for the King of Snow—and not caring to hear Lawton's answer to his question—he saw Dalton retching a few steps away.

"That. Was. Bloody. Fucking. Awful," Dalton said, gasping as color came back into his face. "I am never taking a joy ride with you again Lawton Thornwood. Gods save me."

"How was I supposed to know that you got motion sickness?" Lawton said, trying to hold in a laugh.

"How was I supposed to know that when you said you could jump that it was anything like... like... THAT?!" Dalton said, exasperated.

"Gentlemen—" Randolph said, trying to interrupt.

"Gentlemen?!" Dalton spat out, clearly not recovered yet from his bout with vomiting. "Since when are the three of us actually considered gentlemen—titles aside..."

Randolph spun. "You two nitwits—it is time. We have to make a move." His finger followed from a distance mercenaries out of the castle, running toward the forest.

Time to play knight.

Time to play king.

Time to get Charmaine Grimes back.

"Lawton, you jump Dalton inside. Anywhere but the throne room. Remember the chaos of the drawing I showed you, if Finn has any type of ego like I thought... Well, that is where he will be."

"I have to jump again?" Dalton said, though the irritation in his voice did not match the fire that now burned in his eyes.

"Yes, and try your best not to throw up inside. That would be most problematic if Finn found you from a trail of vomit..."

"I do not know *exactly* where we are going to land inside this place," Lawton whispered, unsure of himself. He stretched his hand in and out, flexing as if trying to calm himself down.

Dalton grunted, becoming impatient. The crux of his frustration that he was not looking forward to throwing up again. Gods, he looked terrible. It was clear that he knew that his power had ramifications. Next time he froze something, it would be clear that nobody was allowed to give him shit because Lawton Thornwood and his accursed power merely existed.

Gods, did everyone need a pep talk today?

"Lawton Thornwood, I have seen a lot of power in my day between myself, Randolph, Elena, and Charmaine, but never have I ever seen a power such as yours."

"Oh yeah, and what is that your Majesty? A compliment?" Lawton's eyebrow was raised.

"A power so useful," he whispered. "Now be useful, use it. For your friend. For your kingdom. For New Sarridolon."

Taking the king's ice cold hand, Lawton breathed in and out, focusing, and then melted away into nothingness.

"Take me to Charmaine Grimes," Lawton audibly commanded. *Take me to Charmaine Grimes.*

A cold hand landed on his shoulder, and snow began to fall most steadily again, like a beating heart. "I know what to do," Dalton said seriously.

Dalton extended his hand, bracing himself mentally to go through the wringer once again. And then he was gone.

Taking a deep breath to recenter himself, to prepare to confront all that he had left behind, Randolph broke into a run.

And made his way toward the secret entrance to the kitchens.

RANDOLPH STOPPED dead in his tracks. Throwing open the door with haste, his sword drawn, hands heating up, he was confronted with none other than the cook herself.

"Mrs. Knox?" he asked, his voice filled with grief as if he were mourning the woman in-front of her as she lived.

Covered in flour from head to toe, her face erupted into a smile as tears began to clear the path to skin under her white-covered face.

"I never thought I would see the day," she said through sobs, her voice nearly bringing Randolph to his own.

Embracing her in a silent hug, Randolph let himself be covered in flour, and let the smells of what he remembered about being home in a positive light wash over him.

"I never thought I would see the day either, Mrs. Knox," he whispered back, emotion flowing out of his voice despite his best efforts to remain neutral. He did have a mission to attend to.

But it could wait one more moment.

He pulled back, regaining himself and refocusing on his mission. "You need to leave Mrs. Knox—"

"You know he is here?" she asked, though it came out as more of a statement. "She is in her chambers, they returned her about an hour ago. But the castle is under attack—" She burst out laughing, clearly putting two and two together. "But where will I go?"

"Anywhere, safe-harbor will be granted in the town, I promise you that." Randolph thought of a few places immediately that used to provide shelter to him while his father had been... Well, his father. Pushing the memory away, he reminded her of a few noble families, and exactly what to say. "They will take care of you, their allegiance always lied with his children."

His.

No names.

No, he would never name his abuser ever again. Not while he lived.

Without another word, she threw her arms around him one more time. The smell of fresh baked bread and pastries washed over him once again, and he was confronted with the most beautiful memories of his life in this castle. He prayed as he walked down the hallway that he could hold onto them.

Parting ways suddenly, he made his way through the entrance to the kitchen, and did not look back.

MEMORIES.

Fickle things.

Flashes launched themselves into the forefront of Randolph's mind with every step. He was no longer seeing the hallway as it was now, filled with nothing but darkness, but only saw moments of his life that had since come and gone.

Blink. Three year old Randolph running down the hallway, play sword in hand.

Blink. Six year old Randolph and toddler Reine playing with wooden horses, envisioning and dreaming of themselves riding them one day.

Blink. Randolph walking down the hallway at ten after getting his first tattoo. A memoriam to his princely training being underway. His first lesson? Taking a life. Hand to hand combat.

Blink. Randolph five years ago, standing in this very hallway in silence and darkness, contemplating what he knew he must do to save his sister from harm.

With a deep breath in and out, Randolph lit a flame that existed between his pointer and thumb and lifted the tiny flame high enough so that he could see in-front of himself. Their mission was depending on secrecy, and stealth, and he had to get to her before everything went to hell.

As he made his way down the long hallway, he came to the all too familiar round-about staircase that reminded him so much of his former life that all of the wind was suddenly knocked out of him.

Memories, it would seem, were more alive than he could have ever anticipated. They breathed, they sang, and they existed within the walls of places that lived beyond the second that they had happened. And that within itself was really powerful, and something that he would never ever forget again, as long as he may live.

Before he knew it, he was at the door. Her door.

His heart thundered in his chest. Mrs. Knox said that she would be here, and that was a woman that he would trust with his life. She had looked after him so many times in her own life: tended to his wounds, listened to his silent sobs and only handed him a slice of pie as comfort, and been there truly for it all. So when she had told him that Reine was behind the door, this door, in her chambers, well, he knew it was truth in its rawest form.

Lifting a shaking flowered hand, he paused. What was he to do? Knock? Barge in? He did not want to get flamed by his own sister.

A smile curled his lip at the thought, those memories flooding back over him like water.

With a decisive breath in and a long exhale out, he slowly pushed open the door, figuring if now was an inconvenient time, that Reine would blast him into oblivion.

"Bairre, if that is you again, I want no more to do with your little introductions as if we are girls in a playgroup."

Randolph paused, shocked to hear her voice. She had grown up, her tone more firm and confident.

Like a Queen.

Tears began to steadily fall down his face. He imagined that if one looked close enough, that they contained scenes of what he imagined his sister to be like before he left.

He responded by opening the door, and to seeing his sisters back. She was turned around, doing what he did not care, and did not bother himself to figure out the details. Her hair had gotten longer than he had last seen her, sitting now at the lower part of her back. She wore a red gown, though he could tell by the way that she carried herself that this was something she was forced to do.

A soft smile expanded across his face, it was so like Reine to be resentful about doing something that she did not want to do. The blood of a queen through and through.

"Bairre, I do not like when you are all creepy like this. I know that is not really what is in your heart—" A pregnant pause filled the air, and Randolph gasped as the girl with dark brown hair turned around.

An unrelenting sob broke out of him as he met the gaze that was all too familiar, flower tattoos meeting flower tattoos as they seemingly ran toward one another, unaware of their own movements as though they were not their own.

"I am here," Randolph said, hands shaking as he hugged his sister so deeply that he was sure that he was crushing her.

"How? Why?" she said, pulling apart slowly so that she could look him in the eyes. Her gaze was filled with regret and longing and complete surprise. "How did you get here?"

"It is a long story," Randolph said. "But I am here to get you out. This place is—"

"You know he is here?" Relief flooded her voice, as if she was glad that she did not need to recant the story of how King Finn took over their families castle.

Randolph only nodded his head. "Grab your sword sister, we are leaving."

Chapter Thirty-Two

With a thud, Dalton blinked and he was once more on his knees. Sickness washed over him, though after gagging once he felt no longer like he did the first time.

As if reading his mind, Lawton put a hand on his shoulder.

Damn, he was starting to really like this kid.

"It gets easier with time," Lawton said gently. Now that they were one on one, it was clear that Lawton was not as confident and sassy as he was when Randolph was around. In this moment, they were merely king and knight, working together on a mission.

There was no time to be sentimental. Dalton needed to get moving and quickly.

Taking Lawton's hand to help him rise, he smiled softly. A silent thank you.

"Where will you go as I..." Dalton did not need to finish his sentence, Lawton knew. As he went to go and find Charmaine.

"I think I can be useful scouting," Lawton said firmly.

"There have to be more prisoners here than just the ones that we are aware of. I am going to try to get as many people out as I can without arousing suspicion."

With a nod, Lawton turned to head the other direction. Before having a chance to evaporate for a third time, Dalton whispered loud enough for him to catch it, "Thank you."

"Go and find her, Dalton Saphirrus," Lawton said with a half-smile. "Go and find her, and bring her home."

CHAPTER THIRTY-THREE

Creeping through the darkened castle alone, Dalton held out his shaking hands, trembling for the first time of this whole excursion with the weight of the truth.

King Finn was here and he was to be the cause of the demise that was prophesied. It rang through his head, thrumming like a drum set would at a king's coronation. Or funeral.

The King of Snow is coming. He will Rise from the death of his Father. The Ten Kingdoms will fall. Fire will scorch the lands. A Violet Queen will Reign, and the light that holds the Kings of Old will go out.

In order to take himself anywhere other than his nerves, Dalton began to reason through it. One, the King of Snow is coming. Well, that was rather self-explanatory. It was not as if King Cian was to rise from the death. Two, he will rise from the death of his father. Surely, that one had come and passed as well. Three, the Ten Kingdoms will fall.

Dalton snorted. Well, this surely felt like the beginning of the fall of his continent. Check.

Fire will scorch the lands was an interesting one to him. He had assumed it was war itself that was to overtake the land, but the gleam that was in Randolph's eye earlier while launching at a fireball at his own castle reminded Dalton that maybe not everything in the prophecy was as simple as it was made out to be. Could the fire be a person, rather than something so literal?

And surely that last line was the most complex and damning of them all.

He smiled to himself softly. He had only figured out part of that one thus far, and was not ready to delve into that latter half.

One obstacle at a time.

And this was a rather large obstacle that he was in to begin with.

Silently cursing himself, he dreamt of what it could have been like to make a deal with Kai where he could have flown in and burned the whole place to the ground, the evil king from a century ago with everything else.

But that was not the plan, nor a part of the deal which he had so devastatingly made. The part that Randolph did not even know... He smiled to himself. The deal that was going to get him in a lot of trouble for when his friends all found out what he was up to.

The bond that he had made at his coronation—one to protect those that he loved—had been quelled since he had begun this journey to find Charmaine. It had satisfied its need. Now though, this in place with such darkness, it bloomed and blossomed into something else that was all too familiar.

The draw that ever lingered between himself and Charmaine Grimes.

With a final smirk he reset his face and mind, his hands returning to shaking. It was a miracle that snow did not flow out of him just out of pure malice and sheer tragedy. It was a miracle within himself that he had even come this far, in his life, without being so out of control.

He was dangerous, he just needed to remember it.

Kai did.

That is why he had agreed. Kai would do his bidding, once the time was right, but he would have to set him free. A dangerous bargain, indeed. But Dalton needed insurance, should things go as wrong as he anticipated them to.

Gliding down the hallway silently, Dalton pushed out a cold breath of air, appearing in front of him as a true puff of smoke. However, Dalton knew the truth, it was pure ice, and that type of power had made different claims to the same type of old power.

Depending whom was doing the looking.

Rounding the corner, Dalton knew what he was going to find. And he welcomed it.

There he was. Standing before him. A legend but oh so very real.

King Finn's red hair was tied behind him, his gaze the same as it was in the hall of portraits. His mind demanded to wander to the memory of being in there with Charmaine when he first came to the castle, pinning her up against the wall—

Focus, he commanded himself.

And focus he would. There was too much on the line to play games. Despite how much they loved him, and how much he loved them back. There would be a time and a place for that, but not now.

Rounding a corner, he paused. A long black cloak and red hair stood before him, and it took every muscle in his body at once to stop him from running.

"And who are you?" King Finn whispered, uneasy at the

sight of the boy which he did not know, yet should. Shadows twirled in the air, searching for danger.

"Well, well, well," Dalton said softly, doing what he did best.

Making shit up.

Clearly, Finn was hesitant. He had not killed him on sight, so this was promising,

"I thought you would know me. Remember me?" With a quirked up eyebrow, King Finn gasped, and Dalton's face melted away at the words that came next. He was merely playing—

"Cian, I thought you were dead—"

Silently, he laced his hands behind his back, pivoting in his plan entirely.

If he was to be Cian like everyone wanted him to be, then Cian he would be.

Well, this was already much easier of a feat than he had ever even thought possible.

"It is nice to see you, old friend," Dalton probed, thinking back to the diary entries that he had read from Ciara all those weeks ago. What would he have said? What could he take from Ciara's words and turn it into reality? This was the only person to ever survive the wrath of the dark king, the only one who had traveled into the shadows and found his way back.

If King Finn was not to be scared of Dalton, then he would certainly be afraid of Cian.

Let him use it.

The dark hair, the swagger, it came together in one go.

And Dalton was transformed.

Long live the fucking king.

"How are you here?" Finn demanded, his face contorting in rage.

However, Dalton could see it living and breathing

behind the facial features that commanded him. They were hidden, those emotions that actually existed, and breathed more deeply than the others.

Fear.

Hatred.

They coexisted. Dalton knew this because of Ronan. They lived and breathed through him too, and when mixed together they created not just a monster, but a weakness.

One which Dalton was going to exploit.

He was not the prince of snow anymore.

He was the king of everything.

And he would give everything to set the world right again.

Bowing, he knew it would piss of Finn the most. "The same way you are here, I suppose," he drawled, sounding bored, despite his heart racing so hard he thought it might burst from his chest. "Magic and destiny."

"I never expected us to meet again," Finn said. "I thought she had been the one to make sure of that."

Dalton had no idea what Finn was referencing, only assuming that he meant some type of magic that Ciara had done to keep Cian safe. A part of Dalton suddenly felt guilty, tampering with such old love. But there was some part of him that knew that it was what was right to be done.

Ignoring the statement, he took his opportunity, and said, "You have something that I want, and I am not leaving without it."

"To what is that?" Finn said, his interest suddenly peaked. "I am afraid that I do not have anything to give."

"A girl. Violet eyes. Dark hair." He figured he was here, Finn already believed him to be the dead king.

Might as well just fucking go for it then.

Finn raised a red eyebrow, shadows beginning to curl at his fingertips that had not been there a moment before.

Dalton breathed in and out, readying his mind and body to give everything that could possibly be given.

"Why do you need Charmaine Grimes?"

He nearly fell to his feet, scrambling at just the sound of her name. So she was here. He took her. Rage bubbled within him before he let it boil over and fizzle out. The draw thundered within him, and he knew that he only had a few more minutes before it overtook him completely. To be so close... And for it to be confirmed...

"Why do you need Charmaine Grimes?" Dalton pressed, irritation flowing through him as the power began to build.

"I suppose I no longer have any use for her," Finn said, though he was skeptical at best. "But what do I get in return for giving you a girl with such gifts?"

Had he seen her use her gifts? Or worse, had he made her? He would kill him—

No, Dalton thought, focus.

Wait, could he even be killed? Was he not dead himself?

No.

Focus.

Later.

These questions could be asked *later*.

He was running out of time. And getting impatient.

Dalton suddenly remembered a key detail from Ciara's journal, one which actually did link him to Cian directly. Some key personality detail that kept them both so close to Cyril's heart, one which made them rather unrecognizable from one another.

There were citizens of the continent who did not understand Dalton for who he was. They called him immature, bratty, and spoiled. They had called Cian the same things, though, he had nothing that Dalton had of spoils.

The secret to both of their powers was their ability to

turn their turmoil, their spoils, into pure unadulterated chaos.

The real power, Kai had silently taught him before he left, was the inability to let go of the things that kept one straight and narrow sometimes.

Chaos was beautiful.

And it should be erupted.

Raising his no longer trembling hands, Dalton flashed his most devilish smile, and said with all the command that he could muster, "You get to be cold."

And the worst winter storm to ever be conjured exploded out of his hands, barreling straight for King Finn.

HE WAS RUNNING down the hall, ice and wind and snow like a tornado of death behind him. He could feel the depletion in his magical body, feeling quite what he imagined it to be like to be completely and utterly normal.

He found in that moment that he did not hate it.

Instead, he focused on the one thing that he knew was truth, for he did not know how long his chaos would keep King Finn at bay.

The draw.

Her.

Her.

Anything to get to her.

So he kept running, and turned left down the hallway, and knew she was closer than he could have ever imagined.

CHARMAINE GRIMES FELT *WEIRD*.

There was a pang in her chest, something familiar yet

something completely and utterly remote. She felt like her heart was reaching for something. Her breath was coming in short stagnant breaths: ragged and unnatural.

Something was happening.

Was something here?

She attempted to stand, get to the door, yell for help—

Yes, maybe Bairre would help her. Since he had been trying to do so...

As she began to stumble toward the door, it flung open, a peculiar mist flowing in as it shut behind her. Icy air hit her like a ton of bricks. The breath completely leaving her, and she looked up as she stumbled to her knees before the strange boy who entered the room. There was something familiar about him, the deepness of his eyes and the smile that graced his face were shockingly familiar yet completely foreign as they were matched with a hair so dark.

Dalton did not have dark hair.

Yet, this version of him did. It could not be—

"Cian?" she whispered, her throat suddenly raw. He looked just like he had in the dream he had visited her in, though there was something more aloof about him. She backed up, wary of his appearance. There had been so many tricks up this point, she was not sure what to believe before her very eyes.

Smoke continued to cloud in-front of her, lingering as the fire had raged on the one side of the castle. Things had erupted into chaos, this was a perfect and opportune time for Finn to play his tricks on her again, to try to bend her to his will.

No. She would not have it.

She began to lift her hands defensively...

He knelt down to be level with her, taking her hands in his own. Interrupting her thoughts completely as a steady heartbeat thundered between them. "Why does everyone keep bloody calling me that?" he said with a tearful laugh, tears beginning to flow from his eyes.

Taking a deep breath, Charmaine Grimes threw her hands around Dalton Saphirrus and sobbed.

"I am here Char, I am here," he said softly, rubbing his hands along the small of her back.

Lifting her gaze to meet his own, something caught in her throat. She was unable to speak, even breathe, for a few heartbeats. "Breathe with me," he said, his deep blue gaze never once leaving her own. "Breathe with me, it is alright. I am here. I am not going anywhere, darling."

Slowly, following his commands, her breath came back to her as her heart began to settle under his control. Always his control. Always him. It was *always* him.

"Why—why is your hair black?" She half-laughed and sobbed.

He spat out a laugh, his head tilting to this side as if he truly wanted to laugh with her. "I guess I should have led with that story, though it is very long."

"I like it," she said, nearly covering her own mouth. Something about him always had her blurting stupid shit.

"That is a tale for another day," he said kindly, affection clouding in his blue eyes. "Unfortunately, I do not know how much time we have."

Pulling back, her face soaked from the relief of her tears, she asked, "Are you really here?"

"Yes, and I had to share a bed with Randolph to get here beautiful, an act which I do not wish to participate in again in this life. He took all of the covers. It was tragic."

Taking his hands in her own, she breathed out slowly, trying to steady herself of his presence.

Her anchor.

Her savior.

Her king.

He was here.

He was really here.

Then where was—

"Everyone else?" she asked, knowing he could read her on this. He could always read her, even if she did not know he was capable of doing such a thing. "*Wait, did you say you had to share a bed with Randolph?*"

"Somewhere. You know Randolph and Lawton are like two peas in a pod. They followed me when I left the castle," he said unreassuringly, leading her toward the door. Clearly, she was not going to get this one bed story out of him right now. Time. They had time. She took another deep breath. "Do you have protection on you?"

She shook her head, "I have not had any weapons on me. They have not allowed it."

"I told you that women should have daggers around castles," he said teasingly, taking her back to that moment in the rose garden.

"There is still so much unsaid between us," she said.

"Later," he said, commanding. "There will be a later."

"How can you be so sure?"

"Because my name is Dalton Saphirrus," he said confidently, though something was off about him. Was he afraid? Was he hurt? He did not look hurt— "And I am never wrong."

With an eyebrow raise as they left her chambers, she decided that was utterly false, but could not bring herself to argue.

He was here.

Her friends were here.

She was going home.

And that was wherever Dalton was.

Chapter Thirty-Four

Randolph felt the ground shake as shadows began to crowd themselves in the room, an unwanted friend amongst them, and coming for them.

And then she looked up at him, like she did when she had been a child looking for direction when the smallest of moments required such support. "Randolph..." she started, unsure where to even begin, but it was a start.

"Reine," he finished, answering all of her questions without even beginning to scratch the surface.

She nodded, and that was the pure joy of being a sibling, of sharing blood. The mind worked in wondrous ways, but that blood and familial connection ran deeper than all the rest. That level of love and friendship, no amount of time could erase it. No matter of sin could fully remove the stain of what it was to once be there for one another without rehashing the entirety of their relationship.

And fortunately for Randolph, there was nothing left to burn between them. There was only ash, and what lay beneath it.

So he lifted his hand, waiting for her to take it and accept him for all that he had become.

And she gave him his, and he held back a small sob.

All he ever wanted was to be accepted, and now, here with her... it had become reality.

"Thank you," he said. Thank you for forgiving me.

"Anytime," she said, blinking back tears. There was nothing left to forgive.

As he made headway for the door, his sword at the ready, Reine said, "Wait."

"What? Reine, we do not have time to catch-up unfortunately, time is of the—"

"Essence, I am sure," she said, finishing his sentences as if she were children. He naturally found himself falling into old rhythms, almost rolling his eyes when she said far too seriously for her to be kidding, "There is someone we have to get on our way out, Randolph. And I need you to be honest with me, did you come alone?"

"No, I came with friends," Randolph said, unsure if he was ready to tell his sister that he brought the King of the First Kingdom with him. She would not be angry of course, but there was already enough going on. He was simply trying to take this one step at a time.

Step one for him had been to get Reine.

Step two for him had been to get her out.

And he had yet to figure the rest out.

"Friends?" she asked, huffing out a laugh. "Randolph, tell me you did not bring *him* here."

Randolph could not help but smile, though his confidence in bringing the continent and prophetically famous king here began to wane. "You are going to have to be specific about who *him* is."

"Gods," Reine said, cursing. "If he gets his hands on him—"

"He will not. He is cunning."

"And so is Finn." Taking her brother's arm with her hand, Reine began to pull him toward the door again with haste. "We have to get her now then."

"Who is her?" Randolph said, his turn to be puzzled.

"His sister, of course," Reine said with a smirk.

"WHAT?" he roared, pausing. His breath left him. There was no way—

Reine looked at him with that same childish mischief that she had seemingly never lost and said, "You just told me time is of the essence, hurry up brother."

And then she began to tear down the hall.

CHAPTER THIRTY-FIVE

Despite the hallway's darkness, her eyes were more violet than he remembered.

"Why did you come for me?" she asked, pausing as she leaned so close to him against the wall as they listened for noise.

Dalton was not sure whether they should make a run for it, or if they would run into Lawton or Randolph by chance. He did not want to depend on anything when he was planning this, and truly was not even sure that he was going to make it to this point to begin with.

But now he was here. He was with her. And for a moment, that would be enough.

"Are you kidding me, Charmaine Grimes? Who would not come for you?" He smirked, shielding her slightly behind him on the wall. "Nobody takes what is mine and does not suffer the consequences."

"And is that what I am then, I am yours?" she said, softer than he could bear.

Spinning around to face her, nose to nose in the hallway, Dalton craned over her. He forgot how much taller he was than her, especially in this compromising position. He should be keeping look-out... Finn would not stay frozen for long. But instead he found himself entranced by her, mesmerized by the way that her lips parted when he looked at her and how her eyelashes fluttered as if in awe that he was really here. "If you will have me," he crooned, whispering in her ear.

Closing her eyes, she breathed him in. He leaned downward, his mouth angling at the perfect direction to catch her own, when suddenly that feeling was back.

Her violet eyes shot open, and he snapped up.

She felt it too.

The one that Dalton had not experienced in many months at this depth—maybe he had never experienced it at this depth—terrifying and weightless and confused all at once. It consumed him, his hands shaking as if he had been completely and utterly undone, yet it was the look on her face of complete and utter terror combined with endless wonder that kept him walking forward.

Shadows began to crowd at the end of the hallway, gathering like a storm cloud ready to surge.

King Finn wailed behind them, his shadows exploding all over the castle in the feverish search for the Violet Queen and the King of Snow. But there was nothing to find. They had vanished into nothingness. Together.

Now and forevermore, they would be together.

Charmaine, once again, had taken him with her.

Shocked, Dalton could barely speak, afraid that he would be heard somehow. Though, every sense within him could feel the heaviness of her power as it draped over him. Every nerve in his body that had the power to turn to ice was numb, dulled down, overtaken even by the extreme power that she beheld.

Had it been like this forever? Since when had she learned to access it?

As if in an answer, she turned to face him, her hand still holding his own. "I have been...avoiding this." Though the hesitation did not come from pain, rather from a hesitance.

"Have you?" he choked out, almost unable to breathe. It was not new to him that Charmaine was not comfortable with her power, it had taken many a training session to even get her to consider using it, but this felt different. The transition to power had been easy for her just now, but it was the remaining, the control, that was what scared her.

"Just once or twice," she whispered, as if she too understood that there was a chance that someone could be listening. That this invisibility was not as full-proof as one might discern. However, it was clear it was out of precaution, for the shadows that swarmed below them feverishly did not react as they stepped through it.

Finn ravaged by them, his shadows trailing and dispersing wildly as he shouted "FIND THEM! FIND KING CIAN AND THE GIRL!"

They held their breath in unison as he tore down the hall, disappearing as his shadows exploded behind him in a wall of darkness.

Almost as if on cue, down the hallway of the Seventh Kingdom's castle they went, slowly, fearful, and angry as they searched for an exit. Any sign that they could leave—

"How did you get in?" she asked, her violet gaze forward. Always driving. Always strong in silent strength.

He was so fucking proud of her.

But later, it would have to wait for later.

First, they would get out of here.

Next, he would worship her.

But the getting out of here was critical to his success on step two...

"Where did you go?" she asked, her head still facing forward. "We have to stay focused... He could be anywhere..."

"To devious places," he mused, unable to keep his chaotic ego out of his tone.

He could feel her smiling as they walked down the hallway, further and further into Randolph's home, but further from the source of the dark magic. Further from Finn. Hand-in-hand they kept moving forward, Dalton looming behind her with a hand on his blade.

"I got in by Lawton," Dalton said, answering her prior question before his mind had drifted. "He jumped."

A moments pause passed before she answered, "I am proud of him."

"I am proud of everyone," Dalton found himself saying. "It is not easy to live up to the power that lives within."

As they made their way down the corridor, she paused.

A dead end.

The shadows that had been around them slowed, beginning to crawl their way up the walls.

"Do they think that we can climb bricks on a wall?" Dalton asked, exasperated. How were they to escape?

"No," Charmaine replied. "No, I do not actually."

Extending her free hand, Charmaine touched the darkened stones, and the shadows began to turn away, almost on instinct. As if they were reacting to her touch...

"Turn around," Dalton ordered softly, a mere suggestion. "I want to see something."

Slowly, she did. Her gaze met his once more, and the wind was nearly knocked out of him as a result. Her violet gaze was filled with fear, but there was something hidden in the deepened hues of her gaze.

Excitement.

"Breathe," he commanded as her breath began to hitch.

He knew it was settling in for her, the weight of all of this, and the realization that her power had gotten them out of Finn's grasp. Dalton knew the feeling, to feel like you were at the mercy of whatever gifts the Gods had given you.

But nobody deserved to feel like that, battered down and controlled.

Especially not her.

Especially not when she was doing what he could not.

He just had to help her believe it—believe in herself. She could do this. She would do this. Grasp her power and use it for good, control it beyond what it naturally wanted to do... which was consume. He knew nothing of the sort. And Gods, he admired her for it.

"Breathe," he commanded again, lifting up his hand to indicate what he was going to do.

"No, do not let go," she said, tightening her grip, eyes clouded by grief.

"You will not," he said, his voice firm. "You can do this, you always could, you just need to believe."

"Dalton..." she said, though her grip loosened slightly.

"You can do anything, be *anything*, Charmaine Grimes." He let go of her hand. "You always could, and always can."

And he remained invisible. He could feel it, his body no different than when he had been physically connected to her, though the heaviness was gone.

There was no fear.

There was only pure power.

She smirked, and for the first time, Dalton felt like he was looking in a mirror, but seeing the girl that he loved.

His eyes widened at his own internal monologue. He used the L word.

Later. He would deal with that thought later.

Opening his mouth, he tried to find the words he

needed to describe this moment, to tell her that he knew that she could do this all along—

And instead of words, he found her mouth crashing into his. Tears flooded down her cheeks, his own eyes leaking the same magical emotion. Pride flowed between them as his tongue found hers, her arms cradling around his neck she shoved him backward, walking into the adjacent wall.

Shadows escaped, fleeing the hallway as he breathed her in. The candelabra that had been shrouded in shadows lit, flames procuring themselves out of nowhere.

Charmaine Grimes had not just been invisible, but now she was freeing the castle from terror.

CHAPTER THIRTY-SIX

Lawton wandered the halls with his hand on his hips. He had jumped from nearly every room to the next. Sweat brewed on his brow-line, threatening to fall onto his eyelashes as he tried to remain focused and calm. This was not the time to falter, for he was beginning to slowly de pleat. He had heard Randolph and Dalton speak often of what they referred to as the "well" of their power. They often pondered whether it had a limit.

Maybe that was a part of the whole trick of the thing. He did not have almost the bottomless source that the two of them did. Not being royal, maybe that was the punishment, for he had somehow cheated the system.

As he came to the end of yet another very dismal, red-wallpapered colored hall, he made a mental note that Randolph (should he ever reconquer his throne) should really commit to some studying about interior decorating.

This was the last room that he had not entered in this wing, everything else empty. As he approached yet another grand door, he noticed it was slightly ajar. Hesitantly, he debated jumping through the wall just to get a leg up on whomever might be inside, but he decided it was not worth his time.

He would enter, and not risk depleting himself further.

Pushing the door open as quickly as possible to remove himself from any more anxiety, he was confronted with pink hair and chains.

"T-Titan?" He blurted out, dropping his sword suddenly. "What in the name of the Gods are you doing here?"

Titan's eyes widened, his energy immediately filling the room in an aura of warmth and welcome. "I told you we would meet again."

"WHAT THE FUCK?" Randolph was seeing double.

But in the form of a woman.

"How?" he asked for about the third time.

Carinthya Saphirrus was nothing like he remembered as a child, though he had to admit to himself that he had only ever seen the Saphirrus children from afar and never quite associated with them. The Seventh Kingdom was not known for their hospitality.

She sat there, ordained in the darkest midnight blue he had ever seen that it was nearly black, hands crossed in front of her and a look of pure confusion on her face. She had been rather stunned when Reine had ushered him into her chambers behind him, and her voice—so eerily like Dalton's but devoid of that chaotic sinister tune—simply asked...

"Did he come with you?"

Randolph had nodded his head, and she had lifted her chin, exasperated. "Did someone invite you here?"

"Even worse," Reine said, "they walked through the front door."

Randolph opened his mouth to explain that he was simply the only one to walk through the door, but then she shot him the most sisterly of sisterly looks, and he stopped.

"We have to leave, while the king is distracted and his power is diverted."

"And where are we going to go?" Carinthya asked, that Saphirrus fire burning brighter and brighter in her eyes with every second. She was clearly no longer the girl that he remembered, some tattered version of a princess who had been locked away for far too long. A part of Randolph's heart broke, despite his incessant need for answers that he would not get. He only prayed silently that Dalton would exert some of the same patience that he was afforded.

Reine smiled, as if she were looking at an old friend. Randolph guessed that Finn kept the two of these princesses —well, Queens in their own right—apart as much as possible. Rubbing her two fingers together, a spark was born from the flames that existed within her. Like brother like sister.

Except Reine always was more of a show-off than Randolph.

"Well, out the front door of course," Reine said.

PART TWO
THE VIOLET QUEEN

CHAPTER THIRTY-SEVEN

They made way for the throne room, the central part of the castle. Charmaine still had Dalton shielded with her power, and surprisingly to her it was as easy as breathing. There was no straining, nor difficulty, that she knew others experienced when they released their power. Unleashed it even. For her, it felt as easy as awakening from sleep in the morning. Natural. A part of her felt guilty, for why was it not this easy for everyone? She knew that Dalton did not feel pain when he used his power, but clearly it weighed on him. Exhausted him. Depleted him in ways that she did not even consider. The emotional piece of things was completely and utterly challenging to navigate, and even though Dalton looked like Dalton, something about him was askew.

Randolph did not use his power enough for her to gauge whether or not it had any depths. She figured though that it did not.

Winter was crueler than the depths of the flame.

Dalton's hair was black for Gods sake—something that

she did not really have the capacity to delve into yet with him. He was forever changed by whatever had happened when she had been taken, and the aftermath of that. He looked healthy though. He looked... Well... *Good*.

"Charmaine Grimes, why in the name of the Gods are you blushing right now?" he asked, his voice so low in her ear that she only felt her cheeks redden more.

"How are you always so keen on what is going on with me?" she asked, trying to play it off. This was no time for flirtation, running for their lives and all in the stay-place of the enemy.

"How could I not notice everything about you?" he whispered, his hands landing on her hips behind her as they continued to walk toward the throne room. "It is down this way," he said, gesturing with his hand to solidify where they were going.

"And you know this, because you know everything?" she asked, her voice steadied with every step they took. She felt deep down like it was because she was taking these steps with someone—together. That was something that she had never really had before. Why her power was so terrifying for her... Well, maybe it was because she never had anyone to share its burdens with. With her mother, she had been told to hide it, to shield herself in protection. That made sense at the time, however, she knew that deep down now it was wrong.

She should never have been afraid to blossom and bloom.

"I know this," Dalton said softly, pointing again at the door just up ahead, "because Randolph drew me a very terrible picture."

❄

"WAIT!" Randolph hissed as Reine and Carinthya began to make their way out the front door. "We should go to the throne room—we are stronger together."

Carinthya looked like she was to be sick. Reine merely looked jested that someone was defying her direct order.

Guess it had been a while since someone had been Reine's equal.

"Is this a part of your rescue strategy?" Reine asked, a dark eyebrow raised in inquisition. "What if it is a trap?"

Randolph put on his knights armor... metaphorically of course. "I was a knight in the First Kingdom, and I know the way that king's think after serving one for so many years." He paused. "After living with one too."

Reine's eyes look sad. Later. They would talk about it later.

Pressing on, his hands extended in a demonstration of ease and compassion, he said, "I know that he will not go to the ornamental place where decisions are made. That would be all too rational for him... No, he will gather wherever he finds his companions. I am sure he has those who serve him."

Randolph could have sworn that Carinthya blushed, but it had to be the trick of the light. There was no way that a Saphirrus could be read that easily.

Blinking it all away, Randolph took a deep breath in and out. "We have to move, and we have to do it quickly."

In the same heartbeat, Reine nodded her head. "Come Carinthya, to the throne room we go. Whatever the king says, goes." Though there was no hurt in her eyes, no flash of disdain or anger.

"Reine—" Randolph said, catching her elbow just before she exited the room. "You do not have to... I relinquished it all."

"I never said I accepted," Reine said with a smirk. "Now let's go, we are running out of time."

"WHAT THE DEVIL are you doing here, truly? My knight in shining armor here to rescue me?" Titan asked, batting his eyelashes in the most absurd manner.

"I actually did not know you were here," Lawton said rather sheepishly. "Sorry to disappoint."

Titan pondered this for a second. "It is actually preferred you did not know, that means that word of my kingdom's destruction has not reached the ears of every corner of the continent."

"Was it truly a destruction?"

"I do not know who sits the throne in my stead. It is most definitely not someone worthy of it," Titan said, fury creeping into his voice. "Some kings and queens, despite their birthright, are not worthy of the crown that they wear. However, I know in my heart that I am enough for mine. And to have it snatched away... All was lost in that moment. My people. My kingdom. My flowers. Gods, there was nothing I could do but comply."

"What did they do to you?"

Titan smiled sadly. "My dearest, no, it was not what they did to me, but what they did to my kingdom. I had been enjoying the evening when I awoke to the sky on fire."

"On fire?" Lawton's voice remained horrified. He had experienced the plight of Finn's destruction with catapults and attacks, but to destroy such a beautiful place with the flame felt utterly intentional. Cruel. "Has he..."

"Touched me? Hurt me?" Titan's voice softened. "Only my crown. I have only been here for a day or so, he has not gotten around to torturing me yet for information. To see what power I may have..."

"And do you have one?" Lawton asked, not even sure if he did.

"Some royals are blessed, I find that I am not one of them."

Lawton rather sighed in relief. He would have been useless to Finn then. Who knows the extent that the king would go if he got his hands on a power like...

"I fear we have dilly-dawdled too much my friend," Lawton said with a sad smile.

"The throne room," Lawton said without much context, as if the thought just popped into his head. "That's where we are to head, after a bit of time..."

"Was a requirement of this journey to bring a watch?" Titan asked. "It might have done you all some good."

"The best laid plans are the ones with no plan at all," Lawton said, extending his hand for Titan to take it. "Can you walk?"

"It is merely my hands that are shackled," Titan said. "I can wait for a time when your friend Randolph is available. His flames could be useful. Or maybe I could go with Dalton... Ice would chip these enough to break it apart."

"You will have your pickings," Lawton said. "Take my hand?"

Titan looked at him with a sinister smile, his eyes shining with the same sort of knowing that Cyril's had when he knew more than he was telling. "No, we walk. You are going to need your strength."

Lawton was speechless, and wanted to ask him to elaborate, but Titan read his face like a book. "I told you when I met you, Lawton Thornwood, that you were destined for something beyond the walls of the First Kingdom. Let me help you, it cannot be far."

"It's downstairs and to the far right," Lawton said.

"Very specific. Did you walk here yourself?"

"No, Randolph drew us a quite terrible picture before we came in here."

Titan bit back a laugh. "When we get out of here, you must show me."

CHARMAINE ENTERED the throne room with a dark expression, terrified of what she may find. Sadness crept into her heart as she looked upon the gorgeous threads of red and gold that adorned the palace, this center of Randolph's kingdom. And her heart broke into even more pieces when she realized that his must be the place, if not the exact room, where Randolph had had to change his fate forever.

To kill his father.

"Quick, I hear someone coming," Dalton said, ushering them into the far right corner of the room to stand along the wall. "Do not unveil us yet, if you can help it, it might come in use to be hidden a bit longer."

Within seconds, right on cue, the doors to the throne room crooned open once more. And it took all within Charmaine not to yelp with joy at the familiar sight of her friend Lawton.

And it took even a bit more within her to not gasp at who he was with.

"Gods," Dalton whispered in her ear so low that she knew that they could not hear her. That was a part of the cloaking she had quickly realized—quite given when Finn had blown past them earlier—but made even more apparent now. "Is that bloody Titan? Why in the name of the Gods is he here?"

Charmaine looked back at Dalton sadly. "Finn took the Sixth Kingdom a few weeks ago, they just arrived back—"

Dalton swore.

As Charmaine prepared herself to have her power melt away, the door swung open once more. Almost on instinct, Lawton grabbed Titan's hand.

Dalton purred in amusement, his bout of swearing over, until he froze as if he had unleashed his own power upon himself. A cry burst forth from him, and she felt him put two hands on her shoulders as if he needed her to hold himself up. She spun to see what was wrong, to ask him what happened, when she turned back herself to see what he was seeing.

Randolph's hands were the first thing that she saw, and she nearly ran toward him if it were not for who was standing behind him that was so shocking. The first girl she did not recognize, but only guessed that it was to be his sister Reine. She wore a gorgeous red gown, tulle flowing effortlessly to the floor and a bodice made of the finest satin she had ever seen. She knew it was to be offensive, probably given to her by Finn as a reminder that she was both a woman and owned by him in this scenario. She adorned the same gorgeous tattoos that Randolph did in essence, tattoos that caressed themselves up her arms like kisses.

But Charmaine's eyes were drawn specifically to the second girl. The one that had caused such a moment out of Dalton. She had the most stunning blue eyes, black hair billowing down to her torso—it clearly had not been cut in my years. But it was the familiarity that stuck with Charmaine. She knew this girl.

The realization hit her like a blast of wind on a winter morning. That the King of Snow and his sister had been reunited once more.

Why had she not told him? Curses flooded through her

mind as it was equally wracked with guilt. There was so much not said between them. Of course she could not have hit him with this information immediately, but she figured she would have had more than a moment's breath to tell him...

"My Gods..." Dalton was shaking, his hands trembling uncontrollably. She turned around, lifted her gaze to look at him, and said with the most courage that she could, "Do you want me to unveil us?"

He closed his eyes, his breath coming in puffs of air. She knew it was snowing inside, could hear the small group by the door beginning to notice, the awkwardness rushing off of them as they held up their hands. As she turned—giving Dalton a moment to think and breathe—she saw only Randolph looking directly where they were standing. Though there was no direct eye-contact. He just knew.

Somehow, he always knew.

"Dalton, we cannot stay here forever, but I will wait for your cue—"

Suddenly, the door burst open, and Finn came barreling in, Bairre on his tail. Dalton's sister backed up instinctively, fear spreading across her face. Randolph's flame burst from his hand, drawing a line on the floor in-front of them as he stood protectively behind it.

"Well, look what we have here—an escape party? Why did nobody invite me?" Finn said, his gaze drinking in each person that stood before him.

Bairre remained silent, calculating. But there was something ticking within him, she could tell that much. His gaze settled on Carinthya, and she could have sworn that he was trying to communicate with her silently. The look that he was giving her—

Finn interrupted her thoughts once more, shouting, "WHERE IS CHARMAINE GRIMES?"

Her heart stopped. Dalton's eyes snapped open.

"Unveil us, Char," he said. A command, not an ask.

"What?" she protested, unsure if this was exactly the right moment.

"Do. It. Now." Lethal energy protruded from him, seeping itself into her very core. For the first time in her life, Charmaine was scared of Dalton.

With a deep breath, she steadied herself. It came quickly, like blinking, and she knew it worked when only a heartbeat later Randolph whispered, "No."

Finn blinked twice. Three times.

Four times.

"How is this—" Then the rage set in. His gaze landed on Charmaine all fury, but then quickly transitioned to fear. "How do you know him?"

She barely had a moment to think before Dalton strode casually toward the king wearing a mask that she had never seen him don before.

"How dare you speak to her! How dare you try to command those who are not your subjects!" He lifted a hand, a shard of ice so long protruding from it now that it looked like a dagger.

"My Gods—" Finn said, clearly wrecked by the sight of Dalton. "Cian, remember how I spared you. Remember how you rose to power and eternal fame. I did that for you. I killed her."

Charmaine was appalled, and only she could tell by the twitch of Dalton's hand that he was just as horrified.

And then it clicked, as she saw in the exact moment that Randolph realized as well.

Finn thought that Dalton was Cian.

And it might just be the one thing to save their life.

But it was clear that Finn was done being appealing, for Dalton's threat loomed all too dangerously with the ice pick. He lifted his hand quickly, shadows swarming behind him like a wave.

Charmaine had enough. She was done being afraid. Done letting Dalton put himself in the way of harm to save those that he cared about.

It was time that she took over. Proved herself.

No, she had already proved herself.

It was time to be who she was destined to be.

With a look of complete and utter disdain, Charmaine ran forward and linked hands with Randolph. He then reached out and grabbed Carinthya, Reine, Lawton, and Titan. Linking them all in a show of force.

Slowly, calculating, Dalton walked over and grabbed Titan's hand.

It was them against King Finn.

And King Finn against the world.

"Bairre! Attack them! Raise your shadows!" Finn shouted, his gaze absolutely livid at the prominent display of resistance.

But Bairre only stood there, and then casually walked over to grab Charmaine's hand.

"No," he said, simply and matter of factly.

Finn's jaw dropped.

Charmaine ran with it.

"You cannot best me." Charmaine's heart clenched at the thought of Dalton. All would be well. She knew it. She just needed to buy them a little more time, time to regroup with their power, time to save for one more battle… "You are not so powerful after all Finn, not in the face of love."

"Love was your downfall the first time, Father, and it will be your downfall once again," Charmaine said, an ancient voice coming through her as she found root in her power.

King Finn fell backward on his heels, as if this voice so

dark and powerful, one which Charmaine knew she had heard once before... but could not pinpoint where it came from...

"No, no, it cannot be!"

"Cian is not here, but I am."

And then she disappeared, her friends following in suit, and they began to run.

CHAPTER THIRTY-EIGHT

Dalton Saphirrus did not look back. He did not look around. He was not ready yet to face who surrounded him, for none of it quite made sense. There were too many lingering questions, too many chess pieces on the board...

No, he had no time for any of this.

He ran as fast as he could. That was his focus now.

Charmaine was up ahead, and he rather found himself shocked at just how fast she was. Gods, she set a blistering pace, sprinting at full throttle as if she were a thoroughbred let loose in the fields. Raven colored hair rose behind her in waves of ebony, a beacon for all of them to follow. She kept a blistering pace as they rounded corners, Randolph slightly ahead of himself. The footsteps behind him told him all that they needed to know.

There was no use in Lawton jumping them out of the castle—not when Charmaine clearly had them under the coverage of her power. She was to be their saving grace after all, it would seem.

Dalton smiled to himself, pride flowing through him in

awe of what she had just done. Standing up to Finn was one thing, he had done it wearing a mask. But Charmaine? No, she had stood up to him completely and utterly as herself.

Way more impressive.

She gave silent commands as they trailed behind her. He was not surprised that she had a good memory of the castle —he imagined the worst that she had only been out of her chambers here only a few times—but it was not without cause that he gave Randolph a bit of room to redirect her if she were to misguide them in their collective panic.

Without a glance behind her, she ducked into a winding staircase and Randolph followed in suit.

Dalton himself refused to look behind him. He could not meet her gaze—

A door appeared at the end of the stairs, faster than he had anticipated. Charmaine gave it a tug and a jiggle, only seconds lost before Randolph's fire erupted from his hands and he blasted the door right off his hinges.

Not even a drip of sweat came off of him, his breath steady.

Dalton decided then and there that he actually hated this man.

"Show off," Dalton murmured.

A chuckle sounded behind him.

He refused to acknowledge it. Though it was tempting. It did not sound like, *her*, so it was probably safe.

But he was not ready.

So through the door he went.

Sprinting to the tree line, once again in full throttle, Dalton heard the silent shifting of the shadows as they exploded from the castle walls. Not that they would be able to detect any of them, for Charmaine's gift was too strong.

He was so fucking proud of her.

As they broke through the tree line, Charmaine

stopped, putting her hands on her thighs as she bent over and breathed deeply. Dalton hesitated, giving her room and the space that she needed. Later. He would tell her everything later. No more secrets. No more hesitation. No more logistics between them.

They were merely a boy and girl, destined to be together.

The lightness about him was freeing, no longer did he feel as though he were wearing shackles and had a weight upon his back. No, he was alive. Free. *Fearless*.

Randolph stepped toward her and put a hand on her lower back. It was the softest of gestures—one of the most pure that Dalton had ever seen in his life—and although softness was not a word he often associated with Randolph, it was touching all the same.

Charmaine lifted her gaze and made a yelping sound, one far different than the cry she had experience when she had seen himself. Throwing her hands around her friend in an embrace of all that they had gone through together, Dalton found himself taking a step backward in a moment of growth. There was no jealousy in his heart. Maybe at one time there would have been such an emotion brewing within him. But now the only thing that existed between the three of them was this bond that was deeper and more knowing than anything else.

Randolph caught Dalton's eye and nodded in his direction. A silent thank you to give them the second that they needed to reunite. There was no denying that Randolph loved Charmaine too—deeply—and for that, Dalton was eternally grateful.

Slowly, they peeled apart from one another. When she turned to face the group that stood behind Dalton, tears streaked down her face. Though what surprised him the most, and had this entire time, was still that there was no exhaustion from power depletion upon her. She was truly a royal after all, it would seem, to not feel any weight of it being expressed.

My Gods, how powerful was she to be—

"We are still veiled," she said calmly, her voice steady.

Dalton did not need to turn around to see that everyone stood behind him, drinking in each of her words.

"I do not know where we are to go, but I can keep us hidden until we are a safe distance away—"

"He will never stop searching, you know. Finn does not take kindly to losing things, especially when those things run away." Bairre appeared before them, walking toward Charmaine, covered in the same shadows that had escaped from Finn.

"What are you doing here?" Randolph asked, venom filling his voice.

Did Randolph know him from somewhere—

"My, my, not even a hello Randolph Eniar?"

Dalton raised an eyebrow in inquisition at them both. Unabashed, Bairre was the first to speak. "Sorry for the lack of formal introduction to our new friends, I am Bairre, Finn's personal Thinker and prior hostage."

"He took a Thinker hostage?" Dalton's question flew out of his lips before he had the chance to really think it through. He supposed suddenly that it was not unlike Cyril, though Cyril's service was a willing agreement between them and the Tenth Kingdom.

And Cyril actually wanted to be there.

"It is quite a long story, something that I will not bore you with today. My situation is not typical though, my aging has been delayed at an incredulous rate due to my service to someone with such terrible intentions. There are three of us, though I will not bore you all with the details of them as well. They are heinous comrades, I am glad to be rid of them finally."

Dalton heard Titan ask, "So you are to come with us then? To what end?"

"I am fleeing with you, of course." He drawled, sounding more bored than Dalton did when Cyril was pestering him. Dalton was not sure what it was about him, but he definitely could see past the facade. Sure, Bairre was self-serving, but he was also not one to make an enemy with.

"No, you are not," Randolph growled, coming forth with his sword unsheathed. "How can we trust you?"

Bairre replied with a gaze at Carinthya, his gaze softening. "Because I have been putting on a show for many years, Randolph, and I desire a new role."

CHAPTER THIRTY-NINE

King Finn had not stopped screaming since he lost the Violet Queen and the King of Snow. It was oddly reminiscent of his worst days, the darkest before Ciara and Cian had defeated him once, not for all.

Bairre had disappeared, gone to the winds, surprisingly. Finn could not be hurt, no not by some betrayal, but it was rather shocking to him.

That no resounded in his head like a bolt of lightning. It played over and over, haunting him with every step he took. Though, it was the betrayal that his shadows had not returned to him which left him most concerned. He had gotten them as a prize from his daughter's dead body, claimed and won fairly in a gamble for life and death. Bairre's had been a gift, something to convince the Thinker that he was to be the one to aide Finn in his conquests. They had been together for many years, so it was different to be trailed by two rather than three. He let it be known as well that the two Thinkers who were in service of him that still remained... Well, they were idiots.

To see him take something from him, and not have to give it back, well, that was most concerning to Finn.

The dark blue Saphirrus Orb in hand, King Finn gazed into it aimlessly. If Charmaine Grimes could not help him with what he would seek, then he would take matters into his own hands.

That was another piece that he was unsure how to tackle. Her power—damn her for playing upon him, thinking her weak—it was undetectable by her shadows. It was unheard of, unprecedented.

Gazing up at his mercenary minions from the King of the Seventh Kingdom's scarlet throne, he smiled cynically. "It is time to give our other friends on the continent a visit, do you not think so?" He growled, his red brows furrowing.

"You want us to go to the First Kingdom, to Dalton Saphirrus?"

"Dalton Saphirrus will be my next target," Finn whispered in finality. "He will see what we can do, and what is coming for him, before he meets his end. The Queen of Frost is traveling with the King of Snow—Cian will not be able to resist me when he sees me next. It is personal between us."

With a smirk, the two Thinkers turned around to rally the troops, and head to the First Kingdom.

"Oh, and my dear friends," King Finn interrupted softly. The mercenaries turned around, confused what else that they were to do. "All are to die, but Dalton Saphirrus. I want him here."

"Why must he live?" Phillis on the left spoke, unsure why the command was necessary.

"Because I have plans for him," King Finn replied. "Big plans."

CHAPTER FORTY

The orders that Dalton gave with Randolph's backing was simple in theory. They were to leave this place immediately. Their destination would be decided soon. They would make way for an inn, the furthest away that they could get, and then settle for the night. Bairre had been insistent that Finn was to strike hard and fast, his pride would keep him from searching every tavern on the continent. No, if he was going to take a stand against their escape it would be something catastrophic in size.

"Lovely," Lawton had said. "That is very comforting."

Everything else, well, they would figure it out as they always did.

On the fly.

It was not a sound plan, but Dalton was not sure what other order to give. At any moment shadows could swarm out of nowhere. Finn could change his mind. They needed to able to pivot and make their way to safety if needed. So for now, that's all that Dalton would give them.

For the most part, they trudged on in silence.

Charmaine walked in front of Randolph, at the ready to

use her power at any moment. With every few minutes, Charmaine would turn around to check-in on the group silently, her eyes always finding Dalton's etched with concern and pride.

Later. He would talk to her later.

Returning a smile, her mouth turned upward as she mouthed "OK".

Dalton still refused to turn behind him, not even sure where his sister walked. He was most definitely not ready to confront her, nor was he interested in hearing what she had to say. He never envisioned a reunion for himself and his sister, for he thought her dead all of these years. He had made peace with it a long time ago, and to see her unharmed in the hands of his enemy should have infuriated him.

However, all he felt was rage that she had never contacted him.

If she wanted to, she would have, he knew it.

There was *nothing* separating a Saphirrus from what they wanted.

HOURS SEEMED to pass in waves, the forest that they walked through seeming to expand. Randolph explained calmly—however, not without annoyance—that it was not in fact expanding, but merely they were now traveling northward to the tip of the continent. Dalton had paused, considering, and obliged that maybe it would be best to not return home immediately.

"That is exactly why we cannot do it. He would be expecting that," Randolph concurred. "The First Kingdom is probably where he will attack first."

Dalton's heart caught in his chest. "Elena—"

"I could jump home and warn her, Dalton," Lawton

said softly. Though when Dalton looked at him, it was clear that just jumping himself and Randolph multiple times in the last day had taken its toll on his body. As enticing as it was to him that Lawton could reach his friend in the blink of an eye, they above all else needed him here.

Elena was a survivor. She would be fine.

"You need rest," Titan's voice chided behind him.

Dalton still refused to look in that direction. Who knew where she was lingering—

Without warning, a breeze picked up overhead. Dalton lifted his gaze to the sky, wondering if the shadows were somehow following them from up above. But they had never been quite this alive before... And frankly never this abrasive. Gasps sounded behind him—surely they were all thinking the same thing.

Charmaine turned to the group—somehow the categorical leader despite the fact that she was with two kings and two princesses—and commanded them with one singular word like a Queen would to her subjects. "Run."

Dalton smirked as he did so, pride filling him up to his brim so quickly that he was sure that he would burst from how happy he was to see her fully herself. The girl that he always knew that she could be. As he let that thought settle, the wind picked up, and he found himself running without another moment to think and reflect.

In unison they took off. Dalton found himself leaping over branches, ducking under tree limbs, all fear gone from him now that he was back with her. He took a few more steps. Duck. He flew by another tree, dodging its branches. With squinting eyes, he looked only forward as Charmaine in-front of him. Gods, when did he get so slow? Or maybe, when did she get so fast? Fighting his competitive nature arising, he began to open up his stride as light began to peer through the thick forest that threatened to swallow them whole.

A clearing existed just up ahead, a clear small break in the wall of forest that they were traveling through. Randolph slowed as he ran, obviously keeping track of those that were behind him, as Dalton pushed forward. He was sure that they were fine, nor was he planning on looking. As he caught up to Charmaine, he urged her to slow as the clearing was merely steps away.

"Dalton—" she urged, warning and hesitation filling her voice. "Dalton, he might be able to see us."

Looking up, Dalton's heart rate began to accelerate, and he knew it was not out of fear. Gods, how could he be so stupid? This was certainly not Finn.

"No, it is not the shadows of Finn that we should fear."

Spinning around to face all that had escaped the castle with him, though keeping his eye-contact steady on Randolph and no one else, he urged them to stop. "I may have made a little deal, and I want to warn you not to be alarmed when you see whom I made it with."

"What the devil are you talking about?"

"Believe it or not, Randolph Eniar, I am not perfect. I am actually far from it. But there was something that we did, someone that we met, before we left the castle, and I have reason to suspect that this little passion project of ours has become a much larger problem."

Randolph's face went green. "You didn't."

"Oh, but I did," Dalton said, fighting the twitch of a smirk across his face.

"Dalton, what did you do?" Charmaine asked, horror projecting out of her.

Without another word, Dalton took a step into the clearing, making sure to keep his hands extended so that nobody else would dare follow him. If he was right, which he surely was, it was important that he only address the beast correctly. This would be critical—beyond critical if there was such a word (he was sure there was one, yet at this moment he was so flabbergasted that he could not find one that would be even possibly suitable to describe what in the name of the Ten Kingdoms was going on)—to his plans.

And almost on cue, dropping from the sky, was Kai.

Landing with a less than gracious thud, his gaze was smug for a dragon, his deep eyes rumbling with some sort of internal laughter that Dalton would only understand.

"Dalton Saphirrus, I was hoping that you would have let me join in on all of your fun." The sound that rumbled through the ground sent a shiver down Dalton's spine. It was easy in the dungeons of the castle to forget the ruthless size of Kai, but out in the open his white scales shone brightly, his shackles making him larger than life. How long had he been following them? Had he been seen? And who in the name of the Gods let him out?

Despite the fear that lived within him, Dalton knew that he was happy to see Kai free. Though, he had not done it himself, which barred the question, it could have only been a...

"I know how your brain works, Dalton Saphirrus." Kai said, that smirk living in his voice. "And I will not tell you how I got out, but please know that you still have a wish that I am willing to grant."

"*What*?" Randolph choked out behind him, though Kai seemed not to notice. He was addressing Dalton directly.

Dalton spoke out of the side of his mouth, "No need to make a scene, Kai." He could not stand to look. At any of them. This was a power greater than any king or queen had wielded in the last few hundred years... A terrifying concept indeed.

He could sense Charmaine's intensity through the draw, her violet gaze hindered on every single one of Kai's movements. It was the greatest secret on the continent, the existence of a dragon, but one that Dalton was not ready to share with anyone.

But clearly one that Kai was willing to share with everyone, and based upon the current situation, it was clear that he was calling the shots.

"Might you—"

Kai's wings flared, the breeze nearly knocking all the trees over in tandem. "Do be careful Dalton Saphirrus, there is only one for which I will let request something of me more than once, and unfortunately that is not you. You have not won any battles yet, my ice king, therefore you have not earned your place upon my back."

With a head swivel in the direction of Randolph, Kai blinked in acknowledgement. It was nearly a bow, and the utmost sign of respect. "Randolph Cian Eniar, it is good to see you again."

"You do not owe him a favor too?" Dalton pressed, seeing how far he could get with the monster.

Kai rumbled, a laugh, Dalton presumed. He turned his head once more, and Dalton's heart stopped dead in his chest. "Charmaine Grimes, my favorite thing about Dalton Saphirrus is that he does not relent. It is a trait that I have found that I no longer wish to refute, for it is the only thing which has kept my heart beating this long indeed."

"So, no favors then?" Dalton said, his smirk firmly plastered on his face.

"None but for you, Dalton Saphirrus." Kai took a step forward, his gazed focused on the trees in front of him as if something were materializing there, out of the gaze of everyone else. However, when Dalton turned his head to look, he saw nothing of the sort. "When you need me, merely command me, King of Snow. I am at your service, and disposal. But you will not ride me."

And with a push off so mighty and strong, Kai exploded into the air and was gone.

Brushing off his pants, nonchalantly, Dalton looked at his comrades and said as calmly as he could despite his shaking hands, "I was *so* hoping that he would give us a ride."

"And where might we be going then, after all?" Reine spoke, her face looking much younger now that they were out of the Seventh Kingdom's castle.

"And you did not think to share with us that a dragon might be on our tails?" Randolph added, clearly still furious that Dalton had not mentioned a thing on their journey thus far.

"The only place to which I can think of that makes sense, dear Reine." He paused, spinning to Randolph. "And to you, other Eniar sibling, did you not just infer that I had no clue that he had escaped? Or been let out?"

"Back to the First?" Charmaine whispered, uncertainty rising in her voice given their suspicions that it is where Finn would strike next.

"To the Ninth," Dalton said, starting to walk forward, decidedly. "Queen Vanellope owes me a favor, just like Kai does."

"The Cloud Castle?" Reine half-shouted. "That will take at least two days to get there!"

Dalton paused, looking back at her with a dark eyebrow raised and eyes full of mischief. "I know you do not know me personally, Queen Reine, but there is something that you ought to know."

He took two steps toward her, closing the gap. Charmaine stood in the middle of them, and Dalton knew that this was somehow her most natural positioning.

Always right there. Always guiding him, whether she knew it or not.

"And what do I need to know about you, King of Snow?" Reine said, her toughness rather impressive. Dalton decided then and there that he liked her.

Much more than Randolph, as far as first impressions go.

"That I am owed many favors."

And then he winked.

CHAPTER FORTY-ONE

The tavern was a good few hours walk from where they had the run-in with Kai. Charmaine was still rather shaken, though she refused to show it to any of her friends. She could feel it, and see it, that quiet dependence that had come over them and onto her with every step that they took in the forest. She knew that she was solely responsible for their escape.

Sure, Dalton and Randolph had organized the rescue, but it was her alone that had the power to cloak everyone. In earnest, she was not even tired.

She was more awake than ever.

The majority of walk was in silence, mostly everyone stunned at the show which the dragon had put on. They had heard its voice rumbling through them, raw power in its finest. Clearly, he was something ancient and had been away for a long time.

And nobody knew how he got out.

Dalton did not say much of anything, aside from his few snide comments to lighten the mood when Kai had flown away. However, Charmaine could see through all of that. It was a surprise to him that the dragon had been released. Charmaine was not even sure how he had figured out that a dragon lived beneath the castle in the First Kingdom and was rather upset that nobody had told her. Randolph had been addressed by name, his betrayal to her not personal yet it stung all the same.

The dalliances of kings would hurt everyone in their path it would seem.

Regardless, Charmaine kept a close eye on Dalton. One thing that she did notice was his reluctance to even acknowledge his sister. Carinthya trailed behind them in the back of the group, Bairre falling at her side with every step. Every time that Charmaine caught her eye, she only saw a deep longing and regret.

Charmaine wanted to go over to her and tell her that Dalton would talk to her when he was ready, but she knew that would not be enough. She tried to envision herself in his shoes, left to survive in this world with cruel parents and nobody to lean on. She would do anything to get James back, to talk to him, but their situation had been different.

For Dalton, finding out that his sister was alive was more of a curse than it was to find out that she was dead. Considering, she thought of holding out her hand on more than one occasion, but she felt it was all too soon.

And she did not know if the draw would be as strong now as it was in the castle before they entered the throne room. If it was, well, it would be best then that they would be alone before any of that picked up again.

Blushing, she caught up to Randolph as they crested the hill. Up ahead, a tavern sat, smoke billowing from the chimney in a home-like way that made her chest ache for all that she had lost in her old life.

"We stay here tonight, keep your heads down and do not cause any problems," Randolph ordered, his voice stern.

"OK, father," Dalton sneered, taking off in-front of them.

Randolph grunted in distaste, but did not repute a comment that normally would have flown out of his mouth. Instead he paused, looked at Charmaine, and nodded as if to say "You need to talk to him. Alone."

Charmaine nodded, walking slowly as they approached the inn.

Upon arrival, Reine offered to tend to the horses, and Randolph paused looking as if he wanted to offer to help her. Before he had a chance to do so, she looked at him with a joy in her eyes and said, "You need to sleep. We can chat in the morning," and he had agreed.

Charmaine grabbed his hand softly before she went in, and said, "Give her time, it was a bit of a shock for everyone today..." Her mind wandered to when Randolph's name had ever been mentioned in-front of Reine by Finn. To put it simply, she had utterly lost it. She felt it pertinent that Randolph learned this information, but this was neither the time nor place. She would let Reine tell him in her own time. If there was one thing that she had learned about Reine Eniar, it was that she was very much like her brother, and that the truth would come out eventually.

It always did.

"You are right," Randolph said, bringing her back to the present. Gesturing with his eyes, he said, "I do not know how many rooms Dalton procured tonight, but you should spend some time with him."

Charmaine could not help herself but to stare at all that Dalton Saphirrus was all the way here. It was not the hair change, though it did nothing but startle her when she first saw him. *No*, it was some way that he carried himself. He had started this shift when he took the crown, when his mother and father were murdered by mercenaries, but this person who rode in front of her was a completely different person entirely.

But was more conniving, sharper than a dagger, and somehow bled all the more mysteriously than he ever had before. She needed to get him alone, and to talk to him, to find out what was really going on. Where was Elena? Where was Cyril? What were they going to do about his sister—

"You look very far away, are you ready to come back to us?" Randolph's voice sounded like an anchor next to her, his horse starting to match her own's stride.

"I am here, but not all the same," she said after a moments pause.

"I understand that more than you know," Randolph said, clearly referencing his own sister trotting mere feet behind him. He had not spoken to her much either, nor had she made any attempts to do the same with him. Charmaine could not even imagine that pain and suffering which had befallen both of them, and now to be confronted with it...

"I think it is going to take time, for all of us, Randolph."

He smiled sadly, rolling up his sleeves to expose his tattooed hands and forearms. The sun glistened above them, shining gorgeously through the breaks in the leaves and vines. "I agree, and think that it is fine. I just do not want to run out of time—"

"I know he is after me," Charmaine whispered. "I could tell I was important to him somehow, but there was something that I was missing... a piece of the puzzle that I had not connected..."

"Why did he give you up?" Randolph asked calmly, though danger echoed in the question.

"He needed me to look into this orb...the Saphirrus orb he called it... He said that I was to be the key to his reign... I am not sure what it all means..."

"Well, did he get what he wanted?" Randolph's gaze was filled with dread.

"I do not think so," Charmaine settled on after a moments pause. "But it would seem that he also got more than he desired. Sure, he lost some valuable leverage who is now traveling with us, but there is something completely and utterly haunting about the fact that he knew about my power..."

"He knew about what?!" Randolph exploded, smoke beginning to pour out of his nostrils. Charmaine knew in an instant what he was thinking, if Dalton caught wind of this... Well, the continent would be entering an eternal winter. But something already told her that he knew this.

"Somehow, he knew about *all* of it." Randolph's face etched with concern, but before he could reply she asked, "How is he?" Leaving the obvious question out of the question was critical. There was still snow on the ground, though it was not cold, just merely existing. That is how she suspected Dalton was at the moment, just going through the motions.

"When you unveiled both of you in the throne room in-front of Finn, it was the most alive he has looked in weeks."

Charmaine gulped, fearful that it had been the case. "When did his hair change?"

"When the snow started, seconds after you were taken... It was an eruption of power that I have never seen before. He was inconsolable, and from that point on it was all that Elena and I could do to help him was to try to keep him under control."

"Not even Cyril was able to keep him in line?" Charmaine jested, though she suddenly felt ill when she saw Randolph's face turn grim.

"Charmaine—" Randolph said, extending his hands to touch hers. They were pulsating, warm, and clearly meant to bring her comfort with whatever he was about to say. "He told Dalton something of prophecy and has been very sick ever since."

"Sick?" Charmaine could barely breathe. She was not sure how Dalton was managing it. Cyril was without a doubt his everything. "Why did you not tell me sooner?"

"We have not received word from Elena in some time, but she said she would keep us updated on him."

Charmaine felt as though her heart was going to cleave in two, for she knew that Cyril was more than just a friend. He was his guardian. A piece of Dalton's soul, and she could not imagine what the world would be like if that spark within him died.

And Elena? Charmaine could only imagine the wrath that she had unleashed on the First Kingdom when she found out that they had left without her. Gods, that had to be difficult. Elena was not a side-liner, no, she was someone who would stand at the forefront of battle for anyone that she loved without a second thought.

"Thank you for telling me," she whispered sadly, releasing herself from Randolph's grasp. "I will see you in the morning."

"Just be there for him," Randolph said. "He lets you in, whereas the door always shuts me out."

CHAPTER FORTY-TWO

The tavern was darker than she had imagined. It was painted in a hunter green, like the forest itself. Very fitting, she considered, given their location. Despite never being here, it oddly felt like home, somewhere where she could truly relax. Even with the world against them, the most evil and fearsome king of all time somehow risen from the dead coming after them, this place gave her solace.

She hoped Dalton felt the same.

As Charmaine walked up the stairs, her breath left her with every step that she took, and the realization dawned on her that she was bloody *nervous*. The last day had been a whirlwind, from thinking that she was to be broken down by Finn to seeing Dalton come to rescue her with her friends—

It was all too much to bear. If any of them had been hurt, killed even, by their attempt to rescue her... She would have never forgiven herself. Rolling her shoulders back, her long dark hair flowing down her back past her shoulders, she recentered herself. She was a survivor. The realization hit her like a ton of bricks that this boy had gone to the corners of their world to bring her back, to reunite them.

There was truly no need to be nervous.

The inn keeper at the bar downstairs had told her where the boy with the black hair had gone, up to his room. The third door on the left. He noted that they did not have enough rooms for all of their traveling companions, but that the boy mentioned that he would be sharing with someone.

That they all would be sharing with someone.

He had given her an all knowing look and her cheeks had flushed. She was not trying to assume anything, that he would even want her at all after all that they had endured, but she had to admit that butterflies were fluttering in her stomach.

As she approached the door now, she took a deep breath. Suddenly, she was hit with a feeling of deja vu as if she were back at the First Kingdom. She smiled to herself, thinking back to the night when Dalton had knocked on her door and chaos had ensued...

The door swung open, as if he were leaving. "Charmaine?" he asked, his voice cracking.

He had knocked on her door very much like this.

Just now, the roles were reversed.

She tumbled into him, where she was merely trying to walk into the room or her body demanded that she collided into him, it did not matter. Nothing was certain except the two of them, in this moment, here together.

With a cry, she threw her arms around him, enveloped in the familiar yet foreign scent of blueberries and snow. He melted into her, returning her affection. Hands drifted down the bodice of her dark simple gown, landing at the strings which she had tied together herself. This gown was reminiscent of her days as a commoner, not a guest of the king.

Or whatever she was to the king. She was no longer entirely sure.

"My Gods, you do not understand what I went through without you..." Dalton groaned in the side of her ear, slamming the door shut with a blast of winter wind.

"Dalton," she said, her eyes closed and drinking in every part of this. Of him. His mouth ran up and down her neck, tracing and worshiping every part of her.

Her mind drifted to them in the throne room, the night of the root of the lily. Then he had been cold, begging her to relieve him of the power which ruined him. This version of Dalton? He was in complete control, relishing in the opportunity to dance with his power, rather than defend himself from it.

Neither of them, ever again, would live in fear of anything.

They had conquered it all. And they would continue to do so.

Dalton inhaled sharply, as if he could not get enough of her. His hands began to run themselves up her neck and to the back of her hair, her loose curls falling through his ethereal fingers. It was feverish, as if he could not touch her enough, despite no part of him not touching her. And she could not get enough of him, her hands wandering up his back, his tunic the only thing separating them from losing it all completely.

He walked forward, her back colliding roughly with the door. "Are you alright?" he mumbled, his lips moving naturally to her jaw. He did not stop to check on her, the draw too strong to get out more than just a few words before it was overtaken again.

"Never better," she huffed out.

A breathy laugh escaped him and he pulled back to look at her. To really look at her. His gaze was heavy, sleep filled, and haunted all the same. Sapphires seemed to loom in his irises, hauntingly dark and whimsical all the same. His freckles seemed dimmer now that the darkness of his hair had come through once more.

Reaching out, she ran a hand through the same loose waves that always fell in-front of his gaze when he was speaking to her. Wild and untamed, he looked at her as if she were the most important person on the continent.

But she knew that it was simply not the truth: he was the most important.

"I thought of you, every day and night," she whispered, her voice breaking. "I tried not to—be affected by it—but it was the draw that held me together, that promise that he had not hurt you."

"He only hurt me by taking you away from me," he snarled, his eyes still soft for her though. "I felt it too, that pulsation. But it was so come and go, so fleeting, that I often wondered if you had left me to be with James, though I never voiced that to Randolph and Lawton."

Stabbing pains shot through her chest. He had thought her dead? "Dalton—" she paused, her hand coming down from his hair to touch him over his heart. "I want you to..."

"To what?" he asked, raising an inquisitive eyebrow. He was dripping with power, his aura radiating through the room like a drum. The draw thundered in her chest. This was a stronger pull than she had ever felt before, the most drunk she had ever felt without even having a single sip of alcohol.

"I want you," she whispered, lifting herself to her tippy toes.

"And where do you want me?" he asked, his mouth

hovering just a centimeter above her own. She was still pressed against the door, though it only gave her the room to stand straight against him, the perfect positioning for all of her wants and needs.

She considered for a moment, teasing him with her mouth slightly agape, and her eyelashes fluttering.

He leaned forward, as if to initiate a kiss, and in return she lifted her pointer finger to his lips.

"I did not answer your question yet," she purred, her voice suddenly raspy and heavy.

"Then where do you want me?"

She rose up another inch, her lips truly just hovering over his own and said with all of the resolve that she could muster, "Everywhere. I want you everywhere."

His eyes became unreadable, and she feared she had gone too far. Had she embarrassed him? Was he not ready? Surely he felt for her like she felt for him—

With a grunt, his hands came under the backs of her thighs and lifted her against the door. Her legs instinctively wrapped around him, her position allowing her to easily stay up without much effort.

Their lips collided, his tongue dancing in her own mouth methodically, ravishing every second that they had together. She turned her head to the side, allowing him to kiss her neck once more.

"Dalton," she moaned. "Dalton..."

"Ten Kingdoms, Charmaine Grimes," Dalton hissed. "I do not deserve you."

Charmaine stopped, breaking apart instantly. Her chest rose and fell quickly, her gaze firmly positioned to meet his own. "We are done speaking like that—even thinking like that—Dalton Saphirrus. You are the most worthy person of happiness I have ever met in my life. You saved me, whether you care to see it or not. Your energy, your commitment to standing by me in a time of hardship... When Finn tried to get me to use my power, I knew I could do it, because of what happened the day that James died."

"Charmaine..." he said sadly, his arms releasing her gently. "You do not have to speak of these things if you do not wish."

"But I do wish Dalton," she said, her arms cupping the sides of his jawline. "I wish very much to speak of the strength that you harbor in your heart so that you can see what I see."

"You speak as if I am perfect," Dalton said sadly, taking a step back. "Yet you know as well as anyone that it is far from the truth. I have not even spoken to my own sister yet."

She inhaled sharply, shocked that he was so open so quickly about this. "I never said you were perfect. That is what makes you *human*, Dalton. Your capacity for imperfection is one of the most beautiful things about you. You are never afraid of failing, never afraid of anything..."

"I was afraid of losing you," he whispered, drawing her lips up to his with a delicate finger under her chin. "Do you know why my hair is so dark?"

"I am guessing it has something to do with the eternal snowstorm outside," she said dryly.

He huffed a breath, the pieces of hair which had fallen in-front of his gaze lifted momentarily. Stepping backward, he flung himself onto his back on the bed, his gaze faced strictly up at the ceiling. At the stars. They seemed to be reflected on his cheeks, constellations that danced so ever honestly and discreetly under his eyelashes when he blinked.

"When you were taken—after we talked so frankly, yet in riddles all the same—I was so shocked. I could not believe that we could be betrayed again, that someone had allowed for this infiltration in the castle. I was broken before you left, and absolutely shattered into hundreds and thousands of pieces when I saw you reach for your power...and were unable to grasp it."

Charmaine recalled, the sickening feeling taking over her as she recalled that moment.

"Randolph asked me to change, and I could not," she recalled out loud.

"And to see that? Compared with today?" He sat up quickly, his hands coming to his knees as if he were out of breath from running. "It was like seeing another person—for the better. You speak of me saving you, but Gods you are the one that saved us all. And the one who is going to save us all."

She blinked twice, her ears not quite registering what he was saying. "What do you mean the one who is going to save us all?"

He lifted his gaze, those strands of hair once again in his eyes, though he seemed not to notice. He suddenly looked paler, as if he were in pain. She wanted to reach out to him, and move those pieces of hair, but he was building up the courage to tell her something, she could tell.

"What is it?" Charmaine said softly. "You can tell me *anything*, you know this."

Then she saw it, the door that Randolph had mentioned. In front of the others, Dalton was closed off, but in front of her she saw that his entire world was wide open. There were no secrets here, not in this room. Free from the constraints of court, they were simply just a boy and a girl, and that allowed for nothing but raw honesty between them.

"Cyril," Dalton said, tears falling from his eyes most uncharacteristically. "Cyril told me something, something that sent me after you. I was going to go anyways, but it was the final straw. He told me that I needed to go after you, because you are the key to all of this."

"All of this what?" she asked, nearly needing to sit down.

"The key to stopping the evil that has somehow risen from the depths," Dalton said firmly. "I know how it sounds, how it is a lot to hear—"

"Dalton, that is madness. I am merely a girl—"

Fast as she blinked, he stood, once again towering over her. "Do not speak of yourself that way, you are so much more than just a girl. You are *mine*."

"Dalton, you are shaking," she said, concern filling her voice as she noticed his hands.

"Gods," he said, sitting down with her assistance. "It has just become too much today."

"Is it the storm, does it weigh on you? Can you make it stop?"

"Ha!" he said, his voice raising an octave. "I do not want it to stop."

"Why ever would you say that?" She tried to keep the horror out of her voice.

"Because it shows him—reminds him—what I can do. I am an ever constant presence when Finn does anything, looming over him like death's shadow."

Charmaine held in a gasp, this was dangerous talk, even for Dalton at his most chaotic. All light was gone from his eyes in this moment, his seriousness almost terrifying her with his intention. It was clear to her now, he wanted to bring about the destruction of Finn. At all costs.

"I know we only have one bed," he said, his demeanor seconds ago leaving him for a much lighter version of himself. "And I do not want to pressure you to stay..."

She waited for it, the invitation that she had always formally dreamed of.

"But I would like to hold you close tonight," Dalton finished. "I would like to talk of happy things and feel your body against mine. If you will have me."

She smiled sadly, joining him on the bed. Damn the improprieties, even if this was the King of Snow.

He was her king.

Hers.

And she was his.

"I will always have you, Dalton Saphirrus."

CHAPTER FORTY-THREE

Wings flapped heavily in the air, the dragon's body rusty from being locked away for so many years. His feet ached, the chains which had bound him were no longer, yet they haunted him like some sort of phantom curse. There were many ghosts about these days, so it was without surprise that this was just another haunting.

Kai had lived a long life, one filled with too many trials and tribulations to reflect on at any given moment, but it did not dull the prosperity of this moment. Its weight was everlasting, a demonstration of all that he had lived for finally coming to fruition. He was not sure that he was ever to be given freedom again. Generations of Saphirrus rulers and rulers of Ciara's line had kept him locked up, a secret passed down from ruler to child for many centuries. Finn had never told Ciara, just as Dalton had never been told by his father Ronan. Yet despite all of the odds, they had suffered the same fate: finding him when they were simply left in the dark about his existence at all.

Chuckling to himself, he beat on, his wings not tiring

but simply waking up once more. The wind on his scales was the most euphoric sense he had in many years; he wanted to relish in it. But it had been too good—an opportunity that he did not want to miss—when he had seen none other than Dalton Saphirrus wandering through the woods.

The Gods, for whatever reason after so many years of hating him, had given him a window of opportunity.

He knew that the boy had a debt to pay to him, but the semantics of Kai's release had him feeling rather soft and resigned. It would seem that Kai *actually* had a debt to pay to Dalton Saphirrus. And he wanted to tell the boy that he could simply cash it in when he was ready.

But only one favor he would get. A dragon's favor was worth more than anything else in the world, and Kai would not be so generous again.

Smoke poured out of his nose at the thought, ravishing in the idea of serving the King of Snow one last time.

As he whipped his head to the sky, surveying the kingdoms below (he believed himself to be in the second, he had not been here in so long though that he was not sure), the wind changed. It was smoky, reminiscent of a candle, though there was no fire in sight.

And then all of his suspicions came true as out of the corner of his eye he saw a flowing river of red hair, sweeping behind her as she ran. *Her.*

"There you are," he grumbled as he swan dived down to greet her.

Cutting her off, he landed on an angle, his wings extended and diverting her to a walk. But whatever was she running from?

"I found Dalton Saphirrus," he announced, as if she cared. He knew why she had released him, and it had been a mistake. He could not get her what she wanted, but she had been exhausting every opportunity. He owed her a favor, and had already tried to give her what she wanted, however, the magic had rebutted and snapped the chains around him as a result before the debt was paid. "Ciara, I cannot give you what you wish."

And as a result, the magic called him to Dalton Saphirrus, where allegiance was set in a cold hard winter.

The woman before him—a mere snippet of who he once knew her to be—stood quietly, as if waiting for more of the story. She stood before him in battle leathers, her red hair whipping behind her and her green eyes flashing with that same impatience that lived within her while she had been alive. But she had none of that same spark, her fire clearly dulled in death. Sadly, he realized with a hot breath of smoke, that she was in fact a ghost. Kai paused, "I only wanted to let you know, for you are the one who awoken me."

"Do not feel pity for what you could not do, I knew I was taking a risk," she whispered, her voice not back to its full caliber. She has half of who she was, that was clear. But she was here, by some magic that Kai did not care to understand. The Gods were in his favor, he best not go around asking questions.

"What are you doing out here alone? You know that you can travel with me as we await more to happen in the kingdoms," Kai urged, feeling rather desperate that he even wanted company at all. Lest a ghost. A shell.

"I was searching for him," she whispered again. The image of her was not fully clear, for she was not completely here. Maybe she had never been, but when she was in the dungeons with him... She had been very much alive in his memories.

"And what did you find?"

"That my job is not finished."

CHAPTER FORTY-FOUR

C yril thought he was going to die.

Until he woke up and realized that somehow this was not the case.

His eyes flew open, as if he were waking up from a bad dream. Sitting up, chest pounding, he moved to speak and found that he had no voice.

Was this a fucking joke?

His hands flew to his throat, as if he were choking. And then his surroundings seemed to explode around him, the realization that he was in his chambers completely and utterly alone.

Not even a note?

He was pissed. *Did anyone care about him at all?*

Memories flooded through him quickly, and without warning he flung himself out of his bed, his feet hitting the cold marbled floors with a sticking sound. He so badly wished to yell, but instead he was forced to sit in silence.

Having a fit like he was a child, he began to rummage the bedsheets around him, angry that they were even touching his skin. How long had he been bloody laying here—

My Gods, the amount of times that he had wished this upon Dalton, now he was not sure.

Dalton.

His mind shifted, his vision snapping from memory to memory for just a second before landing on the King of Snow cradled over him and screaming.

What had happened? Gods—

A pen. He needed a pen. And parchment.

Instead of shifting through his chambers, he stepped outside.

And ran directly into none other than Greyson Althan.

"Cyril?" Greyson's voice was etched with surprise and concern.

Cyril mumbled, as if his mouth were sewn shut when he moved to sleep. As if it would make him easier to understand, Cyril began to flail his arms wildly as if to confirm that he did in fact have sense and had no ability to speak.

"Cyril—it is alright, you are safe..." Greyson said, taking his arm and trying to lead him back to his chambers.

"Fuck!" Cyril mumbled. Definitely discernible, despite it coming out something like "mmmmmMMMMMmmm".

That was enough to throw Greyson off guard, and Cyril did what any sensible person would do in this situation.

He ran.

ELENA ROUNDED the corner of the corridor and slammed into something hard. It had been barreling down the hallway at full speed, all she had seen had been wild arms and heard a lot of grunting. Before she had a chance to look up—or rather look down—and see what in the name of the Ten Kingdoms was going on, she was flat on her back.

Lifting herself up by her forearms, she looked to yell at her assailant for attacking the queen (or soon to be divorced queen, depending on what type of mood she was in), and she nearly stopped breathing all together.

"Cyril?" she asked in one huff, shock radiating off of her. "What in the name of the Gods—"

"MMMMMMM!" he said, or yelled? "MMMMMMM, MMMM MMMM MMMM… MMMMMHMMMM!"

"What?" she asked. "Can you not open your lips?"

"MMMMM!" Cyril said, looking as dismissive as usual.

Rolling onto her knees, she held onto him by his shoulders. "Cyril, I am so glad to see you."

He smiled, his lips parting. Excitement spread across his face as if he had regained his voice, though when he took a breath and sound began to come out once more his lips were completely sealed.

"What type of curse is this?" Elena asked, knowing full well he could not answer.

"Mmmmmmmmmmm" he said, clearly annoyed.

"I am sorry, clearly you cannot—"

"Elena!" Greyson shouted as he ran down the hallway. "Cyril is…"

He paused, surveying the scene before him. "Ah, I see you have been reacquainted with quiet Cyril."

"Mmmmm," Cyril grumbled, eyes rolling.

"Mmm indeed," Greyson said, giving him the eye. He leaned closer to Elena, though was clearly still in earshot of Cyril. "He is fast, my Gods."

Cyril snorted as if to say "of course."

Elena smiled, the first true smile she had felt in a long

time, and threw her hands around Cyril. "Are you ok to walk and listen for a little bit? Greyson, you may leave us."

CYRIL WAS NOT sure what he wanted to do, kiss or kill Dalton Saphirrus.

Elena had explained it all, though he could tell that she had a bit of resentment toward Dalton for leaving her here. Cyril so badly wished that he had his voice in all accounts, but it was more so in this moment that he wished to reach out his hand and tell Elena what she already knew: that Dalton was bestowing on her the greatest honor of all...

Holding everything together. A task that only she was capable of doing.

Elena was steadfast and loyal, but she also felt deeply. Cyril knew that Dalton had probably weighed this heavily when making his decision to leave or stay, but someone had to stay behind. Unfortunately for Elena, Cyril knew that in his heart he would not have made a decision differently. That was the horror of politics in a kingdom, and in a world where magic ran rampant and dark forces conspired, that hard decisions would be made and would hurt anyone who loved anyone.

He held her hand as they came to a final stop, their walk and talk over.

A pang thudded lightly in Cyril's heart, because he knew that there was something to be said for Dalton following his orders. As much as the boy gave him a run for his assets, he could not hide the fact that the boy and him had a special bond that nobody else could possibly understand.

Elena paused, looking Cyril in the eye. "I do not know if they accomplished their goal, and it worries me, but I have to imagine that they are close if they did not do it already."

Cyril grunted, knowing who she was referring to by pronouns alone, and wishing that he had intelligence of their whereabouts as well.

Before Elena had a chance to speak again, Greyson appeared before them, looking just as shaken as he had when Cyril had evaded him. He kind of understood at that moment why Dalton evaded him for all of those years, there was some sort of an allure to it.

It was kind of fun.

Though Cyril was glad he did not have a voice, because he never wanted to give Dalton that type of satisfaction.

"Elena..." Greyson said, his breath heavy.

A first name address? *Interesting.*

"Elena, the scouts reported that there is some sort of disturbance in the citadel below."

Cyril froze.

So Dalton and Randolph had been successful then...

Ten Kingdoms he wished he could speak. Greyson Althan was a great knight, and was very loyal. It was of no question why Dalton picked him to be so personal to Elena, but it was no surprise why he had never been selected by Ronan for anything when Randolph was available.

Greyson was no mastermind.

"My mother—" Elena started. *My Gods, Queen Maria was here?* Clearly, Elena left that out of the story...

"Is safe," Greyson finished for her. "She is somewhere safe, but it is no time we need to—"

Cyril stepped in-front of him, eyes dazzling menacingly. He had an escape plan for Dalton all of these years, just never thought that he would have to use it. With a smirk, he grabbed Elena's hand and beckoned them to follow and prayed that his years of planning for the worst would work in their favor.

Elena ran through the halls of the castle, Cyril and Greyson on her heels. She could hear the thunder outside, rolling dangerously closer and closer. Except she knew in her heart that the sounds of crashing outside were nothing of the creation of the Gods.

It was Finn.

It had to be.

Finn was the impetuous of all destruction.

And she had just received word from Eben, the castles Thinker, mere moments ago, that Dalton himself had sent a message. One word. One that rang loud and clear. The people of the citadel were not to be harmed, no that was where Finn would gain control. The servants too, they would bend the knee out of the necessity of survival. They could endure, they were strong, as were the people of the continent.

But royals? He would have their heads.

The word that he wrote down so simply, and then Lawton had jumped it to Eben, said only...

Run.

Cyril had silently laughed, like some sort of crazed magician that knew all. Well, she supposed that it was actually quite similar to what he was. He did know all, and telling them even a fraction of it had almost cost him his life, and stolen his voice.

Shaking her head, Elena reacquainted herself as they found themselves at Dalton's chambers. Cyril opened the door and turned back, the clamoring in the castle getting more and more loud.

"Cyril... What are we doing in Dalton's chambers?"

Cyril turned around looking like some sort of fallen

angel, his features lit up as he dug through Dalton's clothing dresser so dramatically she was not even sure that she had truly even woken up this morning. Pants, tunics, and socks flew around the room wildly. Cyril's arms picked up the pace before coming to a complete halt and picking up a hand held mirror no larger than a book.

"A mirror?" Greyson said, irritation beginning to cloud his voice. "Cyril, we do not have time to consult a mirror, we need to get Elena to safety."

"Stop," she commanded, her eyes squinting. This was definitely not just some ploy of Cyril's to waste time. Everything with him was intentional, despite the madness of the situation. "Cyril, how is this going to help us?" she asked softly, her voice coaxing him to get a move on it.

They were coming.

Finn was coming.

She could feel it, the air changing in the castle with every moment that passed. Her heart rattled in her chest, her breath becoming unsteady as anxiety began to swim beneath her skin. She had not felt this scared since they had traveled to Brinn, that fear and chaos stirring up the same emotions that she had been fighting so hard to keep at bay these last few months.

No. She would never feel like this again. She would never be controlled again by fear.

She was a Queen for God's sake.

Lifting the mirror to his own height, Cyril looked upon the reflection and lifted his free hand. He began to draw circles, first slowly and then faster and faster until golden sparks began to fly out of his hands.

Elena moved to stand back and Cyril shot her a glance, his eyes darting to his shoulder.

"Grab onto him," Elena said sternly.

"What?" Greyson asked, his voice unsteady.

"Dammit, grab onto him Greyson!"

As they thrust their hands onto Cyril's shoulders, the light exploded with golden light, and then they were falling through time.

Chapter Forty-Five

L ast night had been...something.

Dalton was unable to find the words as he awoke, very unusual for him given that words tended to be his strong suit. He was good at firing them like an arrow, hitting his mark just how he wanted it to land, but right now he was not sure of anything.

A weird sensation, that was certain.

As he rolled over and saw the raven locks of Charmaine Grimes, he remembered that yesterday had been real and beautiful, yet terrifying and hopeless. Finn still remained at large, with no end in sight on how to stop him. And his fucking sister was alive, an unbelievable feat that he knew would have to confront today in some regard.

Everything was falling apart, yet coming together at the same time.

Though he was not sure that if he even had a lifetime to prepare whether he would be ready to truly dive into all of that.

But his time with Charmaine had been damning and beautiful all at once, that fire returned to them once more

and the draw satisfied for the time being. He had been overcome with emotion, his lust for her so heightened that it was
a miracle that nothing else physical had happened between
them.

Other than cradling her up against that door... her legs
wrapped around his...

He nearly choked. Gods, it was too early to be thinking
of all of this. His mind needed to learn how to rest.

It had been so close, closer than the night with the root
of the lily... But he had paused. Stopped himself.

No, when *that* happened between them, he wanted it to
be perfect.

Last night was fueled by what had been left unsaid and
said between them, which frankly was very little and a whole
hell of a lot all that once, since they had last spoken in the
rose garden. There was nothing that he could do last night
but confess all they had been through without action. It had
been a risk, who knew if she still felt the same way with all
that she had been through.

But her response had told him the truth. They still
existed on the same plain. Equals, despite the fact that
society would say something so different about them.

He smiled as he turned to face her, stroking her hair
softly. Unfortunately, it was a new day and the night was
over. And today he had to face his demons, and his sister.
The group was going to want a plan, and Gods knew that he
was going to have to confess some of the workings yesterday
after all that had happened.

"Charmaine," he whispered as she began to blink her
eyes open. "Charmaine, the sun as risen, and I think that
means we should as well. We cannot linger..."

"If we linger, what?" she said, her violet eyes beaming
with the memory of the last time he said that. Damn her.

"You wound me, you truly do, but I fear if we keep

sleeping that we have to confront Randolph, or worse, my sister." He leaned over and kissed her on the forehead.

"You do not have to confront all that you have endured when you go downstairs you know, a little bit at a time. That is what you told me, and it helped me through everything after James died."

"Though you know more than anyone that those types of wounds never seem to heal right," he said, huffing out a puff of air, his hair flying momentarily as a result.

Charmaine sat up, the simple satin black gown she had been wearing now crumpled and clearly in distress after yesterday's affairs. Her hair tumbled over her shoulders, yet she looked at him with the clearest eyes that he had seen in a while. "Wounds can be healed, scars are permanent." She leaned down, his mouth returning a forehead kiss. "Let us go downstairs and confront our fate, like you said, we need to make moves."

VERY MUCH TO Dalton's dissatisfaction, they were the last ones downstairs.

Randolph met his gaze first, an eyebrow raised in curiosity.

"Oh piss off," Dalton grumbled as he took to the head of the table that they had commandeered. There was absolutely nobody else in the tavern at this house, besides the owner himself. Dalton felt no need to filter himself—not like he ever did—due to the fact that they would be leaving within the hour if all went according to plan anyways.

Dalton opened his mouth and all went silent at the table. He made eye contact with all of them at once, even his sister. When their blue eyes connected, she averted her gaze, though Dalton was not stung by this. It was what he expected.

Clearly, her scars were as deep as his.

"So, you are going to tell me how you unleashed a dragon upon the Ten Kingdoms?" Bairre asked, his voice cutting through the air like a knife.

"Well, technically I do not know how he got out..." Randolph said, at the same time that Dalton said, "Well good morning to you too."

"Where in the name of the Gods did you two even find out how to do this?" Lawton asked. "And why did you leave me out of it?"

"The Queen of Fury left very detailed notes. And to open the door you needed to know his name." Dalton was curt in his response; he knew he would have to answer for things of this nature, but he would much rather get a move on this.

"That is it? To wield the only dragon left on this continent..." Reine's voice echoed from the other side of the table.

"That we know of," Dalton corrected, a smirk in his sapphire eyes.

"That we know of," Titan said in irritated agreement. "But that does not stop the fact that someone let him out that was not *you*. Somehow, it would be less problematic if it was you! I would consider that a very big problem if someone knew the inner workings of the mind and history of the Queen of Fury."

"Could it have been Finn?" Bairre asked, more so just speaking aloud.

"No," Carinthya said.

Dalton turned his head. Stiffening.

"It could not be Finn. He is not fantastic at keeping secrets—I should know due to my time with him—if he knew something of Ciara's mind, he would have said something. And his army of mercenaries is not impressive if he were to have a dragon behind him."

"Maybe the Queen of Fury herself did it," Randolph joked. Though, Dalton responded only with darting his head in that direction.

"You have considered the possibility," Bairre's voice drawled, clearly overanalyzing every moment of this conversation. "Could it be possible?"

"And you have not?" Dalton rebutted, surprise coating his voice. "You do cannot sit there and tell me that after all of your years in Finn's service that the question of whether or not she could come back just like he did was completely out of the question."

Bairre considered this, choosing his words carefully. "I will concede that it is not without the realm of possibility, though I was not there at the moment of her death, so I cannot say if it was as final as the legends tell it."

"Answered like a bloody politician," Titan said, his voice finding more strength as the conversation went on. Dalton could only imagine the level of pain and fear that he had endured recently, so he decidedly would give him grace where it was due.

"What do we know of her death, truly?" Randolph said, his sister shooting daggers at him with her gaze as if she could not believe he was actually speaking like this.

"Well, she was stabbed by a very pretty dagger," Dalton drawled, trying to sound bored. "And then I believe she vanished into thin air."

"What?" Charmaine asked, breathless. "There was not a body?!"

Titan laughed out loud at the same time that Lawton said, "Her spirit was gone immediately, though nobody who was there could verify our story."

"So, we cannot keep it out of the realm of possibility," Randolph said in finality.

"I would forget if I did not know that you are who you are, Randolph Eniar," Bairre said with a smirk.

Randolph's face went beet red, and before he had a chance to get hot, Dalton found himself intervening on his friends behalf. "I love when people speak in the oddest of sentences, yet they make sense all the same. Tell me, Bairre, does your allegiance lay with your kings, or does it lay with the dead?"

Bairre only smiled. Dalton could see out his peripheral vision that Carinthya had gone beet red. Was there something going on— No. He could not think of that right now. Not ever. Gods... What the hell had his sister gotten herself into over the last few years?

Randolph chuckled quietly to himself, and Dalton shot him a gaze that should have frozen him on sight. Although he had tried to lighten the mood, he had not mentioned to lighten it so much that Randolph would be laughing. Clearly, he had lost his shit.

"So, what is our plan then? Where are we to go?"

Dalton smirked, his gaze once again landing on each and every one of them. "I think it is time that I share with you something which I learned many years ago."

Carinthya stiffened, clearly unsure what he was referencing.

Looking at her, he said, "When my power erupted, my father learned of a prophecy. Something rather dreary and damning to the continent, and I think it would be in poor taste to not recite it for you all now."

As if he were reciting a poem from memory, Dalton spoke: "The King of Snow is coming. He will Rise from the death of his Father. The Ten Kingdoms will fall. Fire will scorch the lands. A Violet Queen will Reign, and the light that holds the Kings of Old will go out."

"My my my," Titan said, *tsking*. "You are a dirty little secret keeper are you not?"

Dalton smiled villainously. "It was never paramount that I shared this, my father thinking the information would send the continent into a tizzy. One of the few things that I agree with actually."

Reine chimed in. "I am assuming you have overanalyzed this down to the very word."

"Down to the period," Dalton said with a laugh. "But I feel as though spending our time sitting here trying to figure everything out is only a severe waste of our time."

"Well, clearly we are on the 'The Ten Kingdoms will fall' line," Bairre said darkly. "This is a prophecy even I have been shielded from, Ronan must have had some hard alliances made in order to ensure your safety."

Dalton seemed to freeze, though he did not want to show his friends and traveling companions that he was stunned. Ronan could not possibly have—

A hand landed on his shoulder, bringing him back before he had a chance to leave.

Charmaine.

She took a step forward, coming from behind him to stand at his side as an equal. "I am sure all of us standing here have some sort of a role to play in this greater destiny, but I think we need to consider how we move forward. Finn will not wait long before striking, and it is imperative that we make decisions from here on out that will bring us closer to ending this madness."

"And how do you suggest we do that," Bairre asked, curiosity feigning in his gaze. "Violet Queen."

Charmaine blushed, clearly embarrassed to be associated with such a term in an ancient prophecy. Though, Dalton could not blame her. Power, prophecies... They were all damning things after all.

"I..." Her voice seemed to catch her throat. "I..."

"I think we should go to the Ninth," Randolph chimed in gently, helping her as he always did.

Dalton found himself silently grateful for his interference. To display confidence so beautifully in the moment was one thing, but leadership was another beast entirely, and Charmaine deserved to be given grace. Bairre putting her on the spot was a ploy for power, to see whether or not she withstood the test for the title of Violet Queen.

"Finn knew about the prophecy; I feel as though it is null in void at this point," Bairre said, as if this information would not have been important minutes before. "The Ninth would be strategic—"

"Who invited you?" Dalton interrupted, seething. "Like genuinely? Vanellope was welcoming to me at my coronation ceremony, her and her partner are strong and formidable."

"The cloud castle is a great location as well, on the offensive we would be able to see him coming," Charmaine said, finding her legs in the room after a momentary pause.

Atta girl.

"But how do we get there? The cloud castle is a few days ride away still—"

"I can jump us," Lawton said. "We are much closer after a days ride to here."

Concern etched itself over Randolph's gaze, his brow furrowing immediately. "Lawton, I do not want to diminish your gifts, but this offering concerns me no matter how noble it is..."

"We could split up?" Reine offered, shrugging her shoulders. "Finn—realistically—could care less about some of us. Let Charmaine, Randolph, and Dalton go ahead with

Lawton and the rest of us will ride through the night. We should be able to get close enough that if Lawton needs to recover he can do so, and if not we can continue the journey with another days hard ride."

"Finn will not be looking for me," Carinthya said, speaking again and nearly jolting the room with her unsteady voice. "He only used me as a tool to control Ronan, and his hope I think was that he would use my reveal to control Dalton as well. Without that type of leverage, well, I am afraid that I am useless to him."

Bairre raised an eyebrow, as if these words concerned him.

Dalton, despite his better judgement, realized suddenly that his father probably knew about Carinthya all this time. It all made sense, why Ronan had allowed himself to be controlled. It was all for his child.

"Titan should come with us too," Dalton said, after seeing the gaze that Lawton shot Reine for offering all but him. "He is a king of New Sarridolon, and his recount of what happened to the Sixth might be critical for Vanellope to hear."

"Then it is settled then," Lawton said. "Gather what little you have, and we will leave as soon as possible."

CHAPTER FORTY-SIX

Randolph found Bairre quickly when they adjourned and cornered him with a dagger to this throat. He would make this quick, a final warning before they left.

"I know you," Bairre said. "You will not cut my throat. What is it that you want?"

"Lest you forget that I am the King of the Seventh Kingdom, regardless if I denounced my throne. And regardless of your role in taking my kingdom, you took it all the same." He dug the blade closer to this throat, threatening to spill blood. "We met when I was young, and visiting the Tenth Kingdom. I am not sure how you got mixed up in the role that you are in now, but it is clear that your allegiances are skewed and anything but linear. But hear me now, if you harm a single hair on my sister's head, I will not hesitate to take another life."

"Ah," Bairre said, silver dancing around him. "You truly are your father's son. He would be proud of the man you have become, in some circumstances."

"Make me a promise," Randolph hissed. "You will not harm a single hair on her head. You will return her to me."

"I am already at the disposal of the protection of Princess Carinthya, for reasons that you cannot know nor that I care to tell you, so I will make you a promise."

"Sign it in blood," Randolph commanded.

"You are not my king," Bairre growled. "Not my only king, I should correct."

"Then who is?"

Bairre smiled, wicked and evil in nature. Though, Randolph knew that he would not have left Finn just to betray him. There had to be a reason, some sort of motivation.

Something greater than all of this.

"I do not have one," Bairre sneered, using his hand to ever so gently push the dagger away from this throat. Randolph's amber eyes blazed with fury, his hands threatening to expel flames. In a whisper, Bairre hissed, "I do it all in service to my Queen."

Randolph did not yield, keeping his face a mere inch from Bairre's silver moonlight aura.

"And what Queen is that?" Randolph asked through his teeth, smoke beginning of pour out of his nose.

"The one that is back from the dead, of course."

LAWTON SHRUGGED HIS SHOULDERS, his feet finding bounce, and huffed in and out greatly deep breaths. He knew he could do this, but it was going to be a feat indeed. Who knew what he was going to look like when they got to the other side.

When.

Not if.

He was willing to do whatever it took—even die for the kingdoms—if it meant that he could get them all safely to Vanellope's castle. His friend's safety was paramount, especially with so much on the line.

And it meant a lot to him that Titan was to be included in this. Clearly, they had some type of bond and friendship forming. They had spent the night in the same room—for everyone had to share—but Lawton had taken the floor. Titan was extraneous for sure, but oddly curious and so welcoming that Lawton felt like he was wrapped up in his aura every-time they spoke. There was something beautiful about being with someone and seeing all of their colors, that type of relationship rather hard to find.

The conversation had steered from pieces of what Titan went through, to Lawton asking about the content as a whole. Titan's counsel was limited, for he said that he did not have much to say in the affairs of prophecies that controlled all. However, he seemed peaked in interest by Charmaine, for she also had a power without a title too.

"Randolph joked that maybe we were secret royals somehow," Lawton had said half-heartedly.

Titan had then looked very serious. He replied softly, "Be careful what you wish for."

The decision had been made in finality by the King of Snow, they were to travel to the Ninth Kingdom.

The cloud castle was something out of his own dreams, living in the deepest parts of his imagination. He had learned so much about it in stories as a child, the people in the kingdom kind and fair. Vanellope was a just queen, and a young one, though that did not mean that she did any favors for anyone. However, it sounded like she had a soft spot for Dalton.

Unfortunately, Lawton had to agree with the allure.

There were very few on the continent who did not have a soft spot for Dalton Saphirrus.

Breaking through Lawton's inner thoughts, the door to the tavern opened and those who were leaving with him came outside.

"Where is everyone else?" Lawton asked, curious.

"No need to wait for them if we are to be on our way," Dalton said, rather cruel in tone.

Charmaine looked at him with sadness, as if she was rather disappointed that he was not awaiting anyone. Lawton figured with context that she probably had tried to convince him to talk to Carinthya before they were separated, though it was clear by his demeanor out here that it had been without success. Lawton could not blame Dalton for being as he was, for he had been in Ronan's presence for a long time as well.

He understood. There was nothing else to it.

"Lawton," Charmaine said, her eyes wary. Probably for many reasons. "Are you sure that you are able to do this?"

"I do not have a choice," Lawton said, reaching out to hold her hand. "It is either we try, or we die."

"And I would personally much rather die trying than any other way," Randolph said, a smile overcoming him.

"Randolph Eniar, are you smiling?" Dalton jested.

"Over death? Certainly."

Charmaine grunted and asked, "So, how do we do this, Lawton?"

"Well," Lawton started.

"My Gods, I do not know if I can survive this once more," Dalton drawled, his voice dripping in sarcasm.

"Silence," Randolph said. "The moment is over, we have to recenter, focus."

"Because I am so great at that," Dalton sneered.

"Put your hands in the center, all touching," Lawton

commanded, though a smile was encroaching on his face as well.

They did as they were told, begrudgingly. Their bickering was clearly not over. Dalton even rolled his eyes.

"Now when I put my hand on top, you are going to feel like you are falling..."

"Or dying, depending on how you look at it," Dalton muttered.

"I have never jumped this far with this many people, I do not know how long it will take. Normally it feels longer than it is..."

"This is quite the pep talk, Thornwood," Dalton chimed in.

"Will you just *shhh*," Randolph said.

"You are all a very interesting bunch, has anyone ever told you that?" Titan said, speaking for the first time, though it was not without humor.

"Lawton, just take us, I am sure that we will be fine," Charmaine's voice sounded, the voice of reason always. "You will be great. You are strong enough for this."

Lawton looked at her—really looked at her—and prayed to the Gods that they could do this one favor for him. To get all these royals, and the Violet Queen for Gods sake, to safety...

"Well, here goes nothing—"

"Lawton, it better turn into something!" Dalton's voice raised an octave.

And then they were falling once more.

CHAPTER FORTY-SEVEN

Dalton was sure this time that he was going to die. It was worse somehow than the first time he went through this with Lawton. If that was even possible. His hands were tied together by some force—clearly Lawton's power—and it was immovable. He could only assume that the hands of his friends were touching his, though he was lifeless in this fall. His power slammed up against Lawton's, begging for relief, all ice and pure fear. Though it was with no success, Lawton's shielded power was unstoppable once it had been put into force. It was everlasting and untouchable, and Dalton could not help but wonder what had given him such a gift. He could not see anything in-front of him—was not even sure if his eyes were even *actually* open—but could feel the presence of his friends around him.

There was no moment to pause on the bestowing that title on Charmaine, Lawton, Randolph, and Titan, for he was sure that he was going to be sick. He was not sure before Charmaine and James had wandered into his castle that the term friend was even on his vocabulary, unless one was to count Cyril. Though his mind was not ready to explore that yet, not in its full capacity.

Especially not while falling through space.

But death was certainly more plausible than Dalton having everlasting friends. Gods, he was not often so lucky. If he lived through this, he would decidedly tell them that they were indeed his friends.

Maybe even give Randolph a pat on the back, if he were to allow it.

The wind—if that was even was it was—suddenly whipped around his body like a lethal snake, suffocating him from every angle and every inch of his body beginning from relief from this purgatory that he had subjected himself too. The great awe of Lawton's power was that it seemed to bring him to another world, all of them existing in a plane that was not of their own but nothing certainly foreign.

Screams flew by his head, unable to discern who they were though he was sure that they were not voices that were foreign to him. Darkness continued to plunge around him, and he could have sworn he had been existing like this forever, unsure what it was ever like before.

Before he had another moment to consider how he was going to die, and how long he was going to exist in this purgatory of Lawton's power, he hit the ground hard. Stars flooded his vision and his shoulders were immediately heavy, though when he looked up to see where his friends had landed among him, he was met with the great swooping hill before him.

And the white points of the cloud castle raised above the fog.

Lawton had done it.

They had made it.

Chapter Forty-Eight

The cloud castle sat stunning atop the most glistening hilltop. White clouds atop it gorgeously as it framed her beautiful facade, the cream stones glistening in the sunlight dawned the path leading up the gates, and the castle beamed in the wake of it all. It was clear that the cloud castle was to be touched by everything beautiful, exemplifying the old power that graced the Ten Kingdoms.

Very much like all of the legends and the stories.

It was no wonder that Dalton dreamt of coming here for refuge, as it was a powerful message to King Finn to create a standoff at the peak of divinity in New Sarridolon. He wished to pat himself on back as he rose for such an idea, especially since he had survived the jump to this place without projectile vomiting.

Realizing that he had in fact made it with all of his limbs attached and his insides still inside of him, he spun around wildly to ensure the well-being of his comrades.

Randolph lay just a few feet away from him, also rising and looking at the castle with squinted eyes.

"My Gods," Dalton said, walking toward him with dramatic arms and pointing at his face like he was an impetuous child. "Do you need glasses?"

Randolph replied with a fireball launched at his head.

"Treason!" Dalton scoffed, as he made his way over to Charmaine who had walked over to check on Titan. But where in the name of the Ten Kingdoms was—

"Lawton!" Randolph yelled, running over to the jumper about twenty strides away. "Lawton, are you—"

"Projectile vomiting?" Dalton offered. He could hear Charmaine on his tail with Titan.

"Yes," Lawton said gruffly. "But we made it here."

"I am positively thrilled that my limbs are intact!" Dalton chimed in, suddenly feeling lighter after being out of the Seventh Kingdom.

Lawton gave him a look that screamed: *You are welcome.*

"Me too," Titan chimed in. "But I had no doubt that it could be done. It is destiny that we are all here together. Lawton, your power truly is a gift from the Gods."

Dalton caught Charmaine smiling proudly, acutely aware that she understood more than anyone that if you are not royal and not trained in some capacity the depths of struggle that come with wielding such a power.

Standing, it was clear however that Lawton was unsteady on his feet. He swayed slightly, and Randolph gave him a hand to help him stay upright.

"You cannot seriously think that you could go and get the others at the checkpoint," Titan said as if he could read the expression on Lawton's face. Determination. "You did us a great service, your power exceeding what you even thought you were capable of, but it is time now to rest."

Charmaine gestured to the cloud castle. "Titan is right, Lawton, our greatest battles have not even begun yet I am afraid."

Dalton smiled at Lawton. "Let us meet with Vanellope, and if you are feeling strong then tomorrow you can jump to them and bring them back. They have survived a great feat so far—and they have Bairre with them for what it is worth—so they will be fine."

"And they have horses," Randolph chimed in. "Their travel will be less tedious with just a few of them. Though the journey will be weary."

Begrudgingly, Lawton agreed. "Fine, but tomorrow I reevaluate whether or not I am good to go back for them. Nobody should be left behind, especially all that they have been through."

THE HIKE up to the castle was just that—a hike. For such a magical land and place, it was rather shockingly ordinary.

The Ninth Kingdom was different from the First in so many ways, but most notably the villages and towns of the Ninth were spread out. There was no citadel under the cloud castle, similar to castle dead in the Seventh. Knights were poised at the top of the castle's road, blocking the entrance with their white armor and long swords.

"And who might you be?" a knight asked, skepticism beaming in his dark blue eyes. "Claim yourself."

Unsurprisingly to absolutely nobody, Dalton spoke first. "I am King Dalton Saphirrus of the First Kingdom, and I wish to speak with Queen Vanellope."

The guard adjacent to him began to laugh. "We have heard the stories of the famous King Dalton, and certainly you cannot be him. Do you think us fools? His white hair and snow powers are legend."

He extended his hands as if to make his point, gesturing to the eternal light snowfall that they had experienced all over the kingdom. It did not even stick to the ground, nor was it cold outside. The snow just fell, as if it were the most natural and normal thing in the world.

Dalton sighed, exasperated. "Must I send out a newsletter to all in New Sarridolon that I have dyed my hair?"

The two guards looked at one another, as if to say: *what in the name of the devil are we to do with this idiot?*

In an answer with a grand smile on his face, Dalton extended his hand lazily and froze the guard's armor who had laughed at him. The guard began to scream, the shock of being frozen obviously beyond his cognition.

Dalton stepped forward, feeling more himself by the day. In a voice laced with boredom, he spoke directly to the other knight. That mask of cruelty slipped on once more, and Dalton felt comforted in knowing it was something that he could so easily remove. There had been a moment in his life where he was not sure that it was something that could be taken off at will, but now that he knew that was not the case, he was to wield it as he pleased.

"Let us try this again," Dalton purred, crossing his hands behind his back. "My name is Dalton Saphirrus, and I am the King of the First Kingdom. I would like to see my friend Queen Vanellope."

"Y-yes, your Majesty," the knight said, teeth chattering.

"And a word of advice," Dalton said, now speaking to the other knight directly. "Never laugh at a king."

THE KNIGHT BROUGHT them through the hall quickly, obviously terrified of Dalton. In a sick way, it brought Dalton joy to see people cower in his wake. It was a risk exploding his power like that, he knew that Vanellope would not appreciate it, but the circumstances were too dire for him to have sat there and begged to be let into the castle.

As Dalton rounded the corner, he ran into a young woman who had clearly also been in a rush. The knight stopped, and gasps sounded behind him from his friends.

"I am so sorry—" the voice sounded, so familiar that Dalton could not even believe that it had really come from this girl. There was no way—

A noise of surprise and happiness came from Dalton as he looked up at his best friend, and ex-wife, Elena LeClair.

Without a heartbeat between the recognition, they threw their arms around one another. Dalton ran his hands through his friend's auburn hair, unsure how she was really here. They touched one another feverishly, though there was no desperate romantic hunger. No, it was only the lust that existed between friends, who desperately craved one another's presence and comfort to maintain all that was right in the world.

"I am so sorry," he whispered into her ear. "I am so sorry I left you there."

"It is ok," Elena whispered. "You did what had to be done, as a king should. I was angry at first, upset that you would not take me, but I understand that to leave me at your home was an honor."

"Then what are you doing here?" Dalton asked, as they broke apart. "How did you even get here?"

Elena smiled past him sadly, taking in those behind him. He could have sworn he saw her blush, but concern was etched so much in her face that he did not have time nor the energy to decipher it. Had she been hurt? Had Finn's men come to attack? He had not heard anything of note in the short amount of time that he had walked away from his crown to get everything that mattered to him back. He silently prayed for his people, for despite his recent actions they did in fact mean quite a bit to him.

"Elena, what are you doing here? Where is—"

Dalton's eyes wandered past her to Greyson Althan striding down the hallway. Though, it was not Greyson that drew his eye, it was the small man who strode beside him, arms flailing in that angry way that caused a laugh to explode from Dalton in a way that he had not felt in weeks. It took everything in Dalton right then and there not to crumble to the ground in a heap of hysterics.

"Gods," Dalton said, darting his way past Elena to give Cyril the biggest hug that Dalton had ever given.

Wrapping their arms around one another, Dalton found that his eyes were spilling emotion, and he cursed himself for letting his emotions come out in-front of this random guard who he had just been so king-ly too.

Well, he guessed that kings did cry.

But still.

"Cyril, what in the devil are you doing here?" Dalton pulled apart from him. "How are you?"

Cyril looked at him with his deep blue eyes, his hands coming to his mouth and gesturing in the same wild manner that he had just before. Though this time, Dalton realized that it was not out of anger or impatience, but out of pure frustration.

"Dalton..." Elena said sadly, coming up behind him. His friends followed her, silent as if they were watching something that they were not allowed to be a part of. "Dalton, we should go see Vanellope. She will want to talk to you."

"Cyril?" Dalton said, whipping his head around to face his oldest and dearest friend. "Is something wrong?"

Elena's hand came to Dalton's shoulder, and she whispered sadly in his ear, "The Gods took his voice for helping you."

Dalton's rage was palpable. Darkness swept across the hallway, the white walls of the castle becoming jagged with shards of ice as if they had entered a cave of winter's most evil aura.

Dalton saw out of his peripheral vision that Charmaine moved to get closer to him, to reach out a hand to calm him. Though Randolph put his arm in-front of her to stop her, as if he were saying: Cyril has got this.

Cyril stood in-front of him, steadfast and immovable.

Maybe the anchor of his life was Cyril after all, challenging him and grounding him. He did not need his voice, for the look that he gave Dalton was easily readable: *Stop*.

Before Dalton had a chance to listen, a petite woman with shoulder length white hair and a crown made of clouds stormed down the hallway. Elemental in her own rage, her voice carried like a thunderstorm as she growled, "Dalton Saphirrus—and friends—please join me in my throne room, and leave this place to melt."

QUEEN VANELLOPE SAT before them on her throne and gazed upon them as if they were ants.

Dalton knew that this was just a play, one that he would have taken from his own playbook if the roles were reversed. But it was *he* that was standing at her feet, begging for refuge.

Especially since he just froze her hallway by accident. He was not sure how many times he had muttered something along the lines of, "I am so sorry" and "Thank you for your hospitality", though it was null-in-void. Clearly, she was annoyed.

Though, everyone was always a little annoyed at Dalton,

so by all accounts this rage of hers would dissipate and she would become amiable again.

"Best friends forever," Randolph muttered under his breath.

If Dalton was not literally on thin ice, he would have turned to hit him with a snowball.

Rage still flooded through him, though it was not toward anything but himself. He had allowed *this* to happen, his emotions to overtake him like he was still the prince of snow. Finn should have been stopped. He should have looked for the signs that there was some evil at work with his father. Clearly, over the years, there had been an extreme change that was unstoppable and a force that nobody could understand. His father had been an extremist in his views: locking him up for five years because he came into his power, beheading a girl because she had a magical weapon in her vicinity, instilling fear in anyone who was anything other than perfectly ordinary... Dalton seethed, even thinking about it now. His father had been so preoccupied with preventing magic, but he had it all backwards. He should have been encouraging it. Letting it flourish the way that it was meant to.

Magic was the only power that was going to be able to save the world.

He knew how it sounded, that is why he had left Randolph to do the explanation.

Eniar had started off at the beginning for context, bringing Vanellope through their trials and tribulations as a group since the fire in Brinn. He recounted running into James and Charmaine outside of the village, bringing them refuge in the First Kingdom. The story recounted the major points, leaving the dramatics and the flares to the imagination. But the core of all was that the signs had been there all along: King Finn was back, and he was coming for them.

"...which brings me to the greatest ask of all, Vanellope." Randolph kneeled before the queen, beckoning that Dalton do the same. Begrudgingly, he followed in his lead. He could not get out of his own way and wished so deeply that he had been the one to execute the whole story to Vanellope.

Oh, she would have been laughing thunderously at his recount of the time that Cyril followed him out of the—

"What is your ask?" Vanellope asked, her white hair shining in the ethereal way that Dalton's was used to.

Randolph paused. Of course now the bastard would stutter.

Dalton had enough. Standing up, he crossed his hands behind his back and began to pace back and forth nonchalantly.

"As my dear friend has explained so insightfully, Vanellope, it is clear that war is imminent."

"And you bring it here?" She gestured to Elena. "She left impending war in your kingdom!"

"It is everywhere, your Majesty." He paused, looking her directly in the eye. Quickly, he had put pieces together that Elena was here because the First Kingdom was no longer safe. He had no time to let his heart cleave in two, yet he grieved the world that he once knew and lived in. Though, it was clearly not Finn's style to kill civilians, if he did he would have nothing to rule over. Brinn was different, he told himself, because Brinn was the home of Charmaine and that was who he was looking for. "Instead, I ask you for something that I myself have had the pleasure of hosting."

"Dalton—" Randolph growled, still bowed like a servant.

In that moment, Dalton realized why Randolph annoyed him so. It was not that he was never wrong, or that he was dim-witted. No, it was because he did not seize the moment. He lived in the shadow.

Dalton was done existing in a world where shadows dictated.

It was time for the sun to shine.

Thank the Gods that they were in the Cloud Castle.

"I want you to call a council meeting, Vanellope. For tomorrow."

She smirked, understanding exactly what he meant and playing the game with him stride for stride. "Done."

"Then let us prepare the wine!" Dalton shouted, lifting his hands joyously. "We shall need it if Blarquenza is coming."

CHAPTER FORTY-NINE

It was clear to Reine that Lawton was not coming back. She had anticipated this, the power that he wielded obviously had its limits.

She had never tested it, but she knew that her brother and her had almost no limitations to their flames. She had been honing in on her power for years—trained excessively as a child for no reason other than being a tyrant—and her brother had been raised no different. Memories coursed through her constantly of her regrets in her life, they clouded her mind often, taking her from beautiful moments to reflect on when she said the wrong thing. Did the wrong thing. She wished it was not so, for she understood that these moments did not define her, but it hurt to remember her mistakes all the same.

She was a perfectionist, through and through, and anything less than was a regret. It was challenging to live like this, to always come back to darkness, but she knew that she was filled with so much light.

They had rode on for hours before finding a willow tree to rest under for the evening, with a beautiful grassy area for

Dalton, Lawton, and Randolph's horses to graze while they rested.

"We should be able to make it to the Ninth Kingdom by tomorrow evening," Bairre said as he collected some wood. "Eh-hem, Reine, may you?" He gestured to the sticks that he had already collected.

"I do not serve you," she spat before launching a spritz of flame from her pointer finger. The fire caught immediately, immaculate and perfection.

Anything less in-front of Bairre would be criminal. "You are so much like your brother."

"Reine—" Carinthya protested, as if to urge them to get along.

Reine was having none of it. Heat flashed vibrantly from her nostrils. She had witnessed smoke wafting off her brother when he was angry or frustrated, but she found that she herself had always been more expressive. She had stifled a laugh on more than one occasion since being reunited with her brother when she realized that they could not be more different, yet utterly the same.

"I do not know what existed between you two—and what still exists—but you cannot seriously trust him?" The question lingered in the air heavier than smoke.

"Leave her alone," Bairre said. "Believe it or not, I am on both of your sides."

"Then why do you still carry shadows?" Reine asked. "And where are they?"

"Hidden," he whispered in finality.

"You claim to be here, but where is your true allegiance?" Reine asked, her questioning not ceasing despite the pained looks from Carinthya.

Bairre rolled his eyes, his silver hair in this lighting making him look more divine than man. "Reine Eniar, I know that you and your brother both think with your hearts rather than your heads, but listen to me closely. I may be, as you say, confusing. However, I am first and foremost a Thinker, lest you forget."

Reine nearly rolled her eyes out of her head.

Carinthya merely raised an eyebrow, shockingly looking like her own brother in this moment now that Reine had seen him in action. The situation with those knights at the door had most definitely impressed her. She was not sure what Carinthya thought of it, but she was not sure it mattered.

Carinthya loved her brother, just as Reine loved her own, that much was certain.

"And Thinkers," Bairre continued, his gaze narrowed as if he were choosing every word carefully, "Do not have a true allegiance, lest to the Gods and what they allow us to say. Look at Dalton's Thinker, Cyril, voiceless because he said too much."

"And you prevent yourself succumbing to the same fate by saying nothing at all?" Reine asked, truly more pissed off than she had been moments before, if that was even possible.

"Now you are catching on, Reine."

Suddenly, the grass began to blow as if the winter storm was beginning to rage. Was Dalton angry? She had heard so many harrowing rumors, mostly from Finn, about the King of Snow. But it was hard, she had decided after meeting him, to discern the stories of Cian from the reality of Dalton. It seemed that Dalton had inherited all that Cian had held, but there also seemed to be some sort of blockage within Dalton.

Sure, the snow fell dramatically and he flashed his goofy smile and seemed to get whatever he wanted, but there was a depth to him that she was almost certain that level of torment never lived within King Cian.

Cian, from all that she had heard, had been sure of himself.

Hmph, she thought to herself, must be nice.

Bairre began to stand slowly, as if something was approaching them. Carinthya rose too. It took all within Reine not to roll her eyes. Carinthya, for whatever reason, had a rather sad attachment to the Thinker. No, it was not love, it was *certainly* not that.

But it was some sort of lust for the darkness, one that could be controlled.

Carinthya had never really opened up to Reine, but Reine knew the type. Carinthya had lived in Finn's shadows, and Bairre was the impetuous of that power. He was not unkind, but he certainly was not kind. He lived as almost an oxymoron to his own existence.

Kind but heinously rude with not a paternal bone in his body.

Scary but somehow there was no fear when one tried to chastise him.

Handsome but terrifying.

Reine understood the allure, she really did, but she also did not understand it all. She huffed a laugh to herself, maybe she was the oxymoron after all. This would not be the first time that she was a part of the problem.

"Get close to me," Bairre said, extending his arms backwards toward them.

"What?" Reine asked sharply. "You have got to be kidding me—" And then she heard it. The thundering of feet.

Carinthya's blue eyes blazed with fear.

"STOP!" Reine shouted. "I have my fire—"

Bairre whirled on her, Carinthya stopped in her tracks, watching their showdown. "And you think that fire is going to solve this? Those are Finn's men. Fire will only alert them of our location, leave a smoke trail."

Turning to face the forest, he continued, "Take my arm. I will get us to Vanellope's castle."

Carinthya stepped forward, so close that she could touch him. Obedient. Always.

That was what got her into this mess.

"Reine, grab my arm." His command was soft, urgent.

"And what are you going to do to me?"

"We are going to hide." Shadows began to swarm, dark clouds glimmering with secrets. Voice whirled past her head as he extended his free hand, taking Carinthya's with the other.

"And where are we going to hide?" she asked, her voice starting to disappear as the shadows crowded around them, suffocating and beginning to pull them toward where they were meant to go. *What was this* magic?

"In plain sight," he said as impatience took over, grabbing her hand. And then they knew nothing but Bairre's darkness.

Chapter Fifty

The evening had settled down as quickly as it had turned chaotic upon their arrival.

Randolph had decided to keep his energy in check, not fully ready to claim all that he was and who he was. Dalton had seemed to recover quite well—at least he was putting on a good face—from the last few weeks. He was laser focused, not afraid to put on a mask when it served him best. That was something that Randolph was never good at, and why he never played the game as successfully as he did.

For Randolph, despite his best efforts to remain soulless, could not separate who he is and what role he was to play. Even when he served Ronan, he found that he was duty-bound. Dalton bred chaos, he fed off of it. He was not afraid to scare someone, or step on another's toes, in order to move things in the right direction.

At the First Kingdom's castle weeks ago, Dalton had tried to push Randolph to be free. To *think* like this. But it was to no avail, honestly to their mutual disappointment.

He was worried about his sister too, that ever-looming

in the back of his mind. Obviously, Lawton was not going to be able to retrieve the others, but they had their horses and should be able to arrive within the day if they rode hard and fast. Reine was tougher than he could have ever envisioned, though he supposed that he was a part of the reason for this. He had left her to the wolves—his father's court—upon his self-inflicted banishment.

But it brought him comfort to know that she was not angry with him, and that they would get a chance to speak when she arrived here.

In the time between that, however, Randolph knew there was someone that he had to speak to. Someone who had endured quite a bit, and who had oddly enough blushed when he had made eye-contact with her earlier.

All of which lead him to this moment, wandering down the hallway of the Ninth Kingdom in search of Elena Leclair so that they may speak. He had not said many words to her prior to leaving, and it had weighed in the back of his mind when he had seen that she had made it here safely.

He found her where he expected her, hiding out in her chambers and sitting at the bench on the windowsill. She had welcomed him into her chambers quietly, her auburn hair illuminated gloriously in the moonlight that danced through her chamber windows.

"What are you doing here?" Elena asked, nearly sneering. "I rather expected to be visited by my former husband, even Charmaine, before I was to be alone with *you*. Or plotting regarding your sister's appearance at court tomorrow, for I was informed that you had all found her and freed her at Finn's castle."

Randolph stifled a cough. There was a lot to unpack there, but he settled on, "Former husband?"

"He left me a letter of all things," she said with a half-laugh. "A key to breaking everything apart for the betterment of us both. It was a power match made by Ronan, something insignificant to our mutual roles in the universe."

"Spoken like a true queen," Randolph said. "You have come a long way since I last met you, Elena Leclair." He thought to himself, *well, even since the first time we met.*

"And you," she replied, her auburn eyes dancing with challenge and excitement. "Do you remember meeting me when we were children? It took me months to remember after putting two and two together, but you were at the council meeting when all of the king's and queen's met over a decade ago."

"Elena," he said seriously. "I would never forget being in your presence."

There it was again... That slight red flush overcoming her cheeks. Emboldened, Randolph jested, "Why do you keep doing that?"

"Doing what?"

"Blushing."

"I am not blushing!" she said—rather full of rage—turning her face to the side.

"Elena Leclair," Randolph chastised. "Do you have a crush on me?"

Her eyes widened in horror, but there it was again, that flush of tint. Her cheeks reddened, and she turned her head to the other side as if it were to avoid the situation all together. If he did not know any better, he himself would have guessed that she was the one with the fire power.

But no, he remembered, she had the power of water. The power to quell even the most brutal and intense flames, to soothe and to bring life... Randolph nearly stopped in his tracks, of course she was the way that she was.

"Did you not burn while you were away?" Elena's voice was erratic and wavering, two words that Randolph had never associated with her persona before, especially given all that she knew.

"What do you mean?" The words barely left his mouth, they were so quiet against the winds that howled outside the castle hallways. "Elena, I was merely joking."

Her fists were clenched at her side, and he nearly laughed because Elena Leclair was never ruffled. This was a side of her he had never experienced before, and he was almost positive that he was relishing in this, though he would never admit it out loud. He enjoyed his head attached to his body, and he knew if he were to utter that Elena's rattled nature brought him some semblance of peace, that it would cause something within her to rupture.

"It is cruel, Randolph, to make fun of royals." Her voice was lethally calm, though Randolph could tell that he was truly done for. Damn himself, Dalton would have loved a joke like this, but Randolph had none of his bravado.

He could not handle another fire to quell and knew that she was in the same boat, but he could not help what came out of his mouth next. Curiosity driven, he spoke clearly, sure not to show any fear of the princess's temperamental rage.

"Did you miss me, Elena?" His voice was barely a whisper.

She rolled her eyes, yet her dark skin flushed on her cheeks. "Absolutely not, Randolph Eniar."

He stepped closer to her, his leather boots treading heavily with the difficulty of the quest as he took a step toward her. "I think you did."

She snorted, her arms crossed over the bodice of her evergreen gown. The jewels glistened evangelically in the moonlight that peaked through the stained glass white windows, bringing her to light as the Queen that he knew she was. Beautiful. Strong. Fearless.

He silently cursed himself, she had been Dalton's wife after all.

"It was quite dull without your constant peeking in."

Pursing his lips, he dared to push her further. "Your knight, Greyson, he did not entertain you? I thought you were quite close."

"He is like a brother to me. A dear friend," she replied a little too quickly.

Randolph smirked, taking another step toward Dalton's ex-wife. "You know, Elena, I thought you and him had something between you."

"Did you?" She laughed, clearly finding humor in his baiting.

Shoving his hands in his pockets, Randolph took another step. At first, her fire had scared him, but now he realized that he liked the dancing flames that spurred from her being on edge. He made sure to lean in, licking his lips, before whispering, "What was it that made you so *bored*?"

She snarled, obviously insulted by the insinuation that Greyson was anything but boring. He chuckled, stepping back out of her close proximity.

"Did I insult him? I am sorry, I did not realize that you had such a close attachment to knights that were assigned to you."

Elena ran an elegant hand through her fiery hair, the curls falling loosely around her flawless face. Randolph could not help but admire her insistence on being so damn formal, despite how obviously irritated she was with him.

"You did not insult him," she chided, nearly clenching her jaw so hard that Randolph was sure she was to crack a tooth. "You rather insulted *me*."

"Did I?" He kept all emotion out of his voice. Maybe this was fun after-all.

Maybe he was more like Dalton than he even knew.

Oh, Gods.

She stepped forward, her hands crossed and balled into fists over her chest. "I do not have any attachment to knights that are assigned to me. And you should know this, but maybe you have forgotten with your time of sitting a throne behind you, but to make up anything about a rumor can be seen as treason."

"Ah, well Elen—"

"I am not finished," she hissed. "I rather have an attachment to Kings who are assigned to me, it would seem."

Randolph froze, and even though he was not there, he swore that Dalton himself had attacked him with his power.

She laughed at his temporary disarmament, her amber eyes full of life rejuvenated. They shone with loneliness and the deepest friendship that Randolph knew that she was ever-so capable of returning. She was a loyalist above all, the fiercest of friends. "You, you stupid King. I feared for your Gods-damned life while you were gone."

She hit him in the chest with her balled fists. Barring her teeth, she groaned as if she had been holding it in for the last few weeks.

"I stayed up all day and night, dreaming of your stupid way of checking in on me. I stayed up all day and night, replaying the week where you helped Dalton, even planned a way to escape with him. I stayed up and dreamed of you bringing me with you, even though I knew from the start that you would leave me at home. I missed you and Dalton squabbling in the courtyard, and even missed Cyril bitching about how you two knock one another down only to pick one another up again to stand higher than when you fell."

Tears dripped down her face. "I do not know why I fucking thought of you at all, you stupid..." She paused, trying to contain herself. "You have done nothing for me, your kingdom never served mine, yet the last face I saw before I fell asleep was yours. The last voice I heard before I let unconsciousness take me was yours. The hands that I saw in my dreams were covered in tattoos, and I dreamed of them leading me away from the darkness that I had been haunted by for so many years."

"Elena..." He was rather speechless, shocked that his joking had brought her to such an admittance. Did he need to apologize? He did not know she had so much rage in her... He felt terrible. He was a dick.

But she was not done, so he let her continue. She was speaking as if she needed to get it off her chest, needed to speak what had been living inside of her for so long. He had never ever heard of her losing her latch on her 'princess-ness' before. But now, to see her unraveling before him, it did not terrify him—No, it was the most beautiful thing in the world to him.

"I despise you. What you have done to me. At least Dalton has freed me from torment, where you have continued to inflict it." She threw her arms at her sides in exasperation.

"What have I done to you?" He asked as much to her as he did for himself. "Elena, I am so sorry—"

She took two strides toward him, nearly touching his mouth with her own as she hissed, "Make me fucking think about you when you are gone. Make me miss you."

"You know who I am," he said softly, as if that would deter her from what he already knew she was going to do. "You know what I am."

"I don't care."

And then she wrapped her arms around him and kissed him.

CHAPTER FIFTY-ONE

"Your eyes are like amethyst," Dalton whispered. "Has anyone ever told you that before?"

Charmaine sat across from Dalton in his chambers. She had quickly made herself scarce from her own chambers, aware that she needed to talk to him as soon as possible. There had been too much sitting between them, and the night at the tavern did nothing to settle whatever it was *that* was.

Gods.

Gods, help her indeed.

"My mother always said James and I were born of violets," she replied, her heart lurching at her brother and mother's mention. Gone. Both of them. "But I never took her seriously, she was often lost, often urging me to hide my powers. I trusted her—loved her—but I wish if I could go back in time I could choose to not listen to her. I know she just wanted to keep me safe, but there was so much I did not know when James and I came to the castle..." Her voice trailed off. Dalton took her cue, changing subject without hurting her feelings. This was hard to talk about, the truth of her trials and tribulations of all that came before... Well... This life that she now knew.

"I had a dream one night, while we were in a tavern," Dalton said, his eyes not breaking from her own. It was the most laser focused and clear that he had ever been with her. No chaos lingering and no performances to be had. Just him. Purely him. "In the dream, I was observing a queen. She had pointed ears, nothing like I have ever seen before, and white hair like I used to."

Charmaine kept her face neutral, but she was sure that Dalton had seen some fantasy of the mind. There were no queens in this world with pointed ears. Maybe he had gotten into the champagne...

Dalton continued, "I heard her say the word, amethyst."

She paused, not sure how to respond. No, this was not some champagne problem after all. A daydream? Inquiring, she asked, "And how do you know it meant the color purple?"

"Because she was with a baby, and I could see the feeling that floated between her and her king. It was *love*, as much as it was peace. And in that moment, I knew just what it felt like to be in a purple hue. And I knew what it was called."

"That is a beautiful story Dalton," Charmaine said, reassuringly. And she was touched by it, for he never really spoke to her like this.

"Charmaine," he said softly, his blue eyes focused on the ceiling above.

"Yes, Dalton?" she asked, matching the tone and effort of his voice.

"Parents should never dim their child's light, no matter what that light may look like."

She paused, her heart thundering in her chest at the realization of the truth that the two of them were so often afraid of admitting. They were both damaged—that is what he was saying without truly saying it.

Maybe they were meant for one another after all.

They had been getting there in the rose garden before she had been taken, but they never made it there. There was always something bigger sitting between them, whether it be politics or war. She wanted to reach out in touch his arm, as she would have done once, but she knew that she was not ready for even the simplest of those interactions.

They were about to be at war. Surely, there was no normalcy.

They were, rather, living their new normal.

"I do not think it was a story," Dalton said, starting to back-up from Charmaine. Clearly, their conversation was not over. "I think it was very much real, another place and another time really, but surely, that does not mean that something is not real."

"I would like to think that there are kings and queens out there who are happy," she said, quite sadder than she intended. "It has to be possible, is it not, to be free of war and destruction?"

"Finn's resurrection is concerning," Dalton said, suddenly lost in thought. "There are many things about this whole situation which are concerning, Char."

The way he said her name was so natural, she nearly had chills running down her spine. Nobody spoke to her as naturally and as freely as he did. It was purity in its finest, whatever that lived between them existing purely because it was right.

"Charmaine," he said, inching closer very slowly. Methodically. He obviously did not want to shake her, wanted to take his time...

She licked her lips.

Gods.

She was royally screwed.

He needed to—

"Did he hurt you?" His voice cut like ice, though his tone somehow never changed.

"No," she said. "Not in the ways that matter."

"Char, if he hurt you I will freeze his—"

"Dalton!" she interjected, a smile encroaching on her face despite her best effort to try to keep him at least a little bit polite. "He would take me to the throne room and try to get me to make objects disappear. That is most notable to me. It is almost as if he was trying to see how he could weaponize me. I am not even sure how he even knew about my power to begin with."

Dalton pondered this for a second. "Maybe he heard it from the Thinkers who told my father and I when my power erupted?"

"No, I thought of that. I felt like his angle was his own, prophecy aside. He was most definitely acting on his own self-interests and seemed desperate to push me but never actually harm me." She paused, not sure how far she wanted to linger with it, for she truly did believe that Dalton would freeze his you-know-what off. "But it did not mean that it did not... Well...hurt. I do not have good memories of my power, not positive moments associated with it. My mother and father—but most visibly my mother, like I said—always had me hide it, so suppressing for me became most natural rather than expressing it."

"Did you ever do it for him?"

"At first I was so terrified of him that I do not think that I could. There was some sort of block in my mind, a wall that I was not able to climb."

"And then?" he asked, kinking his head to the side ever so slightly as he awaited their answer.

"And then it almost just clicked one day. I realized how

important I was compared to him. He needed me. And I needed nothing of his." She smirked, thinking of the dagger. She debated telling him, but something tugged within her and told her not to. It nagged at her like the draw, but was something that she could ignore.

For weeks the dagger had been strapped to her thigh, or hidden in the sheets of her bedding at Castle Dead, made absolutely invisible by her power. And nobody had found it. Somehow, she knew that it was not its time to be resurrected. Not yet.

"That's my girl," he said most shocking, convincing her with the informality of his tongue.

"When I saw you... Well, it was no question that I was to do it. You all needed me and..."

"And you did what you had to do to save the people you—"

"The people I love." She let that linger in the air for a moment, a confessional all on its own. But if he wanted, it could mean so much more.

It could mean everything.

"You should get some rest," he said. "We both should. Tomorrow should be most intriguing."

She stood, though she could not hide the disappointment in her voice as she said, "I will see you in the morning then."

Walking her to the door, he paused as if he were considering kissing her, though after a moments hesitation he kissed her on the forehead.

Before she left, she turned to face him, and she made sure to make direct eye contact with his icy gaze. "Do not lock me out, Dalton. It will only lead to both of our ruins."

He bowed as she strode out, well aware of the secrets that she kept within herself too, despite what she asked of him.

Chapter Fifty-Two

"Good morning, Rand." Dalton's voice cut through the air like a broadsword.

Randolph jumped as he closed the door to his chambers, entering the hallway to make his way down the hallway.

Recognizing how jumpy Randolph was, Dalton's forehead scrunched. Thinking, clearly. "My Gods," Dalton said with a raised eyebrow in confusion. "What has your leathers in a twist?"

"What does that even mean? Nothing about my leathers are twisted..." Randolph retorted. Rubbing the side of his head with a tattooed hand, he replied, "I thought you were... Erm, nothing."

"Does not sound like nothing," Dalton mumbled.

"And what has your eyebrow all up in judgment this morning?"

"Stop talking to me," Dalton said. Randolph was much more fun at his own castle. Here he seemed, well, on edge. Understandable, but way less fun.

Flabbergasted, Randolph replied in an exasperated whisper, "But you are the one who startled me!"

As Dalton moved his mouth to fire away some other sort of sarcastic remark, the chamber doors down the hallway opened and Elena stepped out at the same time as Charmaine. Charmaine wore black leathers, and Dalton's heart nearly beat out of his chest with how she looked in them. The curvature of her body was absolutely stunning, her legs elongated and her confidence heightened. He was terrified of the prospect of them going to actual battle, but he could not help but admire what blossomed within himself at her coming into her power.

Whatever evil they faced, he knew that they would face it together.

Her dark hair was swept behind her, pulled back off her face into a low ponytail (he had heard her call it this before, women's hairstyles were so rightly named), and tied behind her head with a black ribbon.

Elena, he noticed after a moment of staring at Charmaine approaching, was dressed in similar garb. He had not had a chance to talk to her yet—to make sure that she was ok herself—but he knew that Elena would come to him when he was ready. They had been through so much together in their lives, she was like the gust of wind in the winter for him, always there and never afraid to interject itself. She was his other half, despite the fact that he was certain she had annulled their marriage the first moment that she had the chance to do so. He did not blame her. They both deserved a chance at happiness after this.

Elena's hair billowed down her back, a small tiara sitting atop her head. Dalton found himself rather irritated that she did not wear a crown of larger proportions and jewels, but he did find with some sort of sadness that she was no longer a queen. Now, she was just a princess.

Randolph made some sort of choking sound behind him, and Dalton could have sworn he was flushing red.

"My Gods," Dalton said, confusion riddled in his voice. "What the hell is wrong with you today, Eniar? You cannot take a joke, you are seeming to choke on air... You better get it together."

"I am fine," he croaked out, turning around to seemingly fake cough into his arm.

"It is impossible to find good help these days," Dalton muttered for himself as they made their way to Vanellope's council chambers.

Let the games begin.

THE COUNCIL MEETING HAD BEGUN—NOT unexpectedly—with a lot of yelling.

With a lot of *Dalton* yelling.

Rulers of the Ninth, Seventh, Sixth, Fifth, Forth, Third, Second, and First sat at Vanellope's round table and equally exploded over the circumstances of the continent.

"There is not a chance in this world that Finn has risen from the dead and now marches on our continent!" Blarquenza's fire hair was as red as his ignorant head. Anger blazed off him as if he were some sort of flame itself.

Randolph chimed in, equally irritated. He did not want to display his primal power as Dalton did—nearly freezing the lips off of those who displayed irreverence to his plans—but it was coming more challenging by the second.

King Loe from the Fifth Kingdom sat with his arms crossed over his chest; clearly even he was skeptical of this great horror. Though, he was willing to listen.

"Blarquenza, you know we would not have summoned you in the middle of the day yesterday that today's meeting was critical without reasoning," Vanellope's calm demeanor shattered through the room like a blade. She was practically begging him to hear them, because maybe then everyone else would follow in-suit.

"I would not lie about my kingdom being taken from me!" Titan's blue eyes were practically beaming through Blarquenza's body. "You cannot simply dismiss things that you do not wish to understand in the name of denial."

"I am not in denial! How can this threat be for certain? My Kingdom remains *untouched*." He enunciated the term as if he had invented it himself. Prick.

"Maybe because nobody likes you Blarquenza. He is saving you for *last*." Dalton's voice was sheer ice.

Randolph nearly laughed. Blarquenza caught on.

"And you, Randolph Eniar, you have been away from your kingdom all of these years. How are we supposed to believe a traitor?" He looked to the other rulers, as if looking for backup, but nobody seemed to give him the time of day. Thankfully.

Smoke began to pour out of Randolph's nose involuntarily, and he certainly wished that he was not the one causing the scene. In a panic, he looked to his left to see Dalton smiling. Encouraging the chaos.

Good Gods, save them all.

As Randolph moved to stand, a knife whizzed past his head, pinning Blarquenza to his chair.

"Oh my," Dalton said, his voice laced with sarcasm. "Another meeting among the Ten Kingdoms where Blarquenza gets blasted."

Elena's voice sounded through the air, all of the rulers turning around to face her. She twirled another dagger in her hand lazily, her leathers displaying her true role as the ruler that she was, title or not. "Be careful how you speak about things that you know nothing about, Blarquenza."

"I did not know you could handle a blade like that," Randolph observed out loud. By accident.

Elena's cheeks flushed. "You never asked."

Blarquenza's laugh shattered the air as though there was clearly something askew within it. "Elena Leclair, I almost forgot that you were there. How is your mother?"

Elena paused, obviously not understanding the point his reference. "She stayed behind in the First, keeping the Kingdom in check as Finn's forces invaded."

Blarquenza looked as if he were about to retort, when she continued and interjected with as much venom as she could muster, "I know that must be a foreign concept to you, bravery. She can explain it to you the next time the rulers of the Ten Kingdom's get together, you might learn a thing or two."

Dalton hit the table with his hands, the fit of laughter overtaking his body completely.

Randolph had to admit, that was bad ass.

"Can we get this meeting on without the theatrics?" Vanellope said, though there was humor in her voice.

Randolph nodded, realizing that the smoke had begun to disappear in-front of him. Thank the Gods.

"Randolph," Vanellope gestured. "Elena, both of your kingdoms have been infiltrated by the enemy. Please, recount your tales so we can be done with this misinformation."

Her gaze went directly to Blarquenza, the knife still embedded above his shoulder. He went to move it, but Dalton beat him to it, freezing the blade into the chair. "No, no," Dalton said with a *tsk*. "You deserve to be there a little longer so that you can practice your listening skills."

Elena started first, and it took everything in Randolph not to leave the room. Despite knowing none of it was his own fault, the guilt that overtook him was truly challenging to navigate on his own.

He knew that the best medicine was going to be time, but this was truly difficult to manage. He had been running for so long, the truth felt so distant as it was intermingled with his desire to always fall back on being a knight. But no, he was not a knight after all, and there was no sense in pretending any longer. Dalton looked pained as well, but Randolph felt a lot of pride in how she had been handling things there in the interim. The people needed—deserved— a strong and caring leader like her.

"...and then Cyril took us through a portal..."

"A portal?" King Amethyst of the Third Kingdom's voice sounded for the first time, laced with surprise. Randolph noticed that he and his wife, Elinoah, had been uncommonly quiet the entire duration of the meeting thus far. Charmaine and the both of them had been the only ones to not yet speak.

Titan sat forward, obviously the first time that he had ever heard of such a thing. Or maybe not?

"Yes," Elena said confidently, though clearly she did not have any additional information on the matter. "I do not know why he had access to such a thing..."

Vanellope pondered, but it was Amethyst who spoke. "Cyril is of the best of us, it is no wonder that he had access to old power like that."

"It is no wonder because he was so favorable with Cian and Ciara," Blarquenza shot out.

Dalton gave him a look that said, *I told you to be quiet.*

"It saved us. My mother stayed behind to ensure the safety of the people." Elena's voice was steady, but had no *umph* to it like it had when she was cursing out Blarquenza.

"Have you heard anything since?" Titan asked, hope blazing in his eyes.

"No," Elena said sadly. "But not much time has passed. Finn has not shown a lot of interest in murdering civilians."

"But what about that village in the First Kingdom?" Blarquenza asked.

"So you acknowledge that you have heard of Finn's plundering?" Loe raised a dark eyebrow in inquisition.

"I never said that it was Finn specifically who organized that attack."

"He was after *me*," Charmaine ventured.

Dalton nodded in approval. Randolph gave her an encouraging smile as well.

It was time that she told her story, for the entire royal court to hear.

Every part of her story.

So she started at the beginning. The room was silent, even from Blarquenza as he tried to decipher and take in every magnitude of Charmaine's life. And that was what it was, a life story.

Randolph himself was overcome at emotion at the beginning of the story, never quite hearing it in its full. She held strong the whole time: from the recounts of her mother having seer power to her father passing away, and even stretching to that first night in Brinn when a fire so terrifyingly awoke her.

As she began to wrap up her tale, she told of darkest days in her capture from Finn and what he had to do. She detailed the fear of trying to do what she believed was impossible: using her power on command, but the terror had gripped her every which time. She had never been truly motivated, never felt like the stakes were high enough. And unfortunately, she still had no clue what he had planned for her. It could only lead to the assumption that the prophecy had some wiggle room—or Finn thought it did anyway— that if the Violet Queen was able to hide an army or something, maybe that would be the way to conquer the kingdom after all.

Wrapping up her story, Randolph gazed around the room to see them all truly moved, each in their own individual way. His gaze however, settled on Amethyst and Elinoah, who truly looked mystified. Elinoah had tears silently falling from her eyes, and Amethyst did not look away from Charmaine for even a second, as if he did that, she would disappear from them forever.

When she finished speaking, she paused and looked every single one of them in the eye. It was the most regal thing that Randolph had seen from anyone in a while. That quiet control was something that basically none of them in the room had, for the trait evaporated into chaos every-time that it was provoked. But no, Charmaine felt stead-fast onto it. It was her anchor. And she was to be there's. "I am sorry to just dump all of you on it, but I hope now you can understand the severity of the situation. It would seem that this has been in the works for Finn for a very long time, something that none of us can even comprehend. Somehow, I am a missing piece of his puzzle, though I seem to also be the piece."

Vanellope stood first, the rest of them falling in line. Randolph stood at the same time as Dalton did, last and with their faces beaming with pride. That was not easy, to stand before strangers and friends alike, and tell them the most private truths of your life.

As Vanellope moved to speak, her dark eyes filled with warmth and that same level of respect that seemed to radiate through the room, King Amethyst moved to speak. He seemed, rattled, the gaze that he exchanged with his wife concerning.

Randolph noted that Dalton kinked his head to the side,

rather surprised that Amethyst would interrupt Vanellope for something.

"I do not mean any disrespect, but I feel as though I must tell a short story of my own for some context."

Charmaine nodded her head, for Amethyst was speaking directly to her. But instead of Amethyst taking the floor, it was Elinoah. Her golden eyes shone with tears, her beautiful face clearly overcome with emotion. "Eighteen years ago, Amethyst and I received some haunting prophecies from the Thinkers who lived in our castle. They promised war and death, the omens telling us that the child which we were about to have would live a life of similar doom if they were to stay with us."

Loe nodded in recognition with Vanellope, as if they remembered her being pregnant.

"We had to make a terrible choice, risk our child's safety or give her the best chance that we could." She closed her eyes, as if the words were too painful for her to say.

Amethyst took over, acknowledging and sensing his wife's turmoil. Obviously, they had not made this decision with haste. Grabbing her arm, steadying her, he spoke once more. "On the night of her birth, we sent her away with a member of our castles staff. She was a gifted sight-seer, her abilities convinced us after many years of service that she could keep our daughter safe. She had a child of her own— even with the same colored eyes and of a comparable age— so we sent her away in order to give her the best chance of life."

Amethyst leveled his gaze at Charmaine, and Randolph felt the breath leave him as Amethyst said, "Charmaine Grimes, I believe that you are our daughter. Our heir."

"The Violet Queen," Dalton breathed out in shock, bending his head in a bow. "And the heir to the Third Kingdom."

Randolph froze, as if Dalton's power had reached out and touched every single one of them. Nobody spoke. Nobody even dared breathe. They were watching something unveil before them that was ancient and oh so very private. The reuniting of an heir with her family...

Before he had a second to think, Randolph found himself smiling at the picture before him. He had always known that she was something special, a ferocity that could not be quelled no matter how much she endured. She took it and battled it until she had nothing left to give, never giving up and never losing herself along the way.

Charmaine Grimes, it would seem, was a queen after all.

Even Dalton was frozen in place, his mouth agape like some sort of a character in a fairytale.

Charmaine took a harrowing breath, her hands shaking as she moved to tuck a curl behind her right ear. It was clear that her parents were holding their breath too, stumbling to this realization so naturally that the shock could probably be felt around the entire continent.

Closing her eyes, she took a deep breath in. In and out. In and out. Pride swarmed in Randolph's chest, just like he had taught her all of those months ago. Control.

And just as Randolph thought that he may have to intervene—for clearly Dalton was indisposed and not moving—she took a step forward.

Then another.

Then another.

And then she was moving as fast as she could, throwing her arms around her lost family with a sob of complete joy. The words spoken between them were not able to be understood, nor should they be, for the rulers of the other kingdoms began to stand to move.

But as they got up—all except for Blarquenza, because a knife was still embedded in a chair above his shoulder—

Dalton defrosted, and began to bow. The others followed suit, a silent welcoming of the princess of the Third Kingdom to their council.

AS THE RULERS of New Sarridolon poured out of Vanellope's chambers, three figures appeared at the end of the hallway. Randolph was the first—and only, it would appear—to go over to greet his sister.

Elena noted that Dalton did nothing, not even acknowledge Carinthya at the end of the hall. It was as if she did not even exist, and especially did not acknowledge her like family.

She could hardly blame him though, trauma was fresh in all of their minds. Elena had been keenly aware of how much Charmaine's absence had pained him back in the First, and now that he was here, all of this had been extremely challenging to navigate...especially given the parent reveal that had just happened.

Elena had never known her father, though it was of no consequence to her. Even though her mother had been tough on her, and worked so hard to instill perfection in her, she never once missed the absence of a father. Her mother had done both jobs for her, been there for her.

Parents in the Ten Kingdoms were complicated, and it was a miracle that she ended up with one good one. It could have been much worse... Just look at Dalton and Randolph.

Randolph. Gods. She silently cursed herself for letting her mind really wander there for a second. What in the name of the Gods had she been thinking? Clearly traveling through the mirror had caused her to seriously acquire some serious injury to the head.

"Elena?" Greyson's voice cut through her thick head like a knife.

"Yes?" she said, spinning around to face him.

"I think Cyril was asking for you... It was hard to tell of course."

She huffed out a laugh. "Ah, Cyril, perfect timing."

"Perfect timing for what?" Greyson asked, though confusion most definitely furrowed on his brow.

"Do not worry about it," she said, blitzing past him in the direction of Cyril's chambers. Spinning around, she asked, "Are you coming? I may need an interpreter. And someone fast if he decides to run again."

CHAPTER FIFTY-THREE

After they were given their rooms—each given their own rooms—Randolph seized the opportunity to storm down the hallway and talk to his sister.

He moved through the hall like thunder itself, searching for the one person that he had barely a chance to reconnect with since being reunited with her. There was so much to discuss among them, so many apologies to be had.

And the Gods had given him an opportunity, something that he would not let go to waste.

He knocked twice and heard a soft reply, "You may enter."

Opening the door cautiously, he spoke first, her mouth parted in surprise. "I was not sure if you wanted to see me," he said nervously, his fingers intertwined politely in-front of him. "I know there is much left unsaid between us these years—"

Her answer was to throw her hands around his neck and whisper, "There is nothing that you could do that I would not forgive, Rand."

"Reine, I am so sorry," he sobbed. "I am sorry for everything. Father—"

"Do not go doing that. He deserved death by your blade. You saved me." She pulled apart from him, looking him head on with all of the fury that she could possibly muster. The fury of a queen. "You look at me. You. Saved. Me. You saved the world by ending him, giving us a chance at a better world..."

And with that Randolph broke.

"Rand..." she swiftly said, softer than she had spoken to him in years. It was almost like they were children again, the way that she went to him and cradled him as he was wracked with sobs. "It is OK, let it all out, Rand."

Rubbing his back slowly as if he were once again young, Randolph came back to himself. Memories flashed in his gaze as he sifted through all of the years that they had lived under his father's cruel rule, and all the years that they spent apart.

That he had abandoned her.

"Randolph," Reine said shifting herself to sit in front of him directly. "Randolph, you need to hear it from me."

Warmth oozed from her hands, their power connecting like a candlelight in the darkness which surrounded them. She smiled softly, her amber gaze filled with that same fire that was reflected in his own. There was so much that had lived between them—when they were together and moreso when they were apart.

Randolph had always been internally jealous of the relationship between Charmaine and James, and even more devastated by her loss because he knew what it felt like to lose a sibling. Though the magnitude of his loss was nothing in comparison to the strength of the fire that burned within his heart.

"All of those years ago," he said through shattered

breaths. "All of those years ago, I made a choice. Father was going to marry you off, he was going to hurt you—"

"I know," she said quietly, urging him on to speak whatever it was that lived in him so deeply.

"I did not mean to kill him... That was not my plan."

"He was dangerous, Randolph. Far more dangerous than anyone could have ever imagined."

"I traded one mad king for another."

Reine inched forward, her nose just centimeters from her brothers. She intertwined both of her hands in his and took a deep breath. "You saved us. You saved the world with your choices, Randolph. Father—Gods—who knows the reach that he would have tried to have as the years went on. He was already ruling his kingdom, his children, with an iron fist and with cruelty in his heart. There is nothing to be ashamed of. I am fine. We are fine. Together. I could ask for nothing more."

Without hesitation, Randolph threw his arms around his sister as they forgave one another for everything, yet nothing of malice had lingered between them.

"When this is all over," Reine said. "Do you wish to come home?"

Randolph smiled sadly, pulling away from his sister to hold her hands once more. They glowed, in harmony with one another. Just like the Gods had wished it. "I do not know what or where my family is anymore, I have found over these last few years that family does not necessarily mean those who you share blood with."

Reine smiled. "I saw you with Dalton Saphirrus. You protect him. You look out for one another."

"It is the roll I played for so long," Randolph said, shaking his head.

"No," Reine interrupted gently. "It might have been at

one point, but there is no faking the bond that exists between the two of you."

"Since when did my baby sister get so wise?" Randolph filled with pride.

Reine stood, extending a tattooed hand. "I think us Eniar's have been too heartfelt for too long, my head hurts."

Randolph chuckled as he sniffled and rose to meet her. "A new era for us both, embracing ourselves and our feelings."

"Disgusting," Reine laughed in a huff as she started to make her way toward the door.

"And where are you going?" Randolph asked, raising an eyebrow. Damn, his head really did hurt.

"Going to drop some more wisdom somewhere else, you coming?"

IT WAS NONE other than Charmaine that entered Carinthya's chambers. She by no means anticipated that her brother would be the first to visit her, but there was something oddly surprising about seeing the Violet Queen come on his behalf. She had heard the commotion of the day was chaotic beyond all means, Charmaine finding out that her parents were actually the King and Queen of the Third Kingdom was no small feat. Though, respect built within Carinthya at the realization that Charmaine was really selfless.

A queen indeed. A title more deserving than the one that she had.

"Dalton does not know I am here," Charmaine said as she closed the door with stealth behind her. "Nor would he be rather enthused about it."

Oh, well, there goes the sentiment that maybe her brother had asked her to do this.

"I never meant to give anyone this much grief," Carinthya started. "I honestly never even anticipated seeing any one of these people again…"

"It is ok," Charmaine said, asking with her hands if she could come closer. Carinthya nodded in approval. "It is rather shocking to us all I think, to see a ghost."

Carinthya snorted. "I do wish I stayed a ghost."

Charmaine sighed sadly. "I am glad to see you here."

And Carinthya knew in that moment that she meant it. "Has he spoken to you…of me?"

"Barely," Charmaine answered honestly. *Well, it was better not to lie.* "In earnest, I think you are a wound that he does not want to heal."

"Will he speak to me?"

Charmaine stood up, extending her hand. "There is only one way to find out."

CARINTHYA SAPHIRRUS SAT before her brother in the most awkward silence that she could not have even deeply conjured in her worst imagination.

She often dreamt, in the first few years when she had been taken, of what it would be like to be reunited with her brother. Her mind went to every place, but it always landed the same. They would come running into one another's arms, no questions, only the forgiveness of time which would stand between both of them.

Instead, what she found, was *this*.

He sat across the room, barely within earshot of herself. His arms were crossed over his chest defensively, his eyebrows furrowed and his dimples barely visible. Dark hair swept across his brow line, his eyes still pulsating with an emotion that Carinthya was not sure she could give credit to with descriptive words.

Charmaine had left almost immediately after finding him alone.

Carinthya kicked herself internally for it, but it was certainly best that they were alone. She was not sure what she even wanted from him. She also did not know if he knew her role in Charmaine's capture. If he did... Well, there was certainly no room for forgiveness left in his heart then. These last few days he had not even looked at her—except that one time when addressing the group. She was unbearable to him.

And she knew she deserved it.

She could see hurt, that was for sure. But there was also a level of distrust, rightfully so. How could she explain to him? How could she tell him the truth? She *was* the reason that Charmaine had been taken, and it was clear to her now that what was once important to her brother had been replaced by the girl who had been taken just like she had.

"Do you have anything to say for yourself?" Dalton's voice cut through the air like a knife, startling her.

"I beg your pardon?" she said, stunned that these were his first words to her alone. What did he mean?

"I am awaiting a story, a tall tale of what you endured. Let us get on with it Carinthya, I do not have eons to listen. I have a crown to wear, a king's and queen's meeting to plan."

Shock reverberated through her. All dreams of what she imagined in an epic brother sister reunion had since died. He was colder. Colder than her father had been.

She shook her head from side to side. *No.* This was a trick. One of her brother's games. He was always so good at acting. Lying came easily to him, though she swore as a young girl that he did in fact find remorse from doing it, despite not showing it. Masks were his favorite accessory.

But in case she was wrong—he might not be the brother she remembered—she followed his lead.

"I do not know where to even begin—"

He threw his head back, exasperated. Long fingers ran through his dark hair, like they had when he had been over her as a child. It would have been comforting, except in these circumstances, it stung like a bee sting. Then he had patience. He was just a boy.

Now, he was a king. Patience evaporated.

She dug to find hers, taking a deep breath. She forgot what it was like to deal with someone who was so much very like herself. One had to tip-toe.

How would I talk to myself—

Carinthya took a deep, steadying breath. "I went outside, searching for something that did not lay in the castle."

"I am listening," he egged on, sitting forward, drinking in every word.

Mask beginning to fracture.

"I had heard... a voice..." She paused, thinking of how she could explain this without sounding crazy. "I now know that this was all Finn's doing, but the voice had come to me for a few weeks. It was telling me to do things, to leave, to break items, to make mother and father angry—"

"Do not speak of them. They are not a part of your story, Carinthya, just as they are *not* a part of mine."

She sat up straighter, finding confidence in his words. He believed them, she could tell.

And that meant something to her.

"I do not have an explanation, other than I was controlled. Those shadows that we escaped, they know things, they control minds."

Dalton leaned closer, yet did not come across the room. Mask disappearing.

"I wish I had a better explanation for leaving you like I did, but I do not. I have come to terms with the last six years, brother. And I am so sorry." Straightening her skirts, she looked down. She would not cry, she would not cry, she would not cry—

"How did they know where Charmaine was?" he asked, his voice half filled with questioning and half filled with dread, as if he already knew the answer.

"It was me." She did not stumble over her words. She did not pause before she spoke. She was the one thing that she could be, the one thing that he needed to hear. "I am sorry."

He spoke one word. "How?"

"They had the orb, some relic of our families if you ever can recall. They made me touch it to find who they were looking for…"

"Charmaine," he said, a confirmation.

"I did not know what she meant to you, nor did I even recognize you when I was gifted the vision from the orb." It was the truth, though it did not make it less regretful.

Dalton did not speak for a few minutes, though they felt like hours. Twiddling her thumbs, she breathed deeply to fight off the fear that she was thinking. Finally, he spoke, his voice calm and filled with no hatred that she had anticipated. "I forgive you," he said softly, and sadly.

"You what?" she asked. There was no way that this was going to be this easy between them. He had given her the cold shoulder since he had seen that she was alive. There had been no sibling bond between them, but maybe this was his way of making a start, and reigniting which once had been.

"There was nothing to ever forgive, Carin." Her heart shattered at her girlish nickname from childhood. Nobody had called her that in many years. "It was something beyond either of us, as we seem to fit into the puzzle piece of this world in ways which neither of us yet seem to understand."

He stood suddenly, his hands coming behind his back in a stately way.

She was pretty sure that her jaw had dropped, but she continued to gawk at him nonetheless.

"You are free now, sister," he said with a smile, blue sapphires dancing in his shadowed eyes. "My only hope is that you can continue to break free of your own shackles—I can see how they bind you—and learn how to dance in the sun again. I do not know what you endured all of these last few years, but I can guess that it is along the same lines of what I did."

"Do you not mean snow again? Instead of the sun?" she caught herself retorting, hating herself for falling so easily back into her old taunting ways. She had not meant to be smart, only literal. He used to enjoy that—

The side of his mouth quirked up. Bingo. "The snow can fall in the sun, Carin. That's something that I have learned these last few months."

Turning to go to the door, Carinthya realized that this was respectively over, and that she had survived what she had thought was going to be the confrontation of the century. However, before he had a chance to leave, he paused.

"I have missed you, sister. I am glad you are home."

Home? she thought.

"With your family."

CHAPTER FIFTY-FOUR

In all of Charmaine's life, she never imagined that she really had a place in the world. But as it turned out, she was a princess, and her parents, well, they were the most wonderful people that she had ever met.

After the council meeting died down, Charmaine made her way over to their chambers and asked to see them. They met outside, in Vanellope's cloud garden, and talked for hours. Elinoah and Amethyst answered all of her questions and begged for forgiveness. To Charmaine, however, there was nothing to forgive.

"You gave me the best chance that you could have, that prophecy something evil that I surely would not have survived."

"But you went through so much, experienced so much grief," Elinoah replied. "I am just so sorry that the family we chose for you ended up leaving you more alone than we had ever wanted before. We wanted you to be loved—"

Charmaine interrupted them—interrupted her mother. "I was loved. And my brother... Well, he was my entire world." A single tear began to drip down her face, and her father reached out to wipe it away. "I would very much like to get the chance to know you, especially when this is all over."

"We would like that very much, Charmaine." Amethyst replied kindly. "We would like that very much indeed."

As Charmaine made her way back to her chambers, irritation built in her as she thought of the other night with Dalton, despite the compete joy in her heart. Though, she did understand it. This was a complex range of emotions that she was dealing with, her life laid before all of the people that she knew and did not know, and their judgment had led to the most incredible discovery of all.

And what it taught her was that she never again wanted to hidden away, and she never again wanted to be anything but herself. So she decided right then and there that if Dalton was building up his walls again, and for what purpose she was not entirely sure, that she was utterly pissed.

But she was certain of one thing, as he built them up brick by brick once more, she was going to knock them down one by one.

Making her way back, she stalked right by her own chambers, and entered his. And hoped to the Gods that he was not naked.

He was not.

She found him reading. And Randolph was with him too.

"Charmaine?" Dalton's voice cut through the air like a

jab of ice. She could hear the pain in her name as he said it, splintering like an icicle ready to fall from its stem.

Without turning her head, she answered him, her voice pained and rough still. "I had waited, I waited for someone to rescue me."

Turning, she faced both of them. Randolph's tattooed hands were interlaced behind his neck, amber eyes haunted by the horrors of the last few days.

Dalton looked worse for wear. His usual Saphirrus charm clearly fractured by whatever semblance of control he had lost a grip on.

"I waited," she repeated, her voice breaking with the pain of her throat and the terror that still gripped her. "And you came."

"We did," Randolph said as if offering condolences. "We came for you, Char. There was never a doubt."

Cold tears ran down her cheeks, though she refused to sob. "I thank you for that. I just needed to tell you that."

As she turned again, she could hear Dalton's shoes scuffling on the floor once more. She did not pause as she continued deeper into his chambers, the door thrown open seconds after it clicked behind her by his own doing.

"Charmaine," he whispered, his voice more fragile than she had ever heard it before.

Out of the corner of her eye, she saw Randolph put his book down and make his way out of his room.

Without a word, she began to wash her face. The cold water hitting her was better than anything she had dreamed of before, a reminder as the breath left her with its impact that she was alive. She was here.

And this was all real, it all happened. She had been given another chance with a family. With parents. And even though she could not take any of it back, she had to acknowledge that this was an opportunity that she would embrace fully.

"How can you ever forgive me?" Dalton whispered behind her. "I did not know... I did not know any of it. The prophecy never made any sense to me, I did not know who it referred to other than myself at times—and even then it was rather a guessing game. But I never envisioned in my wildest dreams that there was something else at work...that you had a family out there, waiting for you and hoping that you were alive. What a beautiful piece of destiny to be reunited with...another chance at happiness and life."

She took a deep breath, unsure if she was ready to interject.

Her King continued, "When you were taken, something snapped within me. It was worse than Carinthya... I cannot..." He paused. "I cannot breathe properly without your presence. I cannot laugh without your proximity. I cannot smile without your joy."

She heard him breathe through a sob as he continued to speak. A part of her so deeply wished to turn around and comfort him, but she knew he was not ready. Whatever he had endured in her absence... this was how he was to work through it. And she would let him.

"Upon further reflection, I have deduced that I fell in love with you the moment you put that damned white rose behind my ear. You showed me the horrors of the world in pieces and fragments, telling me your story and of your home." She could almost feel him smiling as he pushed on. "But you also showed me it is resilience. Charmaine, you stand here now as a woman who has been through more in their lifetime than Cyril has in two... You have... You..."

Unable to hold back a moment longer, she turned around and collided with him. Her mouth was hot on his own, her lips starving for the taste of her king. She ran her hands through his jet black hair lovingly, touching him like she had never touched him before. She was drowning and he was sinking—and all they could do is breathe together to stay afloat.

In the past when they had kissed, he had been hesitant in more than one regard. But now? Nothing held him back from his desires.

He spun her, pushing her up against the wall of the Cloud Castle without so much as a second thought. His hands roamed freely over her midsection, fumbling for corset strings.

All hesitations were damned, all that stood was them.

Keeping her hands wrapped around his neck to keep him in proximity, she pulled back slightly. His dark blue eyes searched her face for regret and dismay, and she wished she could paint the joy discovered in them when he realized none existed.

"I was never mad at you, my King."

He bowed his head, resting his forehead on her own. He smelled of soot and ash, the opposite of his usual ethereal nature. Disheveled and broken, he somehow still stood as he always did. "But I was at myself. I should have—"

She cut him off with her index finger pressed against his lips. "You did all you could."

He kissed her gently, his gaze filled with a hope that she did not know the King of Snow was capable of. When he stopped, he pulled back slightly, unlinking her hands from him.

She nearly sagged to the floor in dismay. Did he not want her as she wanted him?

As if reading her mind, he paused, fumbling for the words in the least Dalton like manner possible. "Charmaine Grimes, if I do not stop now, no part of me will be able to. Ever."

"I do not want you to stop. Ever."

He pushed a loose curl off her tired face, though she did not flinch. His touch was pure magic and she would never deny him.

And he knew it.

Smirking, he backed up with his hands raised in resignation. "I must, I am afraid."

She was nearly blistering with rage but tried to keep her voice even. Her emotions were heightened, that mixture of grief and joy so lethal she was surprised she did not inherit Reine and Randolph's fire on cue.

As she opened her mouth to insult him, he reached into his pocket. With a trembling hand, he withdrew the sapphire ring he had given her the night they had been drugged by the Lily root.

"I thought I lost that," she whispered.

"And I thought I lost you."

"You could never lose me," she choked out.

A smile exploded across his face, his white teeth flashing as he said, "And now I will make sure of it."

She gasped, her hands flying to cover her mouth as the King of the First Kingdom got down on one knee. "Charmaine Elizabeth Grimes, Princess of the Third Kingdom, will you do me, Dalton Naoise Saphirrus, first of my name and King of the First Kingdom, the honor of becoming my wife?"

CHAPTER FIFTY-FIVE

Kai was flying at break-neck speed, his queen on his back urging him onward. The Queen of Fury was just that: furious. Her power cracked behind them stronger than lightning and darkness combined, the anger and twisted hatred that befell King Finn stronger now that they had seen the First Kingdom. Now that was three kingdoms he had infiltrated and overtaken: the First, the Seventh, and the Sixth. The Eighth Kingdom had no presiding ruler, it never had, so it was only a matter of time that it had formally fallen as well.

War was ever looming as the shadows themselves, who so ever-effortlessly draped themselves across the skies and grounds from Ciara's soul as they flew faster and faster toward the place where Kai knew that he was.

She had been hesitant at first, fearful of what could happen if she revealed herself too quickly. The Ten Kingdoms rulers were volatile, she knew that had not changed in the hundred years since her rule.

But if it was not now, when would it be?

So Kai beat on, his wings heavy with the promise of war,

but light with the hope that grew in his heart. And as the cloud castle came into his vision, he opened his mouth and let the flames fly, welcoming the Queen of Fury back to court.

She had arrived. And all would bow.

CHAPTER FIFTY-SIX

Dalton has gone out to look for champagne. Something to celebrate.

She touched the white sheets which sat on the bed with a softness. They had but a moment of peace together, before the day broke and the war began officially. They had dreamt of peace with one another for so long and had barely spoken a word of anything about it since they had been reunited. It was all about focusing on the future, moving forward, and defeating evil.

She wished it was not so.

Except that was not how the world worked, and he and Charmaine knew it despite their best judgment. They had a duty to do, for they had been hand-selected by the Gods to do this. To stop evil.

She lightly shimmied off her dressing gown, touching the stitching on the robe again with admiration and disdain.

She heard the door open behind her as she did so, expecting to see Dalton. He had wanted to come and visit her chambers here at the Cloud Castle after a few additional preparations with Vanellope.

However, the girl that stood before her looked no older than she did, and had the same deep green eyes that defined her portrait and fiery red hair that was unmistakable. She looked just like the portraits she had seen. Her aura just like that of the girl who had songs and sonnets written about her. Her hands were neatly crossed in front of her, her smile weak but sincere as if she had been long tired. Darkness crackled behind her as it sealed the door to the bedding chambers.

Charmaine inhaled a breath, keenly aware that she was only in her night dressings.

"Ciara?" Charmaine asked so quiet that it was barely a whisper.

THE DOOR WAS FUCKING LOCKED. Sealed by magic.

Dalton's hands thundered against the wall of his chambers. He was sweating and shaking, his entire body stuck in a purgatory of disbelief and true fear.

He could not lose her again, he would not lose her again.

He was shouting her name, his voice turning raw and crumbling with every single breath he took. *Was this what it was like to have a panic attack?* He tried to steady himself against the wall, his white tunic dripping with sweat down his back as he put his head up against the door.

He feared for the worst, that it was King Finn who had finally come to take her again. *He must have recovered from the Battle when they had left the Seventh,* Dalton thought to himself, manic. *He has come back for her.* A sob escaped his mouth, suddenly feeling as hopeless as the boy who had been sanctioned for doing nothing other than being himself. He felt like he did when his power had erupted, overtaking him and wringing him with the same fear that overtook him now. His hands shook violently as he ran a hand through his black hair, his crown clanging to the floor in an inappropriate display of emotion from the King.

He did not give a fuck.

He breathed deeply.

Once.

Twice.

Three times.

And then he blasted the door with all that he could muster. He felt the familiar tingle of his power, starting from his core and traveling down his veins as it exploded in an icy tundra. The sweat which stuck to his body now felt frozen, his body starting to shiver as he continued to pour himself into the doors structure.

He did not care what he lost right now, all he cared about was opening the fucking thing. No matter the cost. He would get back to her. He had to.

Nobody—and nothing—would take her from him again.

Panting he stood back and looked at his work, his fingers tingling with the familiar power that once overtook him before he had mastered its limits. The door had been frozen over as if the power that he could feel on the other side of it had raged beyond his capabilities. He had been blocked. The door was still sealed shut.

"Gods fucking *BE DAMNED*!" he shouted, screaming as he collapsed to his knees. *What the fuck was it to be the once and future King if you could not best a door?* He felt like he had taken too much of the Root of the Lily, his mind whirling. Instead of blunt desire, he felt only despair, an opening in his chest carved out where his heart was and threatened to rip it from him.

He was drowning, and Charmaine was his only way to the surface.

He heard a scuffle behind him and a voice dropping low

to his ear as someone murmured, "Lord King, what has happened?"

He sagged against the familiar tattooed hands as he breathed in the other man, the grief of losing her again shaking him to his core. He was no longer himself. No longer the King he had allow himself to become.

He was nothing without his Queen.

CHARMAINE GAPED at the once and future Queen. "How did you get here?" she asked, falling to her knees with a thud.

"You do not bow to me," Ciara said, her voice that of the day she possessed Gwendolyn at her execution.

Charmaine felt a chill run down her spine, her memory flashing back to the girl she was then. The fear that she felt. The despair which overtook her.

"You are the once and future Queen," Charmaine said despite her will to remain silent.

Ciara smiled, stepping forward with a soft grunt, as if it were an effort for her to move in this form. "And your King is noted as such a thing? Is he not?"

Charmaine nodded her head, her mind incapable of forming a verbal response.

"I do not have much time," Ciara said softly, her gaze heavy with sadness. She looked like she was merely a painting of herself, not fully and truly whole. Charmaine knew the expression that she now wore, for she had seen it on Dalton many times since she traveled to the castle. "But I need you to listen to me."

Charmaine stood up, rising to meet the fellow Queen which had once worn her crown. Ciara beamed, as if proud of Charmaine's lack of formality. "You wear my crown well," she said softly.

Charmaine blushed as Ciara continued, "He is coming. He is coming for you *soon*. I do not know if I will be able to reach you again, and if I can I do not know when it will be. You must keep your sword close Charmaine and keep your mind sharp. Even I could not best my father in my lifetime, with the help of my Snow King."

Charmaine felt her heart turn to fire at the mention of Dalton. "If even you could not fully beat the King, and you gave your life for it, how are we expected to defeat him?" She could not hide the venom in her voice, despite the respect she held for the legendary Queen.

"Charmaine, do you still have the dagger?"

The dagger is the key.

The dagger is the key.

Voices of the past rang through Charmaine's mind, over and over and over. Charmaine paused, afraid to even speak of it. It had been strapped to her thigh—invisibility cloaking it from anyone even knowing that she had it—and now it was hidden once more, safe in this very castle.

Afraid to utter the words in that paranoid and anxious way that sometimes manifested for Charmaine, she nodded.

Ciara nodded back.

"Ah, but Charmaine, you are not me. And Dalton is not Cian. You will find your way. I so hope that we get to meet again, Charmaine Grimes. And please never forget, that you are stronger than you will ever truly know," she said as she faded into the darkness behind her.

DALTON STOOD UP AGAIN, his sword slashing at the door and ice which caked it's front. His arms burned with the motion, his training had been lacking in the past few weeks in part of the coronation. He cursed himself silently for freezing the Gods damned thing shut, for all he wanted was to blast it to pieces. *What was the reason that he couldn't have been gifted with the power of fire?* Randolph was a lucky motherfucking bastard.

"Dalton," Randolph pleaded behind him, "the door is sealed. There is no use."

"I will not lose her again," Dalton said through heavy breaths and he dropped his sword and pounded on the door with frozen fists.

CHARMAINE COULD HEAR the pounding on the door the moment that Ciara left the room. She collapsed against the chair of the bedding chambers, the crackling of the fireplace returning and warming her back as she sat down for a moment taking in all that had just happened.

Her mind whirled as she poured herself a glass of wine meant for her and Dalton to celebrate their royal bedding. She could only imagine the thrashing outside was him. Her heart lurched as she realized that he was probably terrified that something had happened to her, given all they had happened with King Finn just a few months ago.

She got up quickly, dashing over to her bedside to put on her robe. She felt no shame that she had been entirely naked in front of Ciara. If anything, she felt as if she were oddly enough speaking to an extension of herself.

She ran towards the door, the front of the dressing gown barely covering her and she pulled on the door.

Hard.

She could feel the handles were frozen solid, as if Dalton had tried to blast the door open with his power.

She felt an immense amount of guilt washing over her

that she'd hadn't thought how her absence would have affected him, something which they had both been struggling to deal with since her capture.

She groaned as the doors thrashed open and Dalton stood before her. His chest heaved and his face was flushed with fever. His black hair stuck to his forehead wildly as if he were a caged animal trying to break free. He had his sword raised to the door as if he were about to hack through the wood itself to get to her.

Her heart shattered into a million pieces when she fully took in how much she had wrecked him in this instance, and by the realization that he was utterly broken without her.

"*Char*," he said in a broken gasp as he threw his sword to the ground with a clang.

He ran towards her, touching her face reverently and checking her body for flesh wounds as he slammed the door behind them, separating whom ever had been standing outside from their reunion.

"I am fine," she whispered, her soul cracking at his despair. "Dalton, I am fine."

"Who did this?" he said, his blue eyes meeting hers with an icy fury.

She kissed him in response, meeting him in a hot embrace. They danced with their tongues as they played with one another, her dressing gown barely held together as it was draped off her shoulder slowly.

She made no move to intercept it as it hit the floor with a silent *whoosh*.

They backed up together towards the bedding chamber, well aware that any sort of celebration of their engagement was not going to be taking place this evening. Her head hit the back pillow softly, his hand caressing her on the nape of her neck as if to cradle her from any part of harm.

"Dalton," she begged him, pleading to touch her.

He kissed the side of her neck, murmuring once again, "Who did this, Char?" His voice was laced with a venom which she had not heard ever from him. His eyes did not meet hers as he continued to kiss her, heavy with anger and desire. She noted that his eyelashes had white tips at the end, sending her into a silent panic that he was shifting backwards and losing control again.

"*Dalton,*" she said, more of a warning this time than it was a desire.

"Who did this?" He paused on top of her, his mouth hovering centimeters from her lips.

She hesitated, fear constricting her chest as she muttered the name which she never thought would be the answer to any of their problems, "Ciara."

Chapter Fifty-Seven

Cyril fell to the ground at the sight of auburn hair and leaf-green eyes. He had been wandering about the castle, and then heard Dalton's screams. Horror had blasted through him, and regret too. He had been so certain that he had made a fatal mistake in giving Dalton space since he had seen him. Their reunion had been emotional to say the least, all tears and memories and unsaid things between them.

But one thing was for certain, he was so proud of the man—the king—that Dalton Saphirrus was growing to be. He was not afraid of doing hard things, of confronting evil, and of doing anything and everything to protect the people that he loved.

Which all reminded Cyril of the woman that he saw float out of Dalton's chambers, passing Dalton and Randolph with that same graceful elegance that he could never forget from a hundred years back. *Did nobody see her but him?*

Memories flashed through him like lighting as his body hit the ground.

❄

CIARA'S red hair beamed in the moonlight.

Cyril sat with her at the edge of the rose garden, something which she had reconstructed after the disillusionment of her father's memory. She was haunted by something, he could tell in the short time that he had known her. She often had her hands in multiple different secret dealings, never quite revealing her plans until they were in full swing.

"What are you planning?" Cyril asked her.

"The council is angry, the memory of my father still haunting them. They want weapons, more powerful ones that is. They have found a sword-smith in the citadel below, and they have asked me to retrieve a weapon personally to end all weapons."

"A weapon to end all weapons?" Cyril was not sure he was understanding what exactly she was saying. "The council has asked you to do this?"

Ciara's council was notorious for being untrusting of a woman in power, her position as her father's murderer obviously creating strains, though nobody was exactly loyal to him. She was terrifying. Cyril had seen it at work. If there was a motive for them to have her do this, the motive had to be significant.

She turned to face him, her gaze determined and certain. She would get what she wanted.

She always did.

"Yes, and tomorrow you and I are going to go to the citadel to visit someone named Sean." She smiled deviously.

"And Sean is going to make us this weapon?"

"No, the Thinkers have all but confirmed that Sean just owns the smith. You see, it is his apprentice that we are going to want to see."

"And does this apprentice have a name?" Cyril asked, his

blue eyes beaming with the thrill of adventuring with his queen.

"Cian."

CYRIL WANTED to shout and get her attention, but the second that he went to open his mouth, he was once again noiseless. Grunting in frustration, he looked up to where he had just seen her but was confronted with a confounding reality when she was no longer where she was.

Closing his eyes, he envisioned her as she was that day that she had first mentioned Cian. Poised. Determined. Maybe even a little irritated.

And then he smiled, opened his eyes, and there she was in front of him.

Chapter Fifty-Eight

King Finn approached the Ninth Kingdoms castle with an army of mercenaries behind him. They had been traveling for days, half of the army split to occupy the Sixth, Seventh, and First Kingdom's. His plan all along had been to use Charmaine Grimes to sneak up on the Ninth Kingdom, or wherever in the Ten Kingdoms the most viable option for world domination was.

But now that they no longer had the element of surprise, well, they had nothing to lose.

He had nothing to lose.

"What will you have us do, my liege?" a mercenary spoke behind him, dressed in midnight colored armor. They would take the Ninth Kingdom looking like the shadows that they were, representing their king and his power whole-heartedly.

"I will have you take it all," Finn said as he began to laugh. Extending his arms, shadows began to creep forward, his gaze extending all the way to the castle doors at the top of the castle. "Begin," he commanded.

And so they did.

CHAPTER FIFTY-NINE

The Queen that stood in-front of Cyril was like a shadow of a person.

It broke him.

She was never half of anything in life, and in death her aura had been reduced. Her body was illuminated and did not look as whole as she had in life. She had no shine to her, no spark. In life, she had been as vibrant as the Ten Kingdoms itself. Her hair had shown the most fiery of reds, a deeper and so much more alive than any flame he had ever seen before. Her green eyes had shone with curiosity and fury, green with envy even at times.

But now? The woman that stood in-front of him was lifeless in comparison, like looking at a portrait of his friend where the colors had been muted.

Out of Cyril's peripherals, he saw Dalton, Charmaine, and Randolph stand behind the hallway with a few other knights of the Ninth Kingdom. They were all watching in awe as she approached him. He could almost see through her, the image of her not fully there despite it so clearly being her.

So they could see her *now*.

"Cyril, stand." Ciara's voice commanded him, all power and familiar strength. It washed over him like rainfall in the moonlight, draping him in nirvana and almost breaking a sob out of him.

He had missed his friend so fucking much, and now that she stood here in-front of him—even though she was partially whole—he could barely stand it. *How many years had she been wandering? Had it been the whole time? Where was Cian?* There could not be a scenario in which he could concoct where she would have left him, and that he would have left her.

Cyril stood, the command flooding over him. As he moved to bow his head, she threw her arms around him. It was the most wicked of sensations, for he knew that she was there and could feel her touch, but it was devoid of all warmth.

And then she spoke again, her voice full of every ounce of queenly command that she could muster, and said clear as day, "Speak my friend, it has been too long since I have heard your voice."

"Dalton?"

Dalton fell to his knees, Cyril's voice cutting through the air like an arrow before it landed its mark on a target.

"Your voice—" Ciara said, touching Cyril's face as if he were a young boy. Maybe to her, he was. "Gods... You sound so much older." A laugh escaped her softly, filled with so much kindness and admiration.

Dalton felt like he was observing some sort of intimate moment, but it was hard to look away. He had been afraid to confront Cyril earlier because of his voice, it was enough among the chaos to acknowledge that he was simply alive and well. That he was here. An echo and a reminder of who he was truly at his core. And what if Cyril was angry at him for leaving? For seeing him collapse like that into a comatose state and then just high-tailing it out of the First Kingdom...

Dalton began to stand, shaking those ever-crowding feelings off him like stars shot out of the sky. He did not make any moves to walk toward Cyril, only steadied himself by grabbing Charmaine's hand.

Charmaine Grimes, who was to be his wife.

And he would tell everyone, Cyril included, when the Queen of Fury was not standing in the hallway of his chambers.

He looked at her, a silent beam of excitement and pride, and she nodded in agreement. The draw between them thrummed as if it were pleased, that the two of them finally getting together would solidify all of the aches and pains that they had both been feeling since they met one another.

Charmaine squeezed his hand as they both looked back toward Cyril and Ciara, unable to look away from a moment of two friends reuniting. Maybe Cyril had some sort of physical connection between himself and Ciara like Dalton did to Charmaine, but not out of love.

Out of loyalty.

And maybe that is how their love tested the years and years apart, to lead them to this moment where an old man and a ghost would reunite on the eve of battle to rekindle their friendship.

Cyril huffed out a laugh that bordered a sob. "I might be older, but you certainly have not aged a day my old friend. How is it that you even are here? And what took you so long?"

Ciara turned her head to look at all of them, and a chill washed over Dalton's spine as her green gaze settled on him.

"One hundred years is a long time, my friends. And it would be a very long tale indeed to recount every day since I last saw you, my dearest. I am afraid that we do not have time for that right now, for war is almost upon us."

Dalton flinched. Randolph put a hand instinctively on his sword that sat at his hip.

"But I can answer your question in part, before I go to start what I finished, Cyril."

"And what can you offer me, Ciara?" Cyril's voice was riddled with confusion and sadness, age for the first time becoming apparent in someone who was over one hundred years old themselves and was so full of youthful life.

"It took me so long because I have been waiting and watching. And now it is time. I am surprised I have power enough for this, but when I felt you approaching, well, I thought it was worth the risk."

"Time for what?" Cyril asked, hurt in his voice. "Do not leave me again, Ciara—"

"Time for me to finish what I started one hundred years ago," she said, standing slowly, the image of her starting to gather shadows like a living nightmare. "And it is time to see my dear husband once again."

CHAPTER SIXTY

Ciara had evaporated quickly after that, disappearing into thin air as though she was truly never there at all.

Dalton had run to Cyril, to catch him as he began to sob. Charmaine's heart nearly cleaved in two, for she had never seen anything like that before. Never felt anything like that before.

The power had been palpable in the room, so much so that she felt it electrify the hallway even more-so than she had the room when they had spoken. Decidedly, she felt it was important to keep her conversation with the Queen of Fury to herself for now.

And the most haunting part of it all was the way that the power remained even after she departed, like the whole world was electrified by her power in the moments before chaos sprung in the form of battle.

The castle had erupted into chaos at the time of her departure. For Charmaine validated the queens words, repeating that Ciara only came to talk to her and warn her. It was only Cyril's presence that had reignited her desire to stay in this world, even though it was clear that she was a shadow of herself. A ghost.

Knights began to mobilize, kings and queens began to send notes through the castle thinkers to run as fast as they could because war was close.

Vanellope had secured the castle on all defenses, her clouds beginning to drop and cover the castle's outside in every inch. Draped in secrecy, it would be hard for Finn to navigate unless he was to breach the front door.

But he was already here. Randolph had seen him on a patrol, a large army of mercenaries and shadows crowding itself more and more at the base of the cloud castle. He had come back from the venture with a few knights and Lawton utterly flushed, his normal composure slightly broken.

"I just thought we would have more time," Randolph said. "We did not even have a chance yet to really prepare... the reinforcements will not be here for at least half a day to a day..."

"Randolph," Charmaine said, keeping her voice steady. "I am scared too. Terrified. But we will do this. Together. We will stand together."

Randolph smiled. "There is my girl. You are the greatest friendship I have ever known, the biggest blessing that I found you and your brother in the woods. You, Charmaine Grimes, are the strongest person I have ever met."

Charmaine wiped a tear and turned to see Dalton stampeding down the hallway. He had changed to dark armor, a compliment to his newly found dark features. He looked like a nightmare itself, though the eternalness of him had never dissipated. His sapphire eyes found hers and they were drawn together immediately.

"How is Cyril?" she mouthed as he was stopped by King Loe on his journey to meet them.

"Fine. Resting," he mouthed back before he was swept up in walking the other direction with Loe.

"Charmaine," Randolph said, interrupting her Dalton infused distraction. "Vanellope told me she has something for you. I saw her briefly after I came back in."

"She has something for me?" she asked, confused. What could the queen of the Ninth Kingdom have for her? She did not owe her anything.

"Yes," Randolph said with a smile. "And I think you are going to like it."

CHAPTER SIXTY-ONE

Dalton had been abducted by Loe, in all sense of the word. The knights from the First Kingdom that Maria had sent after Elena, Sixth Kingdom, and Ninth Kingdom were all prepared and at the ready. But he was not convinced it would be enough. The mercenaries were of another breed, powerful and strong and utterly ruthless.

Randolph, Reine, Elena, Bairre, Lawton, Charmaine, and himself had explicit magical powers, and would do everything in their power to expend themselves. Carinthya and Titan were committed to fighting in whatever way necessary. But Dalton could not help but feel nothing but fear in his heart. This was different than some petty council meeting or a flee from the Seventh Kingdom's Castle Dead.

No, this was war.

Complete and total war.

Finn wanted everything. Was ruthless.

He was not sure in what capacity that Ciara was going to be able to help, she looked much like a shadow of herself —a ghost. However, the power that still ripped through the air of the castle had him guessing that she had gone off to recharge somewhere. Maybe even plan and plot against her father. There was something terrifying about that, but thrilling too. If they had Ciara, maybe they had a chance.

Maybe they could win this. Live in peace.

He knew it was selfish, but he wanted Randolph to go with Charmaine. If he was with her the entirety of the battle that he would not be able to be as ruthless as he would need to be. He could not think of her, he knew that she had this...

He paused, the wind nearly knocked out of him at the sight of purple armor and raven colored hair. He looked forward, gazing directly into the amethyst gaze of Charmaine Grimes.

Gods, she was power *exuded*.

He made a move to walk down the hallway, to tell her all that he was feeling—maybe even give her a romantic kiss like what happened in the fantasy novels he had read in his confinement—but he stopped dead in his tracks as the floor beneath him began to rumble. Darkness began to spread through the halls, shadows leaking from the outside world to the inside. He could hear Randolph shouting to breach the castle, to make their way to the door.

So all that Dalton had time for was to nod his head in her direction, and hope that she knew everything that he had not yet said.

The battle had begun.

CHAPTER SIXTY-TWO

D alton was sprinting.

Vanellope's castle had to have a back door somewhere...

Knights and royals and commoners alike flooded the hallway, all running in the same direction. Dalton, true to form, beat to his own drum and ran the complete opposite direction, a smirk wide on his face. He felt like midnight itself.

He had a favor to cash in.

"Dalton Saphirrus?" Vanellope's voice sounded behind him. She was following him.

Dammit.

"Vanellope, now is not a great time. War impending and all..."

"Dalton, where are you going?! The battle is that way." He assumed she was pointing.

He stopped and rolled his eyes before turning to face her. She was dressed in all white armor, her hair illuminated graciously in straight perfection that hit her shoulders. Her dark eyes were mirrors of Dalton's, full of fear and terror.

Vanellope had no powers, not like Dalton did. He could not imagine the position that she was in, and genuinely felt terrible for bringing this here.

Closing his eyes and scrunching his nose in frustration, he said, "I am owed many favors, Vanellope. I am not sure if you noticed, but *I am fucking Dalton Saphirrus.* I am chaos emboldened with a hint of softness and a whole lot of sarcasm. I make bad deals and do whatever I can to save the people that I love." He heaved in a deep breath. "And I made a very interesting deal. One which will save the world if I can enact it right."

"What do you need?" Vanellope asked in wonder. He was not sure if she was horrified or if she simply was holding in a laugh.

"I need a back door."

SOMETHING SNAPPED WITHIN ELENA. It was like the rushing of water over a broken damn, or what she imagined the overflow of a burnt candle to feel like when the wax begins to flow down its side. Elena could only think of one thing. Of one person.

Where was Randolph?

Things had been hideously ugly since she had kissed him. She was rather embarrassed actually. Has one dream about him, fawns over him, kisses him? This was not Elena at her core. Or maybe it was, and she just did not know herself anymore at all. The words escaped her lips before she could even process what was happening, turning around and chasing nothingness but a feeling which haunted her every being. He was hurt, he had to be, it was the only explanation.

As she flew out of the castle's front door and made her

way to the field below, horror crept over more and more with every step. There was a dark haze over the horizon, a thundering in her chest telling her that danger was near.

This was it. Finn had come.

Making her way down, she ran by soldiers from all of the kingdoms that had been able to make it thus far. But there was one voice that she wanted to hear. One face that she wanted to see.

She had been so stupid, so naïve. So very unlike Elena.

James had broken her, but since then it was Randolph that had held her, Dalton, and Charmaine together. He had been the one to silently watch and provide guidance. He had been their everything. The glue that held them together, the foundation that kept them standing. Whether or not she always knew it, whether or not she ever wanted to acknowledge it, she loved the family that they had built together.

And she refused to say goodbye, not today. They would fight for normalcy—for goodness—together. Evil would die today at their hands.

As she got closer and closer, warriors began to run out onto the field as mercenaries poured out of the darkness that sat on the horizon. And almost on cue, the snow began to fall harder.

Light fighting against the dark. The war had officially begun.

With her fire red hair blazing behind her, she took off once more, pumping her arms and extending her fingers as she embraced the cold air around her. Where there was snow, there was water, and where there was water... Well... There was her power.

James flashed in her eyes for just a second, the horror on his face as she had hurt him with her power. But then, only an instant later, there was Randolph. Dalton. Charmaine.

Lawton, even. Sure, power could destroy, it could hurt. But it could also bring joy. It could save.

Flash. Dalton and her snowball fights appeared in her memory. A smile crested over her face.

Flash. Randolph's heat. His warmth. His soul. A tear slipped down her cheeks.

Power was strength.

Power could be good.

Power should be used for good.

She breathed in, pausing at the edge of the battlefield.

And then she heard her name, and took off without a second thought.

There he is.

Distant despite knowing it was coming from close by, her name sounded. However, she could not focus. Could not think of anything but him.

"RANDOLPH!" she screamed, whipping her head from side to side.

"ELENA, YOU SHOULD NOT BE OUT HERE! It is too dangerous—"

Anger flashed through her, her gaze hardening despite his good intentions. She could take care of herself. She always had.

Distracted by her presence, fear living and breathing in his gaze, Randolph was distracted. In ordinary circumstances, she would be flattered. But instead, a scream ripped from her throat as a mercenary appeared behind him, an axe in his hands.

"RANDOLPH!" she screamed again, pointing wildly. *Gods, Elena, maybe you were not meant for battle after all.*

Somehow, Randolph was one with sense. He whipped around, fire immediately pouring out of his hands. But the mercenary was fast—far faster than any human soldier. Were they powered by shadow magic? Elena's mind spiraled, and she took off toward him.

Randolph unsheathed his sword from his back, the blade glistening with golden heat as he channeled his power into it. As he swung, the blade collided with the axe and sparks shot out of it as if it were being welded. The mercenary did not give up, his black armor nearly threatening to melt as Randolph's whole body seemed to light up in flames.

Elena covered her face as she ran forward, the heat nearly too much for her.

The mercenary did not give in as they spun around. His huge body nearly hid Randolph's silhouette, for he was so massive. Darkness swarmed around him, and Elena nearly stopped breathing.

A scream, guttural and unmistakably Randolph's ripped through the air.

"Gods," she whispered, the wind knocked out of her at the sound.

A groan escaped, unmistakable, from the mercenary as Randolph's blazing sword pierced straight through him. Elena let out a gasp, her heart nearly bursting with relief.

And then the mercenary fell forward, the sword still embedded in his middle, Randolph pinned underneath him.

She ran. Her gaze frantically searched for tattooed hands before she felt him. "RANDOLPH!" she screamed, suddenly cursing herself for not being closer, for hesitating instead of just tearing out there. A warrior would not have hesitated. Randolph—even Dalton—would not have waited. Guilt thrashed through her, her mother's harsh criticisms as a child rearing their ugly head in her mind like the devil itself.

With all of her might, she pushed. To no avail, her push did absolutely nothing. Gritting her teeth, she shoved again after taking a pause and a deep breath, recentering her strength. She could do this. Randolph was under him, and she had to get him out. *What if he was—*

The mercenary rolled off of him, and he laid down on the ground, a wound in his side staining his violet tunic a dark red.

"Randolph—" she whispered, her shaking hands searching his face for any other injuries, before quickly wandering to his neck and wrists for a pulse. It was steady. She sighed, her shoulders sagging visibly as relief took over her.

Leaning forward, she put her forehead to his own, well aware that they were in the middle of a battlefield and this was not the time for some romantic fantastical reunion.

"Elena?" he groaned, his voice strained.

"I am so sorry, I am hurting you." she yelped as she sat up straight.

"I did not realize you liked me this much," he said with a tease. "I like the way my name sounds when you are worried about—"

If he was not laying on the ground, bleeding, she would have slapped him.

"Where is your armor?" Elena shouted, panic striking every octave in her voice. She knew her face was probably as red as her hair.

"I did not wear any."

His voice was dim, but the sarcasm was still dripping.

"And why is that?" she asked, confused.

"Because I have my flames."

She sighed. "Idiot."

As he tried to sit up, he groaned and winced, the sarcasm falling away completely and their moment of sadistic flirting well over.

"Wait," Elena whispered, her mind coming back to her.

Amazingly, Randolph listened. He paused, his arms holding himself up as he watched her with complete focus.

Hands trembling, she paused. She could do this.

"Elena—" he whispered, her amber gaze still filled with fire, though it was dimming. Blood. He was losing too much blood.

"Stop talking, I need to focus."

He huffed a laugh, despite the color starting to drain from his face.

"This may sting for just a moment," she whispered, trying to sound strong. As she extended her trembling hands, he stopped her.

"Hey," he said, his voice calm despite the chaos that raged around them. "You can do this. I believe in you."

She smiled softly, the corners of her mouth raising in thanks. She knew he meant every word. Randolph Eniar was many things, but he was incapable of lying.

As her hands collided with his side, he grimaced, and she felt herself start to retract. She was retreating into herself. Closing down her eyes, she breathed deeply. In and out and in and out. "No," she whispered to nobody in particular. "No, you can do this."

Snowflakes landed on her hands, melting on impact. The light of the world—the King of Snow—was fighting back. They could do this. They could win. But they had to do it together.

Elena dove into herself. Let her mind wander. She did not know how long she sat there. It could have just been seconds, but somehow it felt like hours. Memories flooded into her—the happiest ones that she could attach herself too.

Seeing Dalton after he had been released from his father's confines.

Meeting James.

Snowball fights with Dalton.

Hugging Charmaine after she was burned.

Being queen of the First Kingdom, even though she had so desperately wanted out of it. She had done it well. There was pride in that she held onto.

Her mother staying behind, showing her how despite her tough love for her entire life that it was out of love.

Kissing Randolph.

It built within her like a kernel, before that light exploded from her. Simultaneously, her and Randolph gasped in tandem. Her eyes flew open to meet his, and as she looked down, her hands were glowing the most vibrant blue.

"Am... Am I hurting you?" she asked.

Randolph looked down at his side, his mouth agape. A tattooed hand extended, he laid it over her own as the glow faded like a handle that had been blown out.

"Elena..." he said, clearly struggling to find the words.

She froze. Oh, Gods, she had hurt him—-

"Elena, no," he started again, clearly trying to find the words as he sat up without infliction. "Elena, look."

As she removed her hands, they were clean. There was no mark on his side, nothing other than a tear and the remnants of blood that had been there from the wound. The only evidence that it ever existed to begin with.

"You did it," he said in a gasp. "Elena, you did it." And then he threw his arms around her, saying more with one hug then he could ever say right now. Tears flooded in her eyes, the words of validation that she needed to hear more than she even realized.

After a heartbeat, they pulled apart. The snow began to trickle down harder, a warning and a reminder that what lived around them still raged on. Helping him to stand up,

Randolph smiled softly, his brown hair shading his eyes partially.

With a smirk that looked devastatingly similar to that of Dalton Saphirrus, he strode over to the fallen mercenary and ripped his sword out of him. Elena nodded silently, for no words could even come close to expressing what she was feeling right now. Reaching out his free tattooed hand, she took it instantly, and then she began to run again once more.

DALTON WAS NOT sure how to even call a dragon. He tried *everything*. Exasperating sighs turned to grumbles which turned to full blown conniptions.

Thinking.

Wishing.

Yelling.

Conjuring a snowball.

Waving his hands.

Running back and forth.

Jumping up and down.

Cursing.

Nothing was *working*. And he was running out of time. The battle was raging on literally around the corner from where he stood. His friends were throwing themselves in the line of danger—for him, for his legacy, for *their* world.

And here he was, doing his part by standing in a fucking field trying to call some mystical creature because it owed him a Gods-damned favor.

Dear Gods, did King Cian ever have any trials and tribulations this...ridiculous?

"Kai... Come out come out wherever you are..."

The answer was wings flapping in the distance, the trees

and grass rustling, and a fire-breathing dragon suddenly landing in-front of him.

"You know," Kai said, his glistening white scales glittering among the darkness of the shadowed sky. "I heard you when you were just out here thinking... the jumping up and down was not necessary."

"The cursing might have been a little much on my part," Dalton said, nearly smacking himself in the forehead. He was the freaking king of the First Kingdom and he was out here like a fool, rather than a leader. His friends... Gods, his friends had taken off into the battle and he was out here making Gods-damned snowballs.

"I thought about flying around a few more times, but then I realized that your situation must be dire if you were out here while all of your friends were over there." He gestured with his long white spiked tail. "So I must ask you, Dalton Saphirrus, did you meet my queen?"

"Ah, so you serve Ciara." It suddenly all clicked. "Yes, I had the pleasure of being in her presence earlier." Dalton tried to keep all sarcasm out of his voice. He had read the diary entries, and knew none of the truth depths of the deep friendship that had existed between the queen and the dragon. All that he knew was that Ciara and Kai were like magnets, drawn to one another in life and in death.

And that was certainly not something to be messed with.

Kai hummed in approval, smoke beginning to pore out of his nose. "Dragons have many gifts, Dalton. And we do not grant wishes on good will alone. Tell me, what is it that you want?"

"Give it to her," Dalton commanded, dragon tongue pouring out his mouth like hot metal. It was a language that even Randolph had never heard, but being born of flames, hearing it against the wind felt like coming home. A command. Something that he could not refuse.

"How dare you!" Kai shot out, roaring and throwing his head back in betrayal. "To use the ancient tongue with me... You have no right!"

Smoke began to pour out of his nose, but it was clear that no flames would come. Dalton had royally pissed him off, but he won. Kai would give him this. He had no choice in the matter.

"I do not ask for this on good will alone," Dalton hissed. "You know what it is to walk the line of life and death, Kai. And you will give me what you want."

"And why is that? You are going to have to be more specific."

"Because, when this is all over, I will let you do what you really want." Dalton twirled his fingers, a small demonstration—and reminder—of the power that lived within him.

"And what is that?" Kai asked again, his voice keen and intrigued despite the rage he had just shown. "What is it that you think I want?"

"You will get to burn the world down, just like you have always wanted."

Chapter Sixty-Three

Fire blasted from Randolph's hands, his face sticky with sweat and his arms heavy from holding them in fists since Elena healed him. He had not grabbed for his sword since, his flames his most powerful weapon right now.

Mercenaries dodged out of the way as he made his way down the winding path. He could smell the rotting flesh of some that he had burned along the way, hot metal bubbling against skin, while screams simultaneously ensued across the entirety of the battlefield.

He was keenly aware of where the majority of his friends were, but Dalton had eluded him. Charmaine stood at the top of the castle, waiting for the signal that he had designed to suddenly hide their forces. Elena battled just a few feet from him, Greyson had found them and now resided at her side, swinging his sword to hold them back.

"Hold the line!" Randolph shouted, another blast of fire flying from his hands. "Hold the—"

He paused, lifting his gaze to look at sky high above his rising smoke. The sky was dark, the shadows seemingly causing the world to get darker and darker, despite their reach only being the inside of the castle. Squinting his eyes, he found himself blinking twice as he mindlessly continued to play fire balls out of his hands.

Elena noticed his lack of rhythm, his change in pace and aggression. Her voice sounded across the pathway. "Randolph?! What is it?"

"It is…" He paused, making sure that he was right before he descended everyone into mayhem. "It is the dragon."

CIARA WATCHED from the tallest point of the castle. She watched her father from afar, in his prowess, scour the battlefield for anyone who dared to challenge him. Anger built within her at the sight of the shadows which he had stolen from her all of those years ago. It would seem that in death he even had access to things that he had taken from others.

A part of her was more than angry—betrayed—that the Gods would have allowed him to stay alive, in part, these last years. But she also understood, for they had allowed her to live a shadowed life herself. Though she had never been as whole as him, but maybe she did not want to be. Maybe she liked being the way that she was.

Maybe she did not deserve to be whole.

When her father had died, she remembered hearing the winds whip by her head with such raw power that she had collapsed, hitting her head. When she awoke, she felt that chill. Like someone was still there.

Her father was many things, but weak was not one of them. He was not willing to depart this world, even with a knife protruding from his chest. He had never surrendered the ability to… well, live.

In that regard, and only in that regard, was their relation showing.

Lifting her head high, Ciara looked out once more, and then looked above.

Kai had entered the scene.

She smiled softly to herself. The fun was about to begin.

Leaning forward, she watched intently at what he was going to do. She had not given him any commands, not that he really followed her orders, but their bond meant something to both of them.

They had lived too much life together—even if it was a short life—it was a full one. Love like that did not come once in many people's lifetimes, it was a miracle that she had lived such a short life and experienced it three times. Kai, Cian, and Cyril. She had three loves of her life and had been blessed to be reunited with two of them in her re-arrival to this plain of the universe.

She had given up hope decades ago that she would see Cian again. Their rule had been a burning of the hearts until their castle had crumbled around them. Even in death, she had been unable to leave him, watching him for decades until he had passed in old age.

It had hurt, to watch him go through the stages of life without her. But it had also been a gift, and given the circumstances of her life, it did bring her joy. Not many got to follow their soulmates into the afterlife, to get to watch them in their joy and their heartache. In a darker sense, it did bring her some semblance of peace that he had never forgotten her.

Returning her gaze to the battle below, she smiled as Kai continued to fly overhead, not engaging in the war that raged on.

Closing her eyes, she breathed in the air around her and

found that it once again gave her nothing. There were no scents, no feeling...no sensation. She missed life.

As she reopened her eyes, she paused as a bright light began to glow from the clouds above.

And then the Queen of Fury softened, falling to her knees in a bow.

DALTON JOINED THE BATTLE, chaos in full throttle.

He kept an eye on the horizon, praying for some type of daybreak among the shadows. Kai swarmed overhead, rejuvenated yet awaiting the opportunity to fulfill his end of the bargain. Dalton had not been specific as to when this task needed to be performed, but he knew the less specific that he was the better.

He would merely be the vessel for Kai's power, and Kai waited up above to make sure that it happened.

And then he would get what he always wanted.

As Dalton shot a blast of winter's storm into the sky, joining the battle, it replied. Gusts of wind boomed from the storm clouds which loomed and sunk lower and lower into the battlefield below. Screams erupted as the temperature dropped so suddenly that even Dalton felt the keen sting of winter's wrath.

And then a light came down from the clouds, as if the Gods were somehow up above and were descending their fury onto the world below. It was certain that they were angry, that the world was so full of hatred and anger that peace could not be met. And that the evil king refused to accept that death was the only fate that he had ever had the course for.

Blinding, he shielded his eyes as frost covered the lands. His snow had not stuck.

But he quickly remembered—and realized—that this is not his snow. But that meant it could only be one other person's...

My Gods, he was so tired of fucking ghosts coming back to life. Why could they not just die like normal people—

"King Finn!" a voice sounded from the winding castle staircase above him.

Even amongst the battle raging, Dalton could spot King Finn's golden armor. Shadows swarmed around him, a powerful barrier to any harm coming to him. They would take care of any enemies first. It was cowardice as its finest, the armor all for show.

King Finn had no power in the Ten Kingdoms anymore. Not anymore.

For the King of Snow had returned, and he was about to get his vengeance.

CHAPTER SIXTY-FOUR

King Finn howled. Vibrations of horror and rage pulsated through him with a relentless purpose. It had been over a century since he had laid eyes on Cian Saphirrus. The final battle between them...

Well, Finn had always suspected that it was not the end of the war which waged between them.

Finn had been so focused on Dalton—the other Saphirrus king, he supposed—that he had left the door wide open for an old enemy to take him by surprise.

And oh was he surprised.

And it angered him so.

Lifting his arms, his shadows followed in suit. He could see the war slowing around him as the King of Snow landed in-front of him as if he were sent by the Gods themselves. He tried to be nonchalant, but even Cian's greatest time of power had been difficult for Finn to combat. He was the only one to ever truly banish him, and it had taken decades for Finn to regain his strength and power. Him being here now complicated things. But he would not show fear.

No, he would use this as an opportunity to show strength.

One by one, the mercenaries stopped to stare, as did the armies of the Ten Kingdoms. Silence fell over the land, eerie and horrifying.

And then Finn saw his breath. The world went colder. It had been snowing for weeks, nothing that he was not used to. But now the flakes were stronger, the breeze colder, and he could see his breath starting to form in-front of him.

The snow before had been nothing—conjured by a boy in comparison to what was falling before his very eyes...

As the winds picked up, he spun around, commanding his army in panic to not relent. Instinct took over, he no longer felt so royal and godly. "Do not stop! I never told you to stop!" But his voice was lost to the howling winds of the storm that started to rage with the most aggression that he had seen in one hundred years.

Returning to face the front of the Cloud Castle once more, Finn stopped dead in his tracks. Before him the crowd had parted, and a dark figure walked toward him.

Finn blinked twice.

Rubbed his eyes.

And stuck his neck out forward.

There was no possible way that it could be...

But there was.

Somehow.

Someway.

And either way, he was going to have to face the wrath of Old Gods.

"Hello King Finn," the voice sounded as none other than Cian Saphirrus materialized in-front of him.

Finn, for the first time in one hundred years, found himself without words.

"Have you missed me?" Cian said softly.

However, he did not wait for Finn's reply. Extending his arms, ice cold wind and snow blasted from his fingertips, and sent him hundreds of feet behind where he had stood.

And on cue, the world seemed to take a collective gasp before chaos erupted.

CHARMAINE HAD NEVER HAD SO many questions in her life. It was the battle of the ghosts. The battle for the Ten Kingdoms. The battle to find her friends. *Where in the name of the Gods were they?*

People—soldiers, mercenaries—were running everywhere. She found herself bodied at every angle, the noise itself overrunning her senses. There was no way that she would be able to use her power amongst this chaos. Her confidence dwindled at every step, fear beginning to overtake her. Hands shaking, she took deep breaths as she tried to run back toward the castle. She could hear the message being passed along to everyone, a very simple command, probably coming from Randolph himself.

Retreat.

There was no place for war among the descendants of the Gods.

As she got closer to the castle doors, the shoving became worse and worse. She began to struggle, trying to meander her body through the waves of people just as desperate to flee this situation as the next.

Finn had been blown backwards with such power that the whole ground had quaked. Dalton's rage was palpable when his power was the strongest, but *this*? This was other worldly. This was driven by some primal hatred so dark that the whole of the world felt it. This was far darker than anything that Dalton Saphirrus was capable of.

As she continued to try to push herself forward, three knights began to shove their way. Their armor was heavier than hers, their stature more towering, and their shoulders wider. As she lifted her gaze to try to push past them, or at least wait until they had done their shoving so that she could too be on her way. However, they began to shout, the terror being too much for men too it would seem. With the jutting of a shoulder—intentional or not—the next thing Charmaine knew she was splayed on the ground. The wind knocked out of her, she tried to gasp and cry out for help.

She had envisioned the way that she may die thousands of times in her life, but being trampled at the reawakening of the Kings of Old was most definitely not on her list.

After seconds that seemed like hours, two feet appeared before her, and the crowd's chaos began to slow.

"Dalton?" she whispered, sure that he had found her among the chaos. He always did.

Though as her rescuer bent down to help her stand, she was shocked to find long fire red hair and green eyes, far much less ghostly than it had been hours before when she had seen her last.

"Try again," Queen Ciara said as they made their way to stand together, hand in hand.

THE QUEEN of Fury stood before them in shadowed glory. It was as if a mist stood around her, the same shadows that lived around Finn had been stolen from her. All that remained around her was shrouded power. Even her skin seemed to be less gray, as if she herself was an imagining.

But Charmaine knew a real person from a ghost.

And Ciara was very much real.

Her persona was utterly haunting, to see the Queen that legends had sung about for hundreds of years. Charmaine had been most of her young life learning about the young Queen, mourning her, and singing the songs of her life.

And here she was, before them, and asking for help.

"Cian gave me a window," she said, her voice pleading with each and every one of them. "I just need to take another shot at him. My shadows and his... Well, without getting into it... I think that they can turn on him enough to weaken him and his forces."

"And what will that do?" Randolph asked, his eyes wide as if he truly did not believe who he was speaking to.

Charmaine was still reeling that all of this was happening. As she opened her mouth to speak, Kai roared overhead as if he were impatient. What was he waiting for?

Ciara turned to face Randolph, her face returning some emotion that she could not place. It was as if the queen knew him in some capacity. Which Charmaine knew was impossible...

"Randolph Eniar, it will give you all the window to take Finn down once and for all. The war waged between us has been long and hard, with hundreds of years of bloody battles where someone always loses in the worst ways possible. But you all..." She extended her arms regally, gesturing to all that stood before her. The room was filled not with all of the official leaders of the Ten Kingdoms—no, they were scattered due to the nature of the first attacks—but the heroes of Charmaine's own life.

Randolph, Elena, Reine, Lawton, Dalton, and even Carinthya and Bairre crowded around the old queen. A part of Charmaine had wanted to retrieve Cyril, but there was no time. And he was unwell, Dalton had essentially forbidden him from joining them on the battlefield. Besides, his gifts were too precious. He might know something—Dalton had insisted—though Cyril had rather doubted it since they had taken his voice from breaking thinker laws before.

And she did not know how he would react to Cian's return.

"You all are special," Ciara said. "More special than anyone of you could ever know. And more powerful than Finn himself. Think about yourselves and think about you as a collective whole. You come from all walks to life."

She gestured to Charmaine and Lawton. "Two commoner's with a power."

She gestured to Randolph and Reine. "Siblings who have survived it all, who share a lust for the flame and are not afraid of a little heat that the world sometimes brings us."

She gestured to Carinthya and Bairre. "To unlikely friendship and camaraderie, you are a testament to life's reality of shitty circumstances and the strength we must bare in order to survive."

She gestured to Elena. "To the women who rule the world. I know for a fact that it is not easy."

And then she turned to look at Dalton, of whom Charmaine was sure that she was looking directly at Cian, despite the fact that he was on the battlefield. "And to you, who shows over and over again the beauty of finding joy in the darkest of times. Your gifts, Dalton Saphirrus, might be most important of all."

"So I offer to you, my new friends, to take to the battlefield with me. To fight for the world that you want to live in, and the world that I swore I left behind."

Dalton kneeled first, his head bowed in the utmost respect. Soft curls that had been dampened by the sweat of battle hung freely from his forehead. Before anyone else had the chance to follow in-suit, Ciara walked forward him and gestured for him to rise with her sword.

Dalton stood slowly, his gaze filled with wonder and admiration as he gazed upon the most famous ruler that the continent had ever known.

"Dalton Saphirrus," she said. "It is time I am reunited with my husband, and you your ancestor."

CHAPTER SIXTY-FIVE

Ciara watched the battlefield from the lower tower as snow collided with shadow over and over and over again. It took everything in her not to run out there, to get involved... But it was absolutely critical that she stayed hidden. The one advantage that she had over her father this time was the element of surprise that he had over her the last... Surprise. And without surprise, this would all be for nothing.

The years of haunting, watching silently. They had killed her internally. She had been planning this since the moment her father drove that blasted dagger through her heart. Had been envisioning over and over the look of utmost surprise on her face, that she watched her beloved Cian live a half-life without her. It had broken her more times than she could account for, to not intervene or let him know she was there. There had been one instance where she almost did, where he looked the utmost suspicious of her presence because he knew every piece of her, but she had then pulled back. Scared.

Cian was the only person in the world that had the capacity to make her afraid.

Shaking her head, she brought herself back to watching the battle below. She knew that she could bring her father to his knees. She had done it once before, and she would do it again.

Cian, on the other hand, had her breathless whereas her father filled her with rage. She dreamt of running out to him... Touching him for the first time in over a century...

She rolled her shoulders back.

Focus.

She had to focus.

This was the war that she had been waiting for her entire life, and she would not falter. This would be the end of her father. And Gods willing, she could find peace once more.

THEY HAD a window of time to regroup before the battle resumed, Cian's distraction tiring Finn more and more by the second. Ciara gave them half an hour of freedom, and then had disappeared into a swarm of her own shadows.

Dalton had promptly grabbed Charmaine's hand. She whispered, "Where are we going?"

"Out the back door," he said, an eyebrow raised without humor.

"Are we to come back?" she asked, suddenly afraid of his demeanor. She would have expected him to make light of this situation, not to be so serious.

"Certainly," he said softly. "Though I cannot say that I am ecstatic about the possibility."

As they made their way outside, the storm surged, but she was not cold as she had been when Cian first arrived. Dalton's power projected a bubble of a kinder winter around them, a protection from the harshness of the world around them.

"Sit with me Char," Dalton said, gesturing to the ground below. "We might not get another chance."

She sat down without a second thought. "Dalton, you are scaring me."

The bed of snow was not cold, not as she knew it to be.

"Do not be frightened, I just needed to get out of there, for just a moment before we have to go back."

"Do you think Cian is going to beat him?"

Dalton huffed a laugh. "I think my great—however many greats it is at this point—grandfather is just buying us time. Giving us time to regroup. Having fun with him."

"Hmph," Charmaine mumbled. "Sounds like he is your relative after all."

"The resemblance is striking I have to admit."

She agreed with that sentiment wholeheartedly. Extending a hand in front of her, she let the slow falling snowflakes melt on her skin. A refresh of some sorts.

As a girl, there had been times that she had played in the snow, but she had never given it much thought. Snow angels, snowballs... it had been a source of inexhaustible magic. Fun. And when she reflected on it now, she only thought of James and the joyous moments that made up who she was at her core.

Even now, the snowflakes had blended together into a fluffy magic which breathed in the air and melted softly on her skin. They were not just flakes, she realized, they were life itself. Life created by Dalton. Life created by magic.

She had found it to be gorgeously divine, but now the frost the lay on the ground did not bring her any uncomfortable coldness. Instead, it had only allowed her to be more free, and to experience winter the way that it was meant to be experienced.

In beauty.

In joy.

With the ones that you loved.

Hands intertwined, Dalton Saphirrus laid her down slowly on the bed of snow which lain beneath them on the ground. As her violet armor touched the snow, she was shocked to feel that it did not get wet, or was it even affected by the flakes.

"How?" she whispered, but not before he had the chance to answer her.

"Magic."

"I quite like magic," she whispered, in wonder at his deep blue gaze and dark hair.

"I do too," he replied, his mouth centimeters above her own. "When it is being nice."

Much like the first day that she had met him, in the ballroom, it felt very reminiscent of that. He smelled then, as he did now, of blueberries and snow. It was as clean and sweet as the fresh air of winter, awakening while simultaneously taking your breath away.

But when she looked upon him, she no longer just saw the chaotic young prince with the uncontrollable power. Instead, she saw the king, the young man who had overcome so much adversity and trauma in order to rise to who he was today. Yes, his eyes still danced with the same shadows of his past and the playfulness remained, but there was so much more to him than darkness and snow.

He was Dalton Saphirrus: triumphant, fierce, loving, passionate, witty, and completely and utterly hers.

And nothing, no evil, could take that away from them.

"Where did you go?" he asked, his gaze filled with nothing but admiration. "Is it the battle?"

"Nowhere, I did not go anywhere," she said softly. "I was just thinking of you."

He raised an eyebrow, his freckles scrunching across his nose. "What were you thinking about?" Mischief danced in his voice, striking through her like a shooting star. "Specifically, to me..."

With a long finger, he began slowly tracing hearts across her cheekbones. The snow continued to fall softly, landing in her hair before softly fading away to water.

As he drew his second heart on her cheek, she slowly began to sit up. Before he had a chance to combat her with another comment, question, or sweet gesture, she decided that she had enough waiting. They were running out of time, Finn's mercenaries were on the Ninth Kingdom's doorstep, and Cian was only buying them moments...

She had been trying to achieve perfection and feared failure when she fell short. But Dalton had shown her that to be perfection was to be inhuman, and that falling apart was a part of growing.

And that it was okay to be broken.

And that it was just as okay to heal.

So she leaned forward, her gaze never once breaking from his. He tried to lean forward, to kiss her himself, but this was something that she wanted to lead the charge on.

He had healed her, rescued her.

It was time that she rescued him.

Chapter Sixty-Six

When Charmaine's lips touched Dalton's she was transported. Memories flashed in her gaze, her thoughts whirling while her mind left her to go elsewhere. She knew that her body was still kissing him—feverish and filled with everything but goodbyes—but visions began to appear before her.

As Dalton began to run his long fingers through her hair, intertwining and pulling at her raven curls, she felt herself begin to slip away completely. She could not make out what he was saying, but she felt the panic rising in the air around them. Snow swirled—fear blistering in the wind that he had conjured—as her head hit the ground softly, and the vision took over.

SHE KNEW SHE WAS DREAMING, *despite this place looking the same as when she had fallen asleep. Dalton no longer laid beside her; the bed of snow clear from any tracks that he would have left behind him.*

And Charmaine knew that he would never leave her again. He had said it over and over, but there was a different aura around it now. There was no question, no ambiguity. She had just heard him—seen him—panic stricken over her collapse. But now, he was nowhere to be found.

Life or death, Dalton Saphirrus belonged to Charmaine Grimes, and she belonged to him.

Sitting up slowly, she realized that she was colder than she had been with Dalton. Another indicator of a dream. It had been so long since she had one, that she was surprised that she was able to discern the difference between them and reality. Maybe it had been the awakening of her power, and her ability to embrace it, for she could no longer be tricked by fickle things of the mind.

"Ah sister, always a skeptic," a voice that she had not heard in so long sounded behind her.

As she spun and faced the woods, she broke into immediate sobs, for none other than her brother James Grimes stood before her. He looked good. Strong. Healthy. Alive.

Even happy.

Though he was not fully whole, his body a degree softer and lighter than one would be in life.

"You are a ghost," she observed, frozen in place. No longer did she feel the chill of the air, despite seeing her breath. She was alive, and here with him.

And her brother, despite being gone, was here with her.

Extending his arms, he took a few steps toward her. "Give me a hug, Charmaine."

She scrambled to get up, rather ungrateful. "Jamie," she sobbed. "I have been so lost without you." Tears tumbled down her face, her voice cracking with emotion. There was so much to say, she was not even sure where to begin.

"You have not been lost at all, Char," he said, stroking the back of her head in that comforting way that he did. "Your

road has always been difficult, for mother and father always knew it would be. But there is so much that they never told you —that I do not have time to tell you—but you know as well as anyone that you choose your family, despite being born into it."

"Dalton has become my family. Elena, Cyril, Lawton, Randolph..." She paused, tears tumbling down her face. She did not want to hurt him, even in death. "I found that I have different parents."

Softly humming, James put a finger to her lips to quiet her down. "They chose you as much as you chose them. I was so angry when I first left this world, after being promised so many things from visions. But I so quickly realized after I departed that they were just things I saw, never things that I was owed." He backed up, looking Charmaine directly in the eyes. "But you have earned these things Charmaine. You have earned your peace and the life that you are going to live. It is my greatest wish that you live it, and enjoy every day like it could be your last."

"It has been so hard..." she drawled, her gaze tear-soaked. "Jamie, my other parents... We are not brother and sister after all."

Anger flashed in his eyes. "Charmaine, not even the stars and the heavens themselves could make you not my sister."

She smiled as he ran a hand over the side of her head. She could see that he was trying to do everything he could to comfort her. It was working. Nobody knew her like James. "I am happy for you," he said. "Truly. You are blessed to have been given a second chance at a family, Charmaine. I am happy that you get another chance at life with people that love you."

All she could manage was a soft and tearful, "Thank you."

"You have risen above it time and time again," James said. "I am running out of time sister, but I wanted to tell you

to that family—even though it can be found and chosen—can also be literal. Look for those with the violet eyes and trust them. Trust them with your life. The Gods chose you and blessed you, but also ripped away from others to set the course of your path. Trust in the these words. I wish I could be more specific."

"I have never heard of a ghost being anything less than vague," she said with a sad laugh. "Thank you James, for what you did for me in life, and what you do for me in death."

"Sister," he said, kissing her head. Though she could not feel his lips on the crown of her head, she imagined it well all the same. "The pleasure has been all mine."

And then as fast as he had come, he was gone.

Forever.

Charmaine sunk to her knees.

CHAPTER SIXTY-SEVEN

Charmaine had collapsed in his arms, and once again Dalton was helpless in the face of magic. At first, fear controlled him, like it always had when something was completely and utterly out of his control. But then, the dust settled, and he found himself watching her rest. On occasion she would mumble, inaudible, but proof that she was ok. It was the peace of the moment, whatever magic had taken over was giving her something that she needed. He did not need a thinker to understand that something greater was at work here.

After what felt like hours, but he was certain was just a few minutes, Charmaine gasped and sat up.

"Hey," he started, helping her sit up. "Where did you go?"

Charmaine rubbed the side of her head, as if something had impacted it. It took her a moment to piece it together—whatever she had just experienced—and then she spoke, her voice filled with emotion.

"I was with James," she whispered, her violet eyes brimming with tears.

"James?" Dalton could not hide the shock in his voice. "To see ghosts as powerful as Cian and Ciara was one thing, but to be pulled in with a ghost..."

"It was as if he were restless, as if that gave him his power. He just needed to speak to me one last time..."

"Charmaine, do not say it was the last time, you will see him again."

She touched his arm, genuine and soft in her gesture. "I do not think I will, and I think him and I are finally at peace."

"Are you okay?" He was not sure what else there was today. His mind was spinning.

"I will be," she said. "I know what I have to do. What we have to do."

Dalton backed up. "And what is that, darling?"

"We have the kill the king, of course."

Dalton stood rapidly, the storm surging around them and Kai roaring ahead once more. It was time. "I forgot to tell you how much I adore this armor. Violet is your color."

Her cheeks flashed pink. "Later for compliments, Dalton." She turned and looked back at the castle as she stood. Her raven hair flowed in the snowstorm. Dalton so wished that he had the capabilities of capturing the image before him.

Later. He would compliment her later *and* paint it.

"Are you ready for war, Charmaine Grimes?"

She turned to face him. Her gaze all steel and thought. Whatever James must have said to her clearly empowered her. It brought her more than peace, it brought her power.

"I have to run an errand first," she said as she began to trudge through the snow.

"An errand?" He ran to follow, to keep up.

Quickly she spun, catching him as he caught up to her. "It is time I borrowed your chaos a little bit. I will need it."

And then she pecked a kiss on his cheek, before turning to battle her way through the snow once more.

CHARMAINE HAD TAKEN off most suspiciously when they arrived back to the castle. He was tempted to follow her, for chaos called to him in every moment of life. But it was clear that his time to shine, his time to own the spotlight, was dimming. While her light shined brighter, his light began to flicker. And frankly, he was grateful for the change.

Dalton quickly collected his friends as she ran off to do...whatever it was that she needed to do. And as Dalton and his friends walked out of the castle, an army following behind them once more, he smiled.

The battle raged between Finn and Cian, and as they approached the battlefield to rejoin the cause Cian looked behind him. With a smile that hauntingly reminded Dalton very much of himself, he was gone.

Dalton inhaled a sharp breath. Cian... *Just left them like this?*

He shook off his distraught, his fear returning quickly. Cian had been able to hold Finn and his forces off at bay with ease, and now they were left to their own devices.

So Dalton did the only thing that he could think of. He turned to face his friends, and then they ran directly into the line of Finn's power.

JUST AS QUICKLY AS he arrived, Cian left.

Finn found himself laughing as Dalton Saphirrus and his armies emerged and began to charge. Though death's cruel favor was that he was beginning to deteriorate. Maybe

Cian thought that he would be depleted by such a war between the two of them. And sure, it had put a strain on Finn, but now that Cian was gone?

Well, let the battle begin.

Lifting his arms, his shadows called to him. Swarming, they pooled behind him like a deep ocean, almost hissing with anticipation before the attack.

Finn gritted his teeth, his armor fueled by the dark power which lingered in his veins ignited with vengeance. This was the moment. The Ten Kingdoms would finally be his.

And then he paused. His gaze diverting the furthest that they could to the flamed curls and porcelain skin that emerged from the castle gate. Shadows clung to this figure...

His shadows.

Suddenly, the breath left him and he realized that he was truly never fearful of Cian at all. Sure, that had been a good fight, and he had even been surprised by the strength of the battle. But the figure that loomed behind Dalton's forces had him completely and utterly terrified. A face that he never expected to see again.

In over one hundred years, King Finn had never been surprised. Until now.

She held within her hand a dagger riddled with chains and diamonds, the hilt containing a stone the color of Cian's eyes. Slowly, she rose it above her head and smiled the most sinister of all smiles.

Ciara Saphirrus, first and only of her name, called this battle to war.

And Finn was terrified.

OBLIVION.

That was what Charmaine Grimes descended into, dagger in hand after running to her chambers to collect it.

It started as it always did, like taking off a coat on a winters evening. It was fresh at first, and then it became harsh. Ice coated through her veins, her blood running cold until she was not sure it was even pumping beneath her porcelain skin. And then it started. Well, she started.

Inch by inch her power began to seep through her as she let it do what she never did. She lost control.

As she walked onto the battlefield, she let everyone see what she could do.

She could disappear.

Dalton was smiling.

The Violet Queen had come.

And she had brought the Queen of Fury with her.

Ciara had caught up to them quickly, her gaze and challenge fueling with them. It was unlikely that Cian had depleted Finn, for he was relentless. But it had served as the greatest thing of all: a distraction and a chance for her to recenter.

He had given her the chance to succeed. And she would not waste the opportunity.

Mercenaries began to file in, swords clanging and war ravaging. She could see Elena's water flying into bodies, and Dalton working with her by freezing anyone to be touched by her water. Randolph's flames blasted, anguish pouring out of him as much as it was fear.

And Charmaine did what she knew that she could, something that she once feared but now welcome. She changed, let it overtake her.

She turned invisible, and she welcomed it as she strode toward the evil dark king.

He did not see her coming, his gaze focused on wherever he thought his long-gone daughter was amongst the chaos.

And then when she was just within steps of the evil king, she unveiled herself.

She swore she heard Dalton cheering. The whole of the battle seemingly looking over their shoulder as the war raged on, watching her.

Everyone watching the invisible girl, how about *that*.

Gaze on King Finn, she looked up and challenged him with her violet irises alone. Though an emotion that existed on his face was different than what she expected as he was able to meet his match. It was elation, like he had been waiting for this all along. He reached his hands toward her, shadows beginning to fly as she reached for the invisibility coated bejeweled dagger at her side.

The dagger is the key.

And the key needed to be driven through his heart.

And then something—*no*—someone, jumped in-front of her. She screamed as the pain of the realization ripped through her like a dagger would, and the world around them exploded into a light so white and full of winder wonder that it was a miracle that it was not blinding.

But it was not aimed at King Finn—*no*—for it was his face that looked at her in complete and utter wonder. Was it her that had been hurt? Did he win? Was it going to end like this—

Looking up in complete horror at him, she looked down at herself and saw the whole in her chest. Light blasted through her armors violet plated chest, a circle the size of a fist, and she heard someone screaming.

Vision blurring, she saw Randolph at his knees, crawling toward someone who was not her.

A body mere feet from her, someone who had told her that she was going to do this—someone who had believed in her since the beginning of all of this. The one who never doubted her power even for a second.

Dalton Saphirrus.

Her soulmate.

Her soon-to-be husband.

Her king.

Her best friend.

He lay here, his hands outreached as if to say "take it". But take what?

And then she felt it. She saw it. Hands outstretched, they began to frost.

"USE IT!" Elena screamed, running for Randolph as he cradled Dalton's body. "CHARMAINE GRIMES, EMBRACE YOUR DESTINY!"

Dalton. Elena. Randolph. Lawton. Cyril. Ciara. Cian. Gwendolyn. James. Her mother. Her father. Tommy. The people of Brinn. The people of the First. The continent. They all flowed through her, and she suddenly understood the weight that she had tried to help Dalton grapple with.

Except she knew in her heart that it was not a curse for her like it had been for him. It was gift.

All of this, this life.

It was a gift.

One that she was not going to waste.

Lifting her right hand at King Finn, she smirked, suddenly understanding everything and more. It was why she was born, she realized, why she was so drawn to Dalton Saphirrus from the very beginning.

Yes, it was love in its truest form.

But it was also destiny.

And destiny was all.

Lifting her head, her gaze settled on Kai who continued to dance above her, his roar loud and his gaze fixated on them below.

It started slow, her invisibility somehow acting as a

charge, a conduit. She was strong enough to do this. She was all powerful.

She was the Queen of Frost.

As she raised her right hand, surveying where King Finn's heart was located in proximity to her, her left raised in assassination.

And she felt herself suddenly go cold as ice.

And she smiled.

"You have taken everything from this world," she growled, tears flowing down her face as she thought of James. Her mother. Her father. Brinn. "And now you are going to pay the ultimate price."

Speechless, King Finn froze, and she realized that she had already done that. Frost began to build on his cheekbones, his red hair suddenly becoming thick with icicles as if he had been out in a snowstorm. Flurries fell around them in a beautiful array of destiny, and she could not have dreamt up a more beautiful scene.

She suddenly knew what she needed to do, as if Dalton had passed along all of the knowledge that he harbored along with his power. But the secrets, they kept no pain with him. They were liberating. As if they were finally home.

Unsheathing the dagger that sat on her thigh, she strode toward King Finn slowly. She wanted him to see this. She wanted their people to see this.

Everyone was getting their lives back.

For the cost of one.

As he continued to freeze, his eyes wavered as she crouched in front of him, eye to eye.

"This is for James," she shouted as she drove what she knew now to be Ciara's dagger into his shoulder, his body cracking like the ice that sat atop a lake. With a deep breath out, he groaned as he became solid ice, and she raised the dagger which Gwendolyn had been slain above her head.

"And this is for Ciara," she screamed, "Long may she rest in peace, and long may you burn in the shadows!"

Then she drove the dagger into his heart, as he shattered into a million pieces almost instantly.

The dagger is the key. Revenge was the secret. The dagger had killed Ciara, and now it had righted the wrongs of her father's doing. She smiled. It was over.

And as Charmaine Grimes body hit the ground with the force of King Finn's demise, the rest of the world lit up in flames, as the dragon burned all of the mercenaries to the ground.

CHAPTER SIXTY-EIGHT

R andolph stood at the gates of the Ninth Kingdom. He did not even look back, shedding the terrible memories which plagued him there for many years.

This run, the siege, this trip to begin taking back the world as they wanted to now know it... Well, there was something powerful about it.

His power. He felt like he was reclaiming his power.

Sprinting to catch up with the others, he let his left hand fall behind him casually. With a grunt, flames exploded out of his fingertips, and spread in a horizontal line. Commanding, he silently directed them to burn higher and higher, surrounding the castle in a wall of fire.

That should hold them off, momentarily.

Inhaling the smoke from behind him, Randolph found himself to be unaffected. His breath came to him as clearly as it would in all air, a sign that he had truly come to take what was his and give nothing back.

As the tree-line became mere steps away, Randolph paused. Sweat trickled down the side of his temple, though the wind from the chaos he had created only made him feel alive and awake.

As he moved his head to turn, a familiar voice sounded from the trees.

"Randolph?"

Nearly falling to his knees, Randolph beheld Charmaine Grimes. Stumbling, he ran to her and fell at her feet. His head rested gently on her thighs, and he somehow found that he did not care if it would be considered improper.

Improprieties, he decided then and there, did not exist when it came to family.

And that was what Charmaine Grimes was to him, a part of his twisted and messed up family. And oh was he so glad to see her.

Running a hand lovingly through the tops of his brown hair, Charmaine stood there as he trembled. Letting the pain of his life, and recounting all that he had run away from, wash over him, she remained steadfast.

"I am so—" He found himself stuttering through tears, letting the final sobs escape him before beginning to get his breath back. "Proud of you, my friend."

Carefully, she peeled his face off of her legs and crouched down to be eye-level with him. Her violet gaze shone with a light and recognition that Randolph had not seen in her for some time. Despite all that she continued to endure, it was as if she picked up more power along the way.

With a soft smile, she grabbed his hands and kissed them. The breeze picked up around them, as if the Gods themselves had approved of this moment. As if they were watching it.

"You picked me up when I was falling apart," she whispered, tears glistening. "Now let me do the same for you."

With her hands interlaced on his, she heaved and he

went with her. Standing, as he caught his breath, she threw herself around him.

Wind howling, Randolph could not ignore the sounds of destiny. Whatever had happened, and whatever would happen, would remain uncertain. Yet, there was one thing that was positively certain.

Their family was not to be broken up.

Ever again.

THEY WALKED IN TANDEM, hand in hand, to the infirmary where the King of Snow waited. The Dalton version, that was, for the Cian version had yet to be seen after disappearing.

As they walked in, Vanellope stood in recognition. The rest of those who had been sitting followed. The utmost sign of respect.

"Charmaine Grimes," she said. "Thank you."

And then one by one, everyone lowered their heads. As she turned to Randolph, rather in embarrassment, she blushed because he was doing the same.

After a moment's pause—and of minor humiliation— just as they had fallen, one by one they lifted.

"Where is he?" he asked.

"Come," Vanellope said softly. "Let me take you to my healer."

Eithne, the old woman with the hood on, lifted her gaze to meet Charmaine's as they entered Dalton's chambers in the infirmary wing of the cloud castle. Charmaine was immediately taken by how beautiful the woman was, she looked as though she were about thirty years old. However, she had to fight a gasp releasing from her mouth when she removed her hood and unveiled pointed ears. She had never seen such a thing before. Randolph paused beside her as if he were considering, after the turmoil they had been through, whether or not it was even possible.

"My husband had something like you do, a quiet fire that burns steady, and with love. There is much love in your heart."

"Is that why I came here, to hear you say that to me?"

"King Finn wanted something," she whispered, sounding very far away. "It is something unlike another treasure I once knew, yet entirely different. A weapon of murder. A weapon used like none other to take the life of someone, drain them entirely. You know of such a thing, you must?" The question hung heavy in the air.

"Charmaine, I need to know, but I do not want you to speak it in case I am made to speak against my wishes. Is there a weapon you are aware of? One that has taken lives in vain?"

The dagger immediately flashed into her mind, and her heart sunk as it reminded her of Dalton. It was the weapon that she had taken from the mercenaries when they first attacked the castle, glistening and beautiful it had been then. The thing that had been coated in magic apparently, and had let to Gwendolyn losing her life, when it should have been Charmaine in her place.

"That weapon," Eithne said. "That weapon must be buried, so that they may know peace."

"They?" Charmaine asked.

"When he wakes up," she said, acknowledging the body of the king which laid behind the white satin curtain which hung in the corner of the room. "He will tell you, and he will get the chance to say goodbye too."

CHAPTER SIXTY-NINE

Dalton awoke a few hours later.

He felt...*warm*?

As he tried to sit up quickly, he was overcome with seeing stars. And not the stars that he wanted to see. And as he came to vision, he was startled by another sight that he truly was not interested in seeing.

Randolph Eniar.

"Gods," Dalton moaned, rubbing the side of his temple. "Am I dead?"

"No," Randolph said rather dryly, reaching over to assist Dalton to sit up.

"Where is everyone?" Dalton asked. "And what happened?"

Randolph smiled, his eyes darting to about three feet away where Charmaine was asleep in a chair. "Ask her when she wakes up."

Dalton smiled. "So it worked then?"

"What do you mean it worked?" Randolph's voice was calm but laced with concern.

Instead of using words, exhaustion flooding over him,

Dalton lifted his hand and tried to conjure a small icicle. It had been as easy at one point as breathing. Yet, when he called upon his ancient power, nothing came.

And as Randolph raised his brow in confusion, Dalton smiled and threw his head back.

"Thank the Gods," he whispered.

"Dalton?" Panic ensued in Randolph's voice. He was observant enough to understand what Dalton had just tried to do. "Dalton is it—"

"Let us see," Dalton mumbled. He drew upon his power as he had done for many years and extended his arms feverishly—almost comically manic—over and over again as nothing came out.

"Holy shit," Randolph swore after flinching and realizing he was safe from an icy blast. "Are you—"

"I am free," Dalton whispered, looking at his hands in wonder. "Free at last."

"When you jumped in front of her, when you gave her your strength with an outstretched hand... Well, the dragon gave it to you did he not?" Cyril's figure appeared in the doorway.

Randolph just looked confused. "What in the name of the Gods are you two talking about?"

"I did not know if it would work, dragons are most tricky you know."

"So your big bargain with Kai was to give you the power to give your power away?" Randolph's voice was latent with astonishment.

"I knew destiny had some role for me in this," Dalton said, his cheeks flushing with color and excitement. "But I knew that it was never my destiny to kill the King. No, it was always Charmaine's. The Violet Queen always was going to save the world. I was merely the impetuous."

"The King of Snow is coming," Cyril said softly.

"He was risen from the death of his father," Dalton said, fake cheers-ing glasses in the air.

Randolph was utterly speechless. As he opened his mouth to ask another question, Cyril took a step forward and put his old hand on Randolph's shoulder.

"Randolph, if you do not mind, might I request that you give Dalton and I a moment before the celebrations begin."

"Celebrations?" Dalton asked, his voice inquisitive. "I just woke up."

"The King is dead," Cyril said. "Our heroes must be celebrated."

Randolph nodded, clearly seeing something between them that need not be interrupted. As his frame left the room, Cyril said down, his expression grave.

"I hoped Dalton, that I would be able to stay with you forever."

"Well, you can, can you not?" Dalton's voice began to dwindle, like a child's did when they realized they were being punished rather than celebrated.

"Nobody should live forever, Dalton, and I have been around a long time." Tears welled in his eyes, and Dalton knew that this conversation was far graver than he could have ever imagined. "When I first came to the First Kingdom, I was employed by Ciara, before she left us. When Charmaine used her dagger on Finn—ingenious by the way —the magic that had kept Cian and Ciara here, as well as Finn, was broken at long last. I felt it too, for my life has always been tied to theirs, I suppose. In more ways than one."

Dalton turned his body, anchoring himself so that he could hold his old friends hands. He knew what Cyril was getting at without saying it. "There is so much that I want to say to you, Cyril... I thought we would have time. A lifetime. My lifetime." Disbelief clouded in his gaze, he was sure that his lips were trembling with emotion. "Where will you go?"

"You—although the grandest pain in my ass boy—are the greatest achievement of my lifetime. You are a son to me, the fire that I needed before I left this world, and the king of all king's." Cyril took a shuddering breath, saying all that he needed to say and more with that gesture alone. "If I were to sit here and tell you everything that I loved about you boy, I would never leave, and I must."

Seeing Dalton's hesitation, he spoke again. "Dalton, you do not need me anymore. You may want me, and best believe I want to spend more than one lifetime with you too. But I serve the King of Snow, and he has granted me passage to peace."

"Then why do you seem like you are asking me for permission?" Dalton sniffled.

"Because you are the King of Snow too, and I need you to know that where I am going, I will not be able to be reached."

Dalton did not know what to say. He never knew a world without Cyril. How could he repay him? Thank him? Tell him all that he deserved? Dalton stuttered, and Cyril sat there patiently as he always did, waiting for him to find the words that he needed to say.

Quietly, Dalton began to sob, not letting go of Cyril's wrinkly hands. After a few moments, Dalton spoke, his voice barely recognizable as a lifetime of service and friendship was felt between the both of them.

"Cyril?" he asked, his blue eyes an ocean of sadness.

"Yes, my boy?"

"I love you," he sobbed, putting his head to Cyril's hands.

"And I you," Cyril replied softly. "And I you."

CHARMAINE AWOKE TO A SILENT ROOM, alone.

Panic washed over her. *Where was Dalton? Was he alright? Where had Randolph gone?*

As she whipped her head around, Carinthya entered the room. She was dressed in a black gown, her eyes filled with sadness and acceptance. "Charmaine? I was sent to retrieve you."

"Is Dalton okay?"

"He is fine, or he will be." Carinthya extended a hand to grab hers. "I was sent to grab you by him actually."

"Where is your shadow?" Charmaine asked, referring to Bairre. Something had shifted between them, Carinthya stood here now more sure of herself. Was it the battle? Or had something else transpired—

Carinthya's face turned a rather sickly shade of green.

"Oh Gods," Charmaine said, reaching her hand out to grab Carinthya's. "I meant no offense."

"No, I understand completely. I have been rather attached, well, these last few years."

"Can I ask why?" Charmaine could not keep the questioning out of her voice.

"I realized, on our way here to the Ninth, that he did not actually love me. He merely was acting out of duty, a servant of Ciara's."

Pain thrummed in Charmaine's heart. "Carinthya, I am so sorry."

"I never knew what it was like to be truly in love, Charmaine," she said, but not with any contempt in her voice. "For so many years, I was a tool to warp my father's opinions and shape policy. Nobody saw me as anything more than a means to an end."

"But you are back now."

"I am," she said softly, her dark blue eyes looking so much like her brother's that Charmaine felt as though she were speaking to him directly. "And I mean to stay this time, and become me. Whatever that may look like—whoever she may look like—I do not know."

"Come with us," Charmaine pleaded softly. The implication clear. Come to the First Kingdom.

"I would like that very much."

A singular tear rolled down Carinthya's cheek, and Charmaine reached out to wipe it off. As she did so, Carinthya caught her hand with her own, and breathed in with her eyes shut for just a moment. It took all of what was holding Charmaine together to even recognize the power of the moment, two women coming together to make peace with old wounds.

As if reading her mind, Carinthya spoke, "Can you stand? I am afraid if we linger too long talking about the past, we will miss the present."

Charmaine stood shakily, but she was able to manage. When her feet hit the floor, magic pulsated through her. But it was not her feet that went invisible with the change, though the sensation was similar. It came slowly, crept along her bones and through her blood, but when she looked down...

"No," she spoke softly, horror pulsating through her. "It cannot be—"

Where her feet stood, ice pooled like a spider web.

"Charmaine, it is time to say goodbye."

"To who?" Panic thrummed throughout Charmaine's chest. Carinthya had said Dalton was fine—

"To the king and queen."

CIARA AND CIAN stood at the front of Vanellope's throne room hand in hand, looking very much like all of the legends had ever said. They looked more faded, as if both of their souls were on their way from this world. Charmaine felt saddened by this, recognizing that it had been the honor and privilege of lifetime to fight at their side.

But as it went, all good things must come to an end.

Charmaine's breath was caught in her throat as her eyes fell upon Dalton Saphirrus. Tears were streaming down his face, and she found herself completely and utterly stunned. She had never seen Dalton *cry* before and was shocked that he felt that bonded to his ancestors that quickly.

As she turned to ask Carinthya to why this was happening, she quickly understood as she followed Carinthya's gaze to Cyril who she had entirely missed kneeling before his old friends. She made a move to stand by him, but Carinthya held her arm, and Charmaine understood completely and utterly.

This was Dalton's goodbye to Cyril.

Ciara looked down at her old friend as Cian bent to meet him. They rose together, and suddenly Charmaine realized how old Cyril was in actuality. As stunning as Ciara and Cian were as a couple, it was clear that they were frozen in time. They looked more hollow than they had during the battle, and their gazes were fixated upon Cyril. Charmaine caught them in the middle of their speech, thanking those who participated in the battle for their service to not just the crown but to the world.

"...But there is one thank you that we have not yet made, and we need to do so before we depart," Ciara said, her voice ringing throughout the hall. Everyone was on their edge of their toes, leaning to listen.

"Charmaine Grimes defeated my father," she continued. "She was worthy of all of the power that she could harness, a gift from the Gods as it is now a gift to the world that he is gone."

Everyone turned, except to Dalton who kept focused straight ahead.

"We thank her for ridding the world of the evil which would not depart."

Charmaine bowed her head as the crowd roared around her.

Cian lifted his hand and they settled immediately. It was clear that they meant to depart soon.

"And lastly," he said. "There is someone to be recognized today that has served the realm for a lifetime, never faltering and never deviating from those which he has pledged to serve."

He looked down at Cyril, and she could have sworn she heard Dalton whimper. "Cyril has expressed interest to us privately to be able to come with us as we depart today. And we have granted it."

Cyril turned, having nothing left to say. He looked directly at Dalton and smiled, large tears falling from his gaze. "It has been the honor to my life to serve the Saphirrus line," he said. "The honor of my life."

Taking the hand of his oldest friends, Cyril did not look back again before he disappeared forever into a golden archway which had appeared before them. And then Dalton fell to his knees.

Chapter Seventy
A few weeks later...

Q ueen Maria stood before Elena at the highest level of royalty. Suddenly, in this moment, Elena knew why she was the way that she was. She depicted perfection as much as possible, emulating her mother she had realized.

In a dark blue gown, it was clear that Maria was trying to epitomize the Saphirrus bloodline. Paying tribute to her daughter and her finest accomplishment... Marrying into another kingdom and broadening their familial influence. But could Maria really not read between the lines? To see the strife that plagued her daughter day in and day out?

Elena did not love Dalton Saphirrus.

Well, she did, but not the way that they were supposed to be loved.

Marriage was supposed to be a partnership between lovers. Or at least this was how Elena had always dreamt it. She deserved better, as did he, than what cards they were dealt in the game of life.

"Come here Elena," Maria whispered, staring into her

hand held mirror. "Us Leclair women have more magic than meets the eye."

"Whatever do you mean," Elena whispered, coming closer as her mother beckoned her.

"How much magic do you have, Elena?" she asked frankly.

Elena paused, rather surprised that this was the focus of conversation with her mother, when there was so much that stood between them. "More than others, less than others."

Maria furrowed her brows. "How does it manifest?"

"Through healing, through water." Through memories, she thought to herself. Though she no longer thought that there was another to it. That power had evaporated with the death of James.

Her heart hurt even returning to the memory.

"Elena, I heard how you controlled your powers during the battle. You fought bravely."

Elena smiled, her mother's approval reigning through her.

"I heard too, through a rumor of course, that a certain prince-to-be-king and you had a moment amidst the war raging on?" She lifted an eyebrow, which in the past would have been a sign of quiet disappointment. But now, Elena knew it to be out of kindness. She was looking out for her. Maybe she always had been, and Elena was just to blind to see it.

"Who told you that?" she ventured, her cheeks definitely blushing.

Maria laughed quietly. "Your guard, Greyson, is very fond of you. He spoke to me upon my arrival."

"He spoke very plainly then," Elena deadpanned. Greyson had been mostly stationed at the castle gates; she had not seen much of him at the battle at all.

Maria reached out to tuck a curl behind Elena's ear that

had come loose. "I have made many mistakes in my life Elena. I put my kingdom before my family more times than I can count, but you—Elena—you are the best of me. You let love lead your heart and put your family first." Maria gestured outwards as if all of her friends were standing there. "You put your family that you have chosen first." There was no malice in her voice, only regret at what she had never made time for before. "I always wanted you to be perfect Elena, to right the wrongs that I created, and I realized while I was holding steadfast in the First Kingdom that I was oh so very wrong about my own daughter. It nearly cleaved me in two."

Elena blinked away the tears that started to form at the corners of her eyes, but it was too late. Her mother saw. "Mother, we do not have a lot of time for sentiments. We have a coronation to attend to."

"Just know," Maria said softly, giving Elena a hug. "That I am so proud of you."

IT WAS JUST like her dream all of those months ago, but without two of the most important pieces of her life. The room always felt some sort of absence without James, but the void that Cyril had left behind was larger than she expected. It was like a gaping hole, always there. He had functioned as sort of an extension of all of them, always invested and always a part of the scheme at hand.

Taking a deep breath, she tried to push all of that away now. She understood where Dalton had come from all of those times, the cool mask which had come over his face time and now again.

Now she wore it as she bowed at the feet of her King as Randolph Einar placed Queen Ciara's crown on her head.

She felt the spikes of the crown penetrate her hair, settling against her scalp with a cold ferocity. She could hear the gasps of her kings men behind her, as she heard the rustling of clothes as they all got down on one knee to bow at her station.

There would have been a time when she would have blushed at so many giving her so much, but no longer.

She had been tortured and tested.

She had been ripped from all she loved and lost more people than she could bare to remind herself of.

She had no peace left, and was unsure how Cian and Ciara had ever managed to find it amongst the darkness. Maybe there was no peace at all, not until you let yourself have it.

She stood up slowly, the crown on her head suddenly feeling heavy with the weight of the world. It was snow and it was ice, as was the power of the hands which had forged the jewels.

She knew it was decorated with violet hues and black roses. Dalton had told her of its importance and significance this morning as they had arisen from bed, tangled in their sheets. She felt the soft touch of his hand now, just as she had this morning and every morning for the past few weeks, as she rose to meet the destiny she knew now had always been hers. They had laughed together, her power so free and Dalton so completely and utterly enthralled by his chance to be normal. Powerless.

She was the Queen of Snow, crowned before marriage by King Randolph of the Seventh Kingdom, and she was power reincarnate.

She smiled as Randolph kissed her hand softly, the familiar lips of her greatest friend caressing her skin in a warm embrace. His touch reminded her that she was okay, she was here and she was alive.

And that she was never to be in fear again.

She stood up fully, her black gown draping behind her like midnight. She touched the sides of it delicately, conscientious of messing up the traditions of the First Kingdom. Dalton was her King, and had been for many seasons now, and she would not humiliate him in her first act of Queen.

They had already broken sanctions by swearing her into the royal house of Sapphirus without marriage first. She nearly laughed now thinking of what Cyril's contempt at the act would have looked like, his explosive rage when he realized what they were about to do.

But there it was, that hole again.

It had been necessary to stand united against King Finn, one which the world had thought was long gone.

And now Cyril was gone, and Dalton was hanging on by a thread. But he had her, his kingdom, and the whole world at his side to help him rebuild what fragments had been left behind by the Kings of Old.

And they would do it together.

As she looked at him, she saw a build-up of tears threatening to spill over onto his star-dusted cheeks, his lips quivering as he took in everything that was before him; she flashed him a smile and nodded her head.

And then he nodded right back.

EPILOGUE
ONE YEAR LATER...

It was snowing outside. Dalton decided he no longer actually liked snow. Not anymore. It was too cold, too painful when it stung, and had the power to be too vicious. He no longer liked any power at all.

Rather, he liked being powerless.

In the year since the battle, a lot had changed, yet nothing had changed at all. He tried not to reflect too often, for if he thought of Cyril for more than a moment he was immediately devoid of all emotion, and shut himself up in the library to read. It was the only thing that allowed him any peace now-a-days when his thoughts were too loud, to escape into another world and breathe that air for a few hours while he tried to escape his own.

As he made his way through the First Kingdom's castle now, Dalton found it hard to remove himself from all reminders of those that he had loved and lost. For he had lost a lot in his twenty-one years of life, though he had gained much as well. His shoes clicked mercilessly on the white marble floors, the walls gleaming with pristine coldness that he would have enjoyed in years past. Now it just reminded him of snow.

Which he now hated.

Though, the passion for his people was still very prevalent. For he finally had the chance to right the wrongs of all the horrible things that his father's rule had become known for. The execution and persecution of magic was over, for now it was celebrated. Even if he himself no longer had magic.

As he made his way to the throne room for their annual beginning of winter celebrations—which he now hated, if there was any confusion on the subject matter—a smile overtook him at the sight of none other than his queen, Charmaine Grimes.

She had set up a tree from the outer edges of the kingdom, cut down by the kings guard which was spearheaded by none other than Lawton Thornwood, and created a masterful winter wonderland. Far better than anything he would have been able to conjure in his life.

Charmaine's parents had decided to remain in their kingdom, despite Dalton's protests that she could live between kingdoms. He explained to her, though he was secretly terrified that giving her the option would leave him without her on the darkest of his nights, that she deserved to have a family again. To his surprise, and adoration, she had taken his face between her hands—cupped ever so gently—and said, "You are my family too, you know."

That was what a lot of Dalton's last year had been, Charmaine pulling him back from himself. Whereas they used to keep one another balanced, despite the political blocks and magical challenges that they faced, it was now her that saved him time and time again. Since he gave his magic to her, he needed more saving than he cared to admit. But he would not have it any other way. When Finn had lifted his shadows to attack her...he could not bear to watch. Instinct had taken over.

Kai had told him that he could give her the power, only if it was selfless and in the time of most need. This was not a scripted rule book, no, but rather the rules unveiled before Dalton as had watched Charmaine approach him with that dagger in hand.

Dragons were maddeningly frustrating. Never clear.

Dalton was glad that he never needed to work with Kai again. For when he burnt down all of Finn's last standing men, he had fled. Queen Ciara had smiled, as if she was glad that her friend was finally fulfilled in all obligations to rulers.

Dalton wished him well. Though, he would not miss him. The great beast deserved some peace at last.

They all did.

The weapon that had brought Finn down had been destroyed, taken to a secret place where Randolph had placed it himself. Somewhere between the Seventh Kingdom and the First Kingdom. When Dalton had written to Randolph about its disposal weeks later, he could nearly feel the sarcasm dripping off the page as Randolph wrote quite poignantly: It is gone, Dalton.

A smile had overtaken his face then. Safe. His family was safe from its harm. It could never kill again.

He had felt nothing but relief, like a weight was lifted off his shoulders, since he had lost the winter power that had resided him for so long.

Besides, Charmaine was clearly better suited for such a power. As he observed the rest of the room, he smiled as she so easily created a flurry to create an ambience for when the rest of their family arrived.

If he would have tried to accomplish such a task—Gods —someone would have lost a finger or two to frostbite.

His eternal winter had ended as soon as the battle had concluded. When Charmaine pierced the fearsome King Finn with the dagger, his power transferred into her, the winter stopped. The seasons returned to normal.

Life proceeded, as it was meant to without his infliction.

"Dalton?" Charmaine's voice rang calmly from a few steps away, though he could not ignore the sound of alarm in her voice. "Dalton, where did you go?"

"Away for a moment," he answered honestly. There was no point in playing pretend anymore, not with her. This was not some fantasy land that they existed in, this was real life. And in reality, well, it was best to be honest. That had become their code amongst the two of them, for sometime now. Dalton could not remember exactly when it had started, but it meant something deeper than just, "Are you alright?"

They would always go away and come back to one another.

"I am glad you are back," she said as he approached, clearly startling her. "Are they here yet?"

"Am I supposed to wait by the front door?" he said with a chuckle, an eyebrow raised. He felt much more like himself than he did a minute ago.

She looked like she wanted to smack him. Now that he liked.

As he opened his mouth to reply, his sister walked into the throne room, holding a package with a bow on top of it. It was blue and rather poorly wrapped. He almost snickered to himself but held back. He was sure that she wrapped it herself. "I have not seen them yet," she said, joining in on the conversation.

Dalton turned around to grab the box from her, her gaze filled with love and her aura much healthier than this time last year. Carinthya had decided to come back to the First Kingdom with them following the battle, for Dalton realized the importance of both chosen family and blood. Carinthya was blood, and he would choose her over and over again.

When she had first come back with them, terrors had taken her almost every night. Day by day, night by night, Dalton had been there for her, and her there for him. They conquered it together, being back in this castle. And they did it together.

Bairre had returned with them, almost a guardian of hers of some sort. It had been clear that he had been employed by Ciara, but when she had crossed over, his allegiance had ended and it was a new queen which he would serve. He now lived with them as the castle thinker. Though the job he did was sub-par compared to those they had prior employed, if Dalton had anything to say about it.

As Charmaine called over Carinthya to help put the final touches on the decorated tree, Dalton found himself strolling toward the window, looking out over the horizon. His heart had been so empty and so full this year, but there was something that he kept yearning over. Seeing his friends. The ones that had helped them save the world. The ones that he now called family.

Trying to peer out over the castle's overtly large windows to see below, Dalton heard the familiar call of a voice that once reminded him of scraping marble, but now brought an immediate smile to his face. As he spun, it took all within him not to run and tackle the bastard king as Randolph Eniar extended his arms to embrace Dalton in the fiercest of hugs.

"D," Randolph said. "Did you get me a present?"

"Am I to call you R now?" Dalton asked, laughter catching in his throat. With an attempted smack to

Randolph's head he chided, "You know that my mere presence is the present, bitch."

"But then there would be two R's, and how confusing would that be!?" Reine's voice sounded behind them, and Dalton made room in their hug for one more Eniar.

"Are you seriously going to give two hugs and leave me out of it, Dalton Saphirrus?"

Immediately, as if he were a child caught by a disappointed parent, Dalton broke from their Seventh Kingdom filled group hug to move to the arms of his best friend.

Elena LeClair embraced him as she always did, with a golden heart and the ability to read him like nobody else. Well, other than Charmaine.

"I missed you," Elena said. "You look like hell."

Dalton snorted. "I am getting there," he said with as much reassurance as he could muster. "I will get there."

"Dalton, it has been a year," Elena said softly, breaking apart from him and rubbing his arm with understanding.

"I know, I know—"

"No, I mean Dalton, it has only been a year. You have endured more trauma than most. Time is needed to heal wounds. I can feel the reach of your kingdom's goodness all the way from the Seventh."

"How is Castle Dead treating you?" Dalton said, taking her arm and brushing away the compliment, though he buried it in his pocket. He knew that the wound of losing Cyril would take many years to heal, but this was not the time to harp on it as the celebrations were about to begin.

"We have been righting the wrongs of Randolph and Reine's past, ruling together and healing the scars of Finn's temporary stay in the Seventh."

"I can feel the reach of your kingdom too, you are doing great work, Elena."

Elena's cheeks flushed, and she nuzzled her head onto Dalton's shoulder.

As they gathered around the tree, Charmaine looked at all of them with tears beginning to well up in her violet gaze.

"Char, what is wrong?"

"I wish Titan was here," Lawton said sadly. "Though my prestigious king and queen granted me leave—whenever I wish, I might add—to see him whenever I wish." He smirked at all of them, trying to be nonchalant but obviously filled with excitement. "I leave in the morning to visit him."

"How is your letter writing going? Is it still?" Randolph asked, a tattoo hand pointed in both question and inquisition.

"It is certainly...*going*," Lawton said with a smirk, flushing bright red.

"Gods..." Randolph said. "Somehow that was way too much information. Stop moving your eyebrows like that!"

Dalton snorted, turning and giving Lawton a wink. Lawton had chosen to stay in the First Kingdom, and Dalton was ever grateful for it as one of Charmaine's greatest supports, but Dalton also recognized that a piece of Lawton had gone when they had all left Vanellope's kingdom.

That battle had taken a piece of all of them, it would seem.

"Nothing is wrong," Charmaine said, extending a hand to take Dalton's. "I am just happy, that is all."

"Ah!" Randolph said, standing abruptly. "I drew a picture for us, to celebrate the occasion of us being back together, celebrating one another and our friendship."

Dalton bit back a laugh, feeling a bit more like himself. "Randolph, you know you are a shit artist."

"I am not!" Randolph said, smoke beginning to pour out of his nose.

Elena was biting back a laugh as Dalton looked to her for back-up. "He, uh, worked really hard on it."

"Gods," Dalton said, dramatically dragging a hand over his face. "I never miss my powers, I am actually glad to be rid of it, but it did help me to destroy things."

Randolph pulled back the piece of parchment he had pulled from his back pocket—also clearly holding back a laugh—and showed it to the group with closed eyes, looking the other direction.

All at once, they burst into laughter. Dalton held back tears, Charmaine clutching onto him as she gasped for air.

"Randolph, this is worse than your bloody map!"

And as they laughed together, Dalton's grief subsided for that moment, and he felt the one thing that he craved for so long.

He felt peace, with his family.

THE END

KEEP READING FOR A SNEAK
PEEK OF CIARA AND CIAN'S
STORY, A "THE PRINCE OF
SNOW" NOVELLA TO BE
RELEASED

THE QUEEN OF FURY

A SNEAK PREVIEW OF CIARA AND CIAN'S STORY
A "THE PRINCE OF SNOW NOVELLA" TO BE
RELEASED

The brunt force of her father's hand had Ciara's blood spraying across the white marble floors of the throne room. She had been ten years old the first time her father struck her.

And she was fifteen years old the last time her father struck her.

Ciara felt numb, her tiny limbs trembled with the desire to break. She wanted to crumble. She wanted to fall into herself, to forget what transpired. She wanted to forget her father was now a monster, the demons within breaking through the cracks of his soul.

She did not know when she had lost him but she knew that he was gone now.

Her mother watched from across the throne room in horror at her King's fury. Her King *was* different from her husband. This was not the man she married. This was a monster birthed out of a self-righteous bloodline.

Ciara clutched her frail hand to her cheek as the ringing persisted in her ears. The blood that trickled down from her lips was hot, seething to the touch as if it were poison. Her father wasn't looking at her, nor did he even flinch at what he had done. He had touched Ciara before, but he had never wanted to harm her.

This was first time he had drawn blood.

She had seen the string snap within him, it had been strained for so long. She had seen him be stretched, pulled, and smacked around by the lesser nobles. His Kingdom fell out of grasp just as easily as he had come into power. His divinity had been questioned, his throne in jeopardy.

He wanted to solve it with wrath.

At only ten years old, Ciara felt betrayed. The world she had known had fallen from Grace.

She was *alone*. Completely and utterly, *alone*.

She could hear her mother gasping, fumbling for words of kindness or compassion, she was unsure. She could see her father raise his arm as if to strike her, his hand shaking with pure fury at his wife for intervening. It was his wife, not the Queen. This was not the woman he married. She could hear him mumbling words to himself. She caught him uttering "*weakness*" and "*embarrassment*".

He stopped. His hand began to tremble without the blind rage to push it forward. Without the hate in his heart, her father was unable to strike. He was unable to hurt. He was unable to hurt them. He fell to the ground, his knees surely bruising from the impact. He crawled forwards to Ciara, his hands sprawled in front of him. The evil he fabricated overtook him many times, his madness causing him to break like this as of late.

It would be the last time Ciara would be touched.

It was the first time Ciara felt her darkness swarm around her.

Her power was awakened and its depths crept toward her father with purpose. She wanted him to fear her. She wanted him to bow to her power like she had bowed to his hand. She wanted to break him.

She struck.

Her dark power cracked like thunder in the throne room, the white marble walls transitioned to a black so deep the dragons of the Old Religion themselves could not have replicated it.

Her father screamed. She was deaf to his voice now. No longer would his words haunt her nightmares. He would never lay a hand on her or her mother again. He would never scorch the Kingdoms with his fiery hatred.

The darkness seemed to agree with her, this strange part of her awakened by such fury.

Her mother screamed, she could feel the fear that struck deep at her core. Her mother was afraid not for her but of her. She pushed it away and in that moment, Ciara decided if she were to be good, she had to be evil.

ACKNOWLEDGMENTS

When you embark on your author journey, everything feels like it is in hypotheticals.

"Well, maybe someone will read this!"

"Well, maybe someone will like my characters!"

"Well, maybe someone will buy my book and tag me in a picture of it on their shelf!"

This journey has been turbulent and wonderful, filled with endless highs and lows. While all of these hypotheticals ended up becoming true, what surprised me the most about finishing this series was the love and support of the independent author community and readership that I found along the way.

So my first dedication is to you, the reader. Without your compassion, joy, and enthusiasm for the words I have been writing, I am not sure that I would have ever continued beyond TPOS. Thank you for allowing me to prove to myself that I can do this.

To Will, thank you for always cheering me on.

To my family, thank you for buying every version of my books and encouraging me to keep going with this little dream of mine.

To Nicole Platania, one day we will hang out and I will give you a big hug to properly thank you for all you have done for me.

To Chiara Gala, thank you for being the sun. I appreciate everything about you. I cannot wait to see you again, hopefully in London.

To my cats, thank you for being so soft.

A special thank you to my friends: Rowan Redfield, Neena Laskowski, and Marissa Serrao. I appreciate your continued support and friendship.

To my amazing editor, Kay, thank you for lifting me up. Editing is hard. I love you.

To my incredible cover designer, Kelly Carter. I am so glad that I found you. Thank you for creating such beautiful covers that embody my series perfectly.

To anyone that I have not mentioned, thank you. You know that this passion project turned hobby would be nowhere without your love and support.

And to Dalton Saphirrus and Charmaine Grimes, and every other character that I have written, thank you for leading me down this path and allowing me to write your story. Your adventures will live with me forever.

Live laugh love Dalton Saphirrus.

xx,

L.B. Divine

About the Author

L.B. Divine is a young adult fantasy author who drinks way too much coffee and spends too much time telling her cats how beautiful they are. She is constantly waking herself up from dreaming of Paris. She loves all stories, but fantasy ones are her favorite. The Prince of Snow is her first novel. She cannot wait to write all of the others that silently live in her brain. One day, she hopes to unleash them all upon you. L.B. Divine can be found at @lbdivineauthor on Instagram.

www.ingramcontent.com/pod-product-compliance
Lightning Source LLC
Chambersburg PA
CBHW050915030726
47503CB00007BB/2311